Torn Away

by

Vincent Morrone

The Torn Series, Book 1

Torn Away

Cover Art by *Kristian Norris*

The Wild Rose Press, Inc.
PO Box 708
Adams Basin, NY 14410-0708
Visit us at www.thewildrosepress.com

Publishing History
First Mainstream Thriller Edition, 2017
Print ISBN 978-1-5092-1734-2
Digital ISBN 978-1-5092-1735-9

The Torn Series, Book 1
Published in the United States of America

"My father was always mean and cruel,"
Drew said. "And we never knew when he'd strike out.
Smacking us with the back of his hand, giving us a kick
when we didn't expect it, but normally it was quick and
it was done. Those rages he went into, they were rarer.
Sometimes you could go days, other times weeks, but
when they happened, it was legendary. It was three
weeks before it happened again. Something set him off.
Not sure what, but he came home looking for us and we
knew. So I did *almost* the same thing again."

"What do you mean almost?"

"Ashley begged me to hide in there with them,"
Drew explained. "But I knew he'd look for us and
break down the door to get to us. He was already
slamming doors downstairs. So I pushed both of my
sisters in there. And then I locked the door."

Sam blinked. "You had a closet door with a lock on
it?"

"We did then," Drew said. "I'd managed to change
it out after the last time. I didn't want them getting out
again. So I locked my sisters in a closet and dealt with
my father. Ashley is still afraid of enclosed spaces. *I* did
that to her. I knew they'd be stuck in there until I could
manage to let them out and sometimes that was hours
later, but I stuck them in there whenever I knew he was
in a rage. I tried to protect them from my father, but
there was nobody there to protect them from me."

Kudos for Vincent Morrone

1st Place Winner
of the Saratoga RWA Great Beginnings Contest

Dedication

Writing this book made me think about how important being connected to family can be, and in the early stages, I had the chance to reconnect with several members of my own.

Many years ago, when becoming an author was nothing more than a dream, there was an argument within my family. While I was only a witness to the dispute as I was a kid, the actions of the adults in my life affected me greatly. I lost all contact with my aunts, uncles, and all of my cousins from one side of the family. This was before the age of the internet when contact could have easily been maintained on social media sites.

Decades later, my cousin Marcus found me through one of these social media sites. It was amazing talking to everyone, even if I felt a little like a kid who had just found out his face had been on the side of a milk carton for years. Since then, I've had several wonderful conversations with many relatives that were torn away from me at an early age.

First off, thank you to Marcus for finding me! And a special shout out to Gina for those great phone calls.

I want to dedicate *Torn Away* to those family members, in particular to my three aunts that I've been able to reconnect with. I can't tell you how much it means to have you back in my life. Maria, Anna, and Che Che!!! I love you all so much!

Chapter 1
A Free Woman

"Say it. I am a free woman, in charge of my own future and destiny."

Kelli Duncan took a deep breath and used a tissue to dry her tears. "I am a free woman in charge of my own future and destiny."

Diana sat back and appraised her patient. "Now, try saying it like you believe it."

Kelli smiled, but there was no joy in it. She fought against the tears threatening to spill over again. "I don't believe it. I don't feel like I'm in control. If Edward gets out, I'm afraid he'll come for me and Cole."

"You have a restraining order," Diana said. "If he comes into Ember Falls, he'll be arrested again. You've got two friends on the police force."

Kelli knew a restraining order was just a piece of paper.

"You can't control his actions," Diana said. "You can only control your own. What kind of person you choose to be. What kind of mother you want to be."

Kelli's breath hitched as the waterworks kicked back in. "I've failed as a mother. I should have left that bastard years ago, the moment he first raised his fist to me. But I stayed. I was terrified of him. I'm still terrified of him."

Diana nodded. "You had every reason to be, but it

was more than just terror. It's the pattern of your life. Your father was an abusive drunk, to you and your siblings."

"He was always so angry," Kelli explained. "More so after Mom died."

"Then your first boyfriend used and abused you. Left you when you were pregnant with his son."

Kelli shrugged. "Rodger didn't hit me much. He mostly stole from me. And he cheated. But he gave me Cole."

"And then there was Edward Hunter," Diana said. "He isolated you from your family and friends. Beat you in front of your son. You've been conditioned to take it. But you broke away. You left."

Kelli cringed. "He came after me. He was going to kill me and take Cole."

"He has no claim over your son," Diana said. "He never adopted him or even accepted him as his own. Cole doesn't call him 'Dad,' does he?"

Ripping the tissue into tiny pieces, Kelli shook her head. "No. Edward never wanted him as a son."

"How is Cole adjusting to life in Ember Falls?"

Kelli sighed heavily. "I'm not sure. He's quiet. Sullen. He hasn't made any friends. I know he's worried about Edward returning."

Kelli threw away the remains of the tissue, reaching forward and pulled out another one. "He likes living in Lily's house. And the bookstore. Cole always liked books."

"How is he dealing with your friend and sister?"

Kelli smiled. "He likes his crazy Aunt Ashley and she adores him. Lily is so patient. It was so good of her to take us in. If Edward comes here…"

Kelli closed her eyes, imagining her ex hurting her friend or sister. If it happened, it would be her fault.

"If he does, call the police. Your sister is friends with a cop."

Kelli rubbed her arms, even though it was warm. "Ollie's a good man. He's been trying to spend time with Cole. I think Cole likes him, but he won't say it. He's frightened of men, but Ollie's got a way about him. Cole needs that. He needs to be around good men." Kelli dabbed her eyes with the tissue. "I contacted my brother."

Diana's eyebrows went up in surprise. "Oh? Do you think that's a good idea? Are you sure that's not you falling into that same pattern again?"

Kelli made direct eye contact with Diana for the first time all night. "I don't care what everyone says. My brother didn't hurt anyone. He always tried to protect me and Ashley. Dad was always the hardest on him. I think when Dad looked at me or Ashley, he saw a bit of Mom. So we got knocked around a little, but he'd go to town on Drew, mostly because Drew put himself between us and Dad.

"I haven't seen him since I snuck into the hospital. They wouldn't let me into his room, had a police officer stationed at the door. I saw him as a nurse went in. They had him cuffed to the bed."

Diana tapped the pen on her pad of paper. "What does your sister think?"

Kelli folded her arms. "Ashley refuses to even talk about him. He wrote to us." She looked up. "For some time, he wrote letters and e-mails. Ashley refused to read them and sent them back, but she saved the ones that came for me. I believe in him. I've been poking

9

around a little. I owe it to him."

"You don't owe him anything," Diana said. "You owe it to your son to be safe. Is your brother coming back to Ember Falls?"

Kelli sighed. "I didn't actually ask him, but I want him to. I know he hates this town, but I want my brother back. I think he'd be good for Cole. If I ask him, he'll come."

"You're sure that's a good idea?"

Kelli smiled. "There's a lot of things I'm not sure about, but my brother being a part of my son's life? That's not one of them."

Diana instructed Kelli to repeat that phrase in her head, each day, until it started to sink in. *'I am a free woman, in charge of my own future and destiny.'* It sounded good.

Kelli stepped outside, the cool night air refreshing her entire body. She was a free woman, and she intended to stay that way. Kelli failed Cole as a mother, because she allowed fear to dominate her. She had to do better for him. Cole would heal. He had to. He was all that mattered to her.

Yes, life was going to get better. Kelli would make sure of it. She was through being a victim.

She smiled to herself as she reached for the door handle. The promise was still ringing in her mind when his reflection in the car window caught her attention. She had no time to panic before he grabbed her from behind, whispered, "Bitch," in her ear and used a sharp blade to slit her throat.

Her scream drowned in a bloody gurgle as he dragged her to a nearby car, used a key fob to remotely open the trunk, and threw her inside like a bag of garbage. She barely registered the fact the trunk was lined with plastic as he glared down at her with scorn and stabbed the knife into her chest. She prayed her sister, brother and best friend would deliver the promise of a better life for her son. Kelli Duncan died before he slammed the trunk closed, but she died a free woman.

****

"Concentrate," the General snapped, "or you're going to be sorry."

Drew Duncan didn't look up right away. His eyes remained on his cell phone. The picture of a little boy with sad eyes who refused to look into the camera had him captivated.

"What the hell are you staring at anyway? Aren't you a little old to be looking at pictures of girls with their boobs out?"

Paul McAlister, a.k.a. the General, was a tall and sturdy man with gray hair and a square jaw. His old and stern face was offset by sharp blue eyes. He stood with his arms crossed as he waited for an answer, and the General wasn't one to wait.

"If I *ever* get too old to look at boobs," Drew said. "Shoot me."

"Count on it." The General scowled. "So tell me what has your undivided attention."

Drew handed the phone to the General. "I have a nephew."

The General took the phone. "I thought you said you haven't spoken to either of your sisters since that business from your home town."

"I haven't." Drew did his best to ignore the urge to reach for his pack of cigarettes and light up. "I tried to write and e-mail both of them for a while. Never heard back. Ashley returned my letters, ripped up into little pieces. Kelli never responded to hers. Now I know why. She married some asshole. She doesn't go into detail, but it sounds like he was no better than my father. She's left him. Fucker better steer clear of her."

The General arched an eyebrow. "You plan on going to see her?"

Drew's mouth went dry at the thought of returning to Ember Falls. His home town was filled with old nightmares and bad memories. "She didn't ask me, but she wants me to. I can read between the lines."

God, going back to Ember Falls was the last thing he wanted to do, but he wanted his sisters back. Both of them, including the pain in the ass known as Ashley. Plus, he wanted to meet his nephew. Maybe he could convince them to come out to him.

The General held out Drew's phone. "All right, enough with the Brady Bunch routine. We're here to do a job. I need you focused."

Drew took his phone back, gave one last look at his nephew and then shut it down. "Yes, sir."

The General handed a brief case to Drew, who opened it, revealing stacks of hundred dollar bills. "It's all there?"

The General arched an eyebrow. "You want to count it? It's there. One cool million. You remember the plan?"

Drew examined the brief case. "I do. It's not what I'd call a difficult plan."

The General scowled. "It doesn't need to be difficult for it to get fucked up, and I don't want it fucked up. Neither do our clients. You stick to the plan. You're there to make a simple exchange. You show them the cash, make the trade, and get out. Clear?"

Drew shut the briefcase, snapped the locks into place, and grabbed the handle. "Crystal. What could go wrong?"

With a sigh, the General headed toward the door. "I'm too old for this shit."

****

The sun was just breaking into the morning sky, bathing the horizon in a deadly, red hue. Rolling, turbulent clouds blanketed the distance as deep shadows covered the landscape.

Alone in a black SUV, Drew drove out to the rendezvous point. He didn't play any music, making sure to obey all speed limits. He needed to be in control.

Drew struggled to put aside any thoughts of Ember Falls. He was about to face people who wouldn't hesitate to put a bullet in his brain. It wasn't the first time, and certainly wouldn't be the last. Just another day at the office.

Yet the idea of going back to his home town and facing his sisters had his palms sweaty.

Put it away, Drew, put it away. You can't afford to worry about this. Not now. This wouldn't take long and then you can get nice and drunk, and worry then. Right now, concentrate. Get the job done.

He followed the GPS to an old, abandoned drive-in movie theater, the giant screen ripped, and most of the poles bare and rusted. Drew got out and placed the briefcase on the driver's seat. He was dressed in black slacks, a matching jacket and tie, and a white shirt. He hated ties, but needed to project a certain image here. Despite that, and knowing he had a few minutes, Drew reached into his pocket and pulled out a pack of Marlboros. He hadn't taken his first drag before the General's voice sounded in his ear.

"I ought to shoot that thing right out of your mouth, son."

Drew laughed. The General had a strong dislike for cigarettes. He'd promised himself he was going to quit one day, but he hadn't gotten to that day yet.

"Just killing time until the fun starts." Drew blew out smoke.

"Just killing yourself, one lung-full at a time."

"Nah, I'm indestructible." Drew coughed twice and pounded his chest like a ninety-year-old man on an iron lung.

"You're just dumb enough to believe that, aren't you?"

Drew took one last drag on the cigarette before tossing it away. "Not really."

The General chuckled in his ear. "Good, because you're no good to me if you do. Heads up. I see a dust trail. North-west, coming fast. They're almost there."

Drew looked up. The General was right. It was time.

Grabbing the briefcase, Drew headed to the front of the SUV. He placed it on the hood and leaned against the grille, making sure to have his hands in sight.

"No surprises," the General said. "It's a simple exchange."

Two cars pulled up. One was a black sedan, the other a matching van, both very nondescript. They slowed down while still several feet away and came to an abrupt stop. Two men got out from the passenger side of each vehicle, each with a semi-automatic in their hands.

They were extraordinarily large men without any trace of a neck. One was white, covered in tattoos with a clean-shaven head, and several piercings, including a nose ring. The other was Hispanic, had long, black hair pulled back in a ponytail and a Fu Manchu mustache. Each one looked as solid as a brick wall, and probably just as dumb. Drew studied them while keeping a casual expression on his face. 'Tattoo' stared blankly ahead, wearing what Drew considered a good poker face. 'Ponytail' smirked. It was the smirk that worried Drew.

The back door to the sedan opened and a man slowly got out. Only slightly smaller in stature, he wore a finely tailored black suit that hid the bulk of his muscles, with a neatly trimmed goatee, and his eyes concealed behind dark sunglasses.

Here was the guy in charge. His name, learned through their sources, was John Samson. As he approached, he was joined by two other men, each big and brutal looking. They also carried semi-automatic weapons strung over their shoulders.

They reminded Drew of a prison gang, only better dressed and armed.

"Careful, Drew," the General said. "I don't like the feel of this."

Drew's gut instinct agreed with the General.

This was wrong. Exchange, my ass. This was going to be a bloodbath.

Samson stopped a decent distance from Drew. He was the only one not holding a weapon, although Drew could tell he had one under his jacket from the way he walked. "You got the money?"

Casually, Drew nodded. He stepped aside and

placed his hand on the briefcase.

"Show me," Samson ordered.

Hesitating for only a moment, Drew pulled the briefcase off the hood. Without ever taking his eyes off of the men in front of him, he opened up the case, turned it around and lifted the lid for Samson to see. Then he flipped the lid closed, locked it and placed it on the ground.

Samson smiled. "Bring it to me."

Drew shook his head. "No. I showed you mine. You show me yours."

For a moment, Samson did nothing, as if Drew were going to suddenly change his mind and hand over a million dollars if he glared hard enough. Realizing that wasn't going to happen, he snapped his fingers toward the van.

The side panel of the white van opened and another man stepped out, this one larger than the others put together. He took a moment to straighten his jacket before reaching into the vehicle.

Roughly, he yanked a young, teen girl out into the morning air. She was crying hysterically, terrified she was about to be killed. A tiny, wisp of a thing, with long, blonde, hair—dirty and unkempt, wearing filthy clothes and sporting a black eye and swollen lip.

Something about her reminded Drew of his sister, Kelli, when she was thirteen. Perhaps he just had Kelli on his mind. Either way, it took every ounce of restraint not to act on his urge to attack these bastards.

The girl's name was Jenifer Ward. Drew had wanted to know who he was risking life for. She had just celebrated her thirteenth birthday not three weeks ago. Her friends called her Jen, and she was a big fan of pop music, romantic comedies, and books with sad endings. She had a dog named Ralph, and a bunny named Whiskers. Her parents were John and Elizabeth Ward, and she had two younger brothers, Jake and James—both eight.

It was Drew's responsibility to make sure this girl got home to see them again.

Her parents were rich. Not stupid, stinking, filthy rich, but rich enough the kidnappers knew they'd be able to raise a million dollars, which they had. They relied on the General and his team to use that million to get their daughter back.

The huge, tank of a man dragged Jen to Samson, who grabbed her by the hair. "Give us the money, and we'll give you the girl."

Drew smiled and shook his head. "Isn't it a shame in today's day and age, you just can't feel comfortable trusting anyone, including kidnappers. You bring the girl to the halfway mark. I'll meet you there with the money."

Samson tilted his head. "How do I know you won't try something?"

"You don't." Drew shrugged. "Why would I? It's not my money. It belongs to her parents. They made it clear all they care about is getting their daughter back, alive and unhurt. I've got no reason to try anything. *You* do."

The fact was, Drew hadn't talked to the parents. He had no idea how they felt about parting with the money. The General hadn't said anything, one way or another, but the line sounded good. At least, Drew hoped it did.

Samson let go of Jen's hair, snapped his fingers, and handed the girl off to the 'Tank.' He grabbed her by the arm and yanked her forward. Jen winced in pain. When she started to trip, he pulled her back up roughly. She was lucky he didn't dislocate her shoulder.

Drew wanted to demolish him, but that wouldn't be smart and he needed to be smart. Get Jen out; that was his job. These sons of bitches would get theirs. The General would see to that.

Drew stepped forward, briefcase in hand, and went to get a scared, young girl. The 'Tank' held out his hand for the briefcase. Drew held it out and reached for Jen. The moment his fingers grasped the handle, he shoved Jen straight into Drew's arms.

Too easy.

Quickly, Drew put his arm around the girl and guided her back to the SUV. He kept his eyes on the men with the guns as he closed the distance to his car in seconds. "Come on, Jen. I'm taking you home."

"I'm afraid I can't have that," Samson said. With another snap of his fingers, all the men had guns trained on them.

Jen started to weep as Drew shoved her behind him. She shook and buried her face on his back, sobbing, convinced she was about to die. "You've got what you came for. I just want to bring the girl home to her family."

Samson shook his head and grinned, pulling the shades off of his face for the first time. "No, no, no. I'm afraid she's seen our faces. So have you. Really, despite your earlier warning, you are far too trusting."

Drew sent Samson his most wicked grin. "No. I'm not."

As the smile faded from Samson's face, the briefcase exploded, sending the million dollars, now on fire, billowing through the air. The briefcase itself launched straight up and only when it started to fall did the arm detach—the rest of the 'Tank's' body blown in various directions.

Before Samson or his thugs could register the fact their million dollars had gone boom, shots rang out. 'Ponytail's' head exploded, followed by one of the men behind him. Bodies started to hit the ground as Drew grabbed Jen and ran her to the back of the car. He'd almost got to the end when something smashed into him from behind.

Jen screamed louder as someone grabbed her.

Samson.

His shades gone, eyes narrow and wild; like an uncaged animal, Samson raised his gun. Drew kicked him square in the chest, making him stumble back and drop the gun to the ground, which Drew promptly kicked away.

Stumbling back a few feet, Samson reached to the small of his back and pulled out a long hunting knife. Brandishing the blade, he grinned as he lunged forward.

In a lightning-fast motion, Drew lashed out, grabbing Samson's arm. He turned and twisted it sharply. A savage snap mixed with a cry of pain. Drew shifted his weight, smashing his elbow into Samson's face and breaking his nose before turning to face him.

Seizing Samson, Drew launched him forward through the driver's side window of the SUV. Drew repeated the same move, obliterating the backseat window and Samson's face.

Jen peeked out from the corner of the car. Once again, Drew saw his sister in Jen's face, and his father in Samson's.

Drew's fists pummeled that face, trying to erase it from existence, all measure of control gone. Blood gushed out of Samson's nose and mouth. Bones cracked as Drew pounded out his fury.

Drew never heard the General yelling in his ear, or the cars racing up behind him. He would have kept going if someone's hand hadn't grabbed his arm.

"That's *enough*, Marine."

Drew stopped, shocked at the General holding his arm, his eyes grim and concerned.

"You're not doing anything but scaring the girl." The General nodded toward Jen, who stared at him with eyes wide with fear.

With an incredible amount of effort, Drew released Samson, who toppled to the ground in a bloody heap. He moved toward Jen, who backed away from him as she was whisked into the back of a SUV matching the one Drew smashed up using Samson as a battering ram.

"Let's go," the General said. "Now."

The General herded Drew into the back of a black Humvee. Without a word, he held a medical kit and bottle of water. He opened the water and handed it to Drew before going to work on his bloody knuckles.

"Drink," the General said. "Or I'll pour it down your throat."

Drew drank nearly the entire bottle at once.

"Why'd you lose control?"

"Bastard deserved it and more. She was terrified down to the bone, and he was going to kill her even after he had his money."

The General paused a moment. "Yes, he was, but that girl didn't deserve to witness you erasing his face." He waited a moment, and went back to tending to

Drew's hands. "This have to do with your sister?"

Drew closed his eyes. "We were all targets for our father growing up. I tried to protect them, but I was useless in prison. By the time I got out, they'd left him. I thought they were safe. I thought all this time they simply didn't want anything to do with me. Believed I'd…" Drew finished the rest of the water.

"I know what you were accused of," the General said. "I never believed it. If I had, you wouldn't be here. Neither did my grandson."

Drew winced. *Matthew McAlister. Another person he was supposed to protect.*

"I fucked up, and because of it, my sister ended up with some asshole just as bad if not worse than our father."

The General finished with Drew's hands. "We all fuck up in life. Nothing you can do about the past. Just don't keep doing it. Now, I asked you earlier today and you never answered me. You going to go see your sister?"

Going back to Ember Falls was more terrifying than the shootout he'd just survived, but Drew didn't hesitate. "Yes, sir. I think I have some vacation left."

The General nodded. "Son, I don't think you've ever taken a vacation. As soon as we wrap up the legal details from today, consider yourself on leave."

The car pulled to a stop and they got out in the parking lot of the small hotel they'd set up for the op. Drew exited the Humvee just in time to see the parents come out. The husband held his wife as they scanned the cars, looking for their daughter.

With the help of another of the General's agents, Jen slid out of the third SUV. Her parents' eyes filled with tears. They both called her name and they raced to her.

Jen called out for her mommy and daddy like she had probably done when she was a little girl and awakened from a nightmare. They collided in an embrace filled with love.

Drew watched them. The girl would have plenty of nightmares ahead of her, but she'd be okay.

Slowly, he and the General walked over. The family didn't notice them at first. When they did, the mother launched herself at the General and hugged him.

"Thank you for getting our baby back."

The General smiled. "Our pleasure," he said as the father shook his hand. "I'm afraid things didn't go smoothly. We had to sacrifice the money."

Drew watched their reactions, or rather lack thereof. Their smiles never faltered an inch. The money was a non-issue with them. They had their daughter back. Nothing else mattered.

****

The local police had a lot of questions that needed to be answered. It took a little time for Drew to extract himself and head back to the hotel room. He needed a shower, a cigarette, and a stiff drink.

Before heading into the bathroom, Drew opened his sister's e-mail again. He scanned it quickly, pulling out the important details. She'd never gotten his letters until she'd returned to Ember Falls. Ashley was still angry, but Kelli was confident she'd come around. Kelli's mention of her ex was brief, but telling. She never came out and said he'd hit her, but her meaning was clear.

'*He was far more of a monster than Dad ever was.*'

Finally, Drew's eyes found the picture of his nephew—Cole. There was no joy in his eyes. It was as if Drew stared into a mirror of his past.

Whatever Cole's life had been up until now, it was over. Kelli said as much, and Drew swore he'd do whatever was needed to help his sister keep that promise. It was time he stepped up.

Drew hit reply on the e-mail and began to type a response. Moments later, he erased it and started again, and again. When he finally managed to finish, Drew quickly hit send before he had a chance to rethink it too much.

It was done. He'd included his cell phone, so Kelli could call him if she wanted. The thought of his sister's voice made Drew grin as he headed into the bathroom.

As Drew stripped down and climbed into the tiny shower, he realized there was something else stirring within him—joy.

He was an uncle. Wasn't that a kick?

After the shower, Drew dressed and grabbed his phone to see if anyone in the group was up for a drink. He had a voicemail and though he didn't recognize the number, the area code he knew—Ember Falls.

Hitting the speaker button, Drew dialed his voicemail access number, keyed in his password, and smiled as he waited to hear his sister's voice.

"Drew? This is Lily. I don't know if you remember me." Drew did. Who could forget her? Little Lily—small but mighty. She was like an unofficial Duncan. "Drew, something happened to Kelli. They found her today. She's dead. I know she e-mailed you. She talked to me about it. Please give me a call. I'm so sorry."

She rattled off a number, but Drew didn't hear it.

Instead, he fumbled with the phone and replayed the message. He heard wrong. There was no way Kelli could be dead. Not his sister. Not her.

This had to be a joke. A cruel, sadistic joke, or a mistake. A horrible mistake.

But it wasn't. Lily was smart and kind and would never make this kind of mistake or do anything this cruel. Which meant there was only one possibility.

Kelli, one of the two siblings he'd shared a womb with for seven and a half months and a house with for nearly eighteen years, was dead.

Chapter 2
Cell Phones Can't Swim

Paul McAlister was a man who trusted his instincts. From the first time he met Drew Duncan, his grandson's buddy, while he visited them on base, he decided he'd liked him. More so because he learned Drew saved his grandson's life, at great personal risk, on three separate occasions. From the first time the General had shaken hands with him, he thought about having Drew come to work for him when his tour was over. Drew didn't strike him as a career Marine. Again, instinct told him Drew hadn't quite found his place in the world.

The General recognized the signs in Drew, the anger beneath the surface and the self-loathing behind his eyes. He knew what someone looked like when they grew up as someone's personal punching bag, since he'd seen that same look as a teenager whenever he'd looked in the mirror.

Because they both came from ugliness, he understood Drew Duncan from that first handshake. The General always been able to read him before Drew said a word. That's how the General knew his best man was scared shitless about going to his hometown. That's how he knew Drew was going back to Ember Falls and not coming back before Drew came to the conclusion himself.

And that's why he understood the grief in Drew's eyes when he found him pounding on his door.

"I need to borrow a car."

"What happened?"

Drew's jaw tightened, his fists clenched and his eyes closed against tears. "I just got a message. My sister's dead. I don't know anything more than that. I need to get to the airport and get home."

The General placed his left hand on the young man's shoulder, reached into his jacket pocket with his right hand, and pulled out his cell.

"Get the plane ready for immediate takeoff, I'll be there in twenty minutes. We're going to Ember Falls, New York. Make it happen."

Drew trembled and his eyes filled with gratitude.

"Go get your things. Meet me out front in five minutes."

Drew did as he was ordered.

****

In less than a half hour, they were in the air, and the General slid Drew a glass of brandy. "Drink it."

Drew downed the contents. "I don't have... Ashley, my other sister. We haven't spoken since..."

"Do you have that other girl's number? Lily?"

Drew looked up, nodded.

"Call it."

Drew looked back down at his phone blankly.

"Call it, now," the General ordered. There was no softness in his voice, just authority and command.

It snapped Drew out of his trance. He dialed Lily's number and waited.

"Hello? Drew?"

"Yeah." Drew forced himself to breathe. "What the

hell happened? Please tell me it's a mistake. Please."

The silence on the other end was all the answer he needed.

"What happened? Was it an accident? It wasn't, was it?"

"No," Lily said. The anguish in her voice made it clear she'd been crying. "She was killed. We don't know much right now."

Drew's face flushed with anger. He wanted to pound something or someone. "Is that bastard in jail?"

Lily sighed. "It's not that simple. The police don't know who did it."

"How hard is it to guess? Where is he? Where is the son of a bitch?"

"He's in jail," Lily said. "On assault charges, but not on Kelli, or at least not only on her. He's been there for a few weeks. He didn't do this. Couldn't have."

"That doesn't make sense."

Lily gave a weary sigh. "I know, but it's true."

Drew rubbed his hand over his face, pressed his thumb into his left temple and blew out a breath. "Where's Ashley? Is she…how is she doing? And Cole?"

"Ashley is devastated," Lily said. "She just got her sister back. She's in a fury right now, but she's trying to calm down. Cole is…"

Lily's voice cracked and Drew pictured her with tears pouring down her face.

"He hasn't said anything since we told him," Lily said. "He won't talk; he won't eat. Drew, what did Kelli tell you in her e-mail?"

The e-mail had been a flurry of emotions for Drew. Hope he could have a relationship with his sister. Joy he had a nephew. Anger at what Kelli had been through.

Now the hope had been murdered along with Kelli and any joy was drowned out by the anger which now overwhelmed him.

"She told me how her ex hurt her," Drew finally said. "How he kept her from leaving him. She didn't go into details, but there was a lot of self-blaming in there. Kelli always did that. Blamed herself when something bad happened.

"I was going to come," Drew continued. "I'd just gotten her message earlier. I've been busy and I hadn't checked my personal e-mails in a few days, but once I did, I was going to take vacation. Come see her. Meet Cole. God, Lily, if I hadn't been too busy, if I'd called her, maybe I could have…"

"Don't go there, Drew," Lily said. She always had a quiet authority in her voice. "You couldn't have done anything."

Drew pressed the phone against his ear with one hand while the other hand rubbed the back of his head. He sat on the edge of his seat with his head down, certain he was going to be sick.

"I should have been there for her," Drew said, more to himself than Lily.

Lily sighed. "Your sister left behind a little boy who's frightened and grieving over the loss of his mother. Be there for him."

Drew nodded, as if Lily could see him on the other side of the phone. "I'll be there soon. Does Ashley know I'm coming back?"

There was a pause on the other end, followed by an, "Umm."

"I get it," Drew said. "She doesn't want to speak to me."

Another pause.

"It's rough," Lily said.

Trying to frame your answers so she doesn't know that I'm asking about her?

"She's going to have to deal with me. I'll be there soon."

"I know," Lily said. "I agree."

"Can you tell her I love her? And I'm sorry."

Lily sighed again.

"Give me a minute," she said.

The sound on the other end muted. The voice was muffled and he couldn't make out the words, but he was sure it was Lily. Positive she was relaying his message.

He imagined his sister rolling the words around in her head, trying to decide what to say. There was movement and Lily came back on the phone. "Hold on. She wants to talk to you."

Drew's heart caught in his throat. Did she just want to hear him say it himself? He could do that. Did she want to chew him out? He could take it.

He sensed her on the other side, listening, waiting. Her breath the only sound he heard.

"Ashley?"

"Fuck this."

The line went dead.

****

"That was so mature," Lily said. "I'm calling him back and you're talking to him."

"Oh no," Ashley said. "We've got nothing to say to him."

29

She held the phone high in the air, well above where Lily could get it unless she got a step stool. Ashley had long legs and arms. All the Duncan kids were blessed with height, something Lily never was.

While Ashley was just over six feet tall, Lily stood at only five feet six, and that was in two-inch heels. Still, Lily never once let herself be intimidated by anyone taller than her, and she wasn't about the start now.

"Ashley Duncan, give me my phone so I can call your brother back. If you want to act like a little brat, that's your business, but your sister made her feelings clear to me. She was very much hoping Drew would be a part of Cole's life."

"What the hell did she know?" Ashley said. "He's a damn bastard just like the rest of the male species, and Cole doesn't need to have anything to do with him."

Lily refused to play the game of trying to grab the phone out of Ashley's hand. Instead, she crossed her arms, arched an eyebrow, and fixed her best "don't fuck with me" expression on her face.

"I want my phone back, right this instant."

Ashley, who never knew when enough was enough, simply shrugged. "Here, catch."

Ashley tossed it well over Lily's head and across the room where it splash dunked right into the fish tank.

"Jesus Christ!" Lily ran over, found the long, green net used to capture sick and dead fish, and started to scoop for her phone. "Ashley, that's an expensive phone, and it's ruined. I can't believe you did that."

She managed to get it out and wasn't surprised it was dead. Lily had half a mind to chuck it at Ashley, but she didn't. She would have, if her childhood friend

30

wasn't acting out of grief and pain.

Instead, she reached down for patience. "Ashley, he's your brother. He just found out his sister was killed. He's coming back."

"Well, I don't want him to come back," Ashley said. "He's had plenty of time to come back when it counted. Bastard got himself good and gone, he can just stay gone. I never asked him to come back. I don't need him, and neither does Cole."

Lily moved into the kitchen where she used a towel to dry off her phone. "Cole needs his family. *All* of his family. You know Kelli wanted him to be a part of her son's life. He was going to come back before he heard. Something I'm sure is not easy for him." She removed the battery and kept drying. "Drew had good reason to leave. You know that."

Ashley jutted out her chin in defiance. "Yeah, he's a bastard. A selfish, no-good bastard who didn't give a rat's ass about me or Kelli."

Lily sighed as she went into one cabinet, grabbing a small, white bowl, then another where she retrieved a box of uncooked white rice. "You know that's not true. How many beatings did he take for you?" Lily placed the phone in the bowl and started to cover it with rice. "You used to tell me all about it. Your father hurt all of you, but he brutalized Drew. Drew always tried to stand between you and him. How many times were you shocked that your father didn't actually pull the trigger and kill him?"

"Plenty," Ashley admitted, her arms folded across her chest. She was less insolent and more defensive. "He made his choice. He left us."

Lily nodded as she put the rice away. "He did. You

moved in with me. Kelli was living with Rodger after she got pregnant with Cole. I don't think Drew even knew why; he just knew you'd both moved out, away from your father. Look, I'm not saying he shouldn't have said goodbye or wrote, but think about what he'd gone through. A year in jail awaiting trial. God knows what happened in there."

"Don't." Ashley held up a finger in warning. "Don't you dare try and make me feel guilty for not going to see him. I tried. You know I tried."

Lily nodded. "I know. But he probably didn't."

Ashley seemed to consider for a moment, but she wasn't in a mood to feel charitable toward Drew or anyone else. "Who gives a damn? I'm sure the family of Molly Winters doesn't. She's still gone, and Drew is coming home."

Lily remembered Molly. She was one of the prettiest girls in their class, but there was a hardness to Molly that always unnerved her, and Lily wasn't easily unnerved, even back then.

"We don't know what happened with Molly," Lily said. "We never heard Drew's side of it, just what we read in the papers. Heard what everyone else was saying."

Ashley scowled as she leaned against the counter. "I was there at homecoming. They had a rip-roaring fight and he left her in the middle of the dance floor."

Lily moved over to stand next to Ashley, wanting to close the distance between them. "I know. I was there too. She was drunk. They both were acting like idiots. She said something that pissed him off, and when he reacted she slapped his face and laughed. She told him to go and he did. I lost track of her at the dance. I was too busy trying to keep my date from feeling me up."

Ashley smirked. "I was too busy *encouraging* mine to feel me up, and down. So yeah, I remember seeing her here or there, but I couldn't swear when or where."

Lily scooted a little closer. "Neither of us saw Drew come back. Who knows who the hell she disappeared with? Or what happened? We all knew they had a flimsy case against him, accusing him of murder when they didn't even have a body. Nobody knows what happened."

"Except Drew," Ashley said.

"Except Drew, but for all that time he was being held, awaiting trial, you never wavered in your belief that your brother was innocent. And your sister believed it without a doubt."

Ashley rolled her shoulders. "We were the exceptions. Ollie was never sure. The entire town believed he killed her and hid the body. Still do."

"Which is why Drew didn't want to come back, but he is."

"Yeah," Ashley said. "And Cole gets an uncle everyone in town hates. How is that good? How is he going to recover from everything with that hanging over his head?"

Lily took Ashley's hand, and gave it a reassuring squeeze. "Because we'll help him. He's got us. Both of us. And if Drew can help him, we should let him. It's not about us anymore. We've got to do what's best for Cole."

Ashley struggled against the tears. It was easier to yell and scream and be angry at Drew. "My sister was convinced having my brother back would be good for

Cole. I'm not. Cole doesn't need someone coming here pretending to love him and not be able to stick around. Cole needs stability. And that's not my brother."

Determined not to cry, Ashley let go of Lily's hand, pushed off the counter and walked out of the kitchen. She would be damned if she was going to let Drew come waltzing back into town, have Cole start to depend on him, only to break his heart by leaving. Cole couldn't take it.

And neither could she.

Chapter 3
Who Said You Can't Go Home Again?

Sitting in their patrol cruiser as cars went by on the highway, Samantha Rossi wasn't sure what to say to her partner of only nine months. The look on his face let her know he was in a bad place. He'd been in that bad place since the death of Kelli Duncan. It was eating him up inside, but now there was another layer.

Ollie had gotten a text, one he didn't share with her, but it had pissed him off. He hadn't said a word about it. In fact, he'd barely said a word at all since receiving the message and that wasn't like Ollie Miller. Not at all.

"What's the matter, Ollie?"

Ollie glanced over at his partner. "What makes you ask if something's the matter?"

She arched an eyebrow in his direction. "Because you've been stewing ever since you got that text. Who was it? Ashley?"

Ollie nodded.

"She tell you not to come by after your shift?"

"No."

"So, what happened?"

"Old ghosts." Ollie sighed. "Her brother, Drew, is coming back to town. She hasn't seen or heard from him since he left about eight years ago. Kelli sent him an e-mail before she was killed. Now, he's on his way back to Ember Falls. Wants to be a brother again. Be an uncle."

Sam remembered Drew from when she was little, back when she had gone to elementary and middle school in Ember Falls, before she and her parents moved away. Drew was two years older than her, but she still remembered having a severe crush on him that lasted from fourth to sixth grade. She was convinced someday she'd marry him before moving south of Albany.

"You don't think that's a good idea? Seems to me Cole could use all the family he can get about now."

Sam only met Cole a few times. He wasn't much on conversation, but she knew he'd been through a lot, on top of it all to lose his mother. Her heart went out to the kid.

"Cole needs people who will care for him," Ollie said.

"You don't think Drew will?"

Ollie closed his eyes. "I don't know. I know they had things rough when they grew up. Their mom died when they were seven. The father was...*is* an alcoholic. I know he was verbally abusive, but you can't arrest someone for that. When Kelli got back, I talked to her about how her ex was violent toward her. She didn't want to tell me much. She was embarrassed and all, but I told her I needed to know details to help her get that restraining order. She described some of it. Being hit, slapped, dragged through the house by her hair. When Ashley started to curse about how she hated men, Kelli said, 'It wasn't anything new for me.'"

"Their father?"

Ollie nodded. "I asked Ashley about it. She

wouldn't talk. Just said that was then, this is now and how, unlike her sister, she'd never be some man's punching bag again."

Sam thought about her family. Her beautiful, wonderful mother and her supportive and loving father. Seeing their faces in her mind, she said a silent prayer of thanks for what she had with them. "Ashley should be careful how she talks around Cole. Not all men are like that. My father wasn't. I know you would never be. Cole needs to understand being a man doesn't make you violent."

"She knows that," Ollie said. "Kelli said that too. Said something about how Drew never hurt them. Always tried to get between them and their father."

"So, that means he's a good guy, right?"

Ollie frowned. "Not the Drew I remember, no. He took a strong dislike to me for no reason."

"How so?"

Ollie considered the question as he watched a car go by.

"He was a bully," Ollie said. "Tripped me. Pushed me. Called me names. Embarrassed the hell out of me."

"What'd he do? Make fun of your ears?"

"My ears?" Ollie looked in the mirror. "What's wrong with my ears?"

Sam tried to fix a look of wide eyed innocence on her face, but she couldn't help but burst out laughing. "Nothing. I'm just teasing."

The fact was, Ollie was a pretty good-looking guy. He was tall, lanky, with a mess of blonde hair and baby blue eyes.

"Actually, my Nana thinks you're kind of cute."

Ollie stopped studying the reflection of his ears.

"How bad are your Nana's cataracts?"

"Not *too* bad," Sam said.

Ollie scowled at her. "Back when I was younger, I wasn't the fine specimen of manhood you see before you now. In fact, I was a bit of a geek."

Sam put her hand to her cheek and dropped her mouth open in mock surprise. "You? A geek? No. So hard to believe when you've got all that cool stuff at your place. Your light saber and wand, and what was that big thing on the wall? The sharp thing that looked like it could be used to open a really big bottle of beer?"

"A bat'leth," Ollie said solemnly. "A Klingon weapon of honor."

"Right."

Ollie sighed, but continued. "So anyways, back when we were kids, I was also a little on the chubby side. So, I was called fat ass, lardo, doughboy and elephant boy."

"Elephant boy?"

Ollie glanced at his ears again. "Yeah. A few others I'd rather not repeat. Shoved me all the time. Made me miserable."

"I'll bet," Sam said. "So, instead of a good guy, he's coming off as an ass."

Ollie nodded. "Exactly. I don't know if I want someone like him near Ashley or Cole."

"You realize that's not up to you."

"No, it's not." Ollie watched for more cars, but none were coming. "Then there was what happened with him and Molly Winters at the homecoming dance senior year."

Sam knew some of the story. Back when this happened, she heard some of it when she'd come to

38

visit Nana. It had been the talk of the town, after all, but she hadn't lived it, so she let Ollie explain.

"They came to the dance already hammered from a party at the Brooks' house."

Sam blinked in surprise. "That's the big house on Avery. Wasn't there a Mayor Brooks?"

Ollie nodded. "At the time. Now, he's a U.S. Senator with eyes on the White House. Molly Winters knew all the Brooks in school. She'd been the one invited. I'm sure Drew just tagged along.

"They weren't there five minutes before the two of them were going at it on the dance floor," Ollie continued. "They called each other a few rather disgusting names, Molly slapped Drew, and after a moment, he stumbled out."

Sam tried to picture it in her head. Saw them on the dance floor, making out, getting fresh. She imagined maybe Drew Duncan pushed his luck and set things off. Men could be such idiots. Still, it helped paint a picture.

"Was she pissed that he'd left her?"

Ollie shook his head without any hesitation. "Nope. In fact, I'm pretty sure she was screaming at him to go before he turned and left. I tried to ask if she was all right, but I wasn't on her radar. I went my own way, mostly to stand with my back on the wall and stew about what happened. I'd hoped to…" Ollie trailed off, shrugged.

"People said they remembered seeing Molly around here and there. She apparently had several offers to take her home, but by the time the dance was closed out, she was gone. Nobody really thought much of it. She was a popular girl and everyone figured she'd managed to hitch a ride with someone, but nobody knew who. She just vanished."

"And Drew? Did anyone see him around the dance after he left?"

"No," Ollie said. "He didn't have a car that night. Someone else had driven to the dance. They found him in the parking lot of the Wallman's, the old supermarket on the other side of town. It was never open past nine. He had shot something into his veins. Stupid bastard OD'd and nearly died. They rushed him to the hospital. He recovered, but they never found Molly. When they found her blood in the school basement, they placed the son of a bitch under arrest."

"What did they have on him?"

Ollie thought about it a moment. "As far as I know, just what I told you."

Sam took it all in, thought it through. Her fingers started to tap on the car door as she imagined if she had gotten the chance to investigate. Man, she'd have loved that. She was tempted to start poking around, but it wouldn't be right. Why open old wounds now?

"So, he was acquitted?" She knew very well a not-guilty verdict didn't mean innocent.

"Never went to trial," Ollie said. "They held him for nearly a year. Maybe they hoped for a plea, but he never folded. Then the chief had a heart attack and that's when my mom took over. First ever female chief of Ember Falls. I know she didn't think much of the old one. Within a few weeks, Drew was let go. Charges were dropped, and Drew was gone."

"Any other suspects?"

Ollie shook his head. "Not that I'm aware of. I don't think they really looked anywhere else." He looked over to his partner, but she stared out of the window, avoiding eye contact. "What do you think?"

Sam didn't answer at first. She was still running through things in her mind. Old wounds leave scabs. Pick at them and they can get infected.

"Sam, you've got something spinning in that head."

"I've been a cop under a year. And you know the players far better than I do."

"True." Ollie watched more cars go by. "Maybe that's the point. You're more objective. I don't like Drew Duncan, and you've got a good cop's brain in your head. That's why after you finished your six-month probation I asked for them to partner us. I want to hear what you think about all of it."

Sam smiled. "All right, but just remember you asked for it."

Ollie nodded. "Deal."

Sam pursed her lips and took a moment to gather her thoughts. "It's hard to say without more info. Yes, he sounds like he was an ass back then to you, but that doesn't make him a killer."

"I realize that," Ollie said. "It didn't need to be on purpose. He could have circled back, picked her up and things went bad. Hid the body. Maybe he never meant to hurt her. Or he was so out of it he lost his cool."

"Maybe." It *could* have happened that way. "She slapped him."

"So?" Ollie said. "That doesn't give him the right to hurt her. He should have walked away."

"And, according to you, he did. He was pissed, but he *walked* away. The entire idea that he hurt her is based on the idea that he came back, but there's no evidence that he returned to the school that night. Did anyone have to separate them? Did he look like he wanted to hit her?"

Ollie scowled. "No. He was pissed, but he never raised his hand. He walked away. But he was *still* an asshole."

There was no doubt in Sam's mind Drew Duncan earned that title back then. At least when it came to Ollie, and that irked her. Ollie was such a sweet soul. While he was a good, strong, confident cop now, Sam could easily imagine him as a kid too passive to stand up for himself. She'd seen pictures of him when he was younger. He wasn't that heavy, but it was enough she could imagine the ribbing he'd have caught from the wrong kid. Apparently, Drew Duncan was the wrong kid.

She took Ollie's hand. "You're not the same chubby kid you were back then. Maybe Drew Duncan isn't the same asshole, maybe he is, but whatever he is, you can handle him. And this time, you've got me. I've got your back, partner."

****

The driver spotted the patrol car, but even past their field of vision, the General didn't increase speed. It was one of the reasons he insisted on driving. If he let Drew do it, they'd be going ninety miles an hour at the very least.

The General tried to be patient with Drew's smoking. Drew usually didn't chain smoke, but he was in a tremendous amount of emotional distress. From the second he'd shown up at his door, the General could see the grief pour out of him, but the moment they'd crossed into the city limits of Ember Falls, a white-knuckled panic had taken over.

The General had seen Drew in many emotional states, angry, sad, friendly, jovial, and even at times whimsical. He'd never seen him frightened. Drew Duncan faced death the way most men buttered bread, but right now he seemed one step away from a full-blown panic attack.

Now, he sat rubbing his hands over his jeans to dry his palms, fidgeting with his phone, and taking one drag after another.

"At least open a window," the General said.

Drew did. "Sorry."

Now the General was worried. No smart-ass answer meant Drew was really far gone. He understood the sorrow. He'd experienced it himself on more than one occasion, that bitter punch to the gut that comes from finding out someone you loved was ripped from this world. The General understood the grief, but not the fear.

For Drew, home was hell. That much the General understood, but he never expected the boy to be this terrified of his home town. There was something he wasn't seeing, and that pissed him off.

"You're going to chew a hole in your lip."

After a moment of confusion, Drew stopped biting his lower lip, something he was unaware he had been doing. He took a drag, blew out smoke, and tossed away the stub.

"Sorry," Drew said. "I know you hate the stuff. I keep meaning to quit."

"Sounds like bullshit to me. You want to quit, quit."

"It's not that easy." Drew resisted the urge to light up another one. He had a fresh pack in his jacket pocket.

"For a lot of people, you're right," the General said. "Not for you. When you find the motivation you need, you'll quit. You don't do things half way."

Drew didn't respond. He just sat there, nearly trembling in fear, looking ready to vomit.

"Stop it," the General said.

"What?"

"You know what," the General said. "You're taking a stroll down memory lane and not a pleasant one. You're beating yourself up and quite frankly, it's pissing me off. You've got a job to do."

Drew forced himself to look away from the nearby parking lot. "What are you talking about? I'm going to see my family, a nephew who's never seen me, and a sister who'd be happy to never see me again. And I've got to help bury my sister, the only blood relative I have who would have wanted me in their life." Drew closed his eyes and sighed. "Had. Dammit."

The General gripped the steering wheel and tried to resist the urge to slap Drew on the back of his head. "You've got family issues to sort through, a sister who is hurting and is probably going to take that pain out on you, so you need to deal with it. I'm not telling you to be a punching bag, but be patient."

Drew nodded. "It's been a while, but I still know to bring a lot of patience when it comes to Ashley. Even on a good day, she's high maintenance."

"And you're not?"

Drew didn't answer, he just clenched his fists as they approached Ember Falls High School.

"And let's not forget the big picture."

"Huh?" Drew said, forcing himself back to reality.

"What?"

"Your nephew," the General said. "What's his name again?"

Drew pulled out the new pack of cigarettes and began to smack the top of the box, but didn't pull off the cellophane. "Cole."

"I know that," the General said. "I was just seeing if you remembered. He's got to be your first priority. He's going to test you. Push at you. Push *back*. You've got to see him for who he is, not just an obligation to a sister that died. Don't make him feel that way." The General glanced over. Drew was white as a sheet. "You okay?"

"Yeah. I'm fine. Make a right at the corner."

The General glanced down at the GPS. "This is the route to your sister's place."

"It's one route," Drew snapped, visibly shaking. "Just make the goddamned right."

With raised eyebrows, the General hit the turn signal and rounded the corner as directed. As he did, Drew's color came back a touch, although he still looked as if he was going to be ill.

He wanted to ask what they just avoided, but instinct told him not to. Drew wasn't going to give him a straight answer right now. The boy had too many other things to deal with.

So, for now, he allowed the GPS and Drew to take him on the scenic route.

"You know," the General said. "Almost anyone else, if I were tooling around their hometown, I'd be hearing one story after another of their misspent youth. That's where I had my first kiss, that's where I smoked my first cigarette, that's the store that sold me my first nudie magazine."

At first, it seemed like Drew hadn't heard him. Then he looked over to the General and forced a smile. "You're welcome."

The General smirked. *Good to know you're still in there.*

Passing the main shopping area, they came to a bookstore. It was a local shop that boasted a café, internet access, and rare, hard-to-find books. At Drew's direction, they took a right and headed toward a side road.

"At the end of the road," Drew said. "The yellow house."

The General pulled up in front of the house, sliding into a space near the front gate. It was a Victorian, corner house with an elaborate front garden. There was a decent back yard encased with a white privacy fence. The front porch was covered by an overhang.

Directly behind the house was an older home, and to the left was all wooded. A good place, the General thought, for a kid to explore.

"Is this the house you grew up in?" The General asked.

Drew wasn't rushing to get out. "Lily lives here, and now so does my sister. This place belonged to Lily's grandmother, as did the bookstore. She inherited both. Lily always had a love for books and she was close with her grandmother."

The General nodded. "What are you planning on telling Cole about your past here?"

Drew ran his hand over his head. "Not planning on telling him anything. It was nearly a decade ago. No reason to bring that up."

"You think he won't hear it from somewhere?" The General asked. "Better you broach it."

"He wasn't even born yet," Drew asserted.

The General waited, but Drew, who wanted to get here so fast he probably would have gotten out and pushed the plane if he could have, was now making no movement to get out.

"Are we having second thoughts?"

Drew stared at the house. "You should know my home life before the Marines wasn't anything like the family you came from. I did things I'm not proud of."

Drew's appeared haunted as he looked into the General's eyes. "I didn't kill that girl. I can't really remember that night, but *that* I know. But when I lived here, I wasn't a very good person. I didn't know how to be. And I did something that a man like you would never do. I left. I never should have abandoned my sisters, but I really didn't know what else to do. I was weak and afraid. That's the bottom line."

Drew looked back at the house. "I don't know what's going to happen when I walk through that door. I don't know what you're going to hear. I'm not that person anymore. You and your grandson are two of the biggest reasons why."

The General considered Drew for a moment. He had done his homework on him. While he didn't know everything, he could guess a lot of it.

"Son," the General said. "If you think I was under the impression you were an altar boy before you came to work for me, then you're even more of a shit for brains than I thought. Nobody is the same person they were so many years ago. Now, maybe you were a bigger idiot back then than you are now. Hard to believe, but I'll allow for the possibility. That doesn't matter. You can't go back and change it. What counts is what you do now. It's time to step up. I don't need you to show me you can, because I know what your sorry ass is capable of, even if you don't. But I think you need to go prove it to your sister and your nephew. And clearly, you need to prove it to yourself. So, why don't we pull up our big boy pants and get to it?"

Drew couldn't help but grin. "Let's go."

They stood in front of the door. Drew let out a breath and raised his hand to knock when the door swung open.

****

Ashley Duncan looked at her brother and buried the urge to pull him into a hug and cry in his arms. She buried it deep under a ton of anger from all the years of worrying about him and missing him. So, instead of the hug she wanted to give him, she greeted him with a snarl.

"I guess you figured better late than never," she said. "So what's your plan? Blow into town, pretend nothing happened and hightail it out of here? You think you can play weekend hero for that little boy? He needs more than a drive by 'atta boy. He needs stability and that's not exactly your strong suit. So, I'm thinking you should take your pal here and just hit the road."

Drew managed a quick glance at the General, who looked impressed.

"I'm not going anywhere, Ash," Drew said. "I'm here for my nephew. And I'm here for you. You may not want me, but I'm here."

Ashley didn't answer. She couldn't, not without her voice cracking.

"Let them in." The voice came from behind Ashley. Small, gentle, yet full of authority.

Ashley moved aside and let the door slam closed. It opened again, this time with Lily on the other side. She was a tiny thing, barely reaching to Drew's chest even though she was one step up. She had long, red hair that was wavy, and green eyes. She greeted them with a sad smile.

"Drew," she said. "I'm so sorry."

She reached up and pulled him into a hug.

"Please, come in," Lily said.

Drew stepped inside, with the General right behind him.

"This is Paul McAlister," Drew said.

Lily extended a hand. The General took it.

"I'm sorry to meet you under these circumstances," the General said. He turned to Ashley. "And I'm very sorry to hear about your sister."

Ashley nodded. "Thank you."

There was a moment of silence, broken by a sneeze from upstairs. Drew looked up. He realized Cole was up there, listening. He started forward.

"Wait," Ashley said. "Where are you going?"

Drew motioned toward the stairs. "I'm going to see my nephew."

"Just like that? You're going to just go and say 'Hi there, kiddo'?"

"I don't know," Drew said. "I'll figure it out."

Ashley closed the distance and poked her brother's chest. "He's been through a lot. You can't just..."

A series of small sneezes had both Drew and Ashley looking up.

Realization dawned and Ashley sniffed her brother.

"You fucking reek of cigarettes."

"What?"

"You can't go near him," Ashley said.

Drew closed his eyes and tried for patience. "Ash, you can't keep me from him. Kelli wanted…"

Lily crossed the room and put her hand on Drew's arm. "No, she's right. Cole's allergic to cigarette smoke. He goes into a sneezing fit if he's anywhere near the smell. It's really bad."

Drew's eyes darted from Lily, to his sister, to the top of the stairs.

"Here." Lily walked over to a table and went into her purse. "There's an apartment over the garage. It's not much, but you can stay there. Go take a shower. Put on something clean." She pulled a key out of her purse and handed it to Drew as the sneezing continued.

Taking it, Drew slipped it in his pocket. "Thank you."

"You can't be around him and smell like that," Ashley said.

"That's fine," Drew answered. "I just quit."

He started toward the door, but Ashley stepped in front of him. "You can't touch him." She said in a hushed tone.

"Ashley," Drew snapped. His temper was reaching its boiling point. "What the hell do you think I'm going to do?"

"No." Ashley shook her head. "I don't mean… Lily, you tell him."

Drew looked toward Lily. "She's right. You shouldn't try to touch him. Cole doesn't like to be touched. It's not you."

Drew's eyes narrowed as he looked at his sister.

"What the hell did that bastard do to him?"

For the first time since her brother arrived, Ashley didn't answer him in anger. "I don't know."

For a brief moment, Ashley was a terrified little girl looking into the eyes of a brother who would die to defend her.

"I promise you this," he said, putting his hand on her shoulder. "He's never getting near him again. He tries, I'll fucking end him."

Ashley placed her own hand over his and nodded. Then she stepped back so Drew could go shower. As he reached the door, she called out to him. "Drew."

He turned.

"Welcome back."

Chapter 4
Meeting Uncle Drew

"I'm glad Drew is going to try and quit smoking," Lily said. "Besides being better for Cole, it's healthier for him. I hope he's able to."

The General took a sip of water. "He did quit."

Lily laughed. "For about thirty seconds so far. It's not that easy. My mother kept trying to quit. It never took."

"I know it's a difficult habit to break," the General said as Ashley came back down the stairs to join them. "But I know him. He's done being a smoker."

Ashley snorted as she went into the fridge for a soda. "Wanna bet?"

She looked like Drew. Nearly as tall, she had long, wavy dark, hair, the same dimple in her chin, and eyes the color of autumn leaves

"Absolutely," the General said. "And I'll win. If you gave your brother a break, you'd see that."

"The only break my brother deserves is the one I should put in his skull. He was too afraid to come back to town." Ashley slid into the seat near Lily. "By the way, who are you exactly to Drew? His supplier?"

The General blinked several times while Lily's face turned red.

"Ash." Lily tried to give her best friend an admonishing glare.

"What?" Ashley spread her arms out wide. "I have no clue who this guy is or for that matter, what Drew has been up to. I heard he joined the military, but he couldn't get here this fast if you two were still in the Marines. So, what's up? What kind of nefarious business are you and my big bro up to?"

Lily shook her head and buried her face in her hands. "I'm so sorry…"

"No." The General held up his hand. He knew when he'd come on this trip the sister was going to be a handful, but Ashley Duncan wasn't the first handful he'd dealt with. "It's clear you don't know much about who your brother is today."

"Not my fault," Ashley said with a challenge in her eyes.

"Fair enough," the General said. "Allow me to fill in a few holes. My name is General Paul McAlister. US Marines. I have never taken, bought or sold illegal narcotics."

"You served with Drew?" Lily asked.

"No," the General said. "Retired Marine. Drew served with my grandson, Matthew McAlister. The first time I met your brother, I was visiting Matt in the hospital. He'd been injured in downtown Fallujah. He and Drew were buddies. Their unit got ambushed. There were twelve of them together. Four were killed, most of the rest injured. Drew held off the insurgents, mostly single-handedly. If it weren't for him, my grandson would have been killed."

He paused a moment, wanting that to sink in. Ashley held his eyes. She wasn't ready to blink just yet.

"Drew was still pretty rough around the edges, but I saw potential in him. Plus, I was just grateful. I could tell he and Matt bonded. I learned that had actually been the third time your brother had saved my grandson."

"So, why are you here and not Matt?" Ashley said. "Sounds like they're besties."

She started to take a sip of soda when the General sighed.

"Matt was killed a week before they were supposed to come home." He paused, took note of how Ashley froze with the can halfway to her lips. "Their platoon was attacked. They radioed for extraction, but Matt got separated. Drew went back for him. It was too late. Matt was already dead, but Drew risked his life, fought like hell to get Matt's body. Carried my grandson through enemy fire over his shoulder and brought him home to me."

Ashley's eyes broke away.

"I'm so sorry," Lily said.

"Thank you," the General said. "That's something you hear a lot when someone you love dies. I'm sure you've heard it a lot lately. Most of the time, the person saying it means their sorry for your loss. Sorry for the pain you're feeling. Drew said that to me, but when he said those words, I knew it was more than just those same sentiments of condolences.

"Your brother blamed himself. I had already read the report. I also made it my business to talk to the other surviving members of their unit. There was nothing Drew could have done. If it weren't for him, more of them would have been killed. There was no reason for Drew to feel responsible, but he did.

"I asked Drew to join my organization, McAlister Security," the General continued. "I've never regretted it. He's been my point man on dozens of operations. He's saved lives. He's put himself at risk to do so. Do you know where he was when he got the news about Kelli?"

Ashley didn't move, but she couldn't make eye contact anymore.

"We were just across the Mexican border," the General said. "We were there to pay a ransom and recover a thirteen-year-old girl. It was supposed to be a simple exchange, but we both knew there was a good possibility it could go bad. They showed up with the girl and Drew exchanged a million dollars in cash for her, but they didn't want any witnesses. Planned to kill them both. Drew and I had prepared for that. I had him well covered, but there were half a dozen of them and all it would take was one lucky shot. Drew's first action was to shield that girl with his own body to protect her.

"Let me ask you a question. Back in town, the GPS wanted me to go straight on Broadway, but Drew had me make a right by that Mobil station. What would we have passed had we gone the way the GPS was telling us?"

Ashley's face went white. "The house we grew up in."

The General nodded. "What I figured. Everything I know about your brother tells me he's one of the bravest men I've ever known, but he was terrified about coming back here. I'm talking white-knuckled, scared for your life, kind of terrified. I've never seen him scared like that, but he came.

"He made the decision to come before he heard about your sister being murdered. We talked about it. I knew then I was about to lose my best man. He hasn't said anything. He might not have even thought that far ahead. But I know him. He was going to come back for Kelli. He came back for Cole. And you need to believe he came back for you."

Ashley shifted uncomfortably. "You must think I'm a complete bitch, but it hurt that Drew left. I'm not ready to forgive him yet."

The General got up and moved toward her, waiting until she made eye contact.

"Here's what I think." The General's voice softened as he offered her a small smile. "I think you have a lot to be angry about. I think you probably have plenty of reasons to be angry with Drew. Lord knows he's gotten me mad as hell on more than one occasion. He's important to me, but he's also a pain in my ass."

Despite herself, there was a tug at the corner of Ashley's lips.

"I also believe while you might not be ready to forgive him, you love him. And you love that child up there. And he's what's important. If you're anything like your brother, you'll put him first."

The General reached out, put his hand on Ashley's shoulder. "Drew is the last connection to my grandson. He's been like family to me for the last few years. So, that makes you family, and it only follows that you'll be a pain in the ass too, but that's what family is for."

Ashley brushed a tear away. "I'm glad Drew's had you. Just…don't tell him I said that, okay?"

"Deal," the General said.

Drew came through the door. He was freshly showered and wearing clean clothes. "Better?"

Lily sniffed him. "Much."

"All right. I'm going to go talk to Cole." Drew

headed for the stairs.

"Drew," Ashley called out to her brother. "Cole hasn't cried yet. He won't talk to either of us. He understands Kelli's dead, but he's barely said a word since we told him, and he won't eat. See if you can get him to eat something."

Drew nodded. "I'll take care of it."

****

Cole Duncan sat on his bed, holding a book in his hand and ignoring the man who came up the stairs. Cole made no indication he was aware Drew was approaching, even as he stood at the kid's doorway.

Drew knocked on the door frame. "Cole. I'd like to talk to you. Can I come in?"

Cole simply shrugged. Drew took that as an invitation and entered. "I'm your Uncle Drew."

Cole gave a small nod.

"I'm sorry about your mom."

Drew waited, but Cole didn't say anything. He just flipped the page.

"Good book?" Drew was answered by another shrug. "Your mom loved to read. I guess you get that from her. She always had a book with her. I'm surprised she didn't teach you the proper way to read." Drew reached out, tugged the upside-down book out of Cole's hand and turned it right side up. "You might enjoy it better this way."

Cole looked up and gasped. His uncle was bigger than Cole imagined. Cole couldn't help but think how he'd describe his uncle in a story if he were a character. He was massive, like one of those people on the fake wrestling shows that Aunt Ash sometimes watched. He was tall, with short, neatly trimmed brown hair. His arms were huge tree trunks, and solid. There was a black tattoo of sharp, thick lines that ran over the muscles on his right arm. He had a broad chest and blue eyes that were looking right at him.

Cole tossed the book on the bed. Stupid, careless mistakes could get him hurt. Big, strong men didn't like it when boys tried to hide things. He tensed, ready to launch himself off the bed. The problem was, his uncle was between him and the door.

Don't scream. Don't let him hurt Aunt Ash or Lily because you were so stupid.

"So," Drew said. "Let's not pretend like you don't know who I am or that you haven't been listening at the top of the stairs since I walked into this house. Probably watched me walk up to the front door from that window."

Cole's eyes darted toward the door, calculating if he could escape.

Drew gently grabbed a chair and turned it around, straddled it, and then shoved his hands into his pockets. "Is it okay to talk to you?"

Cole relaxed, just a bit. He could escape if he had to.

"I'm sorry I haven't been in your life until now."

Cole shrugged. "I don't give a shit."

"I do," Drew said. "I'm sorry, but I'm here now."

Cole folded his arms. "So what? You weren't here when my mom needed you."

"I know. I wish there was something I could do to bring her back. I can't."

"So why don't you go away?"

"Because your mom wanted me here. And she would want me to be here now more than ever. So I am.

And I'm not going anywhere."

Cole turned away. "Bullshit. Aunt Ash doesn't think you're going to stay either."

Drew nodded. "You're right, she doesn't. So, that's two of you I have to prove wrong. I'm here and I'm not going anywhere. You're just going to have to get used to looking at my ugly face."

Cole glared at Drew. Men made promises they had no intention of keeping all the time.

"Did your mom talk about me at all?"

"Some," Cole admitted. It had been more than some, especially after they had finally gotten away. She said she'd find his Uncle Drew and he'd keep them safe. "She wrote to you a week ago. Why'd you take so long?"

Drew rubbed his hand over his face. "I left Ember Falls when I had just turned eighteen. Things were bad. Your mom left and I didn't know how to get in contact with her. I figured she didn't want me around, but I kept my old e-mail open. I would check it, always hoping I'd hear from either of my sisters, but after years of only getting junk mail I didn't check very often. I just saw your mom's e-mail a few hours ago. I was in the middle of something…"

"That girl you rescued." Cole interjected.

Drew's eyes narrowed. "How did you…?" Despite himself, he grinned. "The General was talking to Lily and Ash. You heard from the landing."

Cole didn't return the grin, but he relaxed a bit more. The fact his uncle didn't get angry because he'd been spying helped.

"Yeah," Drew said. "I was helping to rescue that girl. I got the e-mail right before we went in. I sent back a response when we got back. I went to take a shower and got the call from Lily."

"What did you say to Mom?"

Drew reached into his pocket and pulled out his phone. "Here." He reached forward and held the phone out to his nephew.

Cole hesitantly took it. He hadn't read the e-mail his mother sent, but she had told him about it. He had gotten upset when the Uncle Drew his mother told him about for so long, the man his mother knew, if she could just get in contact with him, would come and help them, hadn't responded within minutes of her sending the e-mail.

He'd asked his mother every day if she'd gotten an answer. Each day he was told, "'Not yet.'" Three days ago, it didn't matter anymore. So why should it matter now?

Cole knew the answer was because it would have mattered to his mother. She would have wanted to read this. So he read it for her.

Kelli,

God, it's so good to hear from you. I'm so sorry I haven't been there. Reading your email, all I can do is say I'm sorry for not protecting you. I fucked up, it's the only thing I can say. I tried to write you both. I thought you and Ashley were ignoring me. I thought you believed everything they were saying about me.

If you'll have me, I want to be a part of your life again. A part of your son's life. I can help if you let me. As soon as I tie up some last-minute details, I'll come see you.

Coming back to that town scares the crap out of me, but knowing you believe in me is enough. I miss my sisters. (Yes, even Ash.) So hang tight and I'll be there. Soon. And please, whatever you do, stay away from Dad. Don't tell him I'm coming back.

If you need anything before I get there, call me. I've been a shitty brother, but I swear I'll make it up to you. I can tell you're worried about your ex. You have my word, I won't let him ever hurt Cole again.

BTW, he looks like you. He has your eyes. I'm sure he's an amazing kid, and I can't wait to meet him. It's pretty cool to find out I'm an uncle.

I love you,

Drew

At the bottom of the e-mail was Drew's cell number. Cole read and reread the e-mail before putting the phone down and slipping off the bed, away from Drew. He went to the window and looked out.

His uncle was big, even bigger than his stepfather, but he could never remember Edward Hunter ever saying he was sorry for anything. Uncle Drew said it. He made a promise to his mother to come back and to protect them. He came back, but it was too late to protect his mother.

Cole turned back to his uncle. He'd listened to that man downstairs talk about how he'd fought in wars and stuff. He could've been killed while saving that girl. That didn't sound like someone who was afraid, but the man downstairs said Uncle Drew was afraid to come back here. Uncle Drew even admitted it.

Cole understood fear. He couldn't remember a time where he wasn't at least a little scared. He never knew when Edward was going to come home or what he'd do. What he'd make Cole watch.

It made him feel a little less like a wuss, knowing a

guy as big and strong as his uncle could be scared. And his uncle still came.

So now what?

Cole stood near the window, his arms folded and his gaze locked on his uncle's eyes. So far, he'd been straight with him. *Let's see how long that lasts.* Cole had questions and it was time he got answers.

"What happened to my mom?"

Uncle Drew looked confused. "She was killed. Cole, she's dead."

Cole let out an impatient breath. "I know that. I'm not a moron. I want to know what happened. Did it hurt? Where is she? Aunt Ash won't tell me. She's my mother. I have a right to know."

Drew appraised his nephew.

"You're right, you do," Drew said. "I can't tell you much because I don't know much. Cole, I found out about this less than six hours ago, and I don't have any details, but I can find out. It won't be easy for you to hear, but if you need to know..."

"I'm not a baby," Cole yelled. "I can handle it. *I'm not scared.*"

Cole was lying, but he did his best to not look afraid.

Drew nodded. "I'll find out."

Cole waited for his uncle to say something like, "and then I'll decide what you can handle" or "but I can't promise to tell you," but he didn't.

"I want to see her," Cole added. "I want to see my mother. Aunt Ash and Lily have seen her, but I haven't. I want to see her."

Drew stood up. Cole retreated back and gasped.

Here it comes, here it comes, here it comes!

He'd pushed too far and now this huge man was going to make him pay.

"Stay here," Drew said. "And Cole, it may take some time for you to believe me, but I swear to God, I'll never hit you."

He walked out of his bedroom and thundered down the stairs.

Cole didn't go to the stairs to listen. He couldn't move right now. All he could was try to desperately try to stop shaking.

Chapter 5
Big Boys Do Cry

Cole didn't need to go to the landing to hear much of what was said downstairs. Aunt Ash started to yell at Uncle Drew within moments of his going downstairs.

And Uncle Drew yelled back.

Cole started sweating, his breaths coming in heaves. What had he done? He liked Aunt Ashley. He didn't want her hurt. Uncle Drew was angry. He was yelling. He expected to hear the familiar sounds of things crashing and his Aunt screaming in pain, and it would be his fault.

Cole wasn't going to let it be his fault again. He opened his eyes and flew down the stairs, ready to do whatever he could to stop his uncle from hurting them.

Aunt Ashley stood in the middle of the room, her hands on her hips and her lip curled at her brother. She didn't look scared or hurt. She *did* look angry.

"Cole, you and me are going to go for a ride," Drew said. "We're gonna go to the police station and talk to someone. We'll see if they'll let us see your mom, but I can't promise that. But we'll get answers *together*. Okay?"

Aunt Ash had her arms folded, and clearly didn't want Cole to go.

"Your aunt is worried because you haven't eaten much for the last few days, so we're gonna swing into a drive thru on the way and you can get something in your stomach before we go, and tonight when we sit down for dinner as a family, you finish what's put in front of you. Deal?"

Without thinking, Cole nodded.

"Let's go," Drew said.

Cole didn't like the way his Aunt looked at him, like she wanted to yell and cry all at the same time.

"Wait." Ashley walked over and knelt down in front of him. "You don't have to look at her. It's okay to change your mind. You can tell your uncle and he won't be mad. Okay?"

Cole glanced up toward Drew.

"And you promise me you'll eat tonight?"

"I'll try," Cole answered.

"What do you want me to make?"

"Why don't we order in tonight? Nobody needs to be cooking here," Drew said as he and Cole moved toward the door. "Besides, kid's been through enough. He doesn't need to be tortured with something you make."

Cole felt a tug at the corner of his mouth.

Ashley sneered, but she held her tongue. "I'll call ahead. Go see Ollie. He knows Cole."

****

"So, what did you hear about me while I was taking a shower?" Drew said.

Cole forced down a bite of a nugget. "That guy, the old man…"

"Paul McAlister," Drew supplied. "We call him The General. Capital T, capital G. Retired Marine."

"He talked about what you did for his grandson. How you saved him. How you saved that girl. But that you were scared to come back here."

Cole waited for his uncle to deny it, but he didn't.

Cole munched on another nugget. "Why'd you come back then?"

Drew hung a left, took the long way to the police station. "Because my sister needed me to."

With his third nugget in his hand, Cole avoided eye contact. "She's dead. You can leave if you want to."

Drew pulled into the parking lot across from the police station and put the SUV in park. "She still needs me here. I'm not going anywhere."

Cole considered the idea that Drew was telling him the truth as he downed the last nugget.

"Okay, here's the deal." Drew killed the engine. "You and I are going to go in there and ask questions. Remember the police may not know much. If at any point it gets to be too much, you tell me."

"I can handle it," Cole insisted as he shoved his empty box of chicken nuggets into the bag they came in. "I'm not a wuss."

Drew sighed. "I know that. Cole, look at me." He waited until Cole made eye contact. "I *know* that. I know you're a tough kid, but this isn't going to be easy on either of us. I know you're scared to go in there because I am. There's no shame in being scared. And there's no shame in crying for your mom."

Cole shifted in his seat. No way was he going to cry like a baby in front of his uncle. Cole reached for the door, but he didn't open it.

"If you're not ready," Drew said. "We can leave. Part of me would be relieved to put the car in reverse and get out of here."

Cole swallowed hard, as if the nuggets were trying

to escape. "You'll stay with me?"

Drew nodded. "Every moment. We're in this together, but it's up to you."

Cole grabbed the door handle and got out.

****

"What the hell is he thinking?" Ollie asked.

Drew and Cole Duncan had come into the precinct, checked in at the front desk and were directed to an interview room in the back where they were waiting for him and Sam.

"Stop it," Sam said.

Ollie didn't take his eyes off the door where Drew and Cole had gone. "Stop what?"

Sam stepped in front of Ollie. "You're not dealing with the bully from when you were a kid. You're dealing with a man who just found out his sister was murdered. He's here with his nephew who lost his mother and is scared and feeling alone. Don't bring your baggage in there. If you need to deal with it, deal with it later. Not while that boy is in there and not when Drew Duncan is about to look at his dead sister. You're better than that."

Ollie unclenched the fist he hadn't realized he made.

"Let's go," Sam said.

When they walked in, Cole jumped. He sat close to his uncle, but never touching.

"Drew," Ollie said. "Why don't we step outside a moment? My partner can stay with Cole."

Drew caught the quick glance from Cole. He shook his head. "I'm sorry, I can't do that. I promised Cole we'd do this together. No secrets."

Ollie glanced at Sam, who held the files. She was

ready to hand them to him, but he wasn't ready to take them. "Are you sure about this? There's no reason to put him through this. I'll be happy to talk to you on your own."

"No!" Cole jumped up. He spun on Drew, his face going red. "You promised me!"

Drew turned to his nephew. He stayed calm and spoke in a quiet voice. "I did and I'm *keeping* my promise. Officer Miller is worried about you, like Aunt Ashley is. And he's thinking this was my idea." Drew turned back to Ollie. "It's *not*. Cole needs this."

Ollie studied both the boy and the man, and understood he'd misjudged the dynamic. *Time to recalculate and adjust.*

He sat down across from Drew, went to speak, but caught the look Drew sent him, directing his glance toward the child. With a nod, he moved over another seat and looked at Cole. Slowly, Cole took his seat again. "Cole, you need to understand that we're still looking into it. Trying to figure out what happened."

Drew leaned in toward the two of them. "We understand you don't have all the facts, and you can't tell us everything. Just tell us what you can. Cole needs to understand what happened."

Ollie nodded as Samantha handed him the file. "Cole, what we know is that she was killed three days ago. That was a Friday. She was last seen at seven in the evening. She had an appointment that ended then. She was walking to her car."

Cole listened, but he wasn't looking at Ollie anymore. He wasn't looking at anyone. "How did she die?"

Ollie shook his head. "You don't need to know…"

"He needs to know if she suffered," Drew said. "Was it quick?"

Ollie sighed. "I don't think she suffered. It wasn't instant, but it wasn't slow. There would have been some pain. She would have realized what was happening, but it didn't last long."

Cole swallowed hard. "I want to see her."

Samantha moved around the table, crouched down near Cole and waited for him to look at her.

"Cole, not too long ago, I lost my mother and father. I had to go see them in the morgue because I had to make the identification. It was the hardest thing I ever had to do. I saw them like that in my dreams for months. Are you sure you want to see her?"

Cole nodded. "She's already in my dreams. I want to see her. I…" He stopped when his voice cracked.

Sam started to say something else, but Drew held up a hand to stop her.

"Cole," Drew said. "The officer is right that this isn't going to be easy. I know you can handle it, but you don't need to. So, the choice is yours and yours alone. Take a moment and be sure. We can always come back, but you can't un-see it. This is your choice."

Cole closed his eyes, and took several deep breaths.

"Please, take me to see my mom."

****

The coroner's office was at the other end of the same building, but in the basement. Nobody said a word as they walked to the elevator and rode down, or as they slowly walked to the far end. Cole, certain everyone in the room could hear his heart slam in his chest as if it were trying to escape, was scared. There was no denying it.

Uncle Drew was scared too. He'd said so. And why say you're scared and make yourself sound like a wuss if you're not, but he was going.

More importantly, he'd kept his word. He let Cole decide. Cole felt confident if he changed his mind, his uncle wouldn't be upset.

They arrived at a pair of doors that swung open each way. There was a man standing there who was old, overweight and dressed like a doctor. He didn't smile, but his face was kind.

"Are we sure about this?" He spoke to Cole directly.

"Yes," Cole said.

The doctor of the dead nodded. "All right. I'm going to explain to you what you'll see before you go in. I want you to understand. Then I'll ask you again. If you still want to go in, I'll take you. All right?"

Cole nodded.

"Your mom was killed because someone cut her throat. It caused her to bleed. It would have hurt, but it would have been quick. She would have passed out from the loss of blood within a minute or two. She's been cleaned up. You won't see her blood, but she'll be paler than you remember. I'll have a sheet over her. You only need to see her face." He paused a moment. "You can't touch her. I know that seems cruel, but for legal reasons, you can't. Do you have any questions?"

Cole hesitated a moment. An hour ago, he was full of them. Now, he couldn't think of any. "No."

"Do you still want to go in?"

"Yes."

Drew stepped in front of Cole. "You tell me when

you've had enough, okay?"

Cole didn't answer with more than a nod, but when his uncle stepped beside him, Cole gripped his hand.

Together they went in.

The doctor went over to a table. There was a blue sheet draped over something. When the doctor went to stand on the opposite side of it and reached for the sheet, Cole realized it was his mother under there.

The doctor took one last look at Cole. "Are you ready?"

Several seconds passed with Cole frozen, until he closed his eyes and nodded. In his mind, he counted to ten, slowly. He wouldn't cry. Only babies cried. He wouldn't cry in front of his uncle, in front of Ollie, in front of his partner or the doctor. He'd been weak too long and he wouldn't be anymore.

When he opened his eyes, Cole saw his mother.

Kelli Duncan was lying on the table, with the blue sheet pulled up to her neck. Her skin was pale and her eyes were closed. Her blonde hair was flat and clean. He couldn't see where the man had cut her, and Cole was grateful for that.

Tentatively, he took a step forward. He searched for something that would allow him to say, "You've made a mistake. That's not my mom." But he knew it was. There was no hiding from it now.

Cole wanted to say goodbye, wanted to tell her how much he loved her, but he couldn't. Not here, in front of all of these people. Men had to be strong. *He* had to be strong. But he wasn't strong enough to stay in this room any longer. He needed to leave, before he broke.

Cole turned to tell his uncle he wanted to leave and

nearly gasped. Uncle Drew, who had been a Marine, had fought bad guys with guns and who was strong and solid, was crying unashamed where everyone could see him.

Finally, Cole was unable to fight the heaves of grief as he wept in his uncle's arms.

Chapter 6
Ollie Drops In

Ashley found Ollie on the front porch, as if he'd been afraid to press the doorbell. The sight of him, as usual, gave Ashley a feeling of warmth and comfort.

"Hey," Ollie said. "I hope I'm not intruding at a bad time."

Ashley pulled him into a hug, her one safe place. "It's never a good time these days. And you're never intruding. Come on in." Ashley grabbed his hand and pulled him forward. "Let me get you a cup of coffee."

Ollie said hello to everyone. Shook hands as he was introduced to Paul McAlister, who he was told to call the General and waited until Ashley brought him a cup of coffee and sat down by his side.

"I wanted to stop by in person and let you know the coroner told me he could release the body to you by the end of the weekend," Ollie said. "I took care of the paperwork, and I'll make sure she's brought to McGuire's Funeral Home first thing on Monday morning. I've talked to Billy McGuire myself. He'll take good care of her."

Ashley covered his hand with hers. "Thank you."

Ollie blushed.

"I suppose we need to plan her funeral," Lily said.

Ashley turned to Drew. "I didn't want to have a big thing. Kelli would have hated it. I had already figured we'd do a small mass, then the burial. I can get some food for here afterwards. That's tradition. You're not going to give me a hard time about this."

Drew didn't object. "Whatever you want is fine, but you should talk to Cole a little bit. Make him feel like he's contributing. It'll mean something."

Ashley shook her head. "He's just a little boy. He can't plan this."

Drew started to respond, but held off when the General raised his hand.

"And you'll make the big choices," the General said. "But there are small ones to be made. When my daughter and her husband were killed by a drunk driver, my wife and I took on my grandson. He was a little older than Cole. Thirteen at the time. We made the arrangements, but my wife had choices to make. Which reading to do? What outfits to put them in? Little things. Simple either-or choices. She consulted Matt so he felt like he was doing something for his parents. Right now, Cole must be feeling so many things. Angry, scared, confused. But also as if he has no control. Little things that you can do to give him some control will do him a world of good. It'll help."

Ashley considered his words. "That's why you took him today. I thought it was just because I had said no, but you wanted to give him some control."

Drew nodded. "In part. But I also understood why he needed to go."

Ashley scowled at her brother. He was right, and that pissed her off.

"There's something else we need to talk about," Ashley said. "Dad."

Drew's face went pale. "What's there to talk

about?"

Ashley shrugged, pretending not to be terrified of contacting him. "She was his daughter. He has a right to be there. I'm not looking forward to having to contact him, but better we prepare than let it just happen. He'll probably want to meet Cole."

"Bullshit," Drew snapped, standing up and jabbing a finger down at the table. "This is a small fucking town. He *knows*. Everyone is talking about Kelli's murder and he hasn't made a single move to contact you, or we wouldn't be having this discussion. And he's not getting anywhere near you or Cole."

Ashley folded her arms and stuck her chin out. "And what are you going to do if he shows up at the funeral? Kick his ass in front of Cole?"

"Your sister is right." The General slanted his eyes toward Drew's chair for a moment. With a huff, Drew sat down. "You can't leave this up to chance. Cole doesn't need to see a confrontation at his mother's funeral. Someone has to deal with it."

Ashley had to admit, she was impressed the General was able to handle her brother so well. "I'll talk to him."

"What?" Drew started to rise, but settled again with another glance from the General. "Why you?"

Ashley shrugged. "It makes sense. We haven't spoken since I…left, but we've seen each other around town. He goes his way, I go mine. It's almost like an unspoken understanding."

Drew started to shake his head.

"He's older now, and I'm meaner." Ashley continued. "I'll let him know. If he wants to go to her funeral, I won't stop him. But he stays away from

Cole."

Drew gripped the table. "No, you don't go near him. I'll do it."

Ashley rolled her eyes. "Please spare me the big brother routine. You made your choice and disappeared from my life. I've managed on my own for years without you. You came back for Cole and maybe he could use you in his life. Maybe I'll work around to forgiving you someday, but I don't *need* you. There's no reason for you to stand between me and Dad anymore. I'll go."

Drew shot up from his chair again, and paced like a caged animal. "No, you won't. Ashley, I get you hate me for leaving and you've managed on your own without me, but things are different now. With everything that's happened, Kelli being killed, me being back."

Ashley snorted. "You really think he'll care?"

"Ashley, please." Drew sat next to her. "Don't go near him. Let me deal with him. Please. I'm begging you. Ashley, if you've ever trusted me, if there's any part of you that still can trust me, trust me on this. He's more dangerous than you realize."

Ashley locked eyes with her brother. There was something he wasn't telling her. That was certain, and she would be damned if she was going to start relying on him. The idea he'd leave her again was too terrifying for her to even put into words.

But she had no great desire to speak to her father.

"Fine," Ashley said. "But on one condition. You don't go alone. He was cruel to me growing up. He fucking brutalized you. I don't want to hear that you got in there and literally tore his head off. Cole doesn't need that. So you go with someone."

"We'll go in the morning." The General turned to Drew. "Don't even bother trying to tell me no, and don't you dare try and go without me." He held his finger up to Drew, a sign the subject wasn't open for discussion. "You need someone to keep your ass in line, Marine. That someone would be me."

Drew nodded. "Yes, sir."

Ashley shook her head. "One of these days, General, you're going to have to show me how you do that."

The General smiled as he sipped his coffee. "Your brother, as I'm sure you know, can be a pain in the ass."

"Yes, I'm well aware of that."

"The trick," he answered with a wink. "Is I'm a bigger pain in the ass."

****

When the General decided it was time to go to bed, he said good night. Lily convinced him to stay with Drew in the guest apartment above the garage. When Lily went to the kitchen and Drew excused himself, Ollie was finally able to talk to Ashley alone.

The two of them went to the front porch and sat on the swing just as the sky turned a deep shade of dark blue. "How are you holding up?" Ollie said.

Ashley didn't answer right away. Her go-to response was "Fine," but they both knew that would be a lie.

"Not good," she admitted. "I'm alternating between being weepy, trying to be strong for Cole, and being a complete bitch to Drew."

Ollie put his arm around her. She rested her head on his chest and he kissed the top of her head.

"Well, it's natural to cry," Ollie said. "You are there for Cole and I'm sure he knows it. And in the grand scheme of things, it's perfectly acceptable to be a bitch to Drew. He deserves it."

Ashley snorted. "Can I tell you what really has me pissed off? Drew's been great with Cole. I mean, really great. He walked in here and just *got* him. Cole's asked over and over again to go see Kelli. Hated the fact Lily and I went without him. I should have taken Cole, but I just kept thinking I needed to protect him. I needed to shield him. But I can't. I can't protect him from the fact Kelli was murdered. What I should have been doing was helping him through it. It's not something I can make better, but I can help *him*. I want to help him, but God dammit, I don't know how. And Drew does."

Ollie forced himself to respond. "I'm glad he's helping."

"Am I being petty in not trusting Drew?" Ashley asked. "I know he's my brother, but there's nobody in the world I trust more than you. You won't piss me off."

"All right. I'm not sure Drew is the best thing for Cole. And it's not just because he left you. That's part of it, but not the whole thing. Back when we were growing up, Drew was an ass to me. He'd push me around and say things. I know I'm not a little kid anymore, but Cole is."

Ashley sat up suddenly and Ollie thought he'd upset her. "Ollie, why didn't you ever tell me? I would have straightened his ass out." She smacked his arm. "It's your own damn fault for being such a nice guy."

"Well then," he said. "Sorry."

She smiled and fell back into his arms. "Don't be.

That's what I love about you."

That's what I love about you.

Her words echoed in his mind. It was almost enough to imagine hearing her say, "I love you." Saying it, and meaning it the way he wished she did.

But Ollie understood she meant it like a friend. She loved him the way she loved Lily. Platonic, friendly, safe love.

Lily appeared at the door behind them. "Hey, Ash. You've got a phone call. Chris Manzullo."

Ashley groaned. "We had a date scheduled. He's been out of town and I'll bet the moron hasn't the foggiest idea what's happening."

Without saying goodbye, Ashley pushed off the swing and went inside. In a few moments, Ollie listened to her talking to Chris, calling him names and explaining with very little detail what happened. When she started to promise to make it up to him after things settled down again, Ollie decided it was time for him to leave.

He should just move on from his idiotic fantasy of ever being with Ashley Duncan. The fact was, she'd never see him as more than just a friend, more than a shoulder to lean on.

More than safe.

He took out his keys and hit the unlock button when someone came out the door. He spun, hoping it was Ashley asking him to stay. Even as a friend.

Instead, it was Drew Duncan. He'd changed out of his jeans into a pair of running shorts. He moved down to his SUV which was parked right in front of his.

Drew nodded toward Ollie. "Heading to the park for a run."

Ollie forced himself to nod. "My partner likes to run at night too." He had no idea why he said that.

Drew looked back to the house. "I wondered if you and my sister hooked up, but I guess not."

Ollie felt his back stiffen. "We're friends. Good friends. I'm always going to be there for her, Drew."

Drew held his keys in his hand, jiggled them a bit. "I get it. You've always been there."

"That's right," Ollie said. "I have been. While you left, I was there for her."

Drew froze. "Do we have a problem?"

Ollie clenched his fist, ready to use it. It wasn't the right thing to do. Certainly not the right time to do it, but he was done being pushed around.

"I suppose that's up to you." Ollie walked over to Drew, stood inches from him and wasn't going to back down. "I'm always here for her, and I always will be. She can count on me."

"And you're saying I won't be?" Drew said. "I'm back and I'm staying."

Ollie sneered. "We'll see. But that's not the point. Things have changed over the last few years. I'm not the same pudgy kid you could push around because you didn't like the fact he was trailing behind your sister. Try and push me around like you used to do, and I'll fucking push back. And you won't know what hit you."

Ollie jutted his chin out, daring Drew to hit it.

"I'm not convinced you're the best thing for Cole *or* for Ashley," Ollie said. "I'm sorry about your sister, I really am, but right now, I'm worried about them. I'll be watching to make sure you're not the same guy who bullied me when we were kids. Because if I get even a hint you're bullying Cole, I'll make you sorry you ever came back to Ember Falls."

Ollie didn't give Drew a chance to respond before he turned and went to his own car. He glared one last time at Drew before he drove off.

Chapter 7
The Best Coffee in Ember Falls

Drew drove way too fast to the park. He didn't give a shit if he got pulled over or pissed off another driver.

He didn't bother to lock the doors to the SUV. He left the keys inside and took off on the trail. Drew wished he was home, where he had access to his gym. He wanted to beat on something. He knew there wasn't a lot of crime here in Ember Falls, but he wished some moron would try and mug him as he cut through the park so he could have an excuse to use his fists and pound out his fury on someone's face.

What the hell was *wrong* with Ollie?

Somebody murdered his sister. Slit her throat and tossed her away like a piece of trash. Whoever that was needed to be found and stopped in the most painful way Drew could think of. He wanted to be the one to find them and take them apart, once piece at a time.

Then there was her ex, the one who kept her isolated and terrified for so long. If he'd known what was happening to her, he would have found her. Drew would have taken Kelli and Cole from that house and kept them safe.

Earlier today, when Drew talked with Cole, he'd gotten up too fast. He'd seen the look of fear in his eyes. In that moment, Cole had expected Drew to knock him across the room.

What Drew wanted to do was find Edward Hunter and knock *him* across the room.

Drew would never hit Cole, but dammit, he wanted to hit someone.

Instead, he hit the brakes as he came to a barrier across the running path.

"What the fuck!"

Wooden barricades blocked his path. Even in the dark, Drew could tell the path way was torn up. He thought about kicking one of them down when he heard someone behind him.

"The city is repairing the pathway. Taking their time about it too."

Drew spun around. She was tall, shapely and stunningly beautiful. Her long, dark hair was pulled back into a ponytail which reached the bottom of her long, slender neck. She wore a running outfit, a black top and gray sweatpants. Her brown eyes, which were the color of milk chocolate, looked him over as she came closer.

Something about her looked familiar, but he couldn't place her,—at least not until she took another step, the light from the moon hitting her face.

"You're Miller's partner," Drew said. "Aren't you?"

She nodded. "Officer Samantha Rossi. People call me Sam when I'm out of uniform. Hell, half of them call me Sam when I'm *in* uniform. I wanted to tell you how sorry I am."

This wasn't the mugger he'd hoped for. "Thank you."

"Do you want to talk?" She said. "Or would you rather I leave you to run? I won't be offended."

He didn't want to talk, but he didn't really want to run either. "I wouldn't be very good company right now."

Sam nodded. "I understand. You had a very intense look on your face as you were running. To be honest, when you turned around I thought you were going to take a swing at me."

"Really?" He thought of how Cole flinched away from him. "You didn't look scared."

Sam shrugged. "I don't scare that easily."

Drew smiled and it was the first real smile he'd had since he'd heard about Kelli.

"You think I'm kidding?" Sam's eyebrows went up. "I'm a cop. I can take care of myself."

Drew shook his head, putting put his hands in the air in mock surrender. "I'm sure you can kick ass. And you're right. When I heard you behind me, a part of me was hoping you were going to demand I give you my wallet."

Sam moved to stand more to his side. "I'll bet. We could go a round or two if it'll make you feel better. I promise not to arrest you for assaulting an officer. Or I could buy you a cup of coffee. I know a place that makes great coffee."

Drew ran his hand over his hair. He really wanted to pound something, but that wasn't going to happen. Maybe he should talk to someone, preferably someone who didn't look at him and see the teen boy who had grown up here.

Besides, despite the grief, the anger, and the fear that gripped him, he looked at Sam and wondered what she would taste like. Right here, right now with that coating of sweat on her.

For now, he decided to go with the coffee.

They ran back out to the park entrance where they got into their respective cars. Drew followed her to a house off Route 9. He was surprised when she pulled into the driveway, but he pulled in behind her.

"I thought we were going to a diner or something," Drew said as he got out.

Sam shook her head as she opened her door. "I had a feeling you'd want more privacy. And this is the place with the best coffee. Trust me."

He followed her inside and looked around as she busied herself in the kitchen. "You live here alone?" He examined the small kitchen filled with pig décor. Pig plates, piggy salt and pepper shakers and even a pink, pig toaster.

"No, my grandmother lives here. I moved to town when she had a heart attack. I wanted to be close to her."

Drew looked at a pig-clock on the wall. It was nearly ten. Not extremely late, but not early evening either.

Sam fiddled with a small device on the counter. She grabbed the handle that was on top and started to turn it clockwise. It made a grinding sound that filled the kitchen.

"Have a seat," she called out over her shoulder. "This is gonna take just a little bit, but it's worth it."

There was a little table off to the side, so Drew took a seat while Sam put the freshly ground coffee beans into a glass container with a black handle. "How strong do you like your coffee?"

"Plenty strong," Drew answered.

Nodding as she continued to work, Sam added

more coffee grounds. By now, a high-pitched whistle filled the room. Sam turned toward the stove and switched off the gas to the front burner before picking up the pig tea kettle. She walked over to the glass container and poured in the hot water out of the pig's snout. She grabbed what Drew thought of as a metal doohickey and placed it on top. There was an elevated handle, like a plunger. Slowly, she pressed it down. Once it went as far as it would go, she took out two large mugs, poured the coffee, and carried them over to the table.

"There's sugar right there," Sam indicated a small pig bowl to the side. "Do you need cream?"

"No thanks." He accepted the cup. The aroma that filled the air was beyond heavenly. Taking a sip, he couldn't help but close his eyes and savor the flavor.

Sam smiled at his grin.

"This is amazing," Drew said. "You were right. It was worth it. I just feel bad. Between the smell and the noise, aren't we going to wake your grandmother?"

Sam shook her head as she sipped herself, having added two tea spoons of sugar. "Not much chance of that."

Drew nodded, drank more coffee, and set his mug down before he finished it all. "Heavy sleeper?"

"She can be," Sam said. "Right now, she's out dancing her fanny off, as she likes to put it. There's a country western dance every Friday. Nana loves her two-step."

Drew's smiled broadened. "And what about you? You like to dosey-doe?"

She grinned over her mug. "On occasion."

Drew was amazed at how comfortable he felt

talking to her. There was something about those big, beautiful, brown eyes. Or maybe it was the coffee.

"It must be tough," Sam said. "Coming back to this town and knowing your sister is gone. I know you two weren't close…"

"Really?" His smile faded into a scowl. "Just what do you know?"

"I'm sorry, I was told you hadn't talked to Kelli or Ashley for some time. I don't know the details, but I shouldn't assume. I didn't mean you didn't care for her. I know you did. It was written all over your face today at the police station."

Drew stared at the coffee mug, fingered the handle and rolled her words around in his head. She had her facts straight. She was right. The devil was really in the details.

"I loved my sister," Drew finally said. "I love Ashley and I loved Kelli."

Slowly, Sam reached out and covered his hand with hers. "People don't grieve the way you are, hurt as deeply as you're hurting right now, if they didn't love. I know Ollie said you're probably just here to bury your sister and move on, but…"

"Is that what he says?" Drew did his best to keep the bitterness out of his tone this time. "For the record, I haven't talked to Ollie or anyone about my plans. Well, almost anyone."

"Oh?" Sam said. "Who have you talked to?"

Drew gulped more coffee. "Cole. I told him I'm staying."

Sam's eyebrows went up. "Just like that? You have a job. A place to live, I assume. A life outside of Ember Falls."

Drew started to trace the top of his coffee cup. "My place is just that. A place I go when I'm not working for the General."

"The General?"

Drew grinned. "General Paul McAlister. Everyone calls him the General. I met him through his grandson when we served together and he introduced me to the General. That's how he referred to him. Even his late wife used to call him that as well. From what I'm told, she was the only one who ever won an argument with the man. He'll kick your ass for fun and you'll thank him for it."

"Ooh," Sam said. "He sounds like fun."

Drew nodded and laughed. "He's great." Drew thought about the man who he'd wished had been his father and smiled. "I was in a pretty dark place when I met his grandson, Matt. I don't know why we bonded the way we did. I think he inherited his Grandfather's ability to just sense bullshit. Plus, I got into a fight right before we shipped out. Asshole hit on this waitress, wouldn't take no. Had his hands on her. I got in his face about it. He didn't like it and neither did his buddies. I'd bitten off more than I could chew, but damn it if I was about to back down."

"You were standing up for someone," Sam offered.

Drew shook his head. "I was looking for a fight. I was pissed at the world and wanted to pound someone. I could have tried to defuse the situation, but I wanted to take him on. I didn't realize he had buddies."

"How many?"

Drew held up his hand with all fingers out, including his thumb. "Figured I was about to get my ass kicked. Still didn't care. Next thing I knew, Matt jumped in. The two of us held our own until the police came. Numbskulls hadn't counted on the fact that the ass they were grabbing belonged to the daughter of a police lieutenant. She was working there, putting herself through college. She told the cops on scene that Matt and I came to her defense, so we didn't get any legal hassles out of it. Girl was okay, assholes spent a few nights in the local pokey and I had a new friend named Matt McAlister."

Drew finished his coffee. Sam got up to refill their cups. When she sat back down and pushed his coffee closer, he ignored it. "We had leave around Thanksgiving one year. I had no place to go." Drew chuckled. "Well, no place where I thought I'd be welcome."

Finally, Drew took the coffee and drank. "Matt was killed in Iraq." He didn't look up to see the sympathy in Sam's eyes. He didn't need to.

"I brought his body home. I'd been injured in the same fire fight. Nothing severe, but I was home and I wasn't going back. We were almost near the end of our tour. Another week and a half and we would have been out of there. Matt was the General's only grandchild. He had two kids. One died before she hit ten. The big C. The other fathered Matt. They left Matt with his grandparents so they could go out of town for their anniversary. He was thirteen. They never made it home. Drunk driver." Drew shrugged. "The General's lost his two kids, his wife to a heart attack and I got to take the last of his family away."

"Drew, you didn't take him away," Sam said.

Drew waved her off. "Before I knew it, I was working for the General. And he's more than a boss. He brought me back here. He'll stand with me when I put my sister in the ground, and then I'm going to tell him I'm leaving. McAlister Security has no interests in Ember Falls. But Cole needs me. I gave my word that I'll stay, and I will. And I know the General. He'll have already figured it out. He probably knew it before I did."

Sam smiled. "You love him."

"Yeah," Drew said. "I do. And I'm going to break his heart."

"Maybe not," Sam said. "You can still keep him in your life. Just because you stay and he doesn't, doesn't mean you have to cut him out completely."

Drew nodded. "And you're wondering if that's what I did with my sisters. What do you know about what happened before I left?"

Sam hesitated. "Some of it. I know a girl named Molly Winters disappeared. She's still never been found. You were arrested. They said you were found close to the scene of the crime. Claimed you didn't know anything. They charged you, which, since there was very little evidence, was stupid. Then the existing police chief died and a new one came in, Ollie's mother, in fact. Charges were dropped. You got out."

"Yeah, I got out," Drew said. "I don't remember most of that night. I was wasted out of my mind. I don't even remember drinking. Molly smoked pot. Pretty sure she was into some harder stuff. I'd never done drugs before then or since. I don't remember doing any that night, but I was probably drunk off my ass. It didn't agree with me. I nearly died.

"They found me OD'd about ten miles from the school, which is the last place anyone can remember seeing Molly. Not that they know that she was snatched from there. Or for that matter that she was snatched, but saying I was found near the scene looked better on paper, and for that matter, in the papers."

"The cops thought you were guilty?"

"The cops *wanted* me to be guilty," Drew said. "So did the DA. Molly's parents were friends with the Brooks. He was mayor back then, not a senator. He had it in for me. And he was buddies with the DA and chief. There was zero evidence. And thank you for not asking, but I'll say it so you don't have to. I'm innocent. I can't prove it. Hell, I can't even remember it, but I know it in here. I wouldn't have hurt her. That much I know. Knowing that, *believing* that, it was one of the few things that kept me going for a while."

Drew stared at his coffee and wondered if she'd slipped something into it to make him so chatty. This wasn't like him, opening up, but he was at the end of his rope. Something had to give, and this was helping. He could feel the knot in his gut loosen just a little bit.

"A little bit after the General buried Matt, I opened up to him. It was probably selfish of me, but I think he wanted to talk about something besides Matt and I needed to get it out. Looking back, I realize nothing I said was a surprise to him. He'd done his homework on me."

Sam smiled. "He didn't just believe you, he believed in you."

"Yeah he did." Drew stood up, walked over to the glass doors that led to the back deck. "Not that he said anything sappy when I told him I was innocent. He just nodded and said, 'Good to know because I need a new man at my company and having you be innocent makes the paperwork easier.'" Drew smiled as he recalled that moment. "That's how he asked me to work for him."

Sam got up and stepped beside him. "He's more than just a boss. He's family now. And you staying here to take care of Cole won't change that."

Drew turned to her, looked into those delicious brown eyes, saw the exquisite curve of her mouth, and he wanted so badly to put his mouth on hers. And then to keep going.

"You want to step outside?" Sam said. "It's a nice night and the fresh air would feel great."

Reluctantly, Drew followed her out to the back porch.

"Did you ever talk to your sisters?" Sam asked as she headed for a small bench swing.

Drew leaned against the back banister and looked out into the dark woods behind her home. "They never came to see me when I was in the hospital or jail. I wrote to them, they never responded. I figured they believed it. I didn't blame them. I heard some of what was going around about me. Stuff they had no evidence of. I'd been seen by over half a dozen people dragging Molly into my car. Nobody knew who these people were, but if you ask someone in town, they're sure they existed. And my sisters had other reasons to be pissed at me."

"Such as?" Sam asked.

Drew turned around and leaned on the banister. He folded his arms as he looked at her, silhouetted in the moonlight.

"I wasn't there for them," Drew said. "I couldn't protect them. That had been my promise. I'd always protect them."

"I've heard things were rough at home for you."

Drew laughed. "*Rough,* huh? Who told you that? Ollie?"

Sam didn't deny it. "Ashley's never really talked to him about the details, but he said every once in a while, she'd slipped and said something about how she wasn't her father's little bitch anymore. Or if she saw your father, she had to resist the urge to run him over just so she never had to worry about her closets anymore. He wasn't sure what that meant."

Drew's face went white.

"Did your father put her in the closet?"

Drew shook his head. His fists clenched, his jaw tightened and he looked out into the night sky, avoiding Sam's eyes. "No, I did."

Drew forced himself to face her. He needed her to see his eyes as he explained this.

"I'd put them both in there," Drew admitted. "When Dad was home, drunk and on a tear, he was in a mood to hurt someone and he wouldn't stop until he did, so I'd put them in the closet and go to him. Sometimes, I'd say something to piss him off even more, focus his attention on me. Sometimes, he'd see me and I knew I didn't need to bother. He'd lay into me. And Kelli and Ashley were safe."

Sam her hand on his heart. "You were trying to protect her. You *did* protect her."

Drew shook his head. "I convinced myself that it was better, but Ashley was afraid of the dark and I…" He took a breath, his lungs on fire. He wished to hell he had a cigarette, but he'd thrown them all away and had no intention of breaking his word. "First time I did that, Ashley came running out. She heard me screaming, so she ran out to help. To stop him. To save *me*. He grabbed her by the throat and I swear I thought he was going to rip her head off. I punched my father in the nuts and he hit me so hard I saw stars. I'm not sure what happened next, but Ashley wouldn't talk for a week."

"How old were you?"

Drew shrugged. "We were seven. Almost eight. It was three days after mom died."

Unsure of what else to do, she put her arms around him. "It wasn't your fault."

Drew moved away from her without returning the embrace. Lord knows he wanted to, but he couldn't. Not yet.

"My father was always mean and cruel," Drew said. "And we never knew when he'd strike out. Smacking us with the back of his hand, giving us a kick when we didn't expect it, but normally it was quick and it was done. Those rages he went into, they were rarer. Sometimes you could go days, other times weeks, but when they happened, it was legendary. It was three weeks before it happened again. Something set him off. Not sure what, but he came home looking for us and we knew. So I did *almost* the same thing again."

"What do you mean almost?"

"Ashley begged me to hide in there with them," Drew explained. "But I knew he'd look for us and break down the door to get to us. He was already slamming doors downstairs. So I pushed both of my sisters in there. And then I locked the door."

Sam blinked. "You had a closet door with a lock on it?"

"We did then," Drew said. "I'd managed to change

94

it out after the last time. I didn't want them getting out again. So I locked my sisters in a closet and dealt with my father. Ashley is still afraid of enclosed spaces. *I* did that to her. I knew they'd be stuck in there until I could manage to let them out and sometimes that was hours later, but I stuck them in there whenever I knew he was in a rage. I tried to protect them from my father, but there was nobody there to protect them from me."

Drew saw the outrage on Sam's face and realized he'd gone too far. He looked to the back of the house, plotted his escape and decided to bolt.

"I should go," he said. "I've laid enough on you for the night. I'm sorry. Thanks for the coffee."

Drew rushed down the stairs of the back porch and off to the side of the house. This was a mistake. He should never have opened up to her. What the hell was wrong with him that he just spilled his guts?

Drew made it to his car, had his hand on the handle, when he heard Sam.

"Drew, wait, please."

He didn't turn to look at her, but he waited, seeing her reflection in his window.

"You didn't ask me if I thought you were innocent," she said. "Maybe you don't care. Or maybe you were afraid to hear the answer, but I'm going to tell you anyway. I know you didn't hurt that girl. That's not you."

Drew let out a laugh, but it held no humor. "I appreciate that, but I don't think you know me well enough to say that. I'm an ass. I've hurt people. Not just my sisters."

Sam leaned against the car so she could see his face. "I know that too."

They locked eyes. "You've been talking to your partner, haven't you?"

"What's discussed in the squad car stays in the squad car," Sam replied.

"Uh huh," Drew shifted around so they were both leaning against his car. "I can't blame you for that. Can I ask you this? How hard is he going to make it to reconnect with Ashley?"

Sam thought about the question. "He's not out to punish you. I'm sure he's got a lot of anger, but in the end, he'll want what's best for your sister *and* Cole. I'm sure if you convince him you're good for them, he'll stay out of the way. He…" Sam hesitated. "He cares for your family."

Drew smiled. *Nicely put, Officer Rossi.* It was a far more diplomatic way to say he's in love with your idiot sister who has no clue he feels that way.

Drew stepped away from the car and turned toward Sam. She was just so damn beautiful in the moonlight. She looked up at him, those big, brown eyes waiting.

And something clicked.

"Bruce Liverman," he said.

Sam started to blink. "What?"

Drew smiled. "Bruce Liverman. He was a snot-nosed kid one grade below me. He picked on Kelli a little when we were in school, until I set him straight. He used to terrorize a bunch of the girls in school."

Sam crossed her arms. "I remember him. Why are you bringing him up?"

Drew took a step closer. "He pulled your hair once. Kept saying a girl shouldn't play football and grabbed you by the hair. You punched him and knocked out a tooth."

Sam arched an eyebrow. "I told you, I can take care of myself."

"I believe you." Drew moved in close, lightly pressing his body to hers. He waited for a sign that she wanted to protest, but there was none. He placed his hand on her cheek, and gave her one more moment to say no.

She didn't.

His mouth was on hers, and the taste of her lips was exquisite. He hardened the kiss, exploring the inside of her mouth.

He heard a soft sigh escape and wanted to scoop her up and carry her back inside. He'd find the first flat surface, lay her down and taste every last inch of her. He wanted to hear her do more than sigh.

After a long moment, she moved her hand to his massive chest and pushed with enough pressure to signal him to stop.

He did, but with disappointment and longing coursing through him.

"Let me touch you," he asked.

She looked tempted, but shook her head. "No. We're not going there tonight. It's too soon. And there are too many...complications."

He nodded and leaned back against the car. "How much of this is because of your partner?"

Sam inhaled the cool night air. "Some. It's also too fast. Maybe not for you, but for me. I'm not into casual trysts. I don't have a problem with them, but they're not my thing. You need to know that. And I need to decide if I'm ready for whatever this might turn into."

Drew didn't look at her. He was trying to get control of himself and looking at her all flustered in the moonlight wasn't going to help.

"I've done casual, meaningless trysts," Drew admitted. "They have their place. But nothing that was going through my mind just then was casual."

She grinned. "Good to know."

Drew moved so he could see her. It was a mistake, because he wanted to pick up where they'd just left off, but he resisted. "Anything else I need to know?"

"Yeah." Sam's eyes glanced toward the road. "My Nana's home."

An old, beat up VW Bug pulled into the driveway. The woman who got out was younger than Drew expected. Her hair was red and her eyes were quick and sharp. Something about her seemed familiar, but he couldn't place her.

Drew saw it. That moment of recognition. He hadn't quite placed where he knew Sam's Nana from, but she knew who he was and she wasn't pleased to see her granddaughter with the likes of him.

"Did you enjoy your dance, Nana?"

"It was lovely, but I was getting a little bored. Most of the people show up in couples and the only singles are either women or old fogeys. But it's better than sitting here, night after night, knitting."

"Nana, you couldn't knit to save your life. This is Drew." She introduced her Nana as Rose.

Drew held out his hand, wondering if Sam's Nana would refuse to take it. Instead, she gripped it firmly and stepped right up to him.

"I recognized you. I'm so sorry to hear about your sister. She was a lovely girl. I remember how much you loved both of your sisters."

Shaken, he didn't know how to respond as the tall

woman leaned in and hugged him.

Rose stepped back and offered a sad smile. "You don't remember me, I'm sure. I can see the blank look on your face."

Drew shook his head. "No, I'm sorry."

"Don't be. It was a long time ago. And I wore a different shade of red back then." She patted her hair. "I worked in the school you and your sisters went to. Administrative office. I also knew your mother, although that was a long time ago."

"Yeah," Drew said. "I guess it was." He studied her face again. She seemed familiar the moment she'd gotten out of her car. He pushed his mind to remember her, her eyes, the line of her jaw, the red hair.

"You were there the day I..." The memory clicked into place. So did the lies. "Ms. Henry. I remember you now. I had to go to the office when the rest of my class had gym because I'd fallen. You used to give me a lollipop."

Rose's eyes narrowed. "Right. You told me you had fallen off the swing at home."

"Yeah," Drew said. "I should go. I've got a busy day ahead of me tomorrow."

"I imagine so," Rose said. "Planning these things is never easy. I don't envy you. I'm glad you're back. Are you just in town a few days?"

Drew shook his head. "No."

Rose smiled. "Doesn't surprise me. I expect you'll stay for your sister's boy. My heart breaks for him. I want you to promise me something." Rose opened up her purse and started to look around inside. "If there's anything I can do to help you or your family, please let me know. It would mean a lot to me to be able to help."

"Thank you," Drew said. "I'll keep it in mind."

Rose found what she was looking for. "You were no stranger to trouble back then. Had a temper and a mouth on you as I recall. You got sent to that office on more than one occasion for getting into a fight. But underneath it all, I knew you were your mother's son. I never believed that nonsense about the Winters girl. I'm glad you didn't let that keep you away. Now you go on and get home. You're going to need some rest. But take these."

From her purse, she pulled out three lollipops. "One of them is bound to be a cherry. I seem to recall you liking those best. Give one to your sister and one to your nephew. I hope to see you around. I'll let you say goodnight to my granddaughter."

She kissed his cheek again, pressing the lollipops into his hand before heading to the house, sending Sam a quick grin as she went.

Drew stared down at the lollipops in his hand, two cherry and one lemon. He wondered which kind Cole would like.

Drew took a deep breath. "You have no idea how lucky you are to have her."

Sam looked toward the house. "Actually, I've got a pretty good idea."

He reached out and gently pulled her into a hug. "Thanks for the coffee and the talk. I guess I needed it."

Sam returned the embrace. "I'm always up for a cup of coffee. I'll see you soon."

Drew nodded and stepped back. He probably should steer clear. He doubted he was any good for her.

But one look at her and he knew that wasn't going to happen. "Ah, screw it." He moved in, pressed his body against hers and kissed her. This time, he didn't hesitate. He just needed one last taste before he left.

When the kiss ended, he rested his forehead on hers. "You *will* see me. I hope you decide you're ready, because ready or not, I want to pick this back up. And soon."

With much regret, Drew forced himself back into his car and drove away.

Vincent Morrone

Chapter 8
Making Deals

Sam found Rose sitting on the back porch, sipping her coffee and enjoying the view.

Rose smiled as Sam stepped outside in her crisp uniform. "That was an awfully yummy man you had in our driveway last night."

"That man has a lot going on in his life," Sam said. "I'm not sure he needs the distraction of a romance."

"Or maybe he could use a little distraction." She grinned.

Sam frowned as she sat down next to her. "I don't know if I need that in my life right now. My partner thinks he's trouble."

"Does he?" Rose took a sip of coffee. "Good. I *know* you can use a little trouble in *your* life."

"Nana!"

"What? It's true. You haven't been out on a single date since you moved here. I go out more than you do. And you're starting to cramp my style."

Sam shook her head. "You're incorrigible." She got up to leave.

Rose raised her coffee cup in salute. "Damn right I am. It's okay to have a life. They would want you to."

Sam sighed. "I know. I'm still working through it all. And Drew is just starting."

Rose nodded, the smile faded from her face. "It's

been a rough road for you. It'll be a rough road for him. Might be rougher for everything else he's been through. That poor boy, I…" Rose turned away.

Sam almost didn't see the tear rolling down her face.

"Nana? What's going on?" Sam moved over to her grandmother, crouched down near her. She reached out, took her hand, despite her grandmother shaking her head.

"Oh sweetie," Rose said. "I did something horrible."

Sam gave her grandmother a hug, and then pulled a chair around. "Tell me."

Sam was going to be late for work.

****

"You made breakfast for everyone," Ashley said as she came into the kitchen to put away the orange juice. "But you didn't eat a bite."

"Not hungry," Drew said. "I just figured with all he's going through, Cole deserved not to eat eggs with burnt pieces of shells in them."

Ashley snarled. "Ha, ha. I've managed to give him breakfast without poisoning him yet."

Drew lifted an eyebrow.

"Okay," Ashley admitted. "So Lily cooks. I can still pour him a bowl of cereal."

Cole finished his bacon, eggs and toast and had gone back to his book. Kid liked to lose himself in stories, just like his mother. He'd been very quiet this morning, but for all Drew knew, that was normal for him. Drew felt like something was off, as if after the progress they'd made yesterday, they'd taken a step back.

"You don't have to rush over there," Ashley said. "It's not like you have an appointment."

"No," Drew said. "But the earlier the better. Less chance he'll be fall-down drunk."

"Have you decided what you're going to say to him?"

"Not yet. I just want him to stay away. He hasn't made any effort to contact you for years. No reason why that has to change. We're done with him. That's the bottom line."

The General came into the room. "You ready?"

"Yeah," Drew said. "Let's get this over with."

They passed by Cole, who was lost in some world with dragons and magic. He didn't say goodbye. As Drew headed for the door, Ashley grabbed his hand. "Drew, he can't hurt us anymore. Remember that."

Drew looked in her eyes, filled with the emotion she was barely holding back. She was still angry at him and that anger spilled out plenty, but she still loved him. Knowing that, seeing that in her eyes, gave him strength.

"I will." He leaned in, before she had a chance to protest, and kissed her cheek. "I won't let him hurt you. And I swear I won't let him make me hurt you again."

****

"You got your head on straight, Marine?" The General said as they pulled up in front of the house Drew grew up in.

Drew felt steadier than he did the day before, but inside he was a small, terrified ten-year-old boy with a broken arm.

"I'm fine." Drew stared at the house he hadn't seen in years. Memories flooded back to him, each more painful than the last. He could almost hear the secrets pouring out of that place. "You sure you want to come in?"

The General smiled. "I wouldn't miss this for the world. You think I'm going to hear anything in there that's going to shock me? You should have realized by now I've looked at you six ways to Sunday. There's nothing I'm going to learn in there that's going to change the way I see you. You'll be the same pain in my ass when we leave as when we go in."

Drew didn't make eye contact. "You might be surprised. Whatever does happen, I'm grateful for everything. And I'm sorry."

"Sorry? You think I need an apology for the fact you're planning on resigning your position with McAlister Security?"

Drew finally looked at him.

"I know you," the General said. "You have a family that needs you here. You're going to put that little boy first. That's the way it should be. That's the way it has to be. If you didn't put him first, you wouldn't be the man I believe you to be."

Drew wasn't surprised. "I'm hoping my not working for you isn't the end of us being in each other's lives. Cole could use a grandfather. He couldn't ask for a better one than you. But that wasn't what I was saying I'm sorry for."

The General frowned. "Then, what exactly?"

Drew glanced back to the house. "You're about to see a very ugly part of me. I know you think you know me, but there are secrets in that house that a man like you, a good and decent man, should never have to come face to face with."

The General nodded. "We all have secrets. Maybe I haven't figured out every nook and cranny of your childhood, but I've figured you out. So let's you and I go in there and take care of what we have to take care of. And when we're done, I'll buy you a beer and you can tell me about the girl that kept you out so late last night."

Drew found himself blinking rapidly. "What are you? Psychic?"

The General simply grinned and reached for the door. "Running my ass."

They walked up to the front door. "Seems strange," Drew said. "Ringing the doorbell of my home."

He didn't wait for a response before he pressed the doorbell. He could hear the familiar buzz from inside. They waited and heard nothing else.

"Maybe he's not home," the General offered. "No car in the driveway."

Drew shook his head. "Dad keeps his truck in the garage. He's here. I can feel it. He'd have nowhere to be this time of day."

Drew pressed the doorbell again, this time holding it in for a few seconds.

He listened, heard nothing, and thought about heading over to the garage to see if he could at least spot a vehicle inside. Before he could move, there was a crash of some sort from inside, followed by a curse. There was more noise. It sounded like whatever had dropped was now being kicked around.

Drew sighed. "Third time's the charm." He rang the doorbell again.

"What the fuck?" Said a hoarse-sounding voice from inside. There was more noise, not crashing this time, but more like someone slamming doors.

"Shit." Drew stepped aside so he wasn't in front of the door. "He's armed."

The General didn't question; he simply slid to the side as well so if a bullet came through the door, he wouldn't be in the direct line of fire.

There were footsteps, heavy and uneven...angry. The door jostled and finally swung open. The General got his first look at Drew Duncan's father.

Frank Duncan was a huge man. Drew's father was ex-military. Army, not Marines. He'd never been an officer, served in the first Gulf war, as did the General himself, but while the General earned a chest full of medals, Frank had been accused of sexual harassment of both civilian and female soldiers alike. None of the charges stuck, but he'd gotten into several brawls, again with both Army and civilians. Eventually, he'd gotten an "Other Than Honorable" discharge. Meaning they wanted him out.

He had blond hair, which although not long, was badly in need of a comb, not to mention a washing. He had hazel eyes red from drinking and although he looked ragged and his pallor was jaundiced, he still seemed solid enough.

Frank Duncan squinted into the sunlight, putting his hand up to shield his eyes as he stared at his son. His other hand was propped on the doorway. No gun was visible. "Never thought I'd see you on my doorstep again."

"I don't want to be here any more than you want me here," Drew said. "But I need to talk with you. You want to let me in, or you want to do this on the porch?"

Frank ground his teeth as he saw one of his

neighbors across the street going for his mail, while a lady from around the block walked her dog.

As he thought it through, his bloodshot eyes found the General. "Who's your boyfriend?"

The General cocked an eyebrow, but refused to be baited. "A friend."

"In or out, Dad," Drew said. "Make your choice."

Frank looked back and forth a few times, shrugged, and walked back inside. Both Drew and The General spotted the bulge in the back of his jeans.

With one last look to the General, Drew stepped inside. He followed his father, who was barefoot and bare-chested, into the kitchen. He went for a bottle of Jack Daniels that was open on the counter, took a swig and leaned against the counter.

The place reeked of cigarettes, and was a filthy mess. There were beer cans and empty bottles of booze on the counters and floors. In the living room to the side, there was an expensive flat screen TV hooked up to the giant satellite on the roof.

Big money items in a shit hole.

"Gotta wonder what you're doin' back here," Frank said as he grabbed a pack of Marlboros. "I thought we had a deal."

The General stepped forward. "Deal?"

Drew ignored him. "We did and I was keeping my end of it. Did you keep yours?"

Frank lit a cigarette, and then shoved the pack into his back pocket. Smoke escaped from his mouth as he laughed. He took another swig, and smiled. "You think I'm the one who killed your sister?"

"It crossed my mind," Drew said.

Frank sneered. "You can rest easy, I'm not the one

that did her."

Drew considered, nodded. "Fine. We'll say I believe you for now."

"You oughta," Frank snapped. "You know I'm a man of my word. And I told you what I'd do. I don't suppose that's what happened."

Drew tensed. "No."

"Well then, there you go." Frank took a drag and the tip of the cigarette glowed bright. "I had nothing to do with it. But this wasn't part of our arrangement."

Drew stepped forward. "I'm changing our arrangement. I'm back and this time I'm staying."

That statement had all traces of humor draining from Frank's face. "That'd be a mistake. You're not wanted here. By *anyone*."

Drew raised his chin in defiance. "I'm needed here."

Frank laughed again, scratched an itch on his arm. "You mean your sister's brat. He's better off without you."

"No," Drew responded. "He's better off without *you*. I want to make sure you understand that. Ashley thinks I'm here to find out if you plan on showing up to the funeral. She thinks you might have an interest in meeting your grandson. I know better. I'm here to make it clear *you* know better. You stay away from Ashley, you stay away from Cole, and I'll stay away from you."

Frank reached back to his neck, rubbed and stretched out. "You've got balls, coming into my home and telling me what to do. I may be a little older, but I can still beat your ass to the ground."

Drew smiled. "Anytime you want to try, feel free. But you stay away from them. Or I'll do to you what you used to do to me."

Frank put his hands on his hips. "You threatening me?"

Drew slowly inched to his right. "You bet your ass."

The two men stared at each other, each waiting for the other to blink.

"Lucky for you," Frank said. "I've got no interest in him. But you want to keep something in mind. Kelli may be on a slab at the coroner's office, but you've still got another sister. And now you've got a nephew to think about. So be real careful about your next move."

"Are you actually threatening to harm your own grandson?" The General said.

Frank's eyes slowly slid toward the General. "Harm? If Drew here steps out of line, I don't think *harm* is the word I'd use. Drew knows what will happen to him." His eyes returned to Drew as he blew out smoke. "He *knows*."

Drew inched closer, further to his right. Staying on his father's left, ready. "You've made yourself very clear. Now let me make something else clear. Anything happens to them. Anything at all, I'll end you."

Once again, Frank was silent. He took one last drag, blew out more smoke and stubbed the cigarette out. Slowly, he reached to his back pocket. "That so?"

Drew waited.

Frank grabbed the gun and swung it toward Drew's head. Blow them both away and claim they threatened him. That was the plan.

The General had his sidearm in his hand, aimed it at Frank's chest, his finger on the trigger.

Drew moved in, twisted the gun out of his father's

grip, grabbed his arm and twisted it behind his father's back, slamming him face first onto the counter. Quickly, he placed the gun to his father's temple. "Well, isn't this something? Seems to me, last time we spoke, our positions were reversed. Except if I recall, you had your gun in my mouth."

Frank started to curse and threaten, until Drew twisted his father's arm tighter. "Let's lay our cards out on the table. I didn't come back here to clear my name. I don't give a shit what anyone thinks of me. I'm not looking under that rock. But if you come anywhere near my family, I'll bury you under one. I'm not the same kid. Despite popular opinion, I hadn't taken a life back then. I've been to war since. I've killed. I know how to do it. I *will* do it and I won't give it a second thought. You stay away."

Drew gave his arm one last twist, took a sadistic satisfaction in the cry of agony from his father, and stepped back. In a quick move, he dropped the clip out of his father's Glock, slid out the chamber and let the pieces fall to the floor. He nodded to the General and together, they headed for the door.

They didn't speak as they left, and neither bothered to close the front door as they headed to the SUV together. As soon as they were inside, Drew slammed the car into drive and took off.

"You want to tell me what the hell that was all about?" the General said. "What deal did you make with that man?"

Drew didn't look at the General as he sped through the streets. "I think you should be able to guess."

The General looked behind them to the house they'd left. "Your father threatened your sisters if you came back here? He threatened to have them killed? And you *believed* him?"

Drew clenched his jaw. "Yes. To all of the above."

"Then how do you know he didn't kill Kelli?"

Drew pulled over to the side of the road, bringing the car to a screeching halt. "Kelli was killed quickly from behind. Her throat was slit. She bled out."

The General waited for more. It didn't come. "And that means what?"

Drew closed his eyes. "She wasn't sexually assaulted. She wasn't raped. If my father had done what he threatened to do, she would have been raped."

The General had no idea what to say. "And you're sure he really would have done it?"

Drew opened his eyes, locked them with the General's and prayed to God he would take his word for it when he replied. "Without a doubt."

****

"You're quiet," Ollie said.

"Hmmm?" Sam replied.

They sat in their squad car, in the parking lot of the station, each with a clipboard, filling out paperwork.

"I said you're quiet. And distracted. What's up, partner?"

Sam didn't want to dump on Ollie, but decided she had to dump on someone. "I was thinking about the Duncan case. Have we looked at the father?"

Ollie was taken aback. "As a matter of fact, yes. He's got an alibi. He was in a bar full of ex-cops. From what I understand, they had to pour him into a cab, which happened about an hour after the time of death window closes. He was too drunk to do much anyway. Why?"

Sam didn't answer. "I guess it doesn't matter."

"Sure it does," Ollie said. "Out with it, partner."

With a sigh, Sam dove in. "I saw Drew last night."

Ollie blinked. "You what?"

Sam rolled her eyes. "Oh, relax. I was jogging in the park. I saw him burst right by. Nearly ran right into the barricades. We talked a little bit and he was pretty on edge. I thought he could use someone to talk to, so I invited him for a cup of coffee. I don't want to go into detail unless it's germane to the investigation."

Ollie did his best to stay calm. "And you're saying what you talked about wasn't germane?"

Sam shook her head. "Not if the father is in the clear."

She went back to her paperwork, with Ollie staring daggers at her.

"Don't let him fool you, Sam," Ollie said. "He's not a good guy."

"He loves his nephew and sister."

Ollie scowled. "He's still a person of interest in Molly Winter's disappearance. You're a cop. Hooking up with him for a thrill isn't going to be good for your career."

"You know damn well there was no real evidence against him. And yes, he was an ass to you, but that was a long time ago. And right now, you don't have room to talk about someone being an ass." She reached for the handle, swung the door open and started to get out. "I know you blame Drew for a miserable childhood and I'm sure he deserves it, but don't blame him for the fact you haven't been able to get together with Ashley. You've had years without him to make that happen and you haven't. I think Drew just may have grown up over the years. Maybe it's time you did the same."

Before he could respond, she slipped from the squad car, slammed the door and stormed into the station alone.

****

That night, Cole did his best to avoid being alone with his uncle. Cole knew when someone was angry and his uncle was supremely pissed, which made him dangerous. He kept waiting for the explosion, but it never came.

At one point, Lily tried lightening the mood by talking about how his mother and Aunt Ash dragged Uncle Drew with them to her house and they all decided to play dress up and made him wear girl clothes. The three of them made him look so silly and his uncle just sat there and looked miserable.

He expected his Uncle to flip out, yelling at them for embarrassing him. Instead, he'd sneered at his sister. "You put me in pink. It's not my color."

Cole had a hard time not smiling a little.

A little later, Aunt Ashley went over the funeral arrangements she and he had made. Uncle Drew listened, nodded and hadn't objected until she got to the point of explaining there wouldn't be a wake.

Aunt Ash looked toward Cole for a brief moment. "We talked about it and decided against a wake. Kelli hasn't been in town for nearly a decade, Drew. And she hated a fuss. It would draw a lot of lookie loos. Cole doesn't know these people. We can invite a few people back here afterwards. We don't need a fuss."

Cole didn't think Drew agreed with their choice and he was about to say it was okay to have a wake, when his uncle nodded. "If that's what you decided, then it's fine."

His tone told Cole he considered the matter settled.

Later on, while cleaning up, Cole accidentally knocked a glass of water down and it had spilt across the table, into his uncle's lap. Aunt Ash thought it was funny because it looked like Drew wet his pants.

Cole nearly wet his waiting for his uncle to punch him.

But he hadn't. He just smirked and said, "You got me good, kid."

He sat in the living room with a book while the others talked, straining to hear each and every word. His mouth went dry when Aunt Ash started to look through her purse. "I could have sworn I had a five in here."

He waited, but she shrugged and finished what she was doing. Slowly, he relaxed. Until he looked up and saw his uncle watching him.

"Good book?" Uncle Drew asked.

Cole nodded. His eyes scanned the page and relief came when he saw that this time, he was holding the book the right way.

"It's getting late, Cole," Aunt Ash said. "Why don't you get ready for bed?"

He nodded, closed the book, and said his good nights to everyone.

Once upstairs, he quickly got changed for bed, brushed his teeth and waited. He knew either Lily, or more likely Aunt Ash, would come upstairs to see him one last time.

He heard the footsteps on the stairs, knew they were wrong. Too loud, too heavy. His body tensed and he was ready to run the moment his uncle appeared at the door.

"I'm just coming up to talk," Drew said. "You can relax."

Cole managed to shrug like he didn't care. The fact was, he wanted to scream his lungs out.

Drew entered the room, pulled the chair closer to the bed and straddled it.

"I'm very angry," Drew said.

"I didn't do shit," Cole said. He knew it was a mistake to talk back.

"I know," Drew said. "I'm not angry with you. You lost a mother, I lost a sister. One I never had the chance to make things right with. So I'm angry at that. And then I went to see my own father today."

"I don't want to see him," Cole snapped. "He's nothing to me."

Drew nodded. "He's less than nothing to you. I was supposed to go there to see if he wanted to meet you. He didn't, but it wouldn't matter. I told him to stay away. I hope that's okay."

Cole shrugged. "Mom told me about him. He was an ass."

Drew smiled. "I doubt Kelli used those words. You've got a mouth on you kid, and I know you didn't get it from her. Maybe it's just a sign there's some of me in you. And almost everyone on this planet has been an ass now and then. My father was far worse."

Cole looked straight ahead, stared at a picture on his wall of a spaceship. "I don't give a shit about him." It was the truth.

"Good," Drew said. "I remember what things were like growing up. My dad being angry meant trouble. Big trouble. Cole, I can't promise you're never going to see me angry, and I'm sure there'll be times when I'm downright pissed off at you. I won't hit you. I'm not going to hurt you because I'm angry. I might yell at you and call you a few well-deserved names like numbskull or something, but I won't send you flying across the room because you spilled a glass of water on me."

Cole's eyes shifted back to Drew.

"Yeah, I saw the look on your face. You were expecting to be hit for that."

"You don't know shit about me," Cole said. "You act like you know me, but you're an ass. I'm nothing like you."

When Drew stood, Cole scrambled away. He wished he could stop shaking. His uncle was about to beat him senseless. He wouldn't cry out. He didn't want to call for Aunt Ash or Lily. His uncle would only hurt them too. He wouldn't make that mistake again, and he didn't want to find out that they wouldn't come.

Oddly, although he was terrified, there was an odd sort of relief. At least he could stop wondering. Stop waiting. Stop hoping.

Drew moved to the foot of the bed, looked down at his nephew, and sighed. He knelt down and reached under the bed.

"What are you doing?" Cole asked, his voice cracking.

Drew's hand found the backpack, pulled it out, and tossed it on the bed. Cole's eyes went wide, but never left Drew's. Walking back to the chair, he sat, scooting closer to the bed.

"Your aunt's missing a five," Drew said. "I noticed the change from dinner last night disappeared. How much you got in there?"

Cole didn't answer. When his uncle reached out, a small cry escaped, but the only thing Uncle Drew grabbed was the bag. He unzipped the pocket where the money was, took it out and counted it. "Fifty-three dollars? Kid, how far do you think this is going to get you?"

"Far enough," Cole said.

Drew laughed.

"How did you know?" Cole said. "When did you know?" There seemed to be little reason to lie now.

"I watch too," Drew said. "I'm just better at it than you. When I came up the stairs before, you knew it was me, right? I sound different coming up than Ashley or Lily, don't I?"

Cole considered telling him to go to hell, but wanted to see where his uncle was going. "Yeah."

"I can move up the stairs without you hearing me," Drew explained. "I saw you snatch the five. I was waiting for it. I wasn't surprised you had this ready. You planning on going, or is this just an 'in case I need it' bag?"

Cole grabbed the bag and held it tightly.

"Cole, I've played it straight with you. Talk to me. Please."

Cole was shaking, but he listened. So far, his uncle hadn't lied yet. "If he comes for me, I won't go. And I won't let Aunt Ash or Lily get hurt trying to protect me."

Drew nodded. "I get that. Is that what you think happened?"

"He's still locked up," Cole said. "For now."

"I'm not going to let him near you. Or Aunt Ash or Lily. I'm here and I'll protect you."

"Bullshit," Cole said. "You don't give a shit."

"Yes I do," Drew said. "I'm going to move. Don't panic. I'm not going to hit you."

Drew reached into his back pocket, pulled out a wallet. Going inside, he pulled out a wad of cash. It was all twenties. He held it up for Cole to see. "This is three hundred." He took the bag back from Cole, shoved it in the front pocket where the other fifty-three dollars was. "That will help. Do you have a cell phone?"

The question took a moment to register with Cole, but when it did, he shook his head. "I'll get you one. We'll program it with numbers. You feel the need to run, you can run. I'll find you because you won't be running from me. You need help, I'll make sure there's help on the other side of that phone." He held up the bag. "You're not going to need this. But if it makes you feel better to have it, you can keep it. No more stealing from your aunt or Lily. Understand?"

Confused, Cole nodded. "You're letting me keep that money?"

"Consider it a loan, kid," Drew said. "I know what it feels like to want to run, and to think running will help protect people you care about. It didn't work out so well for me. You may want to keep that in mind."

While his uncle stowed his backpack under the bed again, Cole thought about that.

Drew moved back to the chair. "Now, you were looking at me weird when you got up this morning. What's up?"

Cole scowled. "You used to pick on Ollie."

Drew's eyes narrowed. "I used to... Where did you...?" He looked toward the window. "Damn kid, you hear everything, don't you?"

Cole waited for the excuses and the lies.

"Budge over." Drew moved the chair off to the side and slid on the bed next to Cole. He managed to do so without having the kid cower away. Drew leaned back, forced himself to relax and waited for Cole to do the same. Or at least come as close to a state of relaxation as he was capable of.

"Yeah," Drew admitted. "I was an ass. I told you earlier anyone can be one. I'm not going to make excuses. Ollie didn't deserve what I did. I was a pissed-off kid and instead of talking to someone or learning to control it, I used him because he was there. It didn't help that he was *always* there."

Cole found himself nodding, the panic fading. "He likes Aunt Ash. I guess he did back then too."

Drew laughed. "Yeah, he sure did. Keep that between you and I. I don't think she's caught on yet."

Cole laughed. "Yeah."

"You're a smart kid," Drew said. "Smarter than I was at your age."

Cole shifted. "I wasn't smart enough to save Mom."

"You didn't fail your mom. If anyone did, it was me. And I'm sorry. But I swear, I won't fail you."

Cole leaned against his uncle. "I like Ollie. He was nice to me and he told me it was his job to protect people. He promised if I called him, he'd come."

"And you're afraid if I'm here he won't come?" Drew said. "I don't think you have to worry about that. He's solid. The man's hung around my sister since we were kids, so that qualifies him as a saint."

That earned a snicker. "She gives him a hard time too. Not as bad as she gives it to you. But he mostly finds it funny."

They both laughed.

"I'll find a way to square things with Ollie," Drew said. "You have my word."

He didn't know why, but Cole believed him. "How?"

Drew shook his head. "No clue. I don't pretend to have all the answers, Cole. But I'll figure something out. Deal?"

Drew held his hand up in a fist. Cole smiled, made a fist himself and bumped it into Drew's. "Deal."

Chapter 9
Burying the Hatchet

"Sam," Ollie called. "Wait up."

When she arrived at the funeral, Sam directed Nana to sit far away from him. She avoided all eye contact, although she was certain he'd seen her when she'd passed by the family on the way out and hugged Drew, giving him a kiss on the cheek.

Now her partner was pushing through the crowd to get to her.

"What, Ollie?"

He managed to catch up and moved in front of her. "Look, give me a minute to talk to you. *Please*?"

Sam considered walking away, but Rose patted her arm.

"I'll wait in the car," Rose said. "Talk to your partner." She passed by Ollie and smiled. "And may God have mercy on your soul."

Ollie groaned and Sam tried not to grin.

"Talk," Sam said. "You've got one minute."

Ollie held his hands up in surrender. "I'm sorry. I'm so sorry. I was way out of line. I don't want to lose you as a partner or as a friend."

Sam rolled her eyes. "Okay, it's a start. Look, Ollie, I understand how you feel."

"No, you don't," Ollie said. "I look at him and I feel like I'm that same acne-ridden, chubby twelve-year-old who he kept telling to get lost. He did everything he could to intimidate me. It's not easy to let that go."

"I know that," Sam said. "And you should talk to him. Show him you're not the same person you were back then. And maybe you'll see he isn't the same person either. But not today."

Ollie started to rub the back of his neck.

Knowing her partner, she grabbed his hand and pulled him off to a more private location. "*What* did you do?"

Ollie groaned. "I went over Friday night to let them know about being able to claim the body. Before I left, I got in Drew's face. I wanted him to understand I wasn't the same geek who he pushed around."

Sam closed her eyes and prayed for patience. "Let me get this straight. On the same day he found out his sister was murdered, that he saw his sister's dead body, you decided that was a good time to have it out with him. You chose that moment to show him you weren't the same guy he bullied when you were kids. And in doing so, you became the bully."

She gave him a minute, let that sink in. She knew he wasn't proud of what he'd done. "I'm going to the house now to pay my respects. Will I see you there?"

Ollie nodded. "Yeah."

"Good," Sam said. "Idiot."

****

At the house, Cole watched people come in, give their condolences and eat food. He didn't know most of the faces and didn't want to talk to anyone, but knew he wasn't supposed to hide in his room. Instead, he sat in the corner and hoped they'd all leave him alone.

"Hi, Cole."

A woman in a black dress, with long brown hair and lips painted red sat near him.

"My name is Diana," she said. "I knew your mom. She and I were talking about things before she was hurt. I wanted to see how you were doing."

Cole shrugged. "I'm fine."

Diana smiled. "Of course. I know your mom was interested in having you meet your uncle. I see he's here. How are you two getting along?"

Cole's eyes found his uncle. He was sitting in the corner, talking to Ollie's partner, Sam, who was looking around the room as if she were searching for someone. A moment later, Sam placed a small plate down and left Drew to head into the kitchen. Cole remembered thinking she was pretty the day he met her. "He's okay."

Diana nodded. "You know if you're afraid of him I can help. I'm always here to help you."

Cole shifted away from her a little. "Why would I be afraid of him?"

Diana smiled. "With everything you've been through, it would be normal."

It was true, he had been afraid of his uncle. He was a big, powerful-looking man. Cole expected the fast hand, the quick fist. It hadn't come. And last night, Cole started to wonder if his uncle was telling the truth.

"We're fine," Cole said. "I'm gonna go."

Without looking back, he got up and went out back.

****

Drew watched as Cole escaped to go out to the back yard. Kid was holding up about as well as anyone had a right to expect, but he knew he had a long way to go.

Not too many people came by. A few childhood friends stopped in, but most didn't stay long. Kelli had always been the quietest out of all of them. She didn't make friends easily. Because their father had been a cop, a few older police officers came in. None seemed shocked that their father hadn't bothered to show.

Ollie was here, staying clear of Drew, mostly following Ashley around. His mother, the chief, put in an appearance, making sure to give her condolences to both Ashley and Drew where others could see her. Sam came with her grandmother and the two of them were floating around here somewhere. Drew decided to go look for Sam.

He found her and Rose standing in the kitchen. Rose was looking out to the yard, crying.

"Do you really think we should say something?" Rose said. "I feel so horrible, but at this point…"

"I'll talk to Drew," Sam said. "But not today. He and his family don't need me to bring that up right now. Not after all this time."

"Bring what up?"

When Drew came into the room, Sam couldn't help but jump. "Drew. I didn't see…"

"I get that." Drew leaned against the door frame. Rose avoided making eye contact. "So tell me what it is me and my family don't need brought up."

Sam positioned herself between Drew and her grandmother. "It's nothing you need to hear right now."

"What has you so worried?" Drew said. "Starting to wonder if you were wrong about me the other night?"

Sam shook her head. "No. Drew that's not…"

A loud sob from Rose cut Sam off. "This is my fault. Be angry with me, not my girl."

Drew moved closer. "Follow me." He led them into a back room used by Lily as a home office. He flipped on the lights and waited until Sam and Rose followed him in. "We'll talk in here. Cole seems to hear everything."

Sam turned to Drew the moment the door closed. "This doesn't have anything to do with Cole."

Drew regarded her coolly. "I'll be the judge of that."

Sam repositioned herself as a buffer. "Drew…"

"No," Rose said. "He's right. You said so before, he has a right to know. It might as well be now."

Drew deliberately stepped around Sam. Slowly, he put his hands on Rose's shoulders. "It's okay. Just tell me."

Rose continued to cry as she nodded. "I suspected." She finally got out. "I never believed you'd fallen down the stairs or gotten hurt on a swing set. It wasn't the first time you showed up to school hurt, and it wasn't the last. I knew you were being abused."

"It was one of those non-secret secrets. A lot of people knew. Nobody did anything."

But Rose just started to shake her head. "I did do something. Or at least I *tried* to do something. I talked to the principal of the school. He said we didn't have any proof. I told him that as mandated reporters, we had to call even if we just *suspected* abuse. So I called."

Drew looked to Sam. None of this made sense to him. "I don't understand. If you called, you did your job."

Rose was crying even more now. Sam came forward and put her hand on Drew's arms. "It was me."

Drew turned to Sam, looked her up and down. "What are you talking about?"

A single tear fell down Sam's face. "Nana called to get an update and was told it was unfounded, but they gave her the runaround when she wanted to know who had gone out and what they found. She realized they hadn't done much of an investigation."

Drew shook his head. "I don't remember being interviewed by a social worker."

Sam sighed. "It's not surprising. Nana wanted to talk with the supervisor. She was told he'd get back to her within twenty-four hours."

"And?" Drew prompted. "Did he?"

Sam shook her head. "No, but that night, she went home and found someone sitting on her couch, watching TV. Waiting. Someone who made it very clear she needed to drop it."

Drew looked to Rose who simply couldn't or wouldn't look at him.

"It was my father, wasn't it?"

Sam nodded. "She was terrified. I was so young. My parents still lived here in Ember Falls. He made Nana believe if she pushed it any further, something bad would happen to my mother and me."

Drew backed away from them, turned and went to the window where he could make out Cole sitting alone on the back porch.

"I know you must hate me," Rose said. "But I believed him. I really believed he would hurt my daughter and my granddaughter. I know you probably find that hard to believe…"

Drew crossed over to her, took her hand and led her to a small chair. He got her to sit and knelt down in front of her.

"No, I find it very easy to believe." He waited until she looked at him. "And I'll tell you something else. I don't know if this will make it easier for you or not, but he would have done it. I'm certain of that. There was probably nothing you could've done to help me and my sisters, but I know without a single doubt in my mind that if you had tried and he found out, he would have done whatever he said he would do. So you may not have been able to help my family, but you kept your family safe."

Rose nodded, wept and looked into his eyes, searching for forgiveness.

Slowly, Drew pulled her into a hug. "I'm sorry that happened to you. You don't have to apologize for protecting your family."

After letting Rose cry in his arms, both he and Sam stepped out of the office to give her a few moments to collect herself. They moved back into the main living room, but found a private corner.

"You were wonderful to her in there," Sam said. "Very gentle."

Drew didn't look at her. "I don't normally kick around old ladies. Not unless it's a real special occasion."

Sam stepped into his vision. "I was going to tell you. I just didn't want it to be today. And yes, I thought you would have been angry. I wouldn't have blamed you if you were. I'm glad you aren't."

"Angry?" Drew snapped in a whispered tone. "I passed angry when I found out my sister was brutalized and murdered. And what your Nana just told me may not have surprised me, but it most certainly did piss me the fuck off. I don't blame her. I wasn't lying, but don't think for a moment I'm not *angry*."

Drew looked across the room, saw Ollie. It only took a moment for Ollie to sense Drew staring at him. They locked eyes.

Drew decided it was time to deal with Oliver Miller.

Sam saw the two men playing a game of blink. When Drew stepped forward, she grabbed his arm. "What are you doing?"

Drew pulled away and strode over to Ollie who was putting down a small paper plate with pigs on a blanket in it. Drew moved to within an inch of Ollie, leaned in. "I need a word with you. Outside. Now."

Drew didn't wait for an answer. He headed to the back through the kitchen and slammed through the door. Ollie followed a moment later, both Ashley and Sam on his heels. The General followed closely behind them, watching and waiting.

****

"This isn't the time or the place for this nonsense," Ashley yelled. "You don't have to go. My brother's an asshole."

Ollie ignored her. He pulled out his sidearm, handed it to Sam who refused to take it at first until Ollie pressed it in her hand. Ollie thundered down the porch, ready to fight, until he saw a pair of wide eyes from under the deck.

"Cole," Ollie said. "Go on inside with your aunt and Sam. Your uncle and I need to work things out."

Slowly, Cole started to move.

Drew pointed to his nephew. "No. Stay where you are. You hear every damn thing anyway. Might as well hear this firsthand."

Cole came out, but didn't head inside. He watched and waited.

"You really think he needs to see this?" Ollie said.

Drew glanced at Cole. "Yeah, he does. He needs to understand something about being a man."

Ollie shook his head. "And you're the one who's going to show him?"

Drew turned to Ollie, stepping closer. "I'm going to be the one to try. And you're going to help. You wanna hit me?"

Ollie grinned. "You bet your ass I do."

Drew held his hands by his side. "Fine. Go ahead. Lord knows, I've got it coming. But before you do, I need you to listen."

Drew stepped closer. "I was an ass to you. I was a bully and I made your life hell. I'm not going to make excuses. I was angry all the time and I took it out on you. It didn't help that you were always hanging around my sister. You told me the other night that you're not going away. Did you mean that?"

Ollie was taken aback, but still ready to fight. "You better believe it. I care about your sister. And Cole."

"I know you do," Drew said, his voice lower. "I know you care and you stayed when I didn't. I had my reasons, but they don't matter anymore. I'm back. And I'm telling you I need *you* to stay."

Ollie allowed himself a quick glance to Ashley who seemed just as confused. "What?"

Drew stepped forward. "I. Need. You." Drew said it slowly, clearly and sincerely. "I don't know what's going on, but I need your help to keep my family safe. My sister trusts you and trust doesn't come easy. She *doesn't* trust me. That's my fault and I'm trying to earn her trust, but it's going to take time. She *trusts* you.

"I'm telling you I'm sorry for everything I did to you," Drew continued. "I know that doesn't make it all right, but it's all I can do. I'm not the same asshole I was back then. My sister thinks I'm still an asshole, and maybe I am, but I'm not the same one I was back when we were in school. Give me a chance."

Drew held out his hand. Waited.

Ollie looked at it. His hands were still balled into fists, but the fight had gone out of him. It was too bad since Ollie was looking for a reason to punch Drew. Doing it now would make him the ass.

Ollie believed Drew meant what he said. With a sigh, Ollie looked toward Cole and understood. Drew was making a point to the kid. He wasn't perfect. He made mistakes. But a man owns up to them, apologizes and does what he can to make amends.

Now it was Ollie's turn. A man, a good and decent man, accepted sincere apologies and gave second chances.

Ollie took Drew's hand and shook. "Jesus, Drew. You could have just bought me a beer at some point."

Drew smiled. "I'll get to it."

They turned to go in. Ashley was standing on the back porch, her arms folded and shaking her head. "I still think you're an asshole," she muttered.

But as she turned to go inside, she smiled.

****

Sam managed to get Drew alone. "That was one hell of a show. I won't ask if you meant it, because I know you wouldn't have said it if you didn't, but you and Ollie should probably have a real conversation."

Drew nodded. "We will. I'd like to have a real conversation with you soon too. Maybe a little more."

Sam grinned. "We'll see. I'm going to take Nana home. I'll call you soon. Take care of your family."

Drew watched her walk off the porch to her car where Rose waited for her. He turned to find Ashley behind him, her arms folded and an eye brow arched.

"Planning on bopping Ollie's partner?"

Drew rolled his eyes. "You have such a way with words, Ash."

"Is she why you're staying?"

"Jesus, Ashley, can you give me a break?" Drew said. "Out of all days, today. I decided I was staying before I even got back. It has nothing to do with Sam. It has to do with what Kelli wanted for Cole. And wanting to make things right with you."

Ashley scowled. "You think I don't want to believe you? Dammit, Drew, it hurt when you abandoned me. Not a word. Not a single word to say goodbye. I was so worried about you. You never returned my letters from prison…"

"You wrote letters to me?" Drew said.

Ashley furrowed her brow. "You're telling me you never got them?"

Drew eyes studied his shoes. "I figured you guys believed I was guilty."

"Oh Jesus, Drew," Ashley said. "You're such a moron." She placed her hand on his heart. "I never believed that. I knew you wouldn't hurt Molly. How could you think that?"

Drew didn't know what to do except shrug. "You

have no idea how bad it was for me in there. I was scared and alone. I had nobody. When I got out, both you and Kelli had left Dad. I figured you were safe and better off without me."

Surprising both Drew and herself, Ashley leaned in to hug her brother. "You are an idiot. How could you think that? You're my brother. I love you."

Drew wrapped his arms around his sister, hugged her back. "I'm back. I'm staying. This time, you can count on me."

****

It took a while to clean up once everyone left. Ashley was a little easier around Drew the rest of the night. She still gave him a hard time in whatever way she could think of, but that was just Ashley. If she wasn't busting his balls, he'd have to check her for a pulse.

The General was using Lily's office for some business and Ashley was watching TV. Drew found it amusing to see Cole and Lily, each sitting on opposite sides of the sofa, each with their own book. Lily's book had the image of a man and a woman on the cover, locked in a passionate embrace, mere moments before they are about turn up the heat. Cole's book had a picture of a zombie about to munch on some poor soul.

What did it say that if he had to choose, he'd prefer Cole's book over Lily's?

Satisfied everyone was content on their own to decompress, Drew made his way up to the apartment over the garage. He wished he had his workout gear, or even his gaming system, something to do so he could just forget. There wasn't even anything on TV like a game that would let him yell at the screen like a moron.

Drew found his mind thinking about Sam. Maybe he'd go for another run in the park and get lucky enough to bump into her again. Might be worth a try.

He got up to get changed when someone knocked on the door. Maybe Sam had come to see him? Drew went to the door, opened it, and was hit in the face by a fist.

Chapter 10
The Dump Site

Drew's head snapped back. He stumbled, tripped and fell on his ass.

"You offered earlier," Ollie said. "And the fact is, I've been waiting for years to do that to you." Ollie offered his hand.

Drew scowled, but took it. "So I did. You get the one. Next time I kick your ass." He let Ollie pull him up. "You come back here just to sucker punch me or is there something else I can help you with?"

Ollie decided not to tell him part of this was a test to see if Drew really could hold his temper. "I thought I'd take you up on that beer. I figured maybe you could use a distraction and I wanted to talk to you. If you'd rather be alone, I'll understand."

Drew shook his head. "I was thinking about going for a run. Beer sounds better, but since you popped me one you can buy the first round."

Ollie grinned. "Deal."

Before long, Ollie had driven them to Dover's pub. The bar itself was nice enough. Homey, without turning up the redneck factor. Ollie and Drew took a seat in the back. In a few moments, a curvy blonde came over. "Hey there, Ollie. Who's your buddy?"

Ollie didn't balk at being called Drew's buddy as he introduced the waitress as Stacey, and gave their orders.

"I meant what I said," Drew said. "I am sorry for how I used to treat you. I wanted to get that part out of the way. It wasn't just for show."

Ollie nodded. "I guess I wondered. Look, I want you and Ashley to reconnect. I want Cole to be close with his uncle. And I guess I'm starting to believe you're not going anywhere, so I figure we should find a way to get along. Because I also meant what I said. I'm not going anywhere either."

"Good," Drew said.

Neither said much else until the beers arrived. Ollie figured since this was his bright idea, he should get the ball rolling. "Okay, since we're being buddies and all, I'm just going to lay it out. The fact that you picked on me was only one of the bugs up my ass about you."

Drew took a sip of his beer. "What's the other?"

Ollie sighed. The next part wasn't going to be easy. "When we were younger, I wanted us to be friends. I thought that..." Ollie looked around as if the right words were going to be floating around the bar somewhere. Finally, he took a long pull on his beer, and dug in. "I was always aware of the fact that I'm a nerd."

"You're not a nerd," Drew interjected.

"Please." Ollie rolled his eyes. "My bet is only one of us ever carried a membership card to the Justice League, a Library card to Hogwarts and picture of the Tardis in our wallets."

Drew couldn't help but laugh. "No, I carried a condom in mine. Okay, you were a nerd."

"Thank you." Ollie decided not to point out that he still carried two out of three of those items in his wallet. "I was a nerd, and you were the cool guy. And I thought we should be able to connect because of what we had in common."

"Such as?"

Ollie was starting to resent being the one doing all the opening up. "If you recall, you lost your mom. I'd lost my dad."

Drew played with his bottle. "I remember. And as an adult, I can get why you thought that."

"But not when we were kids?" Ollie said.

Drew shook his head while he sipped his beer.

"Why?"

"Truth?" Drew said. "I resented the hell out of you."

Ollie's mouth dropped open. He didn't know how to respond to that.

"Ollie," Drew said. "You have to understand when we were kids, it never occurred to me that a father could be anything but a person to fear. You didn't have to hide from yours. I lost my mom, the one adult in my life I thought gave a shit about me and you got your mom all to yourself."

Not sure if he should feel angry at Drew's words or just sad, Ollie stayed silent.

"At some point," Drew continued. "I realized you actually liked your dad. Even loved him. That pissed me off even more."

"Why?"

Drew shrugged. "Part of it was I was always pissed off. I had plenty of reason to be. I never knew when Dad was going to go bat crap crazy on us. Our lives were a nightmare. And I guess I really hated people who didn't have to live in that kind of nightmare. How dare this kid who gets hugs and kisses and hot chocolate with little marshmallows think he knows anything about what my life, my sister's lives are like? And I was jealous as hell. You could go home and be as goofy as you wanted to be. You could screw up. You could go to bed without locking your door at night, without trying to listen for your sister's screams. I guess I hated you for that."

Ollie stared at Drew, completely lost for words. He desperately wanted to say something profound and earnest. Something to communicate to Drew that he understood.

"I don't like marshmallows in my hot chocolate."

It was the best he could come up with.

Relief flooded through Ollie when Drew threw his head back and laughed.

"Dammit, Ollie," Drew said. "I really am sorry. I don't feel that way anymore."

Ollie smiled. "Good. Can I ask you another question?" He waited until Drew nodded. "Do you suspect your father? Because he has an alibi for the night in question. I know he wasn't a good man, but do you think he'd be capable of killing Kelli?"

All humor drained from Drew's face. "Do I think he's capable of killing his own daughter? Yeah, without a doubt."

"I have a hard time believing that," Ollie said. "She was still his daughter. I know he got drunk and violent, but whoever did this probably planned it. It wasn't a drunken rage."

Drew nodded. "I know. And I believe you when you tell me that he's alibied. If my father had a hand in it, he didn't kill her himself. But I'm not ruling out the idea he may have had someone else do it. And neither should you."

"Why?"

Drew sighed. "I don't want Ashley to know this if she doesn't have to. Okay?"

Ollie considered, rolling it around in his head a moment. He decided that he would decide when it was something Ashley needed to know. "Fine."

Drew looked around to make sure there was nobody within earshot, before leaning even closer.

"My father came to see me in prison," Drew explained. "To tell me that I should take a deal and plead guilty. I refused and the message was delivered again. More violently."

Ollie studied Drew's face. "What do you mean?"

Drew just shook his head. "Just trust me. I was tempted to beg them to let me plead guilty, but I was too much of a stubborn SOB to do so. I was convinced I wasn't getting out of there alive. Then the chief died and the new DA dropped the charges and I was told I was getting out.

"When I got out of jail," Drew continued. "I was planning on coming back. Dad was the one who picked me up at the prison, driving a nice, new shiny black truck. Shocked the shit out of me. He told me how Kelli was living with Rodger. She was probably pregnant with Cole, but Dad didn't mention that. He may not have known. Doubt he cared. He also told me Ashley moved in with Lily. Instead of taking me home, he pulled off the road and made me get out. At gun point."

Ollie's eyes widened.

"It wasn't the first time he'd pulled his gun on me," Drew explained. "But this time was different. He wasn't drunk or pissed. If anything, he was very pleased with himself, as if he'd just won the lotto. He made a big deal out of how he could kill me right there and nobody would give a shit. Again, nothing new."

Ollie could see the haunted look in Drew's eyes, and knew how hard it was from him to open up.

"Something changed," Drew said. "He had a different edge. He almost seemed giddy. He told me to leave town and to never come back. He told me if I ever did, if I ever started to come to town and insist I wasn't the one who kidnapped and killed Molly Winters, bad things would happen."

Ollie's eyes narrowed. He started to go into cop mode. "He threatened to kill you if you made inquiries into what happened to Molly Winters?"

Drew shook his head. "Not me, although I suppose that much was implied. He threatened Kelli and Ashley. And he'd promised they'd be raped and killed."

Ollie's fist smashed into the table right before he launched out of his chair. He stalked to the back of the bar and reached into his pocket and pulled out a phone. Drew was by his side in an instant.

"Don't," Drew said. "Don't start making calls and going all cop on me. You do that, you're signing Ashley's death warrant. And probably Cole's too. And I'm not sure that what happened with Kelli is connected."

Ollie wanted to punch Drew again, mostly out of frustration. He shoved his phone back into his pocket. "Why not?"

Drew sighed. "Yesterday when the General and I went to see him, he made it clear if he had been behind it, she would have been raped."

Ollie shook his head in disbelief. He pointed to a

back door. Together they went out into the side alley.

"Jesus Christ, Drew," Ollie snapped. "That's one hell of a fucking bombshell. I'm a cop. I can't just ignore that."

"I'm not asking you to," Drew said. "Ollie, I didn't have to tell you this, but I did. I told you because I know Ashley trusts you, and because I really do need you to help me protect her and Cole. If you're going to do that, you need to keep your eyes open. You need to know what to look for. Dad's threat wasn't an idle one. He meant it. Think about what that means."

"It means," Ollie responded as he paced. "That your father is back on the list of suspects."

"It means more than that," Drew explained. "I don't know how much you know about this town back then, but the police department was pretty damn corrupt. They covered for my Dad plenty. I'm sure he returned the favor. When he told me something would happen to my sister, he didn't mean he'd do it himself. His buddies would."

Ollie stopped pacing. "That was then. My mom has cleaned up the department."

Drew folded his arms. "I believe you, but there's no way to know if she got them all. All it takes is one guy. It wouldn't even have to be a dirty cop, just one who was buddies with one and doesn't know it."

Ollie glared at Drew, cursing him in his mind. "I can't not do anything. I've got to try and figure this out. And I've got to tell someone. My mom will be discreet, but she needs to know."

"I'll trust your judgment," Drew said. "But not in the station. Probably best not to be over the phone."

Ollie scowled. "You really think it can be that bad?

That they'd bug my phone? Or the chief's?"

Drew shrugged. "I don't know. I may be wrong about this entire thing. Kelli's death might not have anything to do with this, but in the time I've worked for the General, I've seen some crazy things. I think we shouldn't take anything for granted."

Folding his arms, Ollie nodded. Drew was right. They had to be careful. He'd talk to his mom alone, at her place, first chance he got. "All right, we'll play it safe. I'm not sure I'm buying what you're selling."

"I'm not asking you to," Drew said. "I may be wrong. I really hope I am, but I'm not willing to take chances with Ashley and Cole."

Ollie nodded. "Neither am I. Don't you think you should tell this to Ashley? She should know why you left. It might help her to trust you again."

"No," Drew answered with a small shake of his head. "I need Ashley to forgive me on her own. Whatever my reasons, I still screwed up. I left her. That was my biggest reason, but not my only one. I didn't ever want to step foot in this damned town again. I wanted to be someplace where people didn't look at me like I'd gotten away with murder."

Ollie scratched the back of his neck. "I get that, but I really think she should know. You should think about telling her. Another thing to consider is that you and I can't be her and Cole's bodyguard's twenty-four-seven. She needs to be on the lookout. You know there's a self-defense class geared toward women that Sam and I give. There's one coming up. I keep trying to get Ashley and Lily to sign up, but they never do. Ashley is just too stubborn and Lily won't go without her."

Drew thought a moment. It would be a good idea

for both of them to take that class, but if he'd suggested it, she'd scoff at the idea. Still, there were ways.

"I can get her there," Drew said with a smirk. "I just need to give her the right incentive. I'll reach out to Sam about that."

Ollie cocked an eyebrow. "I'm guessing you want to reach out to Sam for more than just getting Ashley in that class."

Drew didn't deny it. "Is that going to be an issue for you?"

Ollie sighed. "I guess not. She's an adult and it's her business, but I'm protective. She may not feel she's ready."

"Why not?"

Ollie held his hands up. "That's not for me to tell you."

"All right, fair enough." Drew relaxed. "Feel like punching me again?"

"Maybe."

"Settle for another beer instead."

Ollie smirked. "Deal."

****

Four days later, the General stood in the living room ready to say goodbye. Everyone lined up like troops waiting to be inspected; the one exception was Drew, who waited outside by the car to drive the General to the airport.

He started with Lily, whose eyes only went as high as The General's torso. "Thank you for all your hospitality, Lily."

She smiled broadly. "It was my pleasure and you're welcome any time. I hope you'll be back."

"Count on it," the General said. "Someone has to

come around to kick Drew's ass once in a while, just so he remembers what it feels like."

That earned a chuckle from everyone down the line as Lily reached up to the General and pulled him down to give him a hug and a kiss on the cheek.

"I mean it," she whispered in his ear. "Drew needs you."

The General returned the embrace. When he pulled back, he was flattered by the moisture in Lily's eye. He winked at her before moving on to Ashley.

Drew's sister wore a scowl, but it was clearly hiding a grin. Unlike Lily, she was able to look the General right in the eye as she was only half an inch shorter. "Just so you know, I can and *will* be kicking Drew's ass while you're gone, so don't worry about that."

The General raised his eyebrows in amusement. "I never had any doubt."

Ashley pulled the General into her arms. "But that doesn't mean you shouldn't come back. I think you're good for him. He's not quite as much of an asshole as I remembered."

The General chuckled as he kissed her softly on her forehead. "I'll be back and we can gang up on him. But try and give him a little bit of a break." He lowered his voice to a hush. "He loves you, you know."

Ashley nodded and quickly wiped at her eyes. "Son of a bitch. I hate to cry."

Lily laughed and took her hand as the General lowered himself to one knee to face Cole.

Cole's face was, as usual, passive, but his light blue eyes watched and saw everything. "Thank you for coming, sir."

The General smiled and looked up to Lily and Ashley, both of whom read his expression and stepped into the next room to give the General a moment alone with Cole. The young boy stiffened at the thought of being alone with him, but didn't flinch.

There's a lot of Drew in this one.

"Listen up, kid," the General said. "You've been dealt a bad hand, no use trying to pretend otherwise, but you've got good people here who will look after you. Lily and your Aunt Ash love you. And so does your Uncle Drew. Now I know you're still trying to figure him out, but I know him. I've seen Drew in the worst of circumstances. He's solid."

Cole looked away. "He left before."

The General nodded. "Yes he did. Your aunt is trying to forgive him for that. So should you. I'm not sure your Uncle will ever forgive himself, but I can tell you this. He never stopped loving your mother, never stopped wanting to protect her. He did what he thought was best. He screwed up, but I know without a doubt if your Mom asked him to come back sooner, he would have, and he's here for you. This time, I don't expect him to make the same mistake. He might make other ones. That's one lesson you're going to have to learn now and not later. Adults screw up, even me, as hard as that is to believe." The General sighed, wondering how much of this was getting through. "Here, I've got something for you."

The General reached into his pocket and pulled out a cell phone. "Your uncle asked me to get this for you." He let Cole to inspect it. "It's something McAlister Security manufactures. It's programmed with numbers that should be easy to access. Let me show you."

Tapping a few buttons on the cell, the General brought up the contact list. Cole was able to see it was already programmed with the numbers for his home, as well as the cell numbers of his aunt and uncle. Lily was in there, as was Ollie. There were a few he didn't know. "This one is for the police," The General pointed to the numbers Cole didn't recognize. "This is mine. If you ever don't feel safe, you call me, or use this," He pointed to one marked MS, "McAlister Security. And we'll come for you. Understood."

Cole nodded quickly, not sure what to say.

"Now," the General said. "I took the liberty of programming in a password for it."

With that, Cole found his voice. "It's not something lame, like 1-2-3-4, is it?"

The General scowled. "No, smartass. It's 5-3-5-5-4. Most phones have a four-digit password, but I had this one programmed for you with five. If you look at the letters, you'll see it spells—"

"Kelli," Cole almost whispered. "Mom's name."

The General nodded and handed him the phone. "Right. I assume that's okay with you?" He waited a moment until Cole nodded sadly, his young eyes on the phone. "There's more. You see this?" The General pointed to a red icon with a white exclamation mark in it. "That's a panic button app. You open that up, it'll send messages to McAlister Security and everyone's cell phones. It'll turn on your speaker, so we'll be able to hear everything happening on your side of things, but you won't be able to hear our side unless you key in a code. It's the same code to get into your phone. You'll have to enter that code to call it off, in case you do it by mistake. And they'll only let you do it verbally."

Cole held it in his hand, his eyes locked on the panic button. "What if someone makes me say everything is okay? You won't know the difference."

The General smiled. "That's actually a good question, and it's something we thought of. It's programmed with a dummy code."

Cole squinted in confusion. "A dummy code? What's that?"

"Instead of your mother's name," the General explained, "You enter a different code. It'll send a signal to our group so that even though you say everything is all right, it's not. They may talk to you as if you made a mistake. Might even give you a hard time, just to keep up appearances, but they'll know.

"If you enter the dummy code to key into the phone, it automatically activates the app, so if someone ever takes your phone and wants to check your messages, have them enter the dummy code. It will trigger a message to everyone, we'll know your location, and we'll be able to hear whatever is happening, even if they turn it off." The General tapped the phone in pride. "Your phone won't actually go off, it'll just look like it did."

Slowly, a grin spread across Cole's face. "What's the dummy code?"

The General grinned. "Something I expect you to remember. 1-2-3-4."

The General got to hear Cole laugh for the first time.

****

Drew waited until the General climbed into the car and secured his seat belt before pulling away. "Did you give Cole the phone?"

The General nodded. "Smart kid. Asked good questions. He has a bag packed to run with?"

Drew smiled as he pulled onto the main road. "Yes. He's got some cash, clothes, some candy bars, water and a couple of books."

"Like I said, smart kid." The General said. "I have that meeting tonight with the Blair's, and then I've got to look personally at the security for the Whitmore Foundation."

Drew nodded. "I know you've pushed it off to stay here until after the funeral. I appreciate it more than you know."

They pulled up to a red light. "I wanted to be here for you. Matt would have wanted me to. I'm hoping once I get on that jet, you don't think it'll be the end of me. I'll be back. Probably soon. I expect to see this through."

Drew's grinned. "I know."

The light turned green and Drew released the brake and eased onto the gas. "Maybe next time, I'll show you around. Not too much to see here, but I can show you my old high school. Or challenge you to a game of pool. Or show you where I got my first look at boobs."

The General barked out a laugh. As they drove, the discussion turned more to business. Upcoming jobs, who would be a good replacement for him, and how to handle certain clients Drew worked with.

"You've still got over two months left of leave," the General said. "Have you thought about what you're going to do once that's over? You can't just stay above Lily's garage forever."

"Definitely not," Drew said. "I've got a decent savings. I was thinking of buying a place of my own. I want to stay close to Lily's. Cole seems comfortable there, but I want him to know he can stay with me whenever he wants. There's a few houses in the area."

"You ever fix up a home?"

Drew laughed. "I painted my sisters' room once, when they really wanted to change the color. My father was useless. Once in a while, he'd start to try and fix something, but just ended up getting pissed and drunk, so if we wanted it fixed, I had to do it. But, I wouldn't be up to doing plumbing."

"You might want to hire that out. Not only so it gets done right, but you can hire locally. People will appreciate the business. You haven't interacted much with your community. Have you tried to look up any of your old friends?"

Drew signaled a left turn. "No. You'll notice how few people came to Kelli's funeral. Most don't want to look me in the eye. They think I killed Molly and don't want to pretend I didn't or get into it with me. I'm not here to convince anyone. I'm here for Ashley and Cole."

The General let out a long, soft breath. "Cole isn't going to have it easy, growing up in a town where people think his uncle is a killer."

Drew gripped the steering wheel tightly. "I know. I've thought about trying to get Ashley and Cole to move out of Ember Falls. It's not like the place has great memories for either of us, but Ashley is part owner of the bookstore. She won't leave Lily alone and she'd kill me if I even suggested taking Cole away from her. Besides, the kid needs a stable home. There's nothing wrong with Ember Falls. Just because my childhood sucked doesn't mean Cole's has to."

They sat in silence as Drew navigated onto the highway, heading toward the airport. The General knew Drew didn't want to make waves because it could make things uncomfortable for his sister and nephew, but the fact was Drew wasn't good at *not* making waves. And sometimes you needed to stir things up. A thought occurred to the General, something he wasn't quite ready to share, but something he'd need to look at. He'd have to check on the legality, but it that made him smile.

"Have you thought about what you're going to do for a living?"

Drew did what he could to suppress a snort. "Thought about? Yes. But I haven't figured it out. I made a few calls the other night. Although nobody said it, it felt more or less like a unified, 'don't call us, we'll call you' kind of response. I'm going to have to get a job soon."

"Well, I might have a job for you through McAlister Security," the General said. "Something local that might work out. It won't be permanent, but if it checks out, and the client agrees, it'll give you a paycheck for a little longer. I'll check on it and get back to you."

Drew pulled up to a stop sign, just a few blocks away from their destination. He took a moment to glance at the General, trying to gauge exactly what kind of job he had in mind. As usual, the General had a perfect poker face.

But he did notice Drew looking.

"I can get someone else if you turn out to not be interested," the General said blandly as Drew continued to drive. "But, if it pans out the way I hope it will, I'd consider it a personal favor."

"Of course." Just as Drew pulled the car into a parking spot and killed the engine, his cell buzzed with a text. Drew grabbed it and opened the text.

"Everything okay with the kid?" the General said, instantly reading Drew's face.

Nodding as he read the message, a slow grin appeared on his face.

"Well, now." The General's eyebrows went up in amusement. "I'm guessing that text isn't from or about Cole. Would that be from the young lady you were talking to after the burial? The one that came with her grandmother?"

Drew laughed as he closed the phone. "Yeah. Her name's Sam. She just texted. Her Nana is going out tonight, so she asked if I wanted to come by to talk."

"Ah," the General said with a smug expression. "Is that what we're calling it? Talking?"

Drew scowled. "You've got a dirty mind. She's made it clear she's reluctant to start anything and she's not into casual relationships."

The General smirked. "But you're going anyway."

Drew smiled. "Hell, yeah."

****

"You're not going empty-handed, are you?" Lily stood in the kitchen, seasoning a chicken and looking bewildered.

When Drew texted back, Sam told him to come by about an hour after her shift ended. He offered to bring dinner, but she said she had something to cook at the house.

"Um...yeah," Drew said. "It's not a date. If it were a date, I'd be taking her out to eat."

Lily's eyes widened in shock and utter dismay. "Oh. My. God." She looked to Ashley who sat at the table with a beer in her hand, reading a magazine. "Your brother is a baboon."

Ashley raised her beer in mock salute. "I've been saying it for years."

"Give me a break," Drew said. "She told me she wasn't ready for dating. I got the impression from both her and Ollie that something may have happened. She even used the words, 'come hang out' in her text. If this was a date, I would have called her on the phone at the very least, not made it through a text. I'd take her out to a nice place. I'd bring flowers."

"Yes!" Lily's face lit up. "Flowers. Take her flowers."

Drew rolled his eyes. "I just said…"

"Hush." Lily was thinking about it, tapping her finger on her chin and looking up to the ceiling. "No, not flowers. You're right, too much. Too soon. You'll scare her off."

"Scare her…" Drew was flabbergasted.

"Hush," Lily repeated. "She's cooking, right?"

Slowly, Drew nodded. He was starting to get a little worried.

Lily paced back and forth as Drew sent a puzzled look to his sister who laughed and took another pull on her beer.

"Wine," Lily concluded. "Here, I've got something in here."

Lily disappeared into a nearby pantry. Bottles clinked together as she searched for whatever it was she was looking for. Finally, she came out holding a bottle of Sangiovese in one hand and a bottle of Pinot Grigio in the other. She held up both green bottles to Drew. "What is she serving?"

Drew shrugged. "How am I supposed to know? I offered to bring some food. She said she'd make something. Why are we making a big deal out of this? She might just be grilling up some burgers and…"

"Ahh," Lily screamed as she stalked forward and shoved both bottles in his hands. "Stop. Just stop before you completely break my heart. Take them both. Now…" She looked him up and down. "You're not planning on wearing that, are you?"

Drew looked down at himself. He was in jeans and a black t-shirt. It was the same thing he'd been wearing all day. "I'm gonna say no, only because I'm very frightened of you right now."

Ashley chuckled. "Good answer."

"Go shower and change." Lily took the bottles back and placed them on the counter. She started to shoo him out through the back door. "Nothing too fancy. Jeans are okay if you've something without holes in them. And please tell me you own a decent shirt with buttons and a collar of some sort."

Drew shook his head in disbelief as Lily herded him toward the door. The last thing he heard was Ashley yell out, "If you want to bring something more entertaining, I've got plenty of condoms."

****

Drew found himself walking up to Sam's front door with two bottles of wine, one tucked under his arm and the other firmly in his grip. He'd put on a new pair of dark, blue jeans that didn't—as far as he knew—have any holes in them, and a gray button-down shirt. He imagined he'd open the door and find Sam in sweats, her hair up while she nuked hot dogs for dinner.

He was just about to knock when the door opened.

Rose looked shocked to see him, but her wide eyes quickly melted to joy. "I'm so happy you're here. I almost didn't believe Sam when she told me you were coming over." She stepped back and held the door open, inviting him in.

Drew smiled back as he stepped inside. The moment he sniffed the air, he knew hamburgers were not on the menu. Something spicy wafted through the air, coupled with the scent of tomatoes and wine. Drew started to wonder if he was under-dressed

"Smells great, doesn't it?" Rose said with a broad smile.

Rose was wearing a long, flowered dress and had a small, white purse in her hands. Her feet were clad in shoes that matched her purse, with three-inch heels.

She stepped through the open door. "I've got my poker game. I plan on cleaning up. You go on in the kitchen and have a great time. I won't be home until late, so feel free to get as frisky as you want." She sent him that dazzling smile again before leaving.

Drew headed for the kitchen area. When he opened the door, it hit him. Somehow, he'd died and now he was in Heaven.

If the smell of the food cooking was tantalizing from the door, it was downright mouthwatering from here.

Sam was busy pouring angel hair pasta into a colander as something red simmered in a skillet. Leaving the colander in the sink, she hummed to the slow and sexy country song playing on the radio as she pulled a long, French baguette from the oven.

If the food smelled delectable, Sam looked downright scrumptious. While not in sweatpants, her outfit was simple enough. She wore a pair of tight jeans and a pink blouse that showed off all of her curves. There was something about her, how she glided through the kitchen, her long, dark hair flowing freely behind her as she stirred the sauce in the skillet, her hips swaying to the rhythm of a sultry steel pedal guitar that sent a flock of butterflies aflutter in Drew's belly.

Glancing in his direction, Sam's eyes widened in surprise. Her face lit up as she smiled. "When did you get here and how long have you been standing there?"

Drew closed the distance between them, setting the two bottles of wine down on the counter. "I got here just as your Nana was leaving to play poker and I came in as you were dumping the pasta, so not long. Why? Was the last song on the radio something even sexier?"

Sam grinned. "It was all about a girl's badonkadonk, so no."

Drew laughed. "I don't know, I'm kinda finding your badonkadonk pretty sexy right now." He turned to the stove. "That smells amazing."

"Thanks," Sam said. "It's an old family recipe that was quick and easy to make. You're not allergic to shellfish are you?"

Drew leaned down and pulled her into a kiss. She tasted as delicious as her food smelled, and when she melted into his embrace her body fit his as if she were a part of him that had been missing his entire life, only he hadn't known it until this moment.

When the kiss ended, he thought she trembled. She looked up at him with those big, brown eyes, wide with wonder and a little fear.

"Wow," Sam said. "And you haven't even sampled my cooking."

Slowly, she pulled away from him and went back to the stove.

Drew stood behind her, worried he'd taken things too far. "I'm sorry."

She continued to stir the sauce for a moment, her back tense as she added a sprinkle of salt. Drew thought about excusing himself and leaving when she sighed and turned around. "No, I'm sorry. It was an amazing kiss and it's not like I didn't want to kiss you. Or that I don't like it. I guess it was...more than I was expecting."

"I'm sorry," Drew repeated. "I just..."

"No, please," Sam said. "I have some baggage I haven't told you about. I expected tonight to be very casual and friendly. You make me want to..." she smiled and actually blushed. "Want to leave my dinner on the stove to ruin and do something I might regret. I guess I'm not ready for that yet."

Drew smiled. "I understand. Do you want me to go?"

The lovely blush drained from her face. "No, I definitely don't want that, but dinner's almost ready. Let's eat and talk. Okay?"

Drew nodded.

"Good. I've got to finish this up. What kind of wine... Oh..." Sam picked up the bottle of Sangiovese. "This is perfect for dinner."

Drew sighed. "I've got to be honest. It was Lily's idea which two wines to pick. I don't really know much about it, but she figured between these two, they'd pair well with whatever you were making."

Sam laughed as she handed him the bottle and dug in a drawer for a corkscrew. "Well, she's got perfect taste. I can't imagine a dish I would have thrown together that wouldn't have worked with one of these. Unless I made burgers or hot dogs, in which case beer would be best, but I've got that already."

Drew struggled not to give in to his urge to kiss her again.

"Can you open the wine and get glasses down from the cabinet?" She pointed quickly to the cupboard on the other side of the room. "I'll need a few minutes to finish this up. You want to eat outside? It's a beautiful night."

Drew, thinking the cool night air would do him good right about now, agreed. He put the bottle of wine down on the dark wood buffet under the cabinet so he could open it and retrieve the two glasses. Then with the corkscrew tucked into his shirt pocket, he headed to the door, taking one last look at Sam as she dumped a bowl full of shrimp into the sauce and stirred.

Outside was a small patio table, with two chairs on either side. It was dusk and the sky was a radiant combination of gold and blue auras mixing as the sun began its gentle descent. Drew opened the wine and set it aside to let it breathe. There was a single candle in a small red glass bowl of wax. He dug into his pocket for his lighter before remembering he didn't have it as he no longer smoked.

He headed back to the door to find Sam heading his way. He opened the door and took the breadbasket she was carrying, along with a small tray of butter and butter knife.

"Here." She fished in her jeans pocket. "You might

as well light the candle." She handed him a book of matches. "I'll be right out. Go sit."

Drew took the matches over, lit one and used it on the candle, and then poured the wine. Sam came through the door with two large plates. "I hope you don't mind spicy."

"Not at all," Drew said as he pulled her chair out for her. "This looks and smells amazing."

Sam beamed. "Shrimp Fra Diavolo. One of my favorites." She picked up her fork and speared a big, succulent shrimp and twirled some pasta around it.

Drew enjoyed watching her eat. So many girls hated to eat in front of a guy, but he loved the fact she felt at ease as she savored her own cooking.

Following her example, he sampled shrimp and pasta. "Oh my God." He closed his eyes to relish the taste.

"Too spicy?" Sam said sheepishly.

Drew shook his head. "Not at all. It's…" He took another bite. "It's amazing." He opened his eyes to see Sam flushed with pleasure.

"Thanks." Sam picked up her glass of wine. "It's actually Nana's recipe."

"Yeah?" Drew said. "Well here's the deal, one of you will have to marry me, because this recipe needs to be in my family."

Sam took a sip of wine and smiled. "I'll let Nana know. She'll be thrilled. She may want a pre-nup so to protect her cowboy boot collection."

"Understandable," Drew said. "People have told me all my life I'm nothing but trouble."

Sam's eyes lit with amusement. "Nana's tough. She can handle you."

"What about you?" Drew's tone wasn't quite as playful.

Sam didn't answer and Drew didn't press her. Instead, he spoke of his work for McAlister Security, saying goodbye to the General this morning and shared a few stories of how he was adjusting to life with Cole.

"He's a smart kid," Drew said, the pride obvious in his voice. "Takes after his mom a lot. Loves to read. He tends to be on the quiet side, but he's always listening. You can't get anything by him. But he's scared. He's getting better around me, but whenever I walk in the room, he gets that petrified look in his eyes like I'm going to do something."

Sam nodded. "He's the same way with Ollie. Hesitant. Watchful. We know Kelli was abused by her husband. You think he put his hands on Cole?"

Drew scowled down at his glass of wine. "Yeah, I do. And if he comes near him again, he's going to regret it. But I get this feeling like it's more than that. He likes to give his Aunt Ash a hard time. Lily too, although not as much. But not me."

Sam picked up her own wine, took a sip, thinking about what he said. "You say that like you don't give your sister grief."

Drew shrugged. "Not nearly as much as she busts my balls, but that's not the point. He won't have a go at me. He'll curse at me in anger, but he's afraid to say anything to me. He's still waiting for me to hurt him. Or worse."

"Worse?"

Drew put his glass down, folded his hands and collected his thoughts. "The other night, Ash was having a go at me during dinner. She was telling the story of how in first grade, they had us all in costumes singing TV jingles—"

"What's wrong with that?"

Drew shook his head. "I was dressed like a giant hot dog, singing the spelling of the type of wiener I was." Drew paused a moment to let Sam throw her head back and laugh. There was something about her laugh that lit up her face. When she finally stopped, Drew continued. "Point is, Ashley was ragging on me pretty good. I kept trying to get her to stop."

"Because you didn't want Cole to laugh at you?"

"No, let the kid have a laugh at me. I was laughing myself. I really did look like a moron. Cole should have laughed at me, too, but he was too busy being scared shitless. He even started to shake in his seat. He was certain I was going to do something to Ashley for teasing me." Drew picked up his glass, drank the last of the wine and poured himself more. "He won't talk to anyone about what happened. Lily told me Kelli wouldn't go into details, but at least she was seeing a counselor."

"Maybe you should consider getting him into counseling too," Sam said.

"I talked to Ash, but Cole refuses. Gets angry when you try and bring it up, and she doesn't want to push him. He's ready to run."

Alarm radiated in Sam's eyes. "Cole wants to run away?"

"I don't think he *wants* to," Drew said. "But he's ready to if he feels he has to. He's afraid his stepfather is going to come back for him and he won't go, but he doesn't want Ashley or Lily getting hurt because of him. He's got a bag packed. He'd sneak a few dollars wherever he could find them."

Sam nodded, understanding. "Have you talked to him?"

Drew told her about how he gave Cole three hundred in cash, and the cell phone.

"You're trying to give him a sense of control," Sam said.

"Partially," Drew said. "But there's another side to it, one my sister would rip my head off if she heard me say it. I want to help him so he *can* run."

Sam's eyes grew wide in utter astonishment.

"There way I see it," Drew continued, "Cole knows something he's not telling us. He may understand something about his stepfather we don't. If something happened and he felt the need to hide, I want him to have the means to get away from the house. I told him if he ran, I'd be coming for him and it wouldn't be me he was running from. Like I said before, the kid is smart. I just wish he trusted me enough to open up."

Sam seemed to consider Drew's statement. She traced the top of her wine glass with her finger as she stared at her plate of food, mostly eaten now.

"He's scared because you're a man," Sam said. "So is Ollie. I've met him a few times. He seems to like me. Maybe I should talk with him. I could give him a key so if he needed to get away, he'd have a place to go."

Drew frowned. "It'd be a big help, but the kid isn't a wimp. If he's running, it's because someone is chasing him."

Sam cocked an eyebrow. "I may not have survived battles in downtown Fallujah, but I *am* a cop."

"But your Nana *isn't*. I don't want to put her in the crosshairs."

Sam huffed out a breath and settled back in her chair. "I'll talk to her, but my guess is she'll want to help like that. She's pretty tough for a Nana. She's had to be. Raised my mom on her own. Got pregnant when she was eighteen, and just barely out of high school. The man responsible, I refuse to call him my grandfather, never wanted anything to do with her again. Her parents threw her out when she wouldn't put my mom up for adoption. So, Nana raised my mom on her own. Times were tough, but they made do. Then when my mom was in high school, she met my dad and history nearly repeated itself."

"Nearly?"

Someone lit a fire and the smell of burning wood filled the air. Sam took a deep breath before continuing.

"My mom was pregnant with me before she graduated, but my dad didn't run for the hills, despite pressure from his father to do just that. They married young, but made it work. My father went straight into the academy after school. He was a cop my entire life. I guess I was always a daddy's girl, because I knew that's what I wanted, to be like my dad, in his uniform, coming home every night. I know your father wasn't a good father by a long shot, but mine was. He was my hero."

"I learned a long time ago that my father was the exception, not the rule."

Sam smiled as she rose up, took her glass of wine and went to stand by the edge of the deck. She leaned against the banister as Drew joined her.

"I've only dated four guys," Sam continued. "I told you, I'm not a casual kind of girl. The first two relationships ended on good terms. And then there was

Dylan."

Sam took another sip, stared bitterly into her glass. "He was so nice when I first met him. He knew my plans about wanting to be a cop and was very supportive. I was happy. I never minded spending all my time with him. I started to see less and less of my friends, my family, but that's what happens when you have a serious boyfriend. Then one day, I saw him arguing with some girl named Tracy. I asked Dylan what it was about and he told me she was an ex who didn't want to let go. He hadn't dated her since high school. But he's telling me I was the girl he wanted and next thing I know, he pops out a ring."

Drew's eyebrows went up. "You were engaged?"

Sam smiled. "Yeah. I was engaged. We were half way through our senior year at college and I'm sporting a ring on my finger. Then one day, I get a text that said, 'congrats' on it. It had an attachment which I opened. It was that girl Tracy, and she was with Dylan, in her bed, naked. She must have taken the picture after he'd fallen asleep."

"Oh boy," Drew said.

"Yeah, well," Sam continued. "I went to him, showed him the picture and waited for him to deny it. He didn't even have the decency to lie. Just said she was a good lay, and did things he didn't want the mother of his children to do and this was something men did and I should just not worry about it."

Drew scowled. "Bastard."

Sam laughed and shook her head as if she couldn't believe it herself. "Well, I decided the way to deal with it was to throw my ring in his face and walk out on him. I got half way to the door when he grabbed my arm, swung me around and slapped my face."

Drew's reaction was immediate. His body tensed and his eyes narrowed. "What did you do?"

Sam went to take another sip of wine, but saw her glass was empty. She went back to the table and poured more for herself, took a long drink, and put her glass down. "What do you think I did? I'm my daddy's princess. I balled up my fist like my sweet, doting father showed me and I broke his fucking nose."

Drew smiled wickedly at her. "That's my girl."

Sam nodded. "He tried to get up and come at me, made some noise about putting me in my place." She waved her hand and rolled her eyes in a dismissive gesture. "His life's ambition was to become a CPA. By the time I walked out of that apartment, he had a black eye to go with the broken nose. I worried he'd press charges, but he didn't want to admit he'd gotten his ass kicked by a girl. I heard a rumor he'd gotten mugged, figured that was what he was telling people."

Sam shrugged. "I tried the no relationship thing for a while, but it never felt right to me. I could never get comfortable. It just isn't me, so I stopped dating, and when I was in the academy, I met this guy. He seemed nice, so we dated, but I was reserved. Next thing I know, I'm hearing how I was a slut and I'd banged him in every corner of the academy, and even did one of his friends at the same time. It was humiliating. We didn't even hook up, but you can't un-spread rumors."

Drew shook his head. "Asshole."

"You bet he was," Sam said. "And I was upset, so I called my parents who told me they were going to come in for the week to see me. They never made it."

Drew frowned. "What do you…?" Seeing the look

of pain on Sam's face, he realized what she meant.

"They were run off the road by a drunk driver," Sam said. "My mother was killed right away, but my dad was still alive. I rushed to the hospital, but by the time I got to there it was too late."

Sam grabbed her glass from the table and headed toward the edge of the deck. Drew followed. "I'm sorry. I know how useless that sounds, but…"

She turned and smiled. "You've been hearing it from people for the last few weeks, haven't you? Some say it just to be polite or not sound like an asshole. Some really mean it. I know you do. Thank you."

He gently took her glass from her and placed it on the banister, then took her in his arms. She laid her head on his chest and together, they just stood there in the moonlight.

"You wanna know what really sucks?" she said. "If I hadn't gotten so upset over a rumor that some asshole spread about me, they wouldn't have been killed. So it's my fault."

Suddenly, she was crying in his arms. He never shushed her, just held on and let her cry. When the tears started to ebb, he kissed the top of her head. "It was never your fault, and I'm sure you parents would want you know that."

She nodded in his chest. "I know, but I can't help but feel like it is."

"I get it." Drew still blamed himself for failing to protect his sister. For not even knowing he had a nephew that was being raised in terror, and if he were honest, he always would.

"I'm sorry," Sam said. "You came over here to talk to me about something, not to have me blubber all over you."

"Stop," Drew said. "You've let me unload on you. And I probably will again."

Sam took a deep breath and a step back. She looked up into Drew's eyes. "I'm a mess. You have your chance to run."

Drew smiled. "I'm not going anywhere, and you're right. There's something between us. I want to know what that is. I haven't tried for a real relationship in years. I figured anything I've ever loved never ended up the better for it, but if you want to see where this goes, so do I. I can be real patient, but you should know I want you. And when I saw you in that kitchen tonight, it wasn't a one-night stand that was on my mind."

Sam flushed, pulling him down into a long, deep kiss.

When it was over, she smiled. "I'm a little scared about all of this."

Drew smiled. "Me too. Especially since I know if I screw up you'll kick my ass."

She laughed. "So, what was it you originally wanted to tell me?"

Drew sighed and took her hand and led her over to the swing on the other end of the deck.

"Is this a sitting down kind of thing?"

Drew nodded as they both settled into the swing. "Yeah it is. Ollie came by the other night and he and I talked. I told him some stuff. Stuff I've never told anyone else but the General, who I'd just told recently. I wanted to let you know. You should know, before we take this further because you have a right to know what you're getting into."

Sam squeezed his hand. "You're not gonna scare

me off easy."

"I hope not," Drew said. "Cause there's a little something to do with my sister I need you to help me with."

****

"I don't want to go," Cole said. He was sitting on the living room couch, a book in his lap, with his arms crossed and his face in full pout mode. "It's stupid."

"Cole you have to go to school," Ashley said. "I know it's hard, but you've got to get an education. It's what your mom would have wanted."

Cole refused to look at her. "Everyone there is stupid. The teacher is an ass."

"Cole! You don't use that kind of language," Ashley scolded.

"Why not?" Cole said. "You do. You call Uncle Drew an ass all the time."

Ashley cheeks warmed as her back stiffened. She didn't want to look at her brother, but she couldn't resist. And dammit if he wasn't sitting there, with one eyebrow up and a smirk on his face. Bastard was enjoying this.

"I'm older," Ashley said. "I've earned the right to use that language."

"Oh, I don't know," Drew said. "I seem to recall you using that word more than once when you were his age to describe your teacher. Who was that? Mrs. DeWitt?"

Now Ashley crossed her arms and scowled at her brother. "I don't recall calling Mrs. DeWitt an ass." Ashley recalled calling her a fucking asshole, but she couldn't see how that clarification was going to help her case. "And even if I did, it was inappropriate. And it's also beside the point. Cole *needs* to go to school."

"Why?" Cole said. "Why can't I just do lessons here at home? I've been keeping up, haven't I? It's all stupid and boring anyway."

"But you need to," Ashley insisted.

"Why?" Cole said again.

Ashley clenched her fists and ground her teeth. "Because I said so."

"That's not fair," Cole complained.

"Life's not fair," Drew added. "If it were, the bunch of us would be packing up to go sit on a beach and be served drinks with little umbrella's. But we all have to do what we've got to do. Adults have to work. Kids go to school. The better you do at school, the better chance you'll have when you're done of getting a decent job that you might actually enjoy or at the very least not hate. Your school is out for this week, so come Monday, I'm taking you to school."

Cole pouted. "I'm not holding your hand as we go in. That's baby stuff. But I guess you can take me."

"Gee, thanks," Drew said.

Now it was Ashley's turn to smile. She walked across the room when the doorbell rang. "Sam? What are you doing here?"

Sam stepped inside. "I'm here to pick up Drew."

Drew smiled as Sam walked in. She was not in her uniform. Instead she wore sweats and an Albany University sweat shirt.

"You ready?" Sam said.

"I'm ready." Drew got up, smiled at Cole. "I won't be long. We'll hang out later."

Cole nodded as his uncle headed to the door.

"Wait," Ashley said. "Where are you going?"

"Drew's agreed to give me a hand in a few weeks," Sam said. "But we need to get him fitted."

Ashley frowned. "Fitted for what?"

"Nothing," Drew said. "Forget about it."

Ashley didn't give up. She looked to Sam next. "What's he being fitted for?"

"A training suit," Sam said. "Y'know. One of those outfits men wear with all the pads so they don't get hurt."

Drew headed for the door, but Ashley stopped him. "Hurt doing what?"

Locking eyes with Sam for just an instant, Drew forced an exasperated sigh. "I'm helping out with a self-defense class. Bunch of women learn how to defend themselves. I'm the guy they get to hit."

Ashley smiled. "Really? Is this the self-defense class Ollie's been trying to get me and Lily to sign up for?"

Drew shrugged. "Probably. How should I know?" He tried to step around his sister, but Ashley put her hand on her brother's chest.

"Hold on a moment," Ashley said. "Is it too late for me to sign up for this class? I want a chance to beat the crap out of Drew."

"That's not what this is about," Drew said, sounding impatient. "It's not just about hitting me. Besides, you wouldn't like it. I'll be padded."

Ashley smiled. "Doesn't mean I can't still hurt you."

Drew opened his mouth to say something else, but Sam stepped in. "I'll sign you and Lily up. It's in three weeks on Friday at seven at the rec center."

"Does he have to wear the padding?" Ashley said.

Sam pretended to consider it, tapping her finger on her lips while looking at the ceiling. "Yes. 'Fraid so."

Pouting, Ashley looked like she was reconsidering.

"It'll still hurt," Sam whispered. "If you hit him hard enough."

Instantly, Ashley's face brightened. "Sign me up!"

Sam smiled, grabbed Drew and dragged him out while he displayed his best 'annoyed' look on his face. They closed the door to the sound of Ashley laughing.

****

Drew made sure to keep his scowl on his face until they got into Sam's blue sports car. He waited for her to start the engine and pull away. He looked out through the passenger window and gave one last look of contempt as they passed the house.

When they turned the corner, a grin slowly spread across his face. "Damn, that was perfect. She's itching at the bit to kick my ass."

Sam smiled. "She's likely to do just that."

Drew grinned. "That's the plan."

****

"You sure about this?"

Drew didn't answer as he unlocked the passenger side of Sam's car and got out. If he was being honest, he *didn't* want to be here, looking at the place where his sister's body was found, abandoned like a worthless bag of trash. Of course, he didn't want to be here in Ember Falls at all, but Drew's life seemed to be filled with doing things he didn't want to do.

Yet here he was. Back in this hell-hole of a town, with a sister who still hadn't forgiven him for leaving and a nephew who saw him both as a threat and a savior. Drew wasn't sure which was further from the truth.

"Drew," Sam called as she got out of the car, approaching him. "You there?"

Forcing himself to look at her, he nodded. "Yeah, I'm here. Sorry. I need to look for myself. Can you give me a few minutes?"

Sam sighed. "My phone is on," Sam said before climbing back into her car.

Drew quickly turned away before he changed his mind.

There were no businesses or homes on the long stretch of road where Sam's Camry was parked, just a loud train that rattled by once in a while. Drew climbed through a breach in the old, rusty and dinged-up guardrail that prevented speeding cars from going into the deep ditch. Down below were the tatters of police tape that hadn't been collected.

To bring a body down here would be a task. Gravity would help make the job easier, but it would have been tricky. It had been weeks, but Drew could tell where Kelli's body was dragged to the bottom. He cringed as he forced himself to picture it, her body covered in thick, clear plastic, sliding callously over rocks and tree roots.

Standing at the bottom, Drew wondered if he should say a prayer. Was there a part of his sister's soul trapped in this place? Haunting the nearby trees and rocks? Was she there with him now, asking why he was down in this hole instead of spending time with Cole, helping him through this difficult time?

No. She wasn't here. If any trace of Kelli's soul remained, it wouldn't be wasting time in this would-be grave. His sister would be by her son's side, watching over him and wishing Drew would do the same.

How the hell was Drew supposed to look the kid in the eye if he wasn't doing everything he could to make sure Kelli's killer was caught? Drew pushed those thoughts from his mind. They wouldn't help Kelli or Cole, and least of all himself. All they would do is add fuel to the nightmares he was already having.

Reaching into his pocket, Drew pulled his cell and started to take pictures of everything he saw. The large tree gave cover to whoever was down here from peering eyes should anyone stop to investigate a car on the side of the road. He photographed the dirt disturbed by the killer, who clearly intended on burying Kelli here, never to be found. There was a small alcove of rocks, not deep enough to be considered a cave, but it provided shelter if someone down here needed to hide from a passing rainstorm. Drew checked, and it rained on and off the night she was killed.

Kneeling down, Drew considered the ground. The grass grew here and there in spurts, some of it long and weedy, while in other places short, just beginning to grow. Some of the dirt was broken with thick branches protruding up from the earth, while other places were, while not smooth, certainly more acceptable for digging.

Putting his cell phone away, Drew pulled out a small digital recorder the length of a paper clip. It was black and silver, with a tiny digital display. Drew turned it on, before replacing it in his pocket.

"There are easier ways to get to this spot." Drew did his best to keep his mind focused on the job at hand, and not imagine his sister's body being nearly buried here.

He took a deep breath. "There's a path through the trees, but it would have been very difficult to travel carrying a body through it. Plus someone at the small horse ranch nearby might have seen them. It's up hill and uneven. That's probably the way the teens who found Kelli came from. If I follow the trail in the other direction, it'll come out by the stream. Back when I was in high school, the stoner crowd used to go down there and get high. Is that how the killer knew of this place? Or maybe they weren't aware and that's why they were nearly caught."

Standing up, Drew started to turn around slowly. Twigs snapped every time some animal moved or skittered up a tree, and acorns fell. They weren't far from the main highway, Route 87, known as the Northway. There was an overpass, just around the bend and a train track nearby. It wasn't so close that anyone had a shot of spotting someone down here, but wasn't too far away not to allow for noise from it to travel. What he didn't hear was silence. It wouldn't be hard for someone to sneak up on you here.

The dirt had been displaced where the killer started Kelli's would-be grave, but the hole was only about half way dug. Unless the killer didn't care that the body could be revealed if there was a major storm, the killer would have had to dig a few more feet.

By this point, his sister would have been dead, but the thought that her final resting place would have been a hole in the ground, badly dug, just made Drew want to hit something.

Once again, he forced himself to detach emotionally. He wasn't going to do Kelli any good by getting so angry he'd punch one of the nearby trees.

Moving toward the rock face to his left, around a pair of big trees, Drew scooted down and found an area of dirt and sparse grass much more evenly footed.

Why not bury her here? It would have been much easier than where the body was found. He walked across the small patch of ground and a chill shot down his spine. Quickly, he spun around.

Is someone watching me?

Drew saw nobody through the trees and dense foliage, not that it would be hard to hide from view. After a moment, he turned and headed for the small alcove in the rock face.

Drew bent down and dipped his head to enter. Using an app on his phone as a flashlight, he studied the alcove. Shining it around the interior, he took in the details.

"There's a wall of rock from where the upper road sits. I'm inside a little nook in the wall, right under the highway. Not much light, but I doubt anyone came here to read. There's a large rock near the entrance. It'd make a decent place to sit." Shinning the light over and around the rock, Drew spotted a small reflection. "There's a pack of cigarettes, with a lighter, a few Marlboros from the look of it. Some insect living in there now too and it looks like it's been here awhile, untouched." Drew took a picture, but didn't move it.

He turned and sat on the rock, looking out. "You can't see much, just the piece of ground that's spread out before the entrance to the nook. Perhaps some teenager looking to light up where he or she wouldn't get caught by their parents?" He thought about his words. "No, not a she. Maybe it's sexist, but I don't see a girl coming here regularly. Too many bugs and muck.

It just feels like a guy's thing. Maybe I'll ask Sam."

Sitting in this spot, he felt something was off. He didn't know what it was—the moldy smell, the dampness—but something here wasn't right.

He sat, allowing his eyes to graze over every inch of the alcove, squinting at something on the roof. They looked like scrapes made by a rock. Four lines, side by side, and one strike through them all.

Drew pulled out his cell and took pictures. "There are lines carved into the roof of the cave. You can't see them unless you're sitting in this spot. It looks like a count. Someone was keeping track of something."

With a sigh, Drew got up, careful not to smack his head into the cave top. He was ready to get out of here. Drew never thought of himself as claustrophobic, but something about being in this small nook of stone was suffocating him. It didn't help when the place vibrated as a nearby train went through. He started to back out when something caught his eye.

Rocks, just rocks, piled neatly, on top of and around each other, in the far corner, only three feet away from him, but under the shadow of an outgrowth of the cave wall. Drew snapped a few pictures and went closer to investigate.

Before he could move far, the muzzle of a gun pressed to the back of his head. "You so much as twitch and I'll blow your head off, you son of a bitch."

Drew tensed. His mind calculated his chances of being able to move fast enough. Not here, not in this closed off cave. He had no room. Images flooded his mind. Was Sam all right?

"Come out of there, motherfucker," commanded the man. The voice was young, his own age, but bitter and trying to hide a little bit of fear. "Keep your hands where I can see them."

Slowly they backed up together. Drew kept his hands out, bent up at the elbows.

"What was he doing in there?" Another voice said. This one was older, raspier. "I thought I heard him talking to someone."

"There's no room for someone else in there," the first voice said. "Maybe we should call…"

The question remained unfinished as Drew spun around so quickly it took both men by surprise. Like lightning in a storm, he disarmed the man, twisted his arm and now held the gun to his assailant's head.

The other man, in his mid-forties, overweight and balding, raised his gun, but knew he couldn't get a shot off. He started to shout profanities, ordering Drew to drop his weapon. There was something oddly familiar about him, in his cheap, brown suit and graying mustache.

Drew still couldn't see the face of the younger man but he had a full head of blond hair that was neatly trimmed, was far more built, and wore a blue suit more up to date than his buddy.

"Drew!" Sam raced down the slope, skillfully closing the distance while drawing her gun. She came in with a stiffer arm than either of the men, her eyes full of steel and resolve.

Man, she's beautiful.

"Wilson!" Sam said toward the younger man. "Harrington! What are you doing?

"You know these clowns?"

Sam nodded, lowering her gun slightly, just enough to try and defuse the situation, but not so much to leave herself defenseless. "I work with them. They're half of our detective unit."

"The idiot half, you mean," Drew growled, shoving Wilson away, then moving the gun so he was holding it by the muzzle.

Wilson spun around, his face blotched red with anger and embarrassment. He stalked over to Drew and snatched his gun back. He immediately backed up and raised the gun, aiming it at Drew's face.

"Whoa!" Sam raised her gun as well, aiming it at Wilson. "Lower your weapon."

Wilson glared at Sam. "Your boyfriend just assaulted a police officer and took his gun. He's going to jail for a long time."

"You didn't identify yourselves as police officers," Drew said, calmly and clearly.

Harrington and Wilson exchanged quick glances. "Yes we did. We clearly identified ourselves, told you to put your hands above your head. I'm gonna say it the same way again. Turn around with your hands above your head."

Drew smiled. "All you had to do was ask."

Slowly, he raised his hands above his head and turned around. He wasn't surprised when Wilson shoved him hard into the closest tree and cuffed him. A quick pat down followed, where Wilson located Drew's sidearm.

"Gun," Wilson announced, followed by gratuitous jab in the kidney. "That's for taking *my* gun, asshole.

Sam yelled at Wilson, who took it as an invitation to jab Drew a second time. He swung Drew around, surprising Sam because of the grin on his face.

"What the hell are you smiling about, asshole?"

Harrington asked, noticing Drew's smirk.

He winked at Sam. "You look so sexy with your gun out. Why don't you come get my phone in my pocket? Call the General and he'll arrange for a lawyer to meet me at the precinct as soon as possible."

He held her gaze for a good five seconds, glanced down meaningfully to his pocket.

Sam's eyes lingered on his a moment before she holstered her weapon and walked over. She reached into his shirt pocket and pulled out the contents. "You do know how to show a girl a good time."

Chapter 11
Who's Grilling Who

Sam couldn't stop pacing. If she had insisted on going down there with Drew, then this wouldn't have happened. If she had been down there, she could have had his back. Instead, she let him have his own damn way and stayed by the car, like a good little girl. Now, Drew was under arrest on some trumped-up charge.

What the hell were Harrington and Wilson playing at? Why did they arrest Drew? Were they dredging up Molly Winters again, or could they possibly be stupid enough to believe Drew had something to do with his own sister's murder, even though he wasn't even in the state at the time?

"Will you sit down?" Ollie sat by his desk, while she paced back and forth behind their work area. "You're making me dizzy. He'll be fine. When the General gets here with his lawyer, they'll get it all sorted."

"And when is that going to be?" Sam said. "McAlister Security is based just outside New York City. That's about four hours from here. Five with traffic. If this gets out, it's going to ruin his relationship with Cole. Destroy any progress he's made with his sister."

"Oh yeah..." Ollie said, his face looking down at some paperwork. "His sister."

With widening eyes and pursing lips, Sam glared at her partner. "Ollie, you didn't tell her, did you?"

Ollie smiled sheepishly. "Well, kinda, sorta, maybe a little."

Sam clenched her fists, ground her teeth and closed her eyes. She forced herself to calm down so as not to commit murder in the middle of the police station.

"*Why*," she asked, drawing her words out, "would you do that?"

Ollie shrugged. "She needed to know. She'll find out. Better from me than on the street. She can keep it away from Cole, at least for now. I told her not to worry, that it'll all be cleared up quickly."

Sam sat down opposite Ollie. "So she was worried?"

"Oh yeah," Ollie said with a nod. "Ashley loves her brother, no matter what she says. She wanted to come down here and try to get him out, but I talked her into staying home. We'll handle it."

That news had Sam releasing at least a few of the knots in her stomach. "Thank God. I was so afraid she'd blame him for this and she'd do nothing but yell at him."

"Well…" Ollie said. "She loves him, but I fully expect Ash is going to rip Drew a new asshole the first chance she gets. I wouldn't want to be him for a million bucks."

Sam's mouth dropped open in horror as Ollie stared off into space. Sam assumed he was imagining the coming verbal assault. Slowly, an amused grin spread across his face.

"Ollie!" Sam snapped. "I thought you and Drew managed to put your issues behind you."

"We have," Ollie said, and did his best to hide the grin. "We talked it out. We're good. I just..."

Sam arched an eyebrow. "Just what?"

Despite his best efforts, the grin returned. And it brought a healthy shade of red with it. "Ashley. She's really beautiful when she gets a full head of steam going. As long as it's not directed at me, it's great to watch."

Sam was shocked. "What are you going to do? Sit there with a bowl of popcorn and watch?"

"Well..." Ollie shrugged. "I wasn't planning on making popcorn."

Sam wanted to throw something at him, but that was frowned on in the middle of the bullpen. Not as much as shooting him would be, but still...

Ollie went back to doing paper work, so Sam, using all of her will to stay in her chair and not start pacing again, tried to do the same. She had plenty of reports to catch up on, but the first one she picked up, (Follow-up to a drunken teen who streaked naked into what he thought was his girlfriend's back yard but turned out to be the yard of her elderly neighbors.) had her sighing in desperation. She wanted to see Drew and make sure he was all right.

Sam gazed around the station. Cops in uniform sat at desks, drank coffee and filled out reports. A few walked through the room holding arrest reports, while a sergeant sat at the front desk, ready to log in any officer who walked in with a prisoner.

The room was old, but clean and polished. Large desks sat on top of a black and white tiled floor. One wall was covered in plaques and awards, another with wanted posters and notices. There was an American flag in the corner, and the Ember Falls police crest displayed with distinction nearby.

Sam picked up a pen and threw it at Ollie to get his attention. It hit him on his forehead and bounced onto his desk. Ollie picked it up, looked over to Sam and smiled. "Thanks. I think mine was almost out of ink."

With a scowl, Sam leaned in. "What do you know about Harrington and Wilson?"

Ollie dropped the pen, stood up and walked over to Sam. Looking around the room, Ollie signaled Sam to follow him. She followed him down the hall and into an empty office. Neither bothered to turn on the lights.

"Harrington's been around for almost ten years. He was one of the detectives that actually worked the Winters case." Ollie leaned against the wall and swiped his fingers through his hair. "He's connected too. He was in good with the Brooks."

Sam nodded absently. Why does it seem the Brooks name keeps coming up?

"And Wilson?"

"He was just out of the academy when the Winters case happened," Ollie explained. "I don't know if he's connected, but he's partnered with Harrington, so that's bad enough. Besides… He's kind of an asshole."

Sam leaned against the nearby desk. "I knew that much. He hit on me when I first started."

Ollie's eyebrows drew together. "Isn't he married?"

"Yep," Sam said. "One of the reasons he came off as an asshole. He implied he was connected and that for a good bounce, he'd be able to help me further my career. I heard his wife kicked him out a few weeks ago."

"Ugh." A look of pure disgust displayed on his face. "You never told me that."

Sam shrugged. "Didn't seem relevant." And she didn't want to run to Ollie every time she didn't like the way she was treated, especially with his being the son of the chief. "He bugged me for a while until I convinced him I wasn't interested. He decided I was either banging you or I was a lesbian. Or both."

Ollie scowled. "Bastard. Can't believe any girl wouldn't throw themselves at his feet."

Sam placed a calming hand on his chest. "Don't go doing anything. I don't need you fighting my battles and I don't want you getting hung up over this. It's over, and I don't care what an asshole like Wilson says about me."

"I do," Ollie said. "He shouldn't be able to get away with shit like that and you shouldn't be afraid to call him out."

"I'm not afraid," Sam said, making sure to keep eye contact with her partner. "I'm just choosing my battles. Wilson will get what's coming to him."

Something buzzed and Ollie reached into his pocket for his cell. Pulling it out, a slow, mean grin appeared on his face. "Sooner rather than later. Let's go."

****

The first person Sam saw was the General. There was something about the man that screamed authority and made you want to salute, even though he was dressed in a gray jacket and pants with matching tie.

The next person Sam noticed was the young, extraordinarily beautiful, red-headed woman by his side. She wore a black pants suit that was all business, and gripped a black leather briefcase in her right hand.

The General glanced around for a moment, spotted Sam and Ollie and walked right to them.

Part of Sam wanted to hug the man, because she knew he'd come to get Drew out, but she resisted this urge.

"Officer Rossi," the General said, his tone all business. "Officer Miller."

"General," Sam said. "Drew's in holding. If this is his lawyer, I can have her brought to the back to speak to him."

The General's eyebrows went up. "Oh, I don't think there's any rush. He can cool his heels for a few minutes. Serves him right for letting that pair get the drop on him. I've got a meeting with Chief Miller. Your mother, I believe."

Ollie nodded. "Right this way."

The General started to follow, but paused as the red head stopped to talk to Sam. "Is Drew all right?"

There was something about the familiar and worried tone that put Sam's back up.

"He's fine," Sam said quickly. Maybe a little too quickly. "He's very angry over his sister, but this," Sam indicated the police station, "being arrested, he took pretty well."

She shook her head. "Sounds like Drew. My name's Stephanie Howard." She offered her hand. "Lawyer for McAlister Security. Or one of them, I should say."

Sam nodded. "Were you the only one available at such short notice or did you simply draw the short stick to have to fly to get out here so quickly?"

Stephanie smiled. "Neither. I wanted to come and

help. And I just really wanted to see Drew."

At the General's prompting, Stephanie followed Ollie to an office where Chief Miller waited, leaving Sam to glare after Stephanie, muttering, "I'll just *bet* it was the least you can do."

Sam waited and fumed as she watched Ollie disappear behind closed doors with the General and Stephanie. A few moments later, Ollie stepped out. Walking back to his desk, he sat down and began filling out reports again.

"Well?" Sam said. "What happened?"

Ollie didn't look up. "Not much. I just introduced them to my mom. Stephanie seems anxious to get Drew out. Says she can't stand the thought of him being locked up."

Sam nodded, more to herself than anyone else. Stephanie was worried about Drew, was she?

Looking down at the paperwork waiting for her, Sam knew she was being silly. Of course she was worried about Drew. She knew him. She may have even known what happened before Drew left town. It was normal to become close to people you worked with, and they both worked for the General.

Sam forced herself to pick up her pen and start filling out reports. She'd started to fill out the top of the form, her name, shield number and rank, but when it came time to enter in details, she couldn't concentrate.

She looked back up to see the General coming out of the back office, Stephanie right behind him, followed closely by Ollie's mother. Chief Miller motioned them in Sam's direction.

Sam and Ollie quickly got to their feet.

"Officers," Chief Miller said. "Would you escort

our guests to interview room three? Mr. Duncan will be brought there."

"Yes, Ma'am," Sam said.

Chief Miller turned toward the General. "I guess we're going to see what Drew Duncan is made of."

"I guess we are." The General grinned. "This should be fun."

****

The door opened and the two detectives came in, followed by Stephanie Howard and the General. Both Detectives had empty holsters, as it was procedure not to bring firearms into an interrogation, and they each had their shields clipped to their belts.

Stephanie sent Drew a quick smile, one the detectives didn't see, before putting on her business face. The General leaned into Drew's ear. "You ready for this?"

Drew nodded and sent him a grin to let him know he was not only ready, but eager.

The General took a seat to Drew's left, with Stephanie on his right. The two detectives sat down in front of him.

"Detective Wilson starting interview with Andrew Duncan," Wilson said. "Detective Harrington is also present. Mr. Duncan has representation present. Just for the record, I'm going to read you your rights."

"That'd be a nice change," Drew muttered, earning a scowl from Wilson and a silent chuckle from the General.

As Wilson did, Drew looked toward the big mirror, wondering who was behind there.

"Do you understand these rights?" Wilson said.

Drew locked eyes with the young detective. "Yes."

Harrington leaned in. "So, this seems familiar. A young lady's dead and you're the main suspect."

Drew glared at the older detective. The memory of when he'd seen that face before clicked for Drew while he was being loaded into their car for transport. The last time he'd looked into those eyes, he was a seventeen-year-old boy, terrified and alone. Drew waited a moment, his gaze boring into the detective. He wanted to make sure Harrington knew he wasn't dealing with the same kid when Molly Winter's had gone missing.

Drew took no small amount of satisfaction when Harrington looked away first.

"Oh, I don't know," Drew said. "There are a lot of differences this time. Last time, I was a kid who didn't know not to talk to you without a lawyer. You came and questioned me while I was still recovering in the hospital. Any first-year public defender could have gotten anything I'd said tossed even if I *had* said anything you could use against me. Of course, there are a few similarities. Such as the fact that you've got dick against me and you know it."

Wilson leaned in. "You're going to deny that you've been estranged from both your sisters? I'm guessing there's a lot of animosity between you and your siblings."

Drew crossed his arms and met Wilson's stare, dead on. "You'd guess wrong. Let's be clear. I had nothing to do with my sister's murder. I wasn't anywhere near Ember Falls."

"And I don't suppose you can prove that?" Wilson said.

"As a matter of fact," the General interjected. He reached into a briefcase and pulled out some papers that he tossed onto the table in front of the young Detective. "Mr. Duncan and I, along with several members of my organization, were on the Mexican border, in the middle of an operation to rescue a young girl from kidnappers. Those are affidavits from everyone who can verify that Mr. Duncan was with us. There are other documents that further verify his whereabouts, all of which could have easily been provided if you'd bothered to check into where Drew was while his sister was murdered."

Wilson scowled at the General as he pulled the papers forward. He gave them a cursory glance. "We'll check into these ourselves, but I wouldn't be surprised to find that Drew paid people to give him a false alibi." He looked directly at the General and tried to put on his most intimidating face. "You've got a lot to lose if one of your top men were accused and convicted of murder."

The General raised his eyebrows a little bit, a smile tugging at the corner of his lips. "Do I now?"

Wilson smiled. "Oh, yeah. You've got a lot of clients who'd be very pissed to learn you've got a man working for you that would kill his own sister, one you hired knowing he was the prime suspect in the disappearance and probable murder of his high school girlfriend. Yet you put him in a sensitive position in your organization. If that were to get out, that'd be pretty bad for business."

"Son, I do believe you're trying to intimidate me. It's hard to tell, as you're doing a piss poor job of it. Instead, you're just burying yourself."

Wilson and Harrington exchanged puzzled looks.

"How's that?" Harrington said.

The General shook his head. "Your partner here just told me he knows all about McAlister Security and Drew's position in it, yet you never bothered to even check to see if he had an alibi." The General tapped the folder of documents that were between him and Wilson. "That's what I call shoddy detective work, which I suppose shouldn't surprise me. You see, before I ever offered Drew a position at McAlister, I did *my* homework on him." The General reached into his briefcase again, pulled out another folder, this one thicker than the first. "Knew all about the charges that were brought against him and then dropped as you had shit. I noticed back then, you had no other leads in Ms. Winter's disappearance. What's even more telling is you made no effort to generate any additional leads. Interesting how much of the physical evidence, such as the medical reports on what was in Drew's system, seemed to disappear. Imagine that."

He pushed the folder forward, but Wilson ignored it and shrugged. "It's been several years."

"But it didn't take years for that evidence to go missing," the General countered. "Cases are built on evidence. You had none back then, and as far as I can see, you've got even less now."

Wilson stood up, placed his hands on the table and glared. "Your boy attacked me, took my weapon away from me."

The General, who looked bored, sat back and sighed. "Seems to me you should safeguard your weapon better, son. If one of my men allowed himself to be disarmed, I'd have his head."

"He had a weapon on him," Harrington added.

"All of my men have conceal and carry permits in

all states," the General countered. "But I'm assuming you knew that by now."

Slowly, Wilson sat back down. "Still doesn't give Duncan the right to attack a police detective."

Stephanie leaned forward. "My client had no idea you were a police detective. You didn't identify yourself. You simply put a gun to his head. He defended himself."

Wilson smirked. "We were loud and clear. I showed him my shield, told him who I was and to put his hands above his head and slowly turn around."

"You never identified yourself," Drew said. "You pulled your gun and threatened to blow me away."

Wilson shook his head. "You're a liar and a murderer and I'm charging you."

"No," Stephanie said. "You're not. You're going to apologize to my client and release him."

With a laugh, Wilson shook his head. "You're nuts. Why would I even consider doing something like that?"

Now it was Stephanie's turn to smile. "Because if you don't, you'll regret it."

"Is that a threat?" Wilson said.

"It's a promise." Stephanie leaned in and started to spout off legal jargon about self-defense, improper police tactics, illegal arrests, police brutality and court cases that were meant to illustrate Wilson didn't have a leg to stand on.

"Bullshit," Wilson said, his face getting red. "It'll be our word against his. Two detectives against a twice murder suspect. Who do you think a jury will believe?"

"Well now," Drew said, sitting back in his seat and smiling. "I'm guessing a jury will believe the tape."

Wilson started to respond, pointing a finger toward

Drew with another accusation on the tip of his tongue, but hesitated as Drew's statement sank in. His eyes shifted to Harrington, and Drew could see them both begin to worry.

There was a bead of sweat running down Harrington's forehead, and there was a distinctive look of a panicked animal in his eyes. He rubbed his hand over his stubble and tried to put on his tough cop face, but it was too late.

Wilson, however, was not quite ready to back down. "You're a fucking liar. You killed Molly Winters and got away with it. You lied then and you're lying now. You had no recorder on you and that bitch Rossi was up on the road when we found you. There was no way she could see you, much less record you."

Drew leaned forward, locked eyes with Wilson and narrowed his eyes. "That's a fellow officer you're talking about. You may want to watch your mouth, or someone's going to have to teach you your manners."

Wilson mirrored Drew's posture, lifting his chin as he leaned in, tempting Drew to strike out. "You going to teach it to me? All because I said a mean word about that lesbo? I'd like to see you try." The dare in his eyes was evident, his smirk showcasing his arrogance.

Drew realized Wilson was getting desperate, wanting him to strike out, to commit assault on an officer right here in the precinct. It would give Wilson a reason to charge Drew, not to mention an excuse to hit Drew back.

Oh yeah, Wilson's ego was still sore since he had his service weapon taken from him so easily. That alone was enough to make Drew not take the bait. Stephanie was rubbing his arm, trying to keep him from leaping over the table while at the same time taking Wilson apart verbally, and Drew watched his face grow redder by the moment.

Man didn't like a woman speaking to him that way.

"Let me guess. You hit on Officer Rossi and she told you to shove it, and that's why you're calling her a lesbo," Drew said in an almost amused voice. He sent a glance to his right, winking at Stephanie to let her know he was still in control. "Isn't that what guys with more ego than balls say when they strike out?"

Stephanie smiled. "It's been my experience."

Drew turned back to Wilson, who looked ready to charge, as if he were a bull eager to be let out of the box.

"Of course," Drew added for good measure, "my impression is that Officer Rossi doesn't need me to defend her. My guess is that she could hand your ass to you without working up a sweat. She's certainly smarter than you."

Wilson forced a smile. "Oh? How do you figure that, punk?"

"Because," Drew said, now enjoying himself. "She was smart enough to pull the recorder I was using to take notes for myself when I asked her to take my cell phone. It was in my shirt pocket and I'm fairly certain it picked up every fucking word you said."

Again, Wilson looked to Harrington, who now had a sheen of sweat on his balding head. Harrington cracked his knuckles, not in any sort of pathetic attempt to look tough as that possibility was long gone, but out of edginess.

Wilson, however, was not ready to give up the pretense he'd been nothing but professional during their encounter. Drew wondered if he was the type that could lie about things so effectively they themselves started to believe it.

"You're a lying piece of shit." Wilson was nearly shaking with rage, incensed at the idea anyone might believe someone like Drew over him. "You got away with Molly Winters, but you're not going to skate on this one. Everyone in this town knows you killed Molly and got rid of the body. And before long, they're going to know you fuckin' killed you own sister. I wouldn't be surprised if it was for the same reason. Neither of them would spread their legs for you, you sick fuck."

Stephanie grabbed Drew's arm, knowing that Wilson was still trying to provoke a reaction. "You're out of line," she said. "You've not only got no proof, but you're willfully ignoring evidence that we've presented to you."

She pushed the folder of affidavits forward.

"As far as the tape goes," Stephanie continued. "I've heard it myself. You and your partner did not identify yourselves. Instead, you threatened my client, putting a gun to his head. My client disarmed you which I'm sure pisses you off to no end. And when Officer Rossi did identify both of you as Detectives, Mr. Duncan returned your firearm. So if there are any charges as a result of today's altercation, they'll be directed at you."

Wilson stood again, leaning on the table, pushing his face close to Stephanie, clearly trying to make her uncomfortable by invading her personal space. Stephanie didn't blink. "You better watch your mouth bitch, or you'll be sorry."

Drew started to get up himself, but the General

gently pushed Drew back into a seated position. "Son," he addressed Wilson. "I don't take kindly to idiots who threaten my people and I'm not someone you want to piss off. You're already in over your head and you're only digging yourself deeper."

Wilson turned on the General, his lip curling in disgust. "Listen Grandpa, I'm not even sure why you're in here as opposed to getting your diaper changed in some nursing home, but if you know what's good for you…"

"You moron," Drew said, as he fought the urge to give Wilson exactly what he wanted. "You're speaking to a decorated Marine General. He was in combat situations and running ops while *you* were in diapers, and he could still kick your ass today."

Wilson made a dismissive jut of his chin toward the General, before turning his attention back to Drew. "Let me tell you what I see. I see a guy who's killed before and gotten away with it, coming back and doing it again. A lawyer who's clearly fucking her client. And an old man too feeble-minded to know not to be talked into giving false statements and phony alibis to a piece of shit like you. You're a killer and a rapist and you're going down."

Drew leaned forward, this time offering his own chin in a challenge to Wilson to strike out physically. He planted his most obnoxious smirk on his face and glared at Wilson. "Well then let me tell you what I see. I see a cop who never should have been given a badge. You've already admitted that you saw Officer Rossi on the road, but instead of approaching her and asking what was going on, you decided to sneak up on me, which if it weren't for the noise of that passing train, you'd never have been able to do.

"My guess is that if Officer Rossi wasn't so close by, you would have simply shot me on sight, assuming you have the balls for it. You've come up with some pitiful theory as to what happened with my sister, making little attempt to get to the truth. You've also been very insistent that you identified yourself as a Detective, but you and especially your partner over here are sweating bullets, hoping and praying I'm lying about that recording, which I'm not, and that's gonna get your asses burned. You've given us more information on you than you've been able to get from me, which tells me you just plain old suck at your job and you wouldn't be seen fit to scrub the toilets at McAlister Security. My guess is, whatever game you're playing, you're just too damn dumb to get it right on your own. So I'm wondering who told you to try and pin this on me. Someone smarter than you, not that that's saying much."

Stephanie snickered and Wilson tensed like he wanted to hit her.

"You've also shown a tremendous amount of hostility toward women, directed both at my attorney, Miss Howard, and Officer Rossi," Drew continued. "It's gotta burn your ass to be under the command of Chief Miller. You can't stand the idea of a woman giving you orders."

Drew grinned, leaning in just a little closer. "Me? I'm gonna have me a good laugh when she takes your badge."

Wilson fumed, his eyes locked with Drew's. Harrington, sensing danger, was trying to signal Wilson to leave the interrogation room, and for the briefest of moments, it looked like Wilson was going to go.

Instead he launched out of his chair, his fist was a hammer aimed at Drew's jaw.

Drew knew it was coming and the original thought in his mind was to let Wilson's fist connect, but there was something inside of him that just wouldn't give a bastard like Wilson a free hit.

With reflexes honed in hand-to-hand combat in the most dangerous places in the world, Drew grabbed Wilson's hand, twisted and slammed him face down onto the table. Wilson yelled out like a wounded animal, but Drew held him down. Stephanie screamed, yelling out Drew's name while Harrington rushed over to assist his partner, but jumped back when the door opened and a commanding voice spoke.

"That's enough, Mr. Duncan," Chief Miller said as she walked over to the table. "Let him go now."

With a nod, Drew released him as if he were throwing away a piece of smelly trash.

Wilson sprang up off the table, ready to leap over it and continue the fight, but Harrington pulled him back. Drew stayed on his feet, standing between him and Stephanie, who held her hand over her heart.

The General's face remained all business.

"Stand down, Detective," Chief Miller said. Her voice was low, but stern. Clearly, she was a woman who didn't need to yell to be heard. She wore an air of no nonsense like it was a comfortable pair of pajamas. "I've heard enough. I allowed this little 'interrogation' to go on further than I should have."

Wilson was breathing heavily, trying to calm down. Harrington stepped up, trying to smooth things over. "Chief, we were interviewing Mr. Duncan who's a person of interest in one homicide from years back and was found at the scene of the murder of his sister, interfering..."

Chief Miller held up a hand, silencing Harrington, who flushed red. "You and your partner should know that I was in the observation room for the entire interview. I saw and heard everything, including Detective Wilson's extremely unprofessional conduct. I've also listened to the recording Mr. Duncan made, listened to his notes and heard the interaction on it between Detective Wilson and Mr. Duncan and at no point did Detective Wilson identify himself. Mr. Duncan is a licensed investigator, and the area is no longer considered an active crime scene, so it's only natural he'd want to take a look at where his sister's body was found."

"With all due respect, *Chief Miller*," Wilson said, his voice dripping with sarcasm, "Harrington and I went over that place ourselves. It was nothing but a place for the killer," His eyes slanted toward Drew, trying to reinforce the idea that he still believed his theory that Drew murdered his own sister, to dump his trash.

Without realizing it, Drew tensed and started moving forward, ready to rip the young detective's head off, until he felt Stephanie's hands on his chest, holding him back.

"Don't, Drew." Stephanie turned her body toward Drew, her face inches away from his. "He's not worth it."

Drew nodded, unclenched his fists and took a step back, but kept staring daggers at Wilson.

"What he was probably doing was making sure he

didn't leave anything behind," Wilson added. "A killer always returns the scene of the crime."

The General stepped forward and in front of Drew, in part to keep Drew from reacting himself. "Let me make sure I understand you, son. After all, I seem to be a feeble old man who's just waiting for the early bird special."

Drew turned his head to hide his grin, knowing that tone in the General's voice.

"You believe that there's no chance you and your partner could have missed anything?" The General asked. "No clue that might have been missed?"

Wilson drew himself up, his self-importance in full display like a peacock showing off its feathers. "Not a chance. I don't make mistakes."

The General folded his arms, narrowing his eyes as if he were struggling to understand. "And in your opinion, Mr. Duncan was looking for something that would indicate his own guilt in the matter?"

Wilson, feeling a little more confident, placed his hands on his hips and returned pressed on. "You bet your ass, old man. Wanting to cover his tracks. Bastard dumped his own sister there."

"Is that right?" The General rubbed his fingers over his chin as if he was contemplating the situation, his head slowly nodding. "Interesting." He slowly made his way around the table. "So what was he looking for?"

Wilson started to answer, his mouth froze as he formed his first word, but then his brow furrowed in confusion. He glanced at Harrington, who seemed at a loss as well. Finally, he turned back to the General, annoyance clear on his face. "How the fu..." His eyes slid to Chief Miller for a moment. "How am I supposed to know what he was looking for, Grandpa? What am I, psychic?"

The General shook his head and tapped his index finger on his lower lip. "No, of course not. If you were a psychic, or for that matter a half way decent detective, you'd have understood the implications of my question."

Wilson glared at the General and looked like he might try and take a swing at him. Drew almost wished he would. He'd love to see the General kick his ass.

"What are you talking about, Grandpa?"

The General smiled, but it wasn't a friendly smile. It was the type of smile that let you know you were getting close to having your head ripped off if you didn't remember your place.

Wilson either didn't understand or didn't care. "Look, Grandpa…"

"Do you like your teeth?" the General said.

Wilson started to blink. "Do I…*what?* "

"Do. You. Like. Your. Teeth?" the General asked again. "Because I've got to be honest with you, if you call me grandpa one more time, you're going to lose a few."

Wilson goggled at the General. "Now look…" Wilson started.

"Save it," the General barked. His tone changed from friendly to someone who was getting ready to order you into combat. "For over four decades, every soul on this Earth with a lick of sense has addressed me as General or Sir with two exceptions. My mother, who you are not, and complete morons. So next time you address me, you'll address me with respect. I've been patient because quite frankly, watching you make an ass out of yourself has held a certain amount of amusement for me, but that's getting old, real fast.

"As far as your substandard job, let's be clear here. You royally fucked up. You're an embarrassment to your shield. You stand there and tell me that you checked that area thoroughly, that there's no way you and your partner here who looks like he's about to piss in his pants, missed anything, yet you don't know what my man was looking for? If he was looking for something, surely you would have found it. Yes?"

The General paused a moment, let that sink in. "Clearly you don't. On the other hand, if he was there looking for something you didn't find, then you must have missed something which you've insisted you didn't miss. But I think we can all assume that was just a steaming pile of bullshit."

The General folded his arms, took a moment to look Wilson up and down as if assessing him, before giving him a shake of his head.

"I've always prided myself on being a good judge of character," the General continued. "It's an important quality when you have to send men into battle, to be able to look them in the eyes and see who is tough enough to face death and who's too chicken shit and will more than likely turn tail and run. You've got boat loads of ego, but you've also got your head so far up your ass you should be able to see your tonsils."

Drew snorted while leaning against the wall. Wilson took a step toward him, but Chief Miller moved between them. Her eyes were like daggers, cutting off Wilson from attacking Drew.

"Mr. Duncan is to be released. He is not considered a person of interest in his sister's murder." Chief nodded toward the mirror that separated the interrogation and observation rooms. "Detectives Daniel Wilson and John Harrington," She said, using a tone that Drew imagined used to make Ollie's soul freeze when he was young. "I'm hereby placing you and your partner on suspension. You will surrender identifications, shields and your weapons."

Wilson slammed a chair forward so much that it nearly knocked the table. The movement was so sudden Stephanie jumped closer to Drew who instinctively put a protective arm around her.

The door to the interrogation room opened and Ollie and Sam entered. At the sight of them, Wilson reached down toward his gun holster, forgetting that it was empty; however, the movement was observed by everyone in the room. Ollie and Sam, both of who were armed, had their hands on their own weapons, but refrained from drawing them.

With an icy stare that would freeze hell, Chief Miller stood before Wilson. "I would greatly recommend you keep your mouth closed and contact your union representative. Is that understood?"

Wilson sneered, hatred pouring out of him. He looked like he wanted to strike out physically at the chief, but knew he couldn't. Not here and now, surrounded by all these people.

When Ollie stepped toward Wilson, Drew couldn't help but notice the geeky kid he'd once picked on was light years away. Ollie still had a good amount of nerd inside, but right now he looked like a bull ready to rampage.

Shoving away from him, Wilson stormed out of the room, Ollie quick on his heels. Harrington followed closely behind.

Sam stole one quick glance at Drew, his arm protectively around Stephanie, before following her partner.

Chapter 12
Pickles vs. Potato Salad

When Drew emerged from the police station, he took a nice, long deep breath and grinned to himself. He'd handled it. There was a part of him that wanted to beg them to get him out of that cell when they'd first locked him in. The icy chill of panic in his spine as if he'd been tossed outside on a freezing day, wet and naked, while a snowstorm raged, threatened to bury him alive.

But he managed to push that aside, and was free.

Waiting in that cell had been the worst of it—the helplessness, having no control over his fate. If he could, Wilson surely would have sent Drew to jail, held over for a trial that would never come or at the very least take years to materialize. And while there, he *knew* what could happen.

For a few brief moments, he'd been transported to when he was seventeen, nearly eighteen. He'd made some noises about getting a different public defender, one who actually listened to him and wasn't trying to bully him into giving a full confession for something he hadn't done.

Drew hadn't seen them coming then. He fought like a madman, but there had been three of them and they were all so much bigger. All to deliver a message.

Don't go there. Just don't. It's over.

"You didn't do too shabbily," the General said as he came out of the station to stand next to Drew and slap him on the back, snapping Drew out of his trance. "Glad to see you kept your head in there."

Drew managed a smile. "You weren't too bad in there yourself, *Grandpa*."

The General gave him a scornful glare. "Watch it. I can still kick your ass."

Stephanie groaned as she joined them. "What is it with you two? What is it with men?"

Both Drew and the General laughed.

"Thank you for coming," Drew said, turning to Stephanie. "It means a lot."

Leaning in, Stephanie pulled Drew into a tight embrace, one that clearly showed their relationship went beyond just lawyer and client. "I'm just sorry I wasn't able to be here for your sister's funeral. I'm so sorry for your loss, Drew."

All joy drained from Drew's face as he nodded. "Thank you."

Stephanie hugged him again, but his posture was stiffer. She pulled back and tried to change the subject. "How are things with your other sister?"

Drew started to just say okay, a standard answer like when people ask, "How are you doing today?" It's not that they want to hear how you stubbed your toe, ran out of coffee, were late for work when you lost your keys and got stuck behind a smelly garbage truck in rush hour. They were just being polite.

However, this was Stephanie.

"It's been a rough start," Drew said. "And this probably isn't going to help. She's gonna be pissed at me when I get home, but it's really Cole I've got to worry about."

Stephanie started to rub his arm sympathetically. "I know it's got to be rough for him. I hope I get the chance to meet him, but I've got to get back. Someday, I'd love to meet your family." She leaned up, pulled him into another hug and kissed him. The kiss was quick and gentle, but on the lips and lingered just a moment.

The General turned to Drew. "You okay from here? I've got to get Stephanie back to the airport."

Drew nodded. "I'll see you later."

He watched the General walk off with Stephanie and smiled to himself. They had just reached the car when Stephanie opened the door and started to climb in, but turned to look at Drew one last time. "By the way, the flowers were beautiful. Thank you."

She sent him one last, radiant smile before getting into the car and letting the General drive her away to the airport.

Grinning to himself, Drew decided it was time to find Sam. He was surprised he didn't have to look far.

Sam was standing just by the door to the police station, her arms folded, her eyes closed slits of anger. Drew was taken aback, but assumed she was just pissed at what happened with Wilson. He moved over to her, but saw her stiffen.

"Hey there," he said cautiously. "I was just about to go looking for you."

Sam smiled, but the smile seemed forced and even a little hostile. "Well, here I am."

Drew took a few steps closer to her, but sensed something was wrong. "You really saved my ass, getting that recorder out of my pocket and giving it to

Ollie's mom. If they'd have found it first, I'm sure it would have been erased."

Sam stepped back. "Probably. Listen, I know I'm not technically on duty, but I've got to write up a report on everything all the same. The chief wants all the 'I's dotted and 'T's crossed. You can get home on your own, right? If not, I can see if Ollie can drive you."

Drew frowned. He'd been in that damn holding cell long enough for her to write up a dozen reports and even if she still needed to, he could wait, but Drew was getting the distinct impression Sam was trying to ditch him.

"I can get home on my own," he said. "I was thinking maybe I could swing by your place tonight. Take you out to dinner and thank you."

Sam paused as if to consider his offer. "I don't think I can," she said with a shake of her head. "I've got plans with Nana tonight and I told you I don't think I'm ready to get involved. Besides, I think you have enough on you plate."

Drew tried to formulate some response, but before the words could even form in his mind, she started to go back into the crowded police station. "Oh, and Stephanie was beautiful and seemed very nice," she added before turning her back on him.

Drew stood there a good ten seconds in stunned silence. *Well, damn.*

****

Drew decided to walk home. For the first several blocks, he kept his eyes straight ahead and tried not to think of where he was. Instead, his mind was on Sam.

What the hell was that? Had she decided he was more trouble than he was worth? He walked another half a block as he played the entire thing over in his head, stopped short and shook his head. *Well double damn.*

Having figured out what exactly happened, he actually laughed out loud, causing at least one passer-by to glance his way, probably wondering if he were insane.

Drew passed several stores he remembered from when he was younger, including a small convenience place which would sell him cigarettes back when he first started to smoke. He'd been fourteen and went in to buy a pack as a dare. The store owner didn't even blink. He and his buddies at the time all smoked that afternoon. At first he thought it was pretty gross, but didn't want to be the one to complain about it. By the time he was done with his first cigarette, he'd decided it wasn't so bad.

Since he'd bought the pack, he took them home. His father found them when he'd kicked Drew's bookbag and they'd fallen out. He proceeded to laugh at Drew, mocking him. "So you're a smoker now? You think that makes you a man and not a little Nancy boy?"

Drew of course, answered him back. *"I'm more of a man than you'll ever be."*

That earned Drew a solid punch in the gut, followed by his father pulling his off-duty weapon and placing it under Drew's chin. He'd wanted Drew to beg and plead. Drew, being the stubborn SOB he was, naturally refused.

When his father had grown weary of waiting, he kicked Drew once in the balls, tossed the pack of cigarettes at his son, and went off to get drunk. Drew went outside to wait for his sisters so they wouldn't go inside. He'd smoked half of the remaining pack, trying to get himself to stop shaking. When they'd showed up, he'd sent them off to stay the night at Lily's.

Ever since, Drew had been a smoker. He'd forgotten, or rather chosen not to think about, how he'd picked up the habit, but standing in front of the store, it all came back.

Drew continued to walk as his memory flowed back to that time, remembering the friends he'd taken that first drag with.

Of the three buddies of his who tried their first smoke that day, Jimmy Dugan, nearly puked at the first full puff, stubbed it out and swore never to smoke again. As far as Drew knew, he'd kept that promise, although Jimmy moved out of Ember Falls the following year with his parents.

Scott Middleton, like Drew, picked up the habit. Drew knew Scott remained a smoker when they ran into each other in Iraq. Scott, having decided to believe the stories about Drew killing Molly Winters, refused to speak with him even when they ended up in the same unit. Drew stewed about it for over a week, until he decided enough was enough and vowed to have it out one way or the other with Scott the next chance he had. He knew there was a damn good chance Scott would simply choose not to believe him, but Drew was determined to have his say.

Unfortunately, Drew never got that chance. Scott was killed that afternoon in downtown Fallujah. An IED ended both Scott and his nicotine addiction.

Passing by the old schoolyard, Drew remembered his best friend, the final member of their group to have tried cigarettes that day.

Everyone knew Brooke's mother. She was considered the queen of the trailer trash, often drunk, high or both. She had a quick temper and Drew suspected a quicker hand, but Brooke never talked about his home life much.

When Brooke smoked that day, Drew had the impression it hadn't really been his first drag. Finishing the cigarette silently, Brooke was completely unaffected by it as far as anyone could tell.

For the next year or so, Brooke often lit up when among friends.

Always the consummate non-smoker, Lily gave both Drew and Brooke a hard time about the habit. While Drew used to respond to Lily's lectures by lighting up, Brooke listened and quit, all for Lily.

Drew had been quite sure that the pair of them would be those high school sweethearts that got married, with three or four kids before they hit thirty, but they'd abruptly broken up only weeks before the dance where Molly disappeared.

The last time Drew saw Brooke, things hadn't gone well. Lily refused to discuss what led to the breakup, but was clearly heartbroken. She withdrew, barely eating and often found alone in some corner crying her eyes out.

Drew, who loved Lily like she was another sister, tracked Brooke down. He had ditched school ever since the breakup and was found shooting hoops at their old middle school yard, which wasn't too far from where he lived. Drew didn't go there looking for a fight. He'd meant to just yell at Brooke for hurting Lily, but within moments of arriving, Drew actually punched Brooke in the face.

Funny how so many memories were tied to the first time he'd ever smoked a cigarette.

Down the street from the school, was a deli called Maria's. Drew once tried to purchase cigarettes there when he was nearly fifteen, but the owner, Maria Masci, chased him out and nearly smacked him in the ass for the attempt.

Drew swore never to return, but he couldn't stay away from her potato salad. Upon his return, Maria calmed down. He was treated to a lecture on smoking and how it was wrong and disrespectful to try and purchase cigarettes from her store. When she was done, Maria smiled and waited on him personally. And while Drew kept smoking until returning to Ember Falls, he never again tried to buy cigarettes there.

Funny, he thought, how only now that he was old enough to legally purchase a pack of smokes, he'd just quit. While the urge still plagued him more than he liked to admit, Drew promised himself he'd never light up again.

The sign above the store was the same, although someone replaced the window and door. Maria was well into her sixties when Drew had last been in here and Drew imagined she'd retired and the new owners simply kept the name. Maybe they kept the same potato salad recipe?

Drew walked into the store and made his way to the counter. The lunch crowd was thinning out, but there was still a line of people waiting. The place had gotten a makeover, and there were new faces behind the counter, but the food still smelled heavenly and it still felt like the same store.

There was a pair of large refrigerators behind the main counter that held all the cold cuts—meats in one, cheeses in the other. The counter itself held a large glass case with lasagna, meatballs, olives, pickles, and other assorted deli items. There was freshly baked bread in baskets and cookies on display.

In the back of the store were rows of other foods, many you couldn't get in the grocery store, some brought in from local farmers and bakers. The back of the store held freezers containing items you could only purchase here at Maria's, including her famous clam chowder, which Maria would make at home by the bucket load, freeze and sell in the store. It often went very quickly.

The girl behind the counter was in her mid-twenties and looked familiar. She wore a little too much makeup for Drew's taste, but was very attractive. She flirted in a friendly manner with each of the men who stepped up to the counter.

When it was his turn, the girl turned to smile at him. Her eyes narrowed in confusion as she studied Drew's face, and then widened in surprise as it finally registered who he was. Any and all joy drained from her as she crossed her arms and scowled.

It was the scowl that made it click for Drew.

"Hello, Sandra," Drew said as pleasantly as possible, recognizing Molly Winter's best friend from high school. "How are you?"

For a brief moment, Drew thought Sandra might actually spit on him. Her face was chiseled with contempt and disdain. She didn't answer at first, rather concentrated all her fury into her glare.

Her voice was cold and just loud enough to carry to

the rest of the store. "What the hell are you doing back in this town, Drew Duncan?"

Drew didn't want to make a scene and tried not to lose his temper. "You may not have heard what happened to my sister…"

"Of course I heard," Sandra said, her voice rich with scorn. "We catered the damn wake at your home."

It would make sense that Ashley would have used Maria's, but Drew hadn't eaten anything at all that day.

"I knew you came back into town for that," Sandra continued. "I just thought you would have high-tailed it out of here after."

"Nope," Drew said. "I'm staying for my sister and nephew."

Sandra started to point a finger at Drew, her mouth open with what Drew was sure to be a very nasty little remark, one likely to put him over the edge, when someone else stepped up to the counter.

"That's a wonderful thing, Drew," Maria said with her thick Italian accent. She was coming out of the back holding a large, dry salami. "I think you need to take a break, Sandra, and I'll thank you not to speak to my customers like that again or you'll be looking for work someplace else."

Sandra glowered at Maria, who pointed at her with the salami before placing it on the counter. Sandra gave one final snarl in Drew's direction, and headed to the back.

Maria almost looked the same to Drew as she always had. Her long hair was black, with a few strands of gray showing, olive skin with wrinkles, maybe a few more than Drew recalled, but her face was still vibrant and her eyes looked as young and sharp as ever.

She was beanpole thin, which always amazed Drew since she was a woman who cooked and worked around such delicious food all day. Drew couldn't imagine working in a place like this without putting on a good thirty pounds.

"What are you having?" Maria said, pulled a pencil from the back of her ear, touching the tip to her tongue and then pulling a pad of paper out of her apron.

Drew was going to order just a little something for himself, but instead decided to get for everyone. He started to rattle off different types of cold cuts, a few cheeses, asked for a few olives, pickles and a pound of Maria's famous potato salad. He also asked them to toss in some of their freshly made sub rolls and then, as Maria was writing it all down, changed his mind. "On the other hand, make that two pounds of the potato salad, please."

Maria nodded, smiled and called over to one of her young staff members. "Oy. Bryan, come here." A pimply-faced boy of sixteen came trotting over. "Here, fill this for Mr. Duncan. He'll pick it up in a moment. And don't slice your fingers." She handed the piece of paper off to the young boy who read it quickly before running off to start putting the order together.

Maria turned to Drew. "You, come over here." She motioned toward the end of the counter, and headed down that way. Drew followed, amused but at the same time feeling like the same fourteen-year-old boy who had gotten his head handed to him by her.

When she came out from behind the counter, she wore a smile that made Drew relax. "Andrew, it's been a long time. I was thinking I'd never see you again."

Drew returned the smile. "I couldn't stay away

from your potato salad."

Maria laughed, swatted at him playfully, and looked him over. "You look good. Your sister Ashley is too skinny. She needs to eat more. You could stand to eat more, but you look good." Her Italian accent was still thick, despite having been in this country for at least fifty years.

"Ashley eats more than I do," Drew said, then grinned sheepishly. "Don't tell her I said that."

Maria only laughed, but it turned into a sigh of sadness. "Your other sister. Kelli, so quiet, that one. I want to tell you how sorry I am for what happened. I know how you love your sisters. Whenever you came into my store, you watched them, made sure they were okay. Ashley, she's a firecracker, she could take care of herself. But Kelli," Marie shook her head sadly. "She was shy. She never looked me in the eye. She'd get scared and grab your hand. Not your mother's. I noticed that once, when old Ernie, you remember, the drunk, he came in when you were little. Kelli, she practically jumped into your arms."

Drew couldn't remember that, but it seemed familiar enough that he imagined it happened just that way.

"Such a good girl." Maria made the sign of the cross. "Kelli was such an angel."

Drew nodded sadly. "She was. She was the best. I guess if she was the angel, I was the devil?" He grinned again.

"Ah." Maria did a swatting motion with both hands. "You? You weren't as bad as you wanted everyone to think. Always angry." She stepped forward, put her hand on his cheek. "Still are, I think, but there's more there. You needed a stern hand." She removed her hand and pointed a finger in his face. "But a loving one. But you were a good brother. I always thought to myself, that one? He'll be a good dad someday. A good husband." She touched his cheek gently, before poking him in the chest. "But don't think I've forgot your trying to buy cigarettes here when you were just a boy."

Drew laughed. "I was just thinking about how you threatened to tan my hide."

Maria jutted her chin out. "Don't think I didn't see you around, still smoking. And you can't buy them now. I stop selling them, so there." She flicked her fingertips against the bottom of that chin.

Drew smiled and shook his head. "I quit. Just recently. My sister's kid is allergic. Haven't had one since."

Maria smiled and patted him gently on his chest, right by his heart. "See. Loving a child is good for your health. I'll bet that boy is the best thing for you."

Drew thought about Cole, smiled to himself and decided Maria was absolutely right.

****

Cole's stomach finally lured him out of his bedroom toward the kitchen. Upset over being told he had to return to school, Cole had only eaten a small bowl of cereal for breakfast. He'd skipped lunch and stayed in his room, trying to avoid his Aunt. She was pissed.

Cole didn't know why, but he was pretty sure he wasn't the reason. He'd heard her cursing and using his uncle's name. At first, Cole tried to ignore it. Aunt Ashley was always riding Uncle Drew, but when a few minutes later Aunt Ashley came into his room to check on him, he knew something was up.

Aunt Ashley was just too cheerful, too nice, and way, way too happy to see Cole was enjoying his book. She clearly wanted to keep Cole distracted. The moment she left, Cole tried to listen to a hushed conversation between Aunt Ash and Lily, but he didn't learn much.

"We'll talk later," Lily said quickly. "You remember what Drew told us. Cole's always listening. I can stay here if you want to go."

There had been silence. Followed by a strangled sob. "No. I can't. Not again."

Had something happened to Uncle Drew? Was he dead like his mother?

Cole started to believe that maybe, just maybe, his uncle would really be there for him. He had begun to believe Uncle Drew could be trusted.

Cole desperately wanted to believe the idea that a grown man could not be a monster, because Cole knew someday he'd be a man and he didn't want to be like his stepfather.

How could he come into his life just to leave him? He'd promised to be there for him, to protect him and more importantly to protect Aunt Ash and Lily. Why did he get himself killed?

Why did you, Mom?

His mother promised him a better life. Swore things would be different and they wouldn't live in fear anymore. They'd never have to be afraid.

Ashley appeared again at his door, offering to make him a snack, but he hadn't been hungry. His stomach was feeling sick, thinking not only of what might have happened to his uncle, but upset at himself.

He'd gotten angry at his mother for dying. What kind of monster did that make him?

"You sure?"

Cole nodded. "Where's Uncle Drew?" He tried to make his tone casual.

Aunt Ashley's face went pale, but after a brief moment she'd managed to force a smile. "He's out with Ollie's partner Sam. I'm not sure when he'll be back."

Gripping the book, he forced himself to smile and go back to pretending to read. His uncle wasn't dead. He'd just left. Left him, left his sister…again.

Cole should have known better than to believe him. To hope for someone he could trust. To consider that maybe he'd be like a father.

Eventually the emptiness of his stomach had him silently padding to the kitchen wearing only socks on his feet. Opening the refrigerator, he saw nothing to eat that didn't need to be cooked. No fruit, no leftovers he could stick in the microwave. Cole pulled out an egg and stared at it. Maybe he could stick *it* in the microwave?

Before he had a chance to ponder that question, the front door opened. Cole turned around and promptly dropped the egg, which shattered on the floor and splattered his socks.

Drew smiled at Cole as he entered the kitchen, placing the bags on the counter. "Looks like the yoke's on you, kid."

Cole tensed. "Sorry."

Drew came around the counter, grabbed a handful of paper towels and knelt down to pick up the egg. "Pull off those socks and stick 'em in the hamper. Then grab a wet paper towel and wipe the floor here. Do you even know how to fry an egg?"

Cole shook his head, still nervous and still hungry. "I was thinking about putting it in the microwave."

Drew's eyes widened in shock as he stopped sopping up the egg and looked at Cole, who nearly bolted from the room before he saw the amusement in his uncle's face, just as he started to laugh.

"That would have exploded inside the microwave," Drew said as he finished cleaning up the egg. "Tomorrow morning, you and I can make breakfast for everyone. I'll show you how to cook up some eggs, bacon and English muffins. There's nothing to it. I'm guessing you're hungry?"

Cole nodded just as Ashley and Lily came out.

"Cole, sweetie," Ashley said in that tone that told him he was about to be sent to his room. "Why don't you…"

"No." Drew tossed the paper towels in the garbage. "He's gonna take off those socks, clean the floor and then we're all going to sit down, have some lunch and talk. He's going to hear what happened anyway and quite frankly, I don't feel like telling it more than I have to. Besides, the kid's hungry and so am I."

Ashley scowled and folded her arms, but didn't argue. Lily came in to wash the floor, but Drew shooed her off. "Cole is capable of cleaning up his own mess and it's not a punishment. It's just the right thing to do. And you," He looked at Cole. "Hurry up. You're not leaving me alone with your aunt."

Cole grinned as he pulled his socks off, tossed them in the laundry room off to the side of the kitchen and went to clean the mess he'd made.

****

Drew prepared Cole a sandwich on the softer bread that he liked and doctored it with mayonnaise. Placing it on a plate, he added a helping of potato salad. "Make sure you eat that," Drew said, pointing to the white heap of potatoes on the plate. "It's a sin to waste it. You man enough for a sour pickle?"

Cole nodded, took the offered pickle and sniffed it. Scrunching up his face, he shook his head and handed it back. Drew laughed and took a big bite out of it.

"You going to tell us what happened?" Ashley asked.

"You going to eat?" Drew said to his sister.

Ashley sneered. "I don't know. Is this your last meal?"

Drew laughed as he added slices of meat on his crunchy bread, then started to slather on spicy mustard.

Lily, who helped herself to a small sandwich and just a touch of potato salad, was urging his sister to listen. "Ollie said Drew did nothing wrong."

"Yeah, that didn't stop them from locking him up, did it?" Ashley snapped.

Cole dropped his sandwich. "They arrested you? Why?"

Drew took a huge bite out of his sub, winked at Cole while he chewed, and swallowed. "That's actually a very good question and one I'm asking. And I'm not the only one. Let me start at the beginning. And Cole, some of this is going to be hard to hear, but it's all going to be fine. Trust me."

Slowly, Drew ran through everything. He could tell it was difficult for Cole to hear, as he only picked at his food when reminded, but he wasn't panicked or, at least as Drew could tell, angry with him. In fact, Cole was saving his vitriol for the two detectives who arrested his uncle, but when Drew got to the point of the detectives being placed on suspension, Cole became quiet.

"If they lose their jobs," Cole asked, "Who's going to find out who killed Mom?"

"Chief Miller assured me she wouldn't let your mom's case get forgotten. She didn't say who would take over, but she promised, and I believe her. She raised Ollie and he's as good of a man as you can find. Besides, I don't think either Wilson or Harrington were bending over backwards to get justice for your mom. And I'll keep poking around, see what I can find out."

"You?" Ashley rolled her eyes. "Drew I know your work with the General meant you dealt with some law enforcement issues, but are you really qualified to do this?"

Drew nodded. "I'm a trained investigator. I've run a few murder investigations before, assisted in even more. Normally, we work *with* police, but we've been hired often to look into cold cases. I've dealt with many cops who I've learned to respect and admire."

Ashley smirked. "Yeah, I know you've been admiring Ollie's partner."

The image of Sam filled Drew's mind and he felt like he'd been stabbed in the gut. He dropped his fork and glowered into his plate. He saw Cole, ever so sensitive to mood changes, stiffen. He looked over at his nephew and smiled. "You still haven't touched that potato salad. Trust me, it's amazing."

Warily, Cole sampled the potato salad. Drew wasn't sure if his hesitance was because Cole was still nervous, or if he just hadn't forgotten the pickle. Tasting his first bite, Cole lifted his eyebrows and followed by shoveling a bigger forkful into his mouth.

Drew grinned and was about to say something when the doorbell rang. He signaled to everyone he'd get the door himself and left the table. He walked through the great room, where two leather couches that each sat three to four people, and matching leather chairs all faced a flat screen to go into the small vestibule where the front door was. He wasn't surprised to see Ollie on the other side, but instead of his partner, Drew quickly recognized a different female companion.

"Chief Miller," Drew said. "Please come in. We were having a late lunch. Have either of you had a chance to eat?"

Both Chief Miller and Ollie shook their heads at the offer. "We can't stay long, I just wanted to come have a word with you and your family if I may."

Lily went directly into host mode, reoffering food and refreshment, which were, again, politely refused, until Ashley punched Ollie in the arm playfully. "You love Maria's potato salad, not to mention her pickles."

"Pickles?" Ollie said. He looked at his mother and blushed.

"Eat," she said.

Ollie smiled and sat down next to Cole, saying hello before helping himself to one of the large, dark green pickles.

"What's up?" Drew said, eager to learn the reason for their visit.

Chief Miller motioned for everyone to sit. She was carrying a leather portfolio, which she placed in front of her.

"I assume you've told your family what happened today?" Chief Miller said. "Good. First off, I wanted to personally apologize for my detective's behavior, and to reassure you that you are most definitely not considered a person of interest in your sister's murder. I did check all of the contacts and alibis General McAlister provided, as well as reviewed your record with him. It's very impressive."

"Thank you," Drew said. "And thank you for coming down, but I don't hold what happened against you or your department at large."

Chief Miller smiled. "I know your experience with the Ember Falls Police Department hasn't been good. When I came into office, I worked to get you released. When you were, I had planned on speaking to you directly. I was surprised when you didn't return home with your father."

"What?" Ashley said. "Dad went to pick you up at prison? I would have come. Why did you call him?"

Drew scowled, locked eyes with Ollie who was concentrating on his pickle, trying to keep his face passive. "I didn't call. Dad showed up and felt it best for everyone if I didn't return to Ember Falls. I listened. I'm sorry."

Ashley started to say something more, but Drew held up his hand. "Ash, later."

Chief Miller continued. "As I told Mr. Duncan, I will not let the murder of Kelli Duncan be forgotten. I've spoken to the state. As you know, we're a small department and while we can hire officers who have gone through training, appointing detectives relies on them. I have been requesting to get more detectives assigned or the ability to promote within the department, but that seems to have stalled, something I'm not very happy about. My son is a seasoned and decorated officer. He'll be taking over the investigation."

A weary smile displayed on Ashley's face. "I know Ollie will do right by my sister."

"There's more," Chief Miller said. "Oliver won't be working alone. A private investigator has been hired, and my department will be working with that investigator. A meeting is being scheduled for Monday morning to review all evidence and move on from there."

Ashley frowned. "Wait, a private investigator? The department won't let you hire another detective or promote Ollie, but you can hire a private investigator?"

"We didn't hire anyone," Chief Miller said. "My hands are tied, but I can choose to work with one that's been privately hired."

"Someone is paying to have them find out who killed my sister?" Ashley said, looking confused. "Who?"

Drew shook his head. "If I'm not mistaken, someone we've all been eating with at this table."

Chief Miller nodded. "Yes. General Paul McAlister is hiring his own agency, McAlister Security, to do a full-blown investigation. When he arrived in my office this morning, he handed me a ton of paperwork. He made it very clear he was going to do this no matter what I said, but as a courtesy he wanted to give me a heads-up and offer to have his man work with our department.

"McAlister Security has an outstanding reputation with law enforcement they've worked with. I wanted to do my due diligence before agreeing to have our departments work hand in hand. I made a few calls to verify details and get opinions on the person McAlister Security is assigning and I'm satisfied."

A feeling of gratitude beyond words spread through Drew as he realized what the General had done for him. He looked toward Ashley, who clearly was thinking the same thing.

"Can I ask who he's sending?" Drew said. "I've worked with most of our investigators. They're all good, but I know some are tied up in other cases around the country." He paused for a moment. "Sanders is good, but last I heard she was in Maine working on a case already. Unless she's finished, I've been out of the loop for a couple of weeks. Jordan was nearly done, but his wife was due to give birth soon and he was talking about taking a leave to be with her. I'm surprised that whoever it is didn't contact me the moment it was assigned."

Chief Miller stood up, her eyes showing just the hint of a smile. "Actually, the investigator hasn't been notified as of yet."

Drew frowned. "Any idea when they *will* be?"

"Quite soon," Chief Miller said. "In fact, when I called General McAlister to let him know I planned on working with his agency, he decided I could deliver the notice in person as long as I used his exact words." She picked up the leather portfolio and handed it to Drew. "Consider your leave canceled and your ass back on the clock. And don't dick around because I'm not paying overtime."

Stunned looks were exchanged all around. "I'm being put in charge of the investigation?" Drew said as he slowly rose, accepting the pouch.

Chief Miller nodded. "General McAlister assured

me you'd be able to remain professional. I'll be honest with you, Mr. Duncan, I wasn't convinced it was a good idea. Nobody could blame you for being emotionally invested here and quite frankly, it doesn't look good when it gets to court, so you have to take extra precautions to preserve the integrity of the case.

"You cannot examine a single piece of evidence, interview a single witness, go to a single crime scene, without one of my officers accompanying you. And both you and any officer involved are going to have to wear body cameras."

Ollie looked confused. "Body cams? Since when do we have money in the budget for those?"

Chief Miller frowned. "We don't. They're being provided to us by McAlister Security. And you've got pickle juice on your tie."

Ollie looked down and rolled his eyes.

Chief Miller turned back to Drew. "I was going to ask if you thought working with Officer Miller would be an issue, but…"

Drew laughed. "No, I'm good with Ollie. Looking forward to it."

Ollie looked up, tried to send Drew a smile that said he was too, but then went back to work on his tie.

"Oh, for Christ's sake," Ashley said. "Take off the tie and give it to me. I'll get it clean. You're such a dork." Impatient, she reached over and undid Ollie's tie herself, causing Ollie to blush a light shade of pink. Ashley leaned in and kissed his cheek. "Thank you for what you're doing for my sister."

Chief Miller turned to Drew. "I have to tell you Mr. Duncan, I was against this from the moment General McAlister presented the idea." She smiled.

"That was all before I saw how you handled yourself in that interrogation room. You were a real pro in there, which leaves me with the headache of what to do with Wilson and Harrington."

Drew nodded. "Harrington was farther away. He can claim he simply believed his partner identified himself, although I don't believe that. And they didn't do a good job searching the area. Did you listen to the entire recording?"

Chief Miller nodded, holding his gaze just long enough.

"Drew," Chief Miller said, "Ember Falls may not hold many happy memories for you, but it's a good town with a very low crime rate. The last murder that took place here was…"

"Molly Winters, I know, but let me ask you something. Her case was classified as a murder. What about missing persons?"

Chief Miller pursed her lips. "Yes, I believe we have a few. Why?"

"Any chance you can get those files?" Drew asked. "Anything that indicates a person disappeared?"

She folded her arms, considering. "How far back?"

"Any time between now and the last ten years."

Drew watched as the chief mulled his request over. "We'll talk about it on Monday. I've got to go, but you have a good weekend."

Ollie was replacing his tie that Ashley had cleaned and started to follow his mom out.

"Hey, Ollie," Drew said. "Does Sam know about this particular turn of events?"

Ollie shook his head. "No, she left right after you."

Drew nodded. "That's right. She was doing

something with her Nana tonight, wasn't she?"

Ollie looked confused as he held open the door for his mother. "Nana? No, it's Friday. She'll have her weekly country western dance and she never misses those."

Drew scowled. "Does Sam ever go with her?"

Ollie shook his head. "Just once when she first rolled into town. She kept getting hit on by seventy-year-old Garth Brooks wannabes. I don't think you'd be able to pay her enough to go back."

Drew nodded, more to himself than anyone else. "Right."

Ollie followed his mother out as Ashley and Lily walked back into the kitchen, each carrying the leftovers from their late lunch.

Drew stewed for a few minutes, his hand clenched in a fist, wishing he had something to punch, before he went out the front door.

Chapter 13
The Punching Bag

Cole had watched as his uncle hauled up gym equipment from his truck into the small apartment. It wasn't much, just a few weights and a large punching bag. When Cole heard the blast of heavy metal music emanating from windows, he gave into curiosity and went up to see what was happening.

Cole watched just as his uncle finished his warm-up and stretching exercises.

Cole had never seen his uncle without a shirt on. Although Cole knew Drew had both muscles and tattoos, this was the first time he'd ever gotten to see them so clearly.

Drew's smooth skin was light, his muscles well defined, as he slowly lifted each arm up to his chest, holding a dumbbell Cole would need two hands to move it an inch. As one hand went down, the other came up in easy, practiced strokes. It looked effortless to Cole, as Drew continued to pump for a solid ten minutes.

Cole studied the black tattoo lining his uncle's right arm, circled his right pec and, when Drew shifted, some on his back.

The tattoo had many curves—sharp, black lines that formed the picture of a bird escaping from flames. Drew continued to sweat and his skin started to shine, which highlighted how toned and defined he was.

In the back of Cole's mind, he couldn't help but think how he would simply have no chance if this man, who claimed to love him, decided to attack.

He inched his way farther into the room, moving soundlessly and keeping out of sight. Drew stepped to the side, his eyes fixed now on the small window. There was something about his face, the narrow slit of his eyes, the clenched jaw, which told Cole his uncle was still angry. He'd seen it in the dining room as Ollie and his mother, the police chief, were leaving. Something Ollie said made Drew mad.

No.

Cole continued to watch Drew pump metal while the small iPod dock bellowed out how they were on a Highway to Hell.

No, angry wasn't right.

Uncle Drew was pissed.

And it was that quiet, silent kind of boiling anger Cole feared more than anything. That's when someone was most likely to be at their cruelest and do the most inhuman things.

Aunt Ash got angry all the time, but she yelled and cursed and five minutes later, she'd be laughing again. He'd seen Lily get mad once, at Aunt Ash, but it was mostly funny and when she was mad she cooked and cleaned.

Cole wanted to run, but he needed to know what would happen if he was in the same room with his uncle when he was this kind of angry. So if he had a temper and hurt Cole, at least Cole would know when to stay out of his way.

Yet he stayed there, hidden at the top of the stairs,

able to see and not be seen, as his uncle placed the weights on a rack and headed over to the large punching bag. He grabbed a roll of a white material, and wrapped his hands tightly, starting with the thumbs, moving to the wrists and eventually the entire hand, including the knuckles. Then he grabbed two padded gloves, wiggled his hands into them, and used his teeth to tighten the Velcro. Drew moved to stand directly in front of the punching bag, gave it a few test jabs, and then attacked.

The bag retreated each time a gloved fist slammed into it, but kept swinging back for more punishment. Cole watched how Uncle Drew hit, not just extending his arm out, but using the power of his full body. The muscles in his legs and back flexed as much as his biceps as he blasted the bag over and over again.

Stepping back, Cole was shocked to see his uncle continue his assault with his feet, kicking the bag high enough that it easily could have been a grown man's head. The bag seemed desperate to escape, but had no place to go as Drew continued to pummel it from different angles, with his hands, his elbows, and his feet. But while his tactics changed and evolved, the anger contained on his face didn't. His eyes remained windows to a hellish, cold rage that was as terrifying as it was mesmerizing.

With one final thump Cole felt could kill a man, let alone a young boy, Drew placed his hands on either side of the punching bag and stopped its dance.

Changing his mind, Cole prepared to slip down the stairs. He'd seek the comfort of his books and solitude of his stories where if things became too scary, he could save his place and close the book and look for something happier until he felt courageous enough to try again.

"You planning on coming in or were you just here for the show?"

Cole froze at the sound of his uncle's voice.

Drew used his teeth to open the gloves, pulled them off and tossed them to the side. He walked over to the fridge, opened it up and took out a bottle of water. Twisting off the cap, he took a long pull before putting it back inside the fridge. Drew stretched again, and glanced casually in Cole's direction.

"You ever hit a punching bag before?" Drew asked.

Cole forced himself to speak, keeping himself where he'd have a good chance of dashing to the house. "Doesn't look too hard."

Drew gave an impressed nod. He scanned a table for something and signaled Cole to come up.

Cole took his time, willing his legs to move. Slowly, he managed to climb the rest of the stairs and over to his uncle who was holding something in his hands.

"How long did you know I was there?"

Drew smiled as he sat down on the couch, indicating for Cole to stand in front of him.

"I saw you when you left the house," Drew said. "Show me your hands."

Slowly, Cole held up his hands for his uncle, wondering if he'd get away with just getting his knuckle smacked. Instead, Drew held out the same sort of binding he'd used on himself, only smaller. "I got a pair in your size. Thought you'd might like a go." Hooking Cole's thumb inside the loop, he carefully started to wrap his small hand, gently, but tightly. Once fully wrapped, he used the Velcro tip to secure them. "Too tight?"

Quickly, Cole shook his head, but in reality he knew he wouldn't have complained even if they had been strangling his hands. Drew inspected them to satisfy himself they were both secure and safe before moving on to Cole's other hand.

"You've never come up here to see me before," Drew said as he continued to wrap Cole's left hand. "I figured maybe you were just getting comfortable. I'm aware I'm a big guy and I make you nervous. I'm sorry for that, and I wish I knew a magic way to prove to you you'll never have to be afraid of me, but I'm hoping you'll figure it out in your own time. You're smart." Drew checked both hands one last time. "You're smarter than I was at your age. I know you understand it's more than just you learning you can trust me, it's adjusting to it. Has there ever been a man in your life that hasn't hurt you?"

Cole looked down at his hands, but managed to give a small shake of his head. "For a long time, I could say the same. It wasn't strictly true. I had teachers and coaches that didn't do anything bad, but they weren't a part of the nightmare of my life. For a long time, I thought that's just what men did, hurt women and children.

"I didn't like it, I didn't want to become it, but a part of me figured I'd get to be old enough and even that would change. It's like how you know boys like to kiss girls but you think it's icky and then something pops and you can't think of anything else but planting your lips on one. I hated myself for thinking someday

I'd be violent like that, swore I wouldn't."

"But you've hurt people," Cole snapped.

Drew sighed and nodded. "A few times." Drew put his finger under Cole's chin, gently pushing his head up so the boy was looking the man in the eye. "I can only promise you I'll never hurt you like that. I'm not perfect. I've screwed up. Back when I was younger, I'd lose control easier. Punched my best friend in the face once."

"Why?" Cole said, unable to stop himself.

Drew leaned back on the couch. "He'd hurt someone I loved, someone I always thought of as being sweet and innocent. He didn't hit her. He just...broke her heart."

Cole blinked. "What did he do? Did he hit you back?"

Drew shook his head. "No, and I wanted him to so I'd be clear to pound him. He would have let me. I think, in a way, he wanted me to, but I realized whatever happened between them, he was just as hurt as she was."

Cole scrunched his face up in confusion. "Why'd they hurt each other?"

Drew started to put a smaller pair of boxing gloves on Cole. "I don't know. Sometimes people do. And it's usually to people they love the most. The trick is to forgive, to move on and forget the hurt and pain. Sometimes the hardest part is forgiving yourself. All family will hurt you in some way. Like I told you, Cole, I'm not perfect. Someday I'll upset you and you should always tell me if I do. It won't change the fact I love you and I'll always be there for you. You're family and nothing is ever going to get in the way of that."

It was the first time his uncle had told him he loved him. The first time any man had said it to him. And he knew he should say it back, but he couldn't. The words were just stuck in his throat where they burned.

"C'mon," Drew said, getting up off the couch and directing Cole toward the punching bag. "Like this." Slowly, carefully, he showed Cole how to stand, how to position his hands, guided him on how to make a fist and the proper way to throw a punch. "The power comes not just from your arm."

"You use your body," Cole answered, feeling oddly at ease having Drew so close. "I watched how you did it."

Drew grinned, shaking his head. "Like I said, you're smarter than I was at your age. Of course, I was a moron, so that's not saying *too* much."

Cole laughed. After a few minutes of slowly punching the bag, Drew stepped back and let Cole have a go of it on his own. Drew moved to the opposite side of the bag to hold it in place, gave small instructions, even moving back around to help correct posture and guide his progress, but for the most part, he just allowed Cole to continue to hit.

Pausing for a moment, Cole looked up at his uncle. "You were angry when you came in here."

Drew nodded. "Yes. I imagine you're pretty good at picking up when someone's pissed off. Comes with living with someone whose bad moods meant you're going to have a nightmare of a day. Maybe someday there'll be some kid in our family who won't have that instinct."

Cole took a few more shots, changing his stance as his uncle showed him. "You're not as angry now. Did hitting this thing help?"

Drew smiled. "A little. It's a good thing when you feel the need to take your anger out on something in a physical way, to choose an inanimate object. You helped more."

Cole stopped mid-punch. "Me? I didn't do anything."

Drew stepped to the fridge and pulled out two bottles of water, the one he'd started earlier and a brand new one. He signaled Cole to follow him back to the couch. "That's enough for today, or you'll get sore."

Drew placed the bottles of water on a small table near the couch as he sat down. This time Cole presented his hands without prompting for his uncle to remove the gloves and wraps. "It's hard to understand, but you're a source of joy for me. I like being around you. Seeing you come up to see me meant you were accepting me into your life a little more. I liked that. I *want* that."

Cole nodded. "You're okay too."

Drew laughed and presented his fist for his nephew to bump, which Cole did with a grin. He grabbed the full bottle of water, twisted the top and presented it to Cole. "Always drink a lot of water, especially when you're exercising."

Cole accepted the bottle, took a drink, and wiped his lips with the back of his hand. "Why were you angry?"

Drew shifted over so Cole could sit beside him. Cole slid into place, still wary, but not nearly as afraid as when he'd come up here.

"You know Ollie's partner?" Drew said, as he picked up his own water bottle and prepared to drink. "Officer Rossi?"

Cole nodded as he sipped more water just like his uncle did. "Yeah, Sam. Aunt Ash said you want to get in her pants."

Drew spit out water, which made Cole giggle.

"Oh my God." Drew wiped his mouth. "Ashley said that to you?"

Cole kept giggling as he answered. "No, she was telling Lily and Ollie. They both thought it was gross and told her to stop. I don't get why you'd *want* to. I don't think Sam's pants would fit you."

"God." Drew closed his eyes and let his head fall back as Cole continued to laugh. "I'll explain it another time. I've got to have a talk with Ash. That's a very crass term and it's not polite. I happen to really like Sam and I want to get to know her better."

Cole stopped laughing. "But you're mad at Sam?"

Drew sighed and settled back on the couch. "With everything that happened today, Sam heard a few things and I think she misinterpreted them. She got upset with me, and when I wanted to see her tonight, she told me she was busy, but I'm thinking she lied just so I wouldn't come over."

Cole sat back into the crook of Drew's arm. "And you're mad because she lied?

"I'm angry because she didn't talk to me, and… Well… It's hard to explain."

Cole bit his lower lip. "Sounds stupid."

Drew laughed. "Which part?"

"The whole thing," Cole said. "She shouldn't get mad at you without letting you explain. And she shouldn't lie. It's not nice. But if you know she's just not understanding something, why get mad? Go talk to her. If you like her, isn't that better that being mad?"

Drew groaned. "You really are one smart kid. I better go shower."

****

"Maybe I should stay home," Rose said, even though she was standing in the living room already decked out in her best cowboy boots, a long denim dress with a checkered white shirt, and a rhinestone-studded vest. On top of her head was a white, ten-gallon Stetson. "You're upset."

Sam put on her best smile. "No, you go to your dance. I'm fine. I'm just going to sit down, have a glass of wine, and read a book. It's been a long day and I just want to relax."

That earned a big "hmph" from Rose. "It's a Friday night. You shouldn't be sitting at home reading a book. Why don't you call Drew and go do something." She smiled. "Or better yet, have him come over, stay in, and do something."

Sam's eyes widening. "*Nana!*"

Rose pouted. "Don't you 'Nana' me. Seriously, I'm going to be home late tonight myself. Unless of course I decide to let Mitch Simmons score tonight in which case I'll text you to let you know I won't be coming home until morning."

"Oh, God," Sam said. "Nana, please."

Nana shrugged unapologetically. "I saw the two of you together last night when I came home. You two looked awfully snug under the stars together."

Sam rolled her eyes. "I don't know that I want to be snug with Drew Duncan, but I'll let you know if that changes. Now go to your dance and be a good girl."

Rose kissed Sam on the forehead and got up. "A good girl, huh? Where's the fun in that? I'm leaving."

Sam frowned. "Isn't it your friend's turn to drive? What's her name?" Sam said, watching Rose saunter across the room. "Beverly, right?"

Rose shook her head. "I told her not to come, I'd rather drive myself so if I want to leave with someone else, I can. Ta-ta sweetie." With one last wiggle of her fingers, Rose left.

With a sigh, Sam reached to the side and picked up the novel she'd borrowed from her Nana's collection. On the cover was a young couple, the man playfully nibbling at the girl's neck. The male cover model was rugged with a broad chest, well-defined muscles and a face that was square jawed. The girl was busty, with long dark hair and a look of ecstasy on her face as she seemed to quiver from the slightest touch of her would-be lover. While the guy was naked from the waist up, the girl wore a dress that was practically falling off of her.

With a wince, she opened up the novel and scanned the first few lines.

He ripped off her bra, allowing her lily-white bosom to spill freely into the night air as she moaned his name in his ear, "Marco, I need to feel you deep within me."

He grinned as his hands grabbed at her supple breasts, thrusting his pelvis into hers, making her moan even more. "Hot diggity, let's do this thing."

Sam groaned.

Hot diggity?

If she ever had a man say that to her in the opening throes of passion, she'd probably kick him out of bed laughing. She put the book down and rose from the sofa, heading over to a bookshelf in the corner. She quickly scanned the titles. *The Love Rocket, A Little to the Left, My Lassie*, and *Hot Bum Full of Love* were among some of the less ridiculous ones. Wasn't there anything here without a cover of some girl with crazy big boobs ready to fall out of her dress or corset, or a man who wore a shirt and didn't have pecs like the Hulk, only not green?

There was a rumble of thunder and the night lit up. Sam went to retrieve her cell phone from her pocket and send her Nana a text, telling her to let her know she made it to the dance all right.

Was it wrong to admit she wanted Drew? He was a very attractive man. A real man, not one of those flawless male models with the long hair that looked like it came out of a shampoo and conditioner ad for women, and pecs and abs that were clearly photo shopped to perfection.

Maybe she was being too hard on him. After all, Drew said he was staying in Ember Falls. Maybe he'd ended it with Stephanie and he was trying to move on? But Stephanie hadn't acted like someone broken-hearted over a breakup and Sam didn't want to be the transitional girl who helped him get over the last girlfriend with a sympathetic ear and a good lay.

It could be Stephanie wasn't that broken up. Maybe it was casual. But Sam made it clear she wasn't into casual hookups. She had no problem with people who were, but it just wasn't for her.

Just as the sky finally opened up and started to pour, Sam's cell buzzed. Nana was safe at the dance, where she'd be until the storm passed. If it got too bad, she could always stay at one of her girlfriends' homes. Sam reached for the remote which had somehow fallen between the cushions of the sofa.

Flipping through the TV, she saw one lame romantic comedy after another. Was everything about couples? She even came across a reality show where people went on dates without any clothes on. *Yikes*.

The doorbell rang and Sam groaned. *Great, that's probably Beverly and all of Nana's friends. Probably forgot Nana planned to drive herself. Now they'll all see her home on a Friday night and have their own two cents to put in.*

Sam decided to shut off the TV and not just mute it. She didn't want to have to explain to a bunch of old women why she had a bunch of naked people on the TV with their private's pixilated.

She tossed the remote on the sofa and went to answer the door.

The moment Sam saw Drew, she was hit with a flurry of emotions. A silent thrill made her insides tremble, a little annoyance he showed up when she told him she was busy, a feeling of guilt for being caught in a lie that was like a weight in her stomach and a sudden urge to grab him, kiss…no, not kiss, bite him, and drag him to her bedroom.

"Drew," she said. "Um…what…"

"What am I doing here?" Drew said. "I suppose I could ask the same question to you. Could I come in? I'd like to talk and not drown."

Sam stood there, stunned, unable to come up with a snappy answer or a real reason why not, so she stepped back and swung her arm out as an invitation. He stalked past her, into the living room.

He was soaked. His shirt was wet and matted to his chest and arms, outlining his build.

She had only seen him a few hours ago, but she had already started to miss him. She hadn't realized how much until he showed up at her door, and it not only scared her, it pissed her off.

She had told him to stay away, and he hadn't listened. So why was she ecstatic he was here? And there was something about the way Drew was staring at her. She wasn't sure if he was going to yell or rip her clothes off.

Well, as long as he doesn't say "Hot digitty."

"Do you want coffee?" Sam offered. "Or something to drink? I could…"

"You ditched me," Drew snapped. "You lied to me about your Nana and you ditched me."

Yelling it is. "I shouldn't have lied, but you should have been honest."

"How wasn't I honest?"

Sam looked away. "Stephanie."

Drew closed half the distance between. "I never lied about Stephanie. I never lied to you about *anything*. Stephanie and I are friends. And yes, I've got a past. Did you think I've been living like a monk?"

"No," Sam said. "But if you're in a relationship with someone else, you should have told me."

"This has nothing to do with my relationship with Stephanie," Drew said. "It has everything to do with what happened with you and Dylan."

Sam's hands balled into fists. "Dylan has nothing to do with this! Don't try and bring him into our relationship!"

"I'm not." Drew pointed a finger down to the ground between them. "You put him right between the two of us when you lied to me instead of talking to me."

"No...I didn't..."

"Yeah, you did it," Drew said as he stepped closer, closing the distance even more. "But in a way, I put Molly between us when I got pissed at you and didn't make you talk to me. And it took my eight-year-old nephew to set me straight."

"I don't understand..." Sam put her hand to her forehead. "What do you mean?"

Drew inched closer, while Sam barely had any more room to retreat. "The last time I told a girl I was falling in love with her, she laughed and slapped my face. I didn't want to give you the chance to do the same."

Suddenly, it seemed like the air had been sucked out of the room. Sam's eyes grew wide as the thunder rolled. "You...you think you're falling in love with me?"

Chapter 14
Hot Diggity

For a long few seconds the beating of her heart drowned out the thunder and rain. Had she heard Drew right? Would he say it again or just take it back?

Drew nodded. "Yes. And it scares the hell out of me."

Questions started to whirl in Sam's mind, about his connection with Stephanie, and if either of them was really in the right place to start a relationship, but when Drew took a step toward her, she swept them out of her mind and took what she wanted

A clap of thunder rattled the house as Sam pulled Drew forward. His mouth crushing down on hers sent electric sparks through her body. She tasted the rainwater on his lips as she slipped her fingers behind his neck.

When the kiss ended, she looked into his eyes. "I'm sorry," she said. "I'm scared too."

"I guess we're both a pair of scaredy cats," Drew said with a salacious grin. "What do we do now?"

Sam bit her lower lip. "Let's frighten the crap out of each other."

Taking that as invitation, Drew was on her in an instant, kissing her intensely, his hands roaming over her body, sending tingles through her body where he touched her.

Lightning flashed in the night sky and Sam moaned when Drew brought his mouth down to her neck. She ran her hands under his shirt and laughed.

"You're laughing?" He said, between nibbles.

She pushed him away, but continued to smile. "You're getting me wet."

Drew wiggled his eyebrows. "Isn't that the idea?"

Sam's mouth dropped in a combined shock and laugh. "No, you're all wet from the rain and you're getting me all wet." She indicated her gray sweatshirt which was now damp in the front where he'd pressed his body against her. She could only imagine the wet handprints he'd already left on her ass.

Drew held his hands up in mock surrender. "You want to stop?"

Sam paused for a moment, smiled and shook her head. "Not a chance, but I do want to get you out of those wet clothes."

Drew reached for the bottom of his shirt. "Deal."

"Wait." Sam moved forward and put her hands over his. "Let me."

Seeing his grin, she kissed him again as her hands gripped the bottom of his wet black t-shirt and she slowly started to lift it up. As her hands rose, she felt the firmness of his stomach muscles, the tightness of his ribs. Her hands sensed his well-defined chest, with the small splash of hair.

Ending the kiss, Sam enjoyed the playful desire in Drew's eyes before she attempted to pull the shirt up and off, but she wasn't able to reach high enough to clear his head. Drew's arms had gone up, but the wet shirt got tangled over his face and hands, trapping him within.

"You're too tall," Sam complained while laughing. "Bend over."

"No." Drew tried to wriggle free. "I can do this."

Sam knew she should help him, but it was just too much fun to stand back and watch as he thrashed left to right, fighting to remove the soaked shirt.

After a fierce struggle, he finally escaped from the garment and tossed it to the side where it hit an ugly bird statue, covering its face. The brightly colored figurine tipped over, falling down to the hard wood floor where it cracked into three pieces.

"Shit." Drew looked at the orange, blue, green and magenta fragments, its white eyes staring up at him in horror. "Sorry."

Sam laughed. "Don't be, I always hated that thing. It gave me nightmares when I was a kid."

"Oh." Drew shrugged. "You're welcome."

Sam hooked her thumbs into his belt hoops and pulled him close. "Nana will probably pitch a fit."

Laughing at the look of horror in his eyes, she took his hand pulled him down the hall to her bedroom. She flicked on the lights and gasped.

Her room was a mess, with a pile of dirty laundry in one corner, two bras hanging off the back of a chair, drawers partially open, stuffed past their capacity, and plastic cups filled with varying amounts of water in several spots. Her desk was covered in papers and pens, her lock box with her service weapon, several bobble heads of prominent rock stars and an open box of chocolates where several of the pieces had been sampled and discarded.

She quickly flipped the lights off again, only to have Drew switch them back on.

"Oh. My. God." Drew laughed. "You're a slob. You'd drive Lily insane."

Sam bit her lower lip. "I'm sorry."

Drew kissed her hard and grinned. "I'm not."

Together, they fell on her bed, which although unmade, was covered with stuffed animals. Drew's head ended up lodged between a goofy, blue dog and a squeaking, giant pig. "*This* might be an issue."

"Sorry." Sam punched a big, pink elephant off the bed. It hit the wall and started to wiggle around and sing, "I'm a hunk a hunk of burnin' love" over and over again. "Nana always got me a new stuffed animal every time I came and I can't bear to throw them out. She loves them so much."

Drew was smiling as he examined a fuzzy cat that looked somewhat possessed with one of its eyes missing. "Hey, where are you going?"

Sam slipped to the bottom of the bed and sat up. "I can't be with you in here," she said, thinking about how she'd stayed over here when she was a little girl, playing with dolls and eating cookies with milk, the crumbs of which might still be under the mattress. "Nana has a guest room. Come on."

She watched with glee as Drew knocked aside lions, tigers and bears (Oh my!) to get to his feet.

Taking his hand, she pulled him down the hall to another, small bedroom.

The guest room was painted a powder blue and had an off-white ceiling. There was a basic dresser in the corner and a queen size bed in the middle of the room, covered with a blue comforter that matched the walls. No stuffed animals seemed to have escaped Sam's room and made it this far down the hall.

Brushing aside Sam's long, dark hair, Drew lowered his mouth to her neck while his hands roamed up and down her body.

Sam started to moan, feeling her knees grow weak as Drew's tongue danced on her skin, but she wasn't ready to give herself to him yet.

With a tremendous amount of effort, she turned around and moved his hands. "I'm not done. I want to get you naked. Come here." She gripped his arms and steered him toward the bed, pushing him down on his back. "I'm still undressing you."

Drew grabbed a pillow and shoved it behind his head, interlocked his fingers and did the same with his hands, all the while smiling at the mischievous look on Sam's face.

She went to work on his footwear next. Picking up his leg, she moaned in frustration. "Why did you have to wear high tops?"

As Drew laughed, she untied the laces of each, attempting to remove them. His left one came off easily enough, but the right one took more work. Just as she was wondering if he'd cemented it on, it sprang free. Quickly, she pulled his socks off without comment. There simply wasn't anything sexy about removing a man's shoes and socks.

Sam climbed on the bed and straddled Drew, taking a moment to study him. His eyes still lit up in delight, his fingers interwoven with each other and behind his head. She looked closer at his tattoo, a fierce, black, bird on the right side of his chest, flying from a wall of flames. Its wings stretched toward the shoulder, its talons reached to his pecs and the design of fire stretched down his right arm to the wrist. Sam had never been particularly attracted to men with tattoos before, nor had she ever thought of them as a turnoff. This tattoo however, very much suited Drew. It was dark and bold, fierce and mysterious.

"Something catch your eye?" His smile faltered, and she wondered if he was becoming uncomfortable with her staring.

Slowly shaking her head, Sam smiled down at him. "Just enjoying the view, and I'd like to enjoy it even more."

She reached down to his belt buckle and slowly undid it, all the while holding eye contact. Her mouth parted slightly, with the tip of her tongue planted to the roof of her mouth. Once the belt was undone, she popped open the button at the top, slipped her hand into the top of his jeans and started to push them down, taking his underwear as well. Lowering them just so the top of his pelvic area was exposed, Sam placed her hand just below his hard stomach. Slowly, she let it slide up, tracing the lines in his abs, the indentation of his pecs.

She lowered herself, her dark hair falling to one side, as she slid her body up and began to kiss him. Her hands found his as he responded to the kiss. He stiffened beneath her and she imagined being in this same position once they both shed their clothing. As she deepened the kiss, exploring the inside of his mouth as he tasted hers, she moved her lower body on him. His hardness became more pronounced until he moaned. The sound of him thrilled her and she felt her own body respond.

Her mouth left his, finding his neck. Alternating between kisses and nibbles, she started to work her way down.

"God, Samantha," he said in a low, almost painful voice. "You're killing me here."

It was the first time she recalled hearing him use her full name. She enjoyed how it sounded when filled with such need. "At least you'll die happy."

Her gyrations were also having an effect on her. Dull stabs of pleasure shot through her as she continued to move downward. Her hands slipped from his and slid down to his jeans. Sitting up, she undid the half way open zipper of his jeans and tugged his pants down just a touch more. Low enough where she could see the outline of him, trying to escape, desperate for release.

Sliding off him, she lay at his side, nuzzling into his neck, while her right hand glided under the jeans. With a small layer of fabric between them, her fingers brushed the top of his erection.

Drew turned his head toward her, his eyes barely open. "Please, Samantha," he whispered.

She kissed him, knowing this would be the last real kiss before she finally stripped him naked, then moved off the bed. She offered him her hand. Taking it, he stood.

Putting a hand on his chest, she slowly walked behind him. She slipped her free hand down the seat of his jeans, feeling his hard ass while tasting the skin on his shoulder. She noticed there were small areas on his skin, under the tattoo, that were rough, but she didn't dwell on his imperfections. Instead, she moved both hands to his hips and pushed his remaining clothing down. As they fell down to his ankles, she took a moment to admire the view from behind before moving to face him.

Drew's face was almost unreadable to her. No embarrassment at being nude, and yet he seemed vulnerable as he stepped out of and away from his pants. Finally, she allowed her eyes to look at the whole of him. Seeing he was fully ready to take her sent a tingle down her skin.

She stepped closer, putting one hand on the back of his neck and pulled him into a long, hard kiss, while her other hand wrapped around his hardness. He gave a soft spasm as pleasure shot through his body and she gripped him tightly. His breathing was heavier and she relished touching him, squeezing him, hearing him moan.

She kept her eyes on his as she pushed him back onto the bed, where he sat on the edge, waiting...wanting.

Quickly, she pushed her sweatpants off, letting her panties fall with them. She grinned as his eyes went down, only to find her oversized sweatshirt fell down and covered her like a dress. Slowly and playfully, Sam reached down to the bottom, grinned impishly, and then pulled it down even further.

"Hey..."

Sam wagged a finger at him as she stepped back.

Holding the sweatshirt in place, she managed to wiggle out of her thick, wool socks using only her feet and toes. Once she was barefoot, Sam turned away from Drew to take off the sweatshirt, grateful she removed her bra earlier.

Gripping the bottom of the sweatshirt, Sam slowly pulled it up. She heard a small, muffled grunt of delight as her bottom was exposed, but didn't pause as she pulled the sweatshirt above her head. She held it in front of her body, letting it drape over her front, while Drew enjoyed her from behind.

Sam turned around, and Drew was even more excited. His eyes pleaded for her to finish stripping so they could touch. With a seductive half grin, she dropped the sweatshirt.

Drew's hungry gaze wandered over her for a few moments, and then slowly she walked to the bed. Reaching down, she grabbed him again, feeling his erection, the heat that told her he was more than ready.

She started to move in to kiss him, when he pulled his head back.

"Um..." Drew mumbled. "Do you have...you know..."

She blinked as she drew back, her hand still wrapped around him. "Wait, don't you have a condom?"

Disappointment flooded his face. "No. I was on assignment when I came to Ember Falls, I never expected...And I didn't think this would happen when I drove over..."

Sam frowned. "I don't..." She shook her head in frustration as she sat on the bed, next to Drew. "I haven't dated since I came to Ember Falls, despite Nana's complaining that I..." Sam's eyes lit up. "Nana!"

She started to get up, but Drew grabbed her hand. "Wait, you're not going to call her, are you? I could run to the store."

Sam laughed. "Good luck getting that into your jeans again. Besides, it's pouring out there. I don't want you on the road. Stay here." She leaned down, kissed him hard while stroking him softly for a moment.

"Exactly where and *how* you are."

With one last kiss, she ran out of the room, laughing as Drew groaned from down the hall.

Moments later, she returned, carrying a shoebox.

"Not that I have anything against stiletto heels," Drew said, eyeing the box she placed on the dresser next to the bed, "But I don't think this is anything that's going to help."

Sam grinned, feeling a little silly now that the mood had been broken and she was still standing naked in front of Drew, although she planned on making that as short-lived as possible.

"These are actually Nana's," Sam said, winking at Drew. "She told me where they were so if I ever, and these are here words, 'got my hot little booty out there and decided to get me some', I'd know where her stash was. She had them in a drawer."

Drew looked surprised. "Your Nana has a box of condoms? And you're okay using one?"

Sam's eyes drifted down. "Nana would never forgive me if I didn't." She lifted the lid. "Besides, I'm trying not to think about it. Or for that matter what else she had in there."

Ignoring the alarmed look on Drew's face, Sam flipped open the box and gasped. "Holy crap, Nana."

The box was a smorgasbord of different types of condoms of every color imaginable, from a cheerful green, to neon pink. A few of the more brightly colored ones advertised the ability to glow in the dark. Others were Christmas themed, with red, white and blue, or one that purported to look like a reindeer with a red tip.

A few were labeled studded or tickling, and some promised to provide a warming sensation when activated by natural body moisture. There was a virtual buffet of flavored condoms, including tastes such as banana, strawberry, chocolate, orange, vanilla, coke and even a mint.

Drew reached in with two fingers and picked up one that was called a French Tickler. It looked like a bright, purple shower cap with little bubble things popping in all directions.

Sam grabbed it and tossed it back into the box. "No. Here, use the black. It's the closest to normal."

Drew took it and ripped it open. "For formal occasions, I suppose."

Sam set the box aside and took the condom. "Allow me."

Gently, Sam slid the condom on. If Drew had lost any excitement while looking through Nana's condoms, he quickly recovered as Sam handled him.

"You keep touching me," Drew said. "It's my turn."

Sam allowed Drew to pull her onto the bed. They lay side by side, their hands slowly exploring each other's bodies as they continued to kiss. Sam gasped as Drew's mouth found its way onto her breast, sending electric jolts of ecstasy through her. His tongue played on her nipple as he reached down between her legs and fondled her gently. The thrill of pleasure radiated through her, and she trembled with excitement.

Before too long, Sam couldn't take anymore. She placed her hand on his shoulder and pushed him on his back. Quickly, she started to reposition. "I need you," she whispered in his ear as she moved on top of him. "Now."

Slowly, she moved down, allowing him to slip

inside of her. His hands reached for her breasts as she crushed her mouth down on his. Gradually, she rose and fell on him as he started to move in concert with her.

Outside, the thunder boomed, shaking the house, but neither Sam nor Drew noticed as they continued to move, both against and with each other. She loved the sound of him moaning from her touch and desperately wanted to hear more.

She adored the fact Drew allowed her to completely control their first time together. Her rules, her choices, and she could tell from the gleam in his eyes and his wicked grin every time she sighed or whimpered in delight how much he enjoyed her pleasure.

Sam had sex before tonight, but until this very moment, she'd never made love. Never been with someone who wanted to please her, where her happiness meant so much. In sync with each other, they both gave as much as they took. Waves of ecstasy rippled through her body as she slowly built to a climax. Drew moved faster, harder and the joy in his eyes was the last thing she saw before she closed hers and threw her head back as spasms of delight ripped through her.

As her orgasm subsided, Drew slowed, but didn't stop. She wanted to say something, but couldn't quite catch her breath. She collapsed on him, as his hands gently caressed her. Her mouth found his and she could tell he hadn't yet had his fill.

They switched positions and Drew was on top of her. He touched her face, kissed her tenderly, and stroked her hair. "I still want more." Drew's voice was full of need. "I need more. Please tell me you're not ready to stop."

"Please," she managed to say in a whisper. "Give me more."

A grin tugged at the corners of his lips as he found his way inside and slowly moved again. She was certain she would never reach that same peak. She'd never been able to go twice before, so why would tonight be different?

Drew patiently kept his pace steady, touching her in all the places she loved to be touched, tasting her skin and whispering in her ear about her beauty, she quickly realized she was wrong. He buried his face in her neck as the intensity built. Her legs curled around him as she felt herself climbed to a new, higher peak.

Drew lost any semblance of control and she lost all sense of reality. She had no idea where she ended and he began. Sam found herself someplace she'd never been before, where the world was only touch and sensation, and pleasure soared through her entire body. She closed her eyes for a moment, losing her sense of self in the indulgence of him, and moaned his name.

He made a noise from deep within, something primal that forced her to open her eyes. Her saying his name pushed him over the edge, as he buried himself deeper insider her than ever before. She was consumed, her body rocking from the intensity of her climax. She screamed as she reached up and grabbed his hair, and he exploded.

His eyes widened in shock as he emptied himself and she took as much delight in his pleasure as he had in hers.

Spent, he collapsed. She felt his weight for the first

time as he continued to stroke and caress her. His lips found hers, her body tingled in aftershock.

Slowly, he moved beside her. She nestled in his arms, snuggled against his chest and smiled contently as he softly whispered her name.

Chapter 15
The Story of the Phoenix

The thunder finally abated, and the only sounds were the gentle fall of a light rain as the storm passed and Drew's heartbeat. Sam had never felt as comfortable in her own skin as she did lying here next to Drew. And that scared her.

Sam knew she should slow things down and not commit her heart, but she wasn't sure if that was possible. Not for her, not after tonight. But the thought of allowing herself to fully and completely fall in love with Drew was terrifying.

Looking up to Drew's face, she realized he was watching her with something in his eyes she couldn't quite place. Amusement? Contentment? More? Or maybe he just wanted to get out of here, like plenty of men did.

"What's on your mind, beautiful?"

"I'm just admiring your tattoo," Sam said. "I like it. I've thought about getting one, but I've never been brave enough."

Drew smiled. "You don't strike me as the type who'd be afraid of a little pain."

"It's not that. Well, maybe a little. I hate needles. But when I've looked at tattoos, I can't decide what I'd want. I mean, it'd be on my body the rest of my life. I'd have to really love it. It's got to be something that really

257

speaks to me, something I'd enjoy looking at on my body for the rest of my life, right?"

"Probably a good idea."

Sam snuggled closer. "What about you?"

"I can honestly say, without a doubt in my mind," Drew moved his face close to hers. "That I *love* your body." He leaned in and kissed her quickly.

"Ha, ha." Not that she minded the compliment. It just added to the warm and gooey feeling she had inside right now. "No, I meant about your tattoo. How did you decide on it? Did you always think about getting a…" She used her finger to lightly trace the face of the bird that was on his chest again. "What kind of bird is that? Not an eagle or hawk. Maybe a really angry chicken?"

Drew looked down at his own chest, amused. "It looks like an angry chicken to you? Original or extra crispy?"

Sam snorted. "You're going to get me hungry. What is it?"

Drew sighed. "It's a phoenix." His voice was quiet as he said it.

Sam re-examined the tattoo and tried to recall what she knew about the phoenix, but beyond knowing they weren't real birds, she drew a blank.

"A phoenix is a mythological creature," Drew said. "It bursts into flames to die and is reborn from its own ashes."

The face of the phoenix looked fierce, even savage. It was completely in black ink, but Sam was still able to see where the bird ended toward the bottom of his upper arm and where the flames took over, an inferno that went to his wrist.

"Why the phoenix?" Sam said. "Was it just

something you thought was cool growing up? Or did it have something to do with your childhood? You know, rising from the ashes and all that."

"Here." He guided her fingers toward his chest. "Feel this here?" Her fingers touched a trio of tiny rough patches on his skin. "And here?" Gently, he steered her touch to the top of the shoulder. Again to three different spots on his upper arm, two places on his lower arm, his wrist.

"What are those?" She realized before he responded that the answer would be much darker. He wasn't looking at her anymore, but rather off into the shadows of the room.

"Every now and then," Drew said, his calm, controlled voice was like being in the eye of a storm, "when my dad was drunk enough and pissed enough to want to hurt us, but not so drunk that he didn't realize my sisters were hiding. He figured they'd never come out if he called them and he wasn't going to chance letting me get away, so he told me to call them. And when I wouldn't, he'd light a cigarette and press it against my skin. He'd tell me he'd stop if I just called them."

A wave of nausea hit Sam bad enough she physically cringed. What kind of hell was it to grow up in that home?

"But they couldn't come even if you called them," she said.

Drew gave a dismissive shrug. "He didn't know, and I sure as hell wasn't going to *tell* him that."

Sam wrapped her arms around him. "No, of course not. You probably just gritted your teeth and took it."

Drew let out a hallow laugh. "No, I really didn't. I

259

fought, but my father's a big guy. The first time he burnt me was actually on my ninth birthday. That was this one." He tapped a spot, now covered by his tattoo, which was located just above his right nipple. "The last time he tried it, I was almost fifteen and I managed to kick him in the balls. But trust me, I screamed. I just refused to call my sisters."

"Didn't anyone ever call the cops?"

"Sure," Drew said. "The house right behind ours was close. They called once. Cops came. Walked up to the door, never knocked or rang the doorbell. They knew my Dad; he was one of them, and the department was pretty damn corrupt at the time.

"About a month later, same thing happened. Same neighbors. Probably the same cops. Same fucking result, but this time, the guy who lived behind us got his ass kicked by my father in front of his wife and son, who I went to school with. Next thing I knew, they up and moved."

Drew looked down at his own body. "When I was in prison, well…You can't really hide crap like this. I even thought about getting inked in prison, but to cover up all of the scars would take forever and everyone had already seen it. Then I got out, and I was on my own. I had finished high school in prison, joined the Marines, but I had a couple of weeks before training started. I was mostly just hanging out, waiting. Saw some place that did tattoos and went in. I didn't think I'd do it, but I figured I'd check it out. That's where I met Dan. He owned the place and he took it really seriously. It was an art to him. When I started to ask about getting a tattoo that would go up my arm to my chest, Dan refused to do it."

"Why?" Sam asked. "Dan didn't like people with big tattoos on them?"

"Are you kidding?" Drew laughed and shook his head. Sam realized he didn't sound as haunted as he had when he'd first talked to her about his past. "Dan was covered in them. Each arm, chest, back. Legs. He was in a tank top and shorts so I was able to see plenty of what he had."

"He didn't think you were tough enough?"

Drew scowled, but there was a playful gleam in his eyes. "Had nothing to do with that. Dan asked me if I had ever gotten any tattoos, which I hadn't. I think he could tell from my questions I was a newbie. You know, people often look at you like there's something wrong with you if you've got ink. So artists tell you start small, but someplace that won't show in business attire or even casual wear unless you wanted it to.

"I was asking to start with this big ass tattoo. Dan told me I needed to be sure. I wasn't in the mood to argue, so I started to walk out, but he called me back. Asked me why I wanted one that big. I hadn't even picked out a design, but he could tell it wasn't just a whim."

Drew grinned, recalling the memory. "Dan was covered in ink, bald with a long beard, yet there was something about him I trusted. I think it was the pictures he had up of his kids and his nieces. So I took off my jacket and showed him. I didn't go into detail, but the moment he saw the scars... I'm guessing he'd seen stuff like that before."

Drew shrugged. "Next thing I know, we're looking at patterns. I just wanted black." He held up his arm, stared at the design. "I guess it just matched my mood about the reason for it. I took a while looking through designs, but couldn't find anything. He asked how long I had and he said we'd have to get started soon if it was going to heal before I went to boot camp, but he made me promise not to pick one unless it felt right.

"He told me to go home and come in the next day. I didn't really have a home, but there was a cheap motel down the road I was staying in for the next two weeks. I went back the next morning and Dan told me he put in a little research. He had over two dozen designs for me to look at, but I never got to most of them. He pulled out one he had custom designed for me. Said he thought it suited me."

Tracing the pattern on his chest with her fingers, Sam had to agree with Dan's assessment. She'd seen some people who had tattoos where it just looked like a collage of various images that didn't match. There were ones that held importance, like the name of a loved one lost, their memory forever etched on their bodies. Somehow, Drew's seemed to be a part of him.

"So, Dan really came up with the idea of the phoenix," Drew continued. "Told me all about it. When I heard it was a mythical bird that rose from its own ashes, well...I was sold. It just looked right. Like an abstract piece of art that you have no idea what it's supposed to be, but it means something to you.

"Took him three and a half days. He really spent a lot of time with me since I was new with it. He was really patient, and he talked to me while he worked. Told me about his kids, his nieces, his family, never asked about my family. It was weird. The more he covered my scars with that phoenix, the more I became determined to be it. To rise from what I came from. It was like putting on a mask, almost. So yeah, I guess you could say it did speak to me."

Listening to Drew explain, Sam started to realize his ink wasn't just sexy and alluring, although it certainly was, it was also quite beautiful. Drew was beautiful. He was a man who grew up with such violence, yet he still managed to become a man who could love and protect. She'd never forget that moment where he'd brought Cole in to see his mother's body and showed the boy it was all right to cry.

Moving her gaze from his tattoo to his eyes, Sam came to another realization. She was so far beyond the falling in love part of the relationship. She had already fallen and now just had to figure out what to do with it.

"You still there?"

Sam smiled. "Yes. I'm just… I keep thinking about what you and your sisters went through. What poor Cole went through, and I wish there was something I could do, but I can't change the past. Your childhood years should be about laughter and smiles and love, not the kind of ugly violence you came from."

Gently, Drew tenderly touch her face. "Nothing I do is ever going to bring back my sister, but what I can do is make sure her son doesn't live in fear anymore. She wanted me back in her life. If I had just checked that damn e-mail account a few days earlier, I would have been here. The General could have found someone else for that last job and he never would have stood in the way of my returning home. Hell, he would probably have kicked my ass if I didn't come." He sighed. "Maybe, Cole would have adjusted to me better if Kelli had introduced us. We're making progress, but it's slow."

Sam placed her hand on his chest. "You're very good with him."

"He wants to be connected to me," Drew said. "He *needs* that connection with Kelli. He knows his mother wanted me in his life, but dammit if the kid isn't still scared shitless of me every time I walk into a room. I've made sure not to surprise him. I haven't raised my voice, even when I caught him stealing, but he still thinks I'm going to turn on him."

Sam caressed his chest. "It's going to take time. He hasn't known you for long. The more you're in his life, the more you do things together, the more he'll trust you."

Drew nodded. "I got home today and found Cole sneaking into the kitchen for food. Kid knew *something* was up and probably spent the day hiding in his room, but he got hungry enough to come out and forage for something to eat. He had an egg in his hand. He was going to stick it in the microwave." Drew paused and turned to Sam, saw her eyes widen in horror.

They laughed together. "*The microwave!* The damn thing would have exploded and made a mess and then he wouldn't have had to worry about me screaming, Lily would have had a fit." Drew shook his head as the laughter died. "I told him we'd make breakfast tomorrow morning for everyone. I'd show him how to make something like scrambled eggs."

Sam forced a smile. "That's good." *I guess the idea of you spending the night in my bed was too much to ask for.*

Drew grinned at the thought, clearly looking forward to it. "I thought about running into that twenty-four hour store near the house, getting a few things.

Cheese, veggies for the omelets. Bacon. We can make a big family breakfast."

Sam did her best to keep the resentment out of her voice. She knew how important this was for his relationship with Cole. "Sounds yummy."

Drew pulled her closer. "I may not be able to cook like you and Lily do, but I know my way around the kitchen. Lily has one of those small skillets that are perfect for making omelets, so everyone can have what they want. I love sweet red peppers, some onion and tomatoes, and a touch of cheese. Maybe even some mushrooms. I know Ash hates veggies. She'll want a ton of cheese, some serious chunks of ham. That's on top of having bacon on the side. I'm not sure about Lily, but something tells me she's one of those feta cheese types with spinach. Nothing I can't handle if I've got the ingredients. What do you like?"

Sam blinked. "Me?"

"Yeah," Drew said. "Whatever you want. Just let me know so I can grab it tomorrow morning at the store. I'll get some English muffins too, oranges for some freshly squeezed juice, make a project out of it. What else should I grab?"

Sam tried to keep up. "Wait, you want me to have breakfast with your family tomorrow?"

"Of course," Drew answered as if it was the only logical possibility. "We'll have to set the alarm to get us up early enough, but I can text someone and let them know to wait. Why? Do you have plans? If so, I'd love it if you could cancel them."

"Um…" Sam was quite sure that if she hadn't been lying down on the bed, she'd probably have fallen. "No, it sounds great."

"Yeah," Drew agreed. "It does."

As the elation of the moment thrilled her, a new idea sprang in her mind. "Are you free the whole day tomorrow? There's a fair one town over. They'll have rides and games. Cole would probably love it. Nana and I go every year since I was little. We could spend the day together."

As she spoke, Drew's eyes lit up with joy at the thought of spending the day together. He enjoyed the idea of the pair of them taking Cole and her Nana to the fair.

Dylan never wanted to do anything with her family. The mere suggestion used to annoy him. He'd pouted when she'd left town to go to the fair with Nana, even though he was invited.

To Drew, the idea was wonderful.

"That sounds perfect," Drew said. "You sure your Nana won't mind if Cole and I tag along?"

"Oh, I won't mind at all."

Sam jumped at the sound of her Nana's voice coming from the bedroom door. She was leaning on the door frame, her arms crossed and wearing an impish grin, her eyes dancing with glee.

It took a moment for Sam to fully understand that her grandmother was standing there as both she and Drew were lying entangled in each other's arms, wearing not a stitch of clothing. Sam wasn't sure what was more embarrassing, her own nudity, or Drew's, who in his current position on his back, was on full and complete display.

Face burning, Sam screamed and tried to cover both herself and Drew with her hands, something that just wasn't working very well. Drew on the other hand, laughed out loud.

"I'd love to share our little outing with both you and Cole." Rose walked into the room. "Just like I'm thrilled to have had the chance to share my supply with my granddaughter." She grabbed the box of condoms off the dresser. "Mitchell wasn't there tonight, but George was. Unfortunately, he's got a roommate who hates when he brings company home, so I invited him here." She turned her back and started for the door. "I'll leave you two alone to finish making plans for tomorrow."

Watching Rose head for the door, Sam started to relax, although it would be a while before she wasn't red.

"Oh, who am I kidding?" Rose scrimmaged in the box. "I'll only need one of these." She pulled out one of the ones labeled as a French Tickler. "He's a fan of these if I recall. You should try one. From the looks of things, Drew's ready to sample any one you'd like. Probably more than one." She placed the box down on a dresser near the door and turned to leave. "Ah, to be young again."

Chapter 16
A Day at the Fair

Cole had been certain his uncle would forget about his promise to teach him how to fix breakfast. It was a small thing, the kind of thing adults forgot because it's so unimportant, at least to them, but Cole wanted to learn. He liked the idea of being able to do something for everyone. He hadn't been able to tell his Aunt Ash and Lily how he liked being here with them. They didn't need to take him and his mother in and must have known there was danger, even before his mom was killed.

No, they couldn't possibly understand how dangerous it really was.

However, Cole didn't want to think of that today, not once he'd gotten a text from his uncle to be ready when he came home with everything they'd need and to not let anyone have a single crumb for breakfast. It was before seven and Lily had to go into the bookstore, but not right away. She was happy to wait. Aunt Ash was still in bed and grumbled like a bear taking a nap when he came in to tell her not to eat anything.

"I'm in bed," she'd snapped. "Do you think I have a buffet under here?"

He wasn't sure what his uncle was getting, but figured it would just be some eggs and bread for toast, maybe a package of bacon. Instead, he had hauled in three huge bags. Ollie's partner Sam was with him, carrying a box with some stuff in it. Had she met him at the store?

"What are we doing with the oranges? You're not gonna put them in the eggs?"

Drew rolled his eyes. "No. Where do you think orange juice comes from?"

Cole matched his eye roll. "A carton."

Drew sighed as he went into a cabinet and pulled out a small metal thing that had a bowl on the bottom and a grooved top that stuck up. It had a metal top with small holes.

Drew placed a small pitcher next to it, and opened the bag of oranges. They nearly rolled off the table and Cole laughed as he grabbed them. "This will be your first job. Start by rolling each one on the counter and pressing them." He demonstrated. "When you're done, I'll slice 'em and show you how to make the juice. I'm gonna start the bacon and Sam volunteered to make coffee for the adults."

Cole quickly started to concentrate on the oranges and Uncle Drew and Sam got to work. Before long there was bacon sizzling, the oranges were sliced and Cole was diligently working through the entire batch, while his uncle expertly chopped veggies and placed them into small piles on the cutting board.

Soon, Cole found himself standing on a small stool as he broke eggs into a white bowl. At first, Cole tried to stir the eggs, but his uncle patiently showed him how to properly use the whisk. Cole figured he'd be watching, but while his uncle insisted on doing the cutting, he allowed Cole to put the eggs in the small frying pan, add the ingredients and even showed Cole how to fold the omelets and moved them to a plate. Sam delivered them to each person.

Everyone seemed very impressed with their breakfasts, and Cole felt a surge of pride fill him as he made an omelet tailored to each family member. Ashley threatened to kick Drew out and make Sam live there so she could continue to make the coffee the way she did.

Lily was the first to leave. Ashley spoke about a few things she had to do, all of which sounded boring. After such a wonderful start to the day, Cole hated the idea of having to be dragged around. He was certain his uncle would want to ditch him for Sam for the rest of the day now that he'd fulfilled his promise.

"You go do whatever," Drew said to Aunt Ash as he poured himself a second cup of coffee and turned to Cole. "How's this sound for the day? You and me are going to join Sam and her Nana. They're going to that fair that's a couple of towns over. You ever been to one of those?"

Cole shook his head slowly, not entirely sure what was happening.

"Great," Drew said. "Let's get these dishes done then we can get ready and head on over."

Less than twenty minutes later, Cole was by his uncle's car, bouncing on his heels as he waited to leave.

"You're not excited are you?" Ashley said as she came out of the back door.

Cole shrugged, trying desperately to look cool and not like a stupid little kid, but it took every ounce of self-restraint not to jump up and down.

Cole never imagined it was possible, that his Uncle Drew simply wanted to spend the day with him. Even now, as Cole waited for his uncle to come bursting through the door on the side of the garage, he couldn't help but think it was all a cruel joke.

Ashley stood beside Cole, messed his hair carelessly, and bumped him with her hip. "I promised Lily I'd run these errands for her, but maybe I'll stop by later."

Cole looked over at his aunt, the feeling of excitement growing even bigger in his eyes. "You and Ollie might come by?"

Ashley blinked as she tried to understand what Cole meant. "You want Ollie there?"

Cole sighed. "Don't you?"

Ashley gave him a shrug. "Sure, why not? He'd love it. But he might have other plans."

Cole frowned. Did she really not get that Ollie liked her?

"Maybe I'll see if Lily wants to check it out after we're done at the shop," Ashley said, rubbing the back of her neck uncomfortably. "I can always text your uncle and we can figure out a way to meet up."

"Yeah," Cole said as he stood on his tippy toes to see if he could catch a hint of activity from the apartment over the garage. How long did it take to get ready to go to a fair?

"Relax," Ashley said. "He'll be down soon. He just had to shower and get dressed."

"Why?" Cole said, now hopping up to see if he could catch a glimpse of movement in the window. "What was wrong with the clothes he was already wearing?"

He noticed his aunt hide a smirk under her hand as she pretended to rub her nose. Clearly she found something funny about what he'd asked, but as far as

Cole could tell, there was nothing wrong with what Uncle Drew was wearing. It was the same outfit he wore the night before.

Cole saw the light change in the window above the garage. Had it just gotten darker? Did that mean…

The door opened on the side of the garage and Sam and Drew came out, each smiling as they walked hand in hand.

"You ready?" Drew said. "I'm tired of waiting on you."

Cole scowled. "I was waiting on you. What took you so long? What was wrong with what you had on?"

"I uh…" Drew's eyes looked toward Sam. "I just grabbed the same clothes I wore last night when I got up. I wanted to get to the store early so people wouldn't be waiting on their breakfast."

"Oh." Cole shrugged. "Makes sense."

Cole noticed his Aunt's hand was back by her mouth. And none of the adults was looking at anyone.

"Let's get a move on," Drew said. "We've got to go to Sam's to pick up her Nana. You met her, right?"

Cole nodded. "She was all right."

"She and I had a lovely conversation last night when she came home early," Drew said. "I thought she was hilarious."

Sam turned beat red as she muttered, "Glad you did."

Ashley was making absolutely no attempt to hide the fact that she was laughing now, convincing Cole he was indeed missing something.

"What's going on?"

Drew just steered him to the back seat of the car. "You're not tall enough to understand. Ask me when you're up to here." He placed his hand on top of Cole's head then brought it up to his chest, only an inch below his neck. "About six years. Maybe less. I've got a feeling you're going to grow like a weed. Now, do you want to stand here and complain or get going?"

Cole got into the car without another word.

Chapter 17
That's Ducked Up

Ashley pushed through the crowd, with both Lily and Ollie struggling to keep up. She wanted to find Cole, see the look on his face for herself, to see him smile for real.

She had been nervous letting Drew take Cole to the fair, worried that Cole would panic around so many strangers. She warned Drew, and he'd promised he would take care.

Drew had sent pictures throughout the day. The first had Cole looking timid, but not terrified. More came, and Cole wore a small grin. It was the ones where Cole had been at the petting zoo, bottle feeding a calf, where Ashley couldn't see any fear in his eyes that had caused her to rush them to the fair.

It was Sam's Nana they spotted first. Rose was looking up at a giant wheel that was slowly lifting and tilting into the air. Upon seeing Ashley, Rose pointed to the wheel. "Your crazy brother and nephew took my equally insane granddaughter on that thing. I think I can hear them scream."

Ashley looked up and spotted Sam, who was screaming as they went up. Drew was grinning on the other side of her and Cole, placed right in between them, was laughing like a little loon. Slowly the wheel of red and yellow cars began to spin. Ashley lost sight

274

of Cole as the ride quickly picked up speed.

Ashley smiled to herself as she imagined Cole squealing in delight and decided she didn't care if the kid had been on every ride already, she was getting a turn with him.

"You couldn't pay me enough to get on that thing," someone said from behind.

Ashley spun to see a woman approach. She looked familiar, but Ashley had trouble placing her. She had long, black hair and wore jeans with a black and white striped blouse.

The woman quickly noticed Ashley's confusion. "I'm sorry." She extended her hand. "We only met briefly at your home after your sister's funeral. I was her counselor."

Ashley nodded and tried to return the smile as she took the woman's hand. "That's right. Kelli mentioned you to me. Diana, right?"

"Yes," Diana said. "Officer Miller asked for a referral from someone in the department and it came to me. I was so sorry to hear what happened. How is Cole holding up?"

Ashley glanced back at the ride where the screams were slowly dying as the ride started to lower itself down. "About as well as can be expected."

Diana came to stand by Ashley's side. "And how is your brother adjusting to being back in town?"

"Fine," Ashley answered. She kept her eye on the ride's exit, desperately needing to see Cole coming out smiling, praying that when he saw her, the smile didn't fade.

"I won't keep you," Diana said. "I'm with my own family and I happened to spot you. I wanted to come over. Here." She pulled out a card. "If there's anything I can do. If you want to talk, or want me to talk to Cole. I've helped children before."

Ashley took the card absently, slipped it into her pocket. "Thank you." Her eyes went back to the exit. A solid mass of people started to come out, breaking into individuals to go their own way. Ashley kept her eye out for Cole.

"Maybe I'll see you guys later," Diana said. "Are you staying for the fireworks?"

Ashley didn't answer. She had no way of knowing how Cole was doing until she saw him with her own eyes.

"I think I see them coming." Ollie pointed toward the exit where the large crowd was starting to disperse.

Ashley spotted Drew first. Being the tallest, he was the easiest to locate. A few feet away was Sam. Bouncing between them was Cole, his face lit up as he laughed and yammered on about the ride they were just on.

"Yeah," Ashley said. "I think we'll be staying for the fireworks."

She wasn't sure if Diana even heard her, and she didn't care. Taking a few steps forward, Ashley sent them a tentative wave.

Drew saw her and smiled. He tapped Cole's shoulder and directed him toward Ashley and the others.

Ashley's eyes met Cole's. She could tell the moment he recognized her. Cole's eye widened, his grin broadened, and he launched himself toward her, skidding to a stop right by her feet.

"Aunt Ash! It was so cool! I've never been on rides

like these. You gotta go. I want to hear you scream." He grabbed her hand. "I'm glad you came. Even Uncle Drew screamed a little. It was cool! Are you here to go on with me? Wait..." He eyed her suspiciously. "You're not here to take me home. Can't I go on a few more rides? *Pleeease!*"

"You don't want to go home?" Ashley said with as straight a face as she could manage. "It *is* getting late." She looked at her watch. "It's going to be dark in a couple of hours."

Cole had grabbed her arm with both hands, pleading with her. "Please, please, *please*. I'll do anything. Just a few more rides."

Ashley grinned, chanced a glance to Drew who was staying back and watching her. "Well, maybe. But there is something else I want to do, so you'll have to go with me to that."

"I will." Cole gave a celebratory grin, but his face turned skeptical. "Wait. Where do you want to go?"

Ashley turned to Diana who was still there, watching the interaction with great interest. "Where and when did you say the fireworks would be?"

Diana smiled. "You'll have to wait, It's going to be at about nine tonight, down by the lake. Probably go for an hour."

Cole gasped. "Fireworks? There's going to be a fireworks show?" He started to jump in place. "Can we watch it?"

"Maybe," Ashley said, grabbing his hand, getting him to stop bouncing. "But first, you've got to go with me on the Thunderstruck ride." She pointed to a big roller coaster to the left of them. It was the biggest of the fair and had three loop de loops."

"Awesome!" Cole did a quick jump in place, grabbed Ashley's hand, and dragged her off.

****

A man sat in a brown car, the engine idling as he sipped cold, bad coffee and waited. He parked the car across the street where the bookshop owner lived, among a long row of cars so he wouldn't stand out. He spent his time using his burner cell to play games, check news reports, and surf for porn.

It was ridiculous to have to sit out here for the last three hours in the hopes of the house being empty. So there was a county fair and maybe the bastard kid might want to go. Hopefully, his uncle would take him, get drunk, and get into a car wreck that would kill them both.

As long as it didn't involve his own kid who was at the fair right now with that bitch of an ex-wife. Not that he'd remembered there had even been a fair today until he got the call this morning, telling him to get his ass to where Duncan stayed. If they could get a bead on everyone in the family, he'd be clear to go in.

He had nearly gone in without the say-so about an hour ago, but just as he'd started down the block, the short chick pulled into the driveway, so he high-tailed it back to the car and waited. Five minutes later the skinny, tall broad followed. They were in there doing whatever, probably getting it on with each other, when that mamma's boy of a cop showed up. Twenty minutes later, they all left together with 'Officer Nancy' driving.

He grabbed the burner and sent a text.

—*The 2 bitches left*

Going in—

He cut the engine and started to get out again when

the cell beeped.

—*R u stupid*
I told u 2 wait til I c them all
I have 2 b able to warn u if they start back
Sit and don't try 2 wink—

Wink? Why the fuck would he wink? Who would he be winking at? That didn't make any sense.

The cell beeped again.

—*Think. Don't think. Ducking auto cucumber.*
Duck—

He laughed. At least that was mildly entertaining.

That had been over a half hour ago, and he had to piss, his back was hurting and he just wanted to just do what he came to do and go home.

If he was going in, he should take the time to plant some evidence that would connect that SOB Duncan with his sister's own murder, but no, that apparently was out of the question. Motherfucker had a rock solid alibi, playing the fucking hero near the Mexico border in California, the chief would know it was a setup, blah, blah, blah.

So instead he was supposed to go in and see if Kelli Duncan accumulated any evidence before her throat was slit.

Taking a sip of his cold, crappy coffee, he remembered sneaking up behind Kelli Duncan, grabbing her from behind. Beforehand, the thought of killing her had been almost repulsive. Roughing her up would have been fine, especially a piece of trash like her. From everything he'd heard, she was used to getting a fist in the face.

If it had been up to him, he would have backhanded her right into the trunk and given her a rough nickel ride past the town limits. He might have even let her buy a ride back with a blowjob since she wasn't too bad to look at. She wasn't a hot piece of ass like her sister, but he'd have been willing to do her a favor.

But the word had been to kill her. Make it clean and quick. He'd enjoyed it, far more than he ever imagined.

Still, in the end it was a major mistake. The whole idea was to stop the bitch from asking too many questions and keep that punk Duncan from coming back to town.

Now they all had blood on their hands, and Duncan was back, asking the questions himself.

So why not off the bastard and make it look like he just up and left again? Apparently, it was fine to kill the girl, but nobody had the balls to take on Duncan, especially when he had that old fool and his company backing him up.

He looked at his watch. It was getting late. It would be dark within the hour. He was wasting his time.

Putting the car into drive, he started to look over his shoulder to see if the way was clear when his phone beeped.

"Crap!" He put the car back into park and picked up the phone, opening up the text app.

—Every 1 @ fair
Go in 2 ck
B careful
Don't duck up—

He scowled as he read the message. "What the hell—" His phone beeped again.

—Don't FUCK up!—

280

With a laugh, he killed the engine and got out of the car. Casually crossing the street, he checked to see if anyone was watching. Satisfied he was in the clear, Kelli Duncan's killer went to break into the home where her son lived.

****

Drew hung back from the next few rides, allowing Ashley and Cole some time together. Lily wasn't interested in some of the faster moving rides. Instead, she talked Nana and Sam into going on the tea cups, dragging Cole along, who acted as if going on such a ride was sheer torture.

Eventually, they stopped to eat. Cole insisted on playing it safe with a hamburger, but at Drew's insistence, Cole tried fried dough for the first time and fell in love with it.

As they finished, Sam and Rose went to find the rest rooms while Ollie mentioned wanting to try some of the stranger fried foods they offered.

As Ollie left the table, a woman ambled up to them with a friendly smile Drew didn't care for instantly. Cole stiffened beside him as she introduced herself as his fourth-grade teacher, Mrs. Collins. She was slightly heavy set, with red hair cut in an unflattering bob style. She wore lime green shorts and a flowered top, with thick rimmed pink glasses that hung around her neck. She continued to wear a grin Drew thought was phony, although he couldn't quite understand why.

"I'm sure you're anxious to go back to school," Mrs. Collins said. "You've been out for nearly two weeks. I'm sure all your friends miss you."

Cole avoided eye contact, concentrating on the half-eaten piece of fried dough on the plate in front of him. "I don't have any friends," he mumbled.

Mrs. Collin's' eyebrows went up as she leaned a little closer. "I'm sorry Cole, what was that?" She said. "You don't have friends? Perhaps that's something you need to work on. You could try being a bit friendlier."

Drew stiffened. His jaw clenched and he was about to say something when Ashley got up.

"Cole is very friendly," Ashley countered. "It's not easy being the new kid in school, especially when you've got a classroom with a bunch of bullies in it."

Mrs. Collins stood straight, her smile still in place and looking more sinister by the moment. "Dear, I'm sure I don't know what you're talking about. I've never observed any bullying in my classroom."

Ashley folded her arms, arched an eyebrow and matched Mrs. Collins' insincere smile with one of her own. "I think maybe you need to keep a better eye on your class, then."

For the briefest of moments, Mrs. Collin's' smile faded, only to be replaced a moment later with one even more disingenuous. "I'm sure you don't mean to say I don't know how to do my job, sweetheart, just as I'm sure you didn't mean to allow Cole to use recent unfortunate events as an excuse to stay home." She reached forward and put a hand on Cole's shoulder, making him flinch. "I know he must have been very sad, but life goes on."

Cole tried to shrug away from her touch as Ashley's fist clenched. She looked ready to come around the table and put her hands on Mrs. Collins when Drew stood up.

"Please don't touch my nephew." Drew's voice was cool, but his eyes were narrow slits.

Mrs. Collins froze, her hand still pressed on Cole's neck. "I'm sorry? Why shouldn't I touch Cole? I'm not hurting him."

"Because," Drew responded, "in case you hadn't noticed, he doesn't like to be touched."

Slowly and warily, as if she were dealing with a growling dog with its hackles raised, Mrs. Collins withdrew her hand and let it drop uselessly to her side. She looked at Drew with an expression that was probably reserved for her most petulant students. "Perhaps part of the problem is Cole needs to understand we don't always get what we like, such as staying out of school for long periods of time because we're feeling a little down. Once he's back in school, he and I can have a conversation about that."

Now it was Drew's turn to smile. "Cole will be returning to school next Monday. I'll be bringing him in myself, early in the morning. We'll discuss things then, with the principal."

Mrs. Collins started to play with her glasses. "It's not your place to speak with the principal. That's a parent's job. Principal Harris is a very busy woman and doesn't have time to…"

"Have her make time," Lily said, speaking up for the first time as she stood as well. "Cole's mother made her wishes very clear and the three of us," She quickly indicated herself, Ashley and Drew, "are now Cole's legal guardians. And we're telling you that Cole isn't going back to class until after we have a meeting with you and the principal. So do whatever you have to do to set it up. Meanwhile, we'd appreciate it if you'll let us get back to family time."

There was an authoritative note of finality in Lily's

words Drew had to admire. For such a short girl who never raised her voice, it was awfully hard to argue with her.

Mrs. Collins must have begrudgingly felt the same way, because with one last, obnoxious smirk, she wandered away from their table, pulling out her cell phone as she sent Drew one last look full of contempt.

Cole looked over his shoulder, stealing a glance at his teacher before turning back to the others who were all sitting back down together. "You guys aren't really all going into school on Monday, are you?"

He was answered with a round of nods, "yeses" and "you bets."

He looked skeptically at his aunt and uncle. "You two are going in there?"

Both Drew and Ashley shared a quick glance. Drew smirked and Ashley rolled her eyes at him before turning to address her nephew. "Cole, your uncle and I may fight like cats and dogs, but we'll both always fight for you."

"That's right," Lily added as she picked up her bottle of water. "And so will I. I'll go to make sure that these two don't go in there like a pair of bulls in a china shop."

Cole's eyebrows drew together as he frowned. "A what in a where?"

"Don't worry about it," Drew said. "Point is, your mom knew what she was doing with the three of us. We've *all* got your back."

Cole didn't know what to make of that and was grateful when Ollie returned with several plates of fried foods, everything from fried Oreo cookies, fried Twinkies, fried watermelon and fried pickles.

"I wanted to try everything." Ollie placed the plates in the middle of the table just as Sam returned with her Nana. "I figured we could all share."

Ashley picked up a fried pickle, which was breaded and sliced thin. "You mean share a ride to the ER together?"

Drew laughed, pulled a fried Twinkie in two, and held it up. "What the hell. We're all in this together." He took a bite, nodded in approval and washed it down with some water. "Bring on the heart attack."

****

"How's your stomach?" Ashley asked Cole, sitting next to him in the backseat.

Cole moaned softly while rubbing his belly. He was in Ollie's car. "I'm okay," he said. He'd tried all the fried treats Ollie brought, enjoyed the fried Oreos most of all and scarfed down nearly a dozen, with a few fried Twinkies and even a little fried watermelon, although he refused to even look at the fried pickles. He'd washed it down with his cherry slushie.

When they passed a ride called the Roundup, Cole had dragged his aunt and uncle onto it.

There were no seats on the Roundup. Instead you were strapped into place while standing as the contraption spun you clockwise, going faster and faster until you were plastered to the back wall of your particular compartment. Cole managed to catch his uncle's eyes and laughed as they both listened to Ashley scream.

He was convinced this was the best thing until the arm started to rise and their speed increased with each inch they rose off the ground. While they spun clockwise, Cole's stomach seemed to spiral counter-clockwise in protest. Uncle Drew started to say something, but Cole couldn't hear the words over the roar of the crowd, his aunt's screams, and the rumble in his belly.

Eventually, the ride stopped spinning and came to a stop. Cole's stomach, however, continued to churn and something tried to escape from his throat.

Hearing his uncle yell, "'Whoa,'" Cole was whisked off the ride at breakneck speed and rushed to a nearby porta-potty wherein the contents of his stomach exploded out.

A cold stab of fear rushed through Cole as his uncle placed a hand on his back, but he was too busy throwing up to protest. When he was done, Ashley cleaned him up while yelling at Ollie for bringing "So much fried junk and putting it front of him." Lily quickly arrived with a few cold bottles of water. The cold liquid from the first bottle helped wash away the awful taste of the formally tasty food from his mouth and the second felt heavenly on his forehead.

That's when the adults started to talk about packing it in for the night, which would mean missing the fireworks, something Cole wasn't willing to give up without a fight.

Insisting he was fine, Cole begged them to find a spot on the lawn and he'd lie still and wait like a good boy for the show to start. After all, what was he going to do once he got home? He'd lie down and relax. He could do that here and still see the fireworks.

Cole believed he'd made a good case and he would have convinced everyone to stay if he hadn't thrown up a second time, this time in a bush and nearly on his uncle's feet.

Next thing he knew, he was being shuffled off to the parking lot. He no longer protested. He couldn't enjoy the fireworks in the sky when there were bigger ones happening inside his gut at that very moment.

Now they were almost home, the storm in Cole's stomach downgraded itself to more of a rainy day. It wasn't bad to deal with, but one wrong turn and someone was going to get wet.

Ollie drove, taking it slow and easy in deference to Cole's upset belly. Ashley insisted on sitting in the back of the car with him and holding his hand and letting Cole lean on her while she stroked his hair, something normally Cole would have protested over, but it was okay for tonight. Lily spent the entire ride spun around in her seat, displaying her smile and reassuring him that he'd feel better in no time and there would be other fairs and more fireworks in the future.

"We'll get you cleaned up and you'll rest and feel better in the morning," Ashley assured him. "All you need is a good night's sleep."

Cole groaned. "I won't be able to sleep. My belly's still all yucky feeling."

Ashley placed her hand on Cole's stomach and gently rubbed in small circles. A sharp stab of panic hit Cole as a dark image pushed against his mind, nearly making him retch again. His breathe quickened and his skin grew clammy. Instinct had Cole pulling away from his aunt.

"I'm really sorry, bud," Ollie said from the front seat. He wasn't able to see Cole jump at the sound of his voice or the sweat forming on his forehead. "I shouldn't have gotten so much junk."

Cole closed his eyes, not wanting to see the pain in

his aunt's eyes.

"Ash," Lily said. "He's sweating. Does he have a fever?"

Cole opened his eyes just as Ashley reached for his head. He couldn't stop the gasp from escaping as he shifted his head, but his aunt wouldn't be deterred. She felt his forehead with her fingers, then flipped her hand and placed her entire palm flat against his skin.

"He's cool as a cucumber," Ashley said. She tried to smile, but she was clearly worried.

Cole tried to force himself to relax, not liking the fact he wanted to jump out of the moving car and run down the street screaming his head off. Wetness stuck in his shirt as the panic continued to build.

"Cole, what's the matter?" Ashley said.

She leaned closer. So much closer. *Why did she have to be so close?*

"What's up?" Ollie said as he slowed down. "Should I pull over?"

Ashley looked toward Ollie, their eyes meeting in the rear view mirror. "Cole's sweating and shaking, but he definitely doesn't have a fever."

"I'm *fine*." Cole's tone was sharp and scared, but he didn't want to stop. He didn't want Ollie to get out from behind the driver's seat and come to check on him.

Lily sent Ashley a concerned look. "Of course you are. And we're all going to take care of you." Her voice was gentle. "We could watch a movie tonight. Would you like that? Y'know what my mother used to give me when my stomach was upset? Ginger tea. It's pretty good. Some of that and a few crackers to nibble on might be good. Would you like Ollie to go to the store after he drops us off and get that stuff? Would that be okay?"

Cole forced himself to nod.

Ollie started to slow the car, pull over to the side and Cole's hand gripped the door frame.

"It's okay Ollie," Ashley said quickly. "Let's get Cole home so he can relax."

"Yes ma'am." Ollie moved the car a little faster. "Hey Cole, would you like to listen to some music? That makes me feel better."

Ollie flipped on the CD player. Skipping around a little, Ollie settled on a fun country song where the singer crooned about how the love of his life had given him an ultimatum: her or fishing. Ollie sang along at the top of his lungs and more than slightly off key, swaying with the rhythm as he drove, making it clear the fish had won. Ashley complained and pressed her hands to her ears and Lily laughed, joining in a key completely off from either the singer or Ollie.

By the time the last notes of the steel pedal guitars reverberated through the car, Cole stopped sweating and even managed a small smile.

****

"Did you see the look in his eyes?" Ashley said to Lily as Cole ran upstairs to get washed and into pajamas. "He was terrified."

Ashley stood at the bottom of the stairs, leaning against the wall and gazing up to where Cole disappeared. Lily stood next to her with her arms folded. In the window behind Ashley the lights from Ollie's truck moved as he backed out of the driveway. He was making a run to the local store to get some ginger tea, saltine crackers, and a few other items for snacking on while they found a movie to entertain Cole until he felt better.

"Yeah," Lily said, keeping her voice low enough so it wouldn't carry upstairs. "I haven't seen him that bad in a while."

Ashley scowled. "You mean since Drew showed up. I know Cole gets nervous around him too, but not like that. I thought we were making progress."

Lily reached out to touch Ashley's arm, ready to say something soothing when Cole sneezed from upstairs three times in succession.

"Great," Ashley said with a roll of her eyes. "He's getting sick for sure."

Lily sighed. "He'll be okay. Kids get sick. You handled it well. Both you and Drew."

"No we didn't," Ashley said. "Sure, we dealt with the puke, but dammit we should have watched what he was eating. I've just gotten so used to Cole just picking at his food that I'm thrilled when he actually eats. But all that fried garbage…" Another sneeze had Ashley starting to climb the stairs. "Damn it. I should be able to go up there right now without worrying about scaring the kid half to death."

Lily placed her hand on Ashley's. "That wasn't you in there. I was watching him. He was okay to lean against you, but it was when you touched his belly his skin went white as a sheet."

Ashley frowned as she recalled the moment Cole tensed. "I thought he was going to jump out of the car."

Lily nodded. "I know. Something triggered a memory. Maybe we need to talk to Cole about seeing someone the way Kelli was."

The fact was they had all taken turns at suggesting

it to Cole when he'd first arrived, but he'd been completely against the idea. Ashley started to wonder if it had been a mistake to make it optional, but she hated the idea of forcing Cole. She herself resisted the idea and got angry whenever someone suggested it. Cole may be a kid, but certainly if he didn't want to spill his guts to some shrink, he shouldn't have to. If it worked for others, fine, but it was ludicrous to think you could force someone to open up their feelings. Unless Cole was ready to talk, he wouldn't get anything from it.

"He's not going to budge on that," Ashley said as she listened to Cole sneeze nearly half a dozen times. "It's not going to do any good if he doesn't want to go and he's made it very clear, he doesn't. We've all talked to him about it. You. Me. Even Kelli before she was killed. Even Ollie and Sam gave it a shot once."

"Maybe we should ask Drew to talk to him?"

Ashley glared at Lily. "Sure, why don't we have big brother do it? Because none of us are able to deal with the kid without him. I would have been fine raising Cole on my own. I love him."

With the same patience one would expect from a teacher dealing with a petulant child, Lily kept her face friendly and her voice calm. "Of course you do. We all love Cole. But Drew seems to have managed to connect with Cole and I know that you want…"

Another sneeze from upstairs, this one so loud it sounded like it hurt. Lily winced while Ashley reached into her pocket for her phone.

"Son of a bitch." Ashley pulled out her phone and stalked to the far corner of the room so she'd be able to raise her voice at least a little bit. "We told him he had to stop smoking."

Midway through the third ring, Drew answered. "Hey Ashley, I'm just getting to Sam's house to drop her off. Do we need anything?"

"Yeah," Ashley snapped, ignoring Lily's urging to calm down. "We need for you to grow a brain and put your nephew first."

There was a moment of silence and Ashley wondered if she'd lost the connection, or if her idiot brother had been stupid enough to hang up on her. "What did I do now?"

Ashley winced as Cole sneezed again from upstairs. "You know damn well what you did, you stupid, selfish son of a bitch! I told you Cole is allergic to the smell of cigarettes!"

"I know that," Drew snapped back. Any trace of patience was gone from his voice. "Maybe he got too close to someone at the fair who was smoking. Or maybe he's just getting sick. I haven't smoked since before I stepped into Lily's house. I quit cold turkey because I won't let anything stand between me and Cole. And you need to accept that. If he started to sneeze on the drive home…"

"No, not on the way home," Ashley said, cutting Drew off. "He started to sneeze like mad the moment he went upstairs. Why is that?"

There was a moment of silence and Ashley sent Lily a smug smile.

"Am I on speaker?" Drew said.

Ashley rolled her eyes. "What difference does that…"

"Take me off," Drew ordered. There was a high-pitched sound in the background from Drew's side of the phone that Ashley couldn't identify. "Now."

With a sigh, Ashley deactivated the speaker function and put the phone to her ear. "Afraid Cole will hear how you fucked up?"

"Listen to me very carefully," Drew's tone was angry and yet controlled. "Is Ollie still there?"

"What?" Ashley shook her head in confusion. "No, he's at the store getting…"

"Ashley," Drew cut in. "Stay calm, but get Cole and Lily out of that house."

Ashley blinked, the anger from her eyes pushed out by confusion "What are you…"

"Ashley." Drew kept his voice calm, yet firm. "You're not alone in that house."

Chapter 18
Don't Step on the Flowers

"Ashley, are you hearing what I'm saying?"

At first, Ashley stood in place, nodding as if her brother could see her from the other side of the phone. Her eyes slowly glanced up to study the ceiling, but it looked like the same ceiling as always.

"Ashley!" Drew's voice was angry with a tinge of terror mixed in.

"Yeah…" Ashley responded. "Um…I don't think that…"

"Ashley, don't repeat what I'm saying out loud," Drew said. "Maybe I'm wrong, but I haven't smoked once in that house so you need to trust me. If there's someone there, they haven't made a move yet. Is Cole and Lily with you?"

"Cole's upstairs," Ashley said, her words coming out a little slower than she normally spoke. She headed toward the stairs slowly, nearly tiptoeing the entire way. "Here, tell Lily what you told me. I've got to make sure the kid brushes his teeth." Handing the phone to Lily, she started up the stairs. She ignored Lily's "uh huhs" and her gasp when Drew explained his suspicions.

Lily started to come up, when Ashley waved her away. They didn't both need to go upstairs.

The floor from upstairs creaked and Ashley's eyes were drawn to the source. It was the ceiling over the living room. Whatever made that noise, it sounded big, too big to be a little eight-year-old boy.

"Cole, sweetie, are you okay?"

There was a flush from the upstairs bathroom, which had Ashley trying to determine if the noise she'd just heard could have been from Cole, but they seemed several feet away from each other.

Different rooms. It was an old house. It makes noise, it could just be settling. It still might be nothing.

Please, let it be nothing.

Ashley slowly climbed the stairs as quietly as possible. Lily was by her side in an instant. "Are you feeling any better?"

She was answered with silence finding the bathroom door closed, but the light on. The sound of running water reached their ears as they stepped onto the top of the landing. "Cole?"

The water stopped and the light turned off. Ashley held her breath and reached for the door. If there was someone here hurting Cole, she didn't care what kind of weapon they had. She'd rip them to pieces.

Just as Ashley's hand was about the grasp the handle, the bathroom door swung open.

Cole blinked in surprise, seeing both Ashley and Lily. Standing in his Spiderman pajamas, he sneezed three times in rapid succession and wiped his nose with his sleeve. "I think I'm feeling a little better." Cole said as he stepped out of the bathroom. "My mouth tasted bad so I brushed my teeth, but now I want a new toothbrush. I know it's too late to go back to the fair for the fireworks, but I don't want to go to bed. Can we watch a movie or..." Another two sneezes, "Something?"

Ashley forced herself to smile, holding her hand out to Cole. Another creak echoed from the left, and she glanced in its direction. Cole's door was ajar.

"Anything you want," Ashley said. "Let's go down and see what movies are available."

Cole started to move toward Ashley, then stopped and turned around, heading back into the bathroom. He flipped on the lights and sneezed yet again as he looked down at the pile of clothes on the floor. "Sorry, Lily," he said as he bent down to get them. "I'll put them in my hamper."

"Just leave them, sweetie," Lily said as she moved up to the landing next to Ashley. "We'll get them later."

"I'll forget later and you'll get upset. Just give me…" Cole's eyes glanced down the hall at his bedroom door and froze. He squinted his eyes.

Ashley and Lily followed his gaze. There was a shadow in the space where his bedroom door was open, which moved and looked like someone staring out at them.

Not waiting any longer, Ashley and Lily reached out, each grabbing one of Cole's hands, forcing him to drop his clothes, and pulled him toward them. As they did, Cole's bedroom door slammed shut.

Cole screamed as they rushed him down the stairs. The sound of tires squealing filled the living room as they crossed to the front door. Drew and Sam burst in, each with a weapon in their hand.

"Are you all right?" Drew said.

Lily and Ashley started to both talk at the same time, screaming about seeing someone, and grabbing Cole to run. They stopped at the sound of heavy footfalls from someone running upstairs, followed by something crashing to the floor.

Drew pointed to Sam. "Stay with them," he ordered and ran upstairs. He didn't slow down when Sam started to yell at him that she was the cop.

Ashley yelled out to her brother to kill the bastard, just before Drew disappeared.

****

Racing to the top of the stairs as silently as possible, Drew came in low and swept the hallway, his Glock gripped tightly in both hands. He checked the bathroom first since it was the closest, but wasn't surprised to find it empty. That left the bedrooms.

Right or left? Front or back of the house?

Before Drew could move, something crashed from down the hall to the rear.

Ashley's room!

Drew smashed into the back bedroom and scanned the room. Ashley's flat-screen TV had crashed to the floor, knocked over as somebody rushed to the open window.

Drew rushed to the window and spotted a figure of a man as he rushed across the back lawn. The intruder, and Drew was sure it was a man, was wearing something over his face and dressed in black, Caucasian, fit, and stood close to six feet tall. He wore black sweat pants, a dark shirt and his right hand gripped a silver gun that he aimed at the house.

Drew withdrew from the window and hugged the wall as two shots were fired; the first one hit the window, sending shards of glass exploding onto the bedroom floor. The second shot hit the mirror that stood on a dresser against the wall opposite Drew. The image of his reflection shattering had him chained to the wall.

A picture on the dresser of Ashley with both Kelli and Cole when they'd first moved in was knocked to the hardwood floor, the glass frame breaking.

With his heart pounding in his chest, Drew tightened his grip on his weapon, took one solid breath and moved back to the window. He lowered himself onto one knee to give the shooter less of a target and scanned for him, ready to shoot.

Where was he? He couldn't have disappeared that quickly.

Drew's eyes scanned the back yard. There was a trail of trampled flowers leading to the back fence which could easily have been scaled. Those few moments Drew pulled back had given him the chance to get out of the yard. Whoever was in that house could be serious trouble.

Drew pushed himself through the window and ran down the sloped roof. Once on the edge, he was low enough to jump into the grass. He followed where the intruder landed and aimed toward the right to avoid destroying any evidence. He landed with a roll and came up with his gun at the ready.

Launching himself toward the back, Drew knew he'd catch hell from Lily for each and every flower he trampled as he made his way to the fence. The wooden enclosure was only chest high and the yard was empty, so he leapt on the fence.

The wood was old, cracked, and an entire section broke and fell forward as he tried to climb over, making an awful racket and announcing his presence. His fingers smashed into the rocked bottom of the fence, scraping the skin off his knuckles.

"Drew!"

Sam burst from the back door, gun drawn and closing the distance as Drew struggled to get up. He ignored her as she checked to make sure he wasn't hurt.

"Ollie's with Cole and the others," Sam said before he could ask. "It's been called in."

Drew nodded. "Bastard took a couple of shots at me before making it over the fence, which he managed to do without breaking it like I did." He moved carefully into the yard of the house directly behind Lily's. He swept the yard to the left, Sam to the right.

The grass was much taller here, reaching as high as their knees. There were large piles of brown leaves scattered about, while several pieces of junk littered the yard. The house's dark paint was peeling and there were no lights. The yard was large and speared out toward both sides of the house. The gate on the right side was swinging open. Drew took off with Sam on his tail.

As they reached the front, the sound of sirens started to fill the crisp night air. The lights to a home across the street turned on and an elderly woman came out to investigate the noise, holding a small yapping dog under one arm.

Seeing the alarm in her eyes, Sam shoved her gun into her pocket and pulled out her shield. "Police, ma'am. Did you see anyone come out from the back yard before us?"

The woman shook her head as she used her free hand to try and calm down the little ball of fur that was letting out high pitched barks. "I heard bangs. Thought some kid had set off fireworks and came out to give them a talking to. There was some foul language, but when I opened the door, I didn't see anything at first until you came running out." She took a small step forward, scowled as she jutted her chin at Drew's direction. "He's no cop. I never forget a face. I remember him from a few years ago. You better not try anything with me. I've called the police. You're not them."

Drew, who had been looking for any sign of which direction the intruder had gone, turned toward the old lady. With a sigh, he dropped his own gun to his side. "No, ma'am. I'm working with them."

The woman's eyes narrowed as she clutched her little dog tighter. "Go away or I'm going to call the police." The Chihuahua barked at Drew and the woman scratched its head, sending Drew a scathing look before she disappeared back into her house.

"I thought you already said you did," Drew muttered under his breath as he shoved his weapon into the back of his jeans and scowled at the house.

Sam turned toward Drew. She placed her hand on his arm. "Forget about her. Are you okay?"

Pulling away, Drew's hand went to his front pocket to pull out a pack of cigarettes that weren't there. He cursed, remembering that he didn't smoke anymore. "No, I'm not okay. Half this town looks at me like I got away with murder. Meanwhile, that piece of shit was in the house. He was in my sister's room."

He started to walk toward the house, with Sam following. He made his way toward the same gate they'd come through on their way out here. "God knows *how* close he came to Cole. I came back to this town to keep him safe and I can't even do that right."

He kicked the gate on the house open and watched with no small amount of satisfaction as it separated from its hinges and fell to the ground. "Now I'll probably get sued by the homeowners."

Sam looked up at the house, with its cracked windows and missing shutters. "Relax. I'm pretty sure nobody lives here."

Drew laughed to himself. "Sounds like a good idea."

"What is?"

Drew gave the old house a hard look. "Not living here. I should pack up Cole and my sister and move them out of this town. Anywhere has to be better than here." He headed back through the yard, not looking back as Sam stood by the gate.

****

Upon arriving back into Lily's yard, Drew was greeted by Ollie and two uniformed officers, all of whom had their weapons drawn and raised toward him. As Drew came to a stop and raised his hands, Ollie recognized him and motioned for the other cops to lower their weapons.

"He's Ashley's brother," Ollie said. "Not the intruder. Drew, where's…Oh, there she is."

Ollie's eyes looked over Drew's shoulder to see Sam running toward them, both hands up, her shield displayed in one. "Where's Nana? She stayed in the car when we pulled up."

Ollie jabbed his thumb toward the house. "She came in when the second squad car arrived. There are two uniforms inside with everyone. McKinley and Brown. Good guys."

"God, your poor grandmother," Drew said, closing his eyes and shaking his head. "She must be terrified, I completely forgot…"

"I'm sure she understands." Sam started toward the house. "I'm going to go check on her."

Before Drew had a chance to say anything else, Ollie was pressing him for details. Drew quickly explained what happened, giving the best description he could of the intruder. Ollie listened intently before turning to the two men with him, ordering them to get the word out and have patrols in the area keep an eye out for anyone who might fit the description.

As the two officers headed around the side of the house toward the front, Ollie looked Drew up and down, taking note of his dirty jeans and bloody fingers. "You okay? You need medical attention?"

Drew looked down at his fingers, noticing the blood for the first time. "I'm fine. Happened when I tried to get over the fence and it collapsed."

Ollie smirked. "Really? Now who's the fat ass?"

Drew shoved a bloody finger toward Ollie's face as his own flushed red. "You think this is fucking funny? That son of a bitch was in the house near Cole, Ashley and Lily! He fucking tried to shoot my head off and all you can do is yuk it up, Deputy-Do-Right?"

Ollie took a step back, holding up his hands. "Whoa. I'm sorry. I promise you, I'm not taking this lightly. When I got the text from Sam I swear I thought my heart was going to explode from my chest. I dropped my basket in the middle of the dairy aisle in the twenty-four-hour mart and broke every speed record on the way here."

Drew dropped his hand and stalked away, cursing himself. He'd been under fire dozens of times. Why was he terrified now?

Slowly, Ollie approached his side. "You all right?"

Drew shook his head. "No, I'm not. I'm scared down to my bones, Ollie. And I'm sorry. I fell right back into taking it out on you."

Ollie ran his hand over his head. "Yeah, well. I probably deserved it this time. Look, I know you're scared of something happening to them. So am I. I already told Ashley I'm spending the night on the sofa."

The two men stood side by side for a few moments, looking out at the yard where the intruder escaped. How long they stood like this, Drew wondered. Both men wanted to be there for Ashley for entirely different reasons. Back when they were kids, Drew should have been happy Ashley had a kid like Ollie hanging around. He was so much of what Drew wasn't. While Drew had gone wild in high school, getting drunk and screwing around, Ollie had been the nice guy who always stood by Ashley no matter how horrible things had gotten, and he'd caught hell for it from Drew.

The amazing thing to Drew was that after years of abuse, he seemed not only willing to put it all behind them, but eager to be friends, which just made him feel even shittier.

"We should go in," Drew said finally. "I'm sure you've got reports to file and Cole must be terrified."

Ollie nodded. "He's a tough kid. He'll be all right. We'll make sure of it. It's really you I'm worried about."

Drew's face grew hot. Did Ollie realize how terrified he'd been earlier that night? Drew thought the one thing he had going for him was the tough guy act, but maybe Ollie had seen right through it.

Smiling, Ollie gestured to the crushed chrysanthemums by the collapsed fence. "Once Lily calms down, she's gonna have your head for crushing her flowers."

Sliding a glance from the destroyed perennials to Ollie, Drew shook his head and laughed. The sad part was Ollie was probably right.

Chapter 19
Don't Forget About Me

When Sam's cell rang, she picked it up. Drew's name appeared on the display. She hesitated a moment, before hitting the decline button and placing the phone in her back pocket, then opened the dishwasher to start emptying it.

"Is there a reason you're avoiding his phone calls?" Rose said as she came into the kitchen.

Sam hesitated, looking closely at the small mug and noticing it still had coffee stains inside. She placed it back in the rack and reached for another, seeing the same thing. "What makes you think I'm avoiding him?"

Rose made her way over to the fresh pot of coffee and poured herself a cup. "Maybe it was the look on your face when you looked at your phone. You started to smile, and then you looked like you were going to cry."

Sam rolled her eyes. "Don't be silly, Nana."

Rose shrugged as she poured a second cup, picked them both up and started to carry them to the kitchen table. "Or it could be because of the fact that after everything that happened last night, you're still here and not with him. You haven't even called to see if his family is all right."

Sam held a plate in her hand, noticing the splotch of gravy on it. She avoided answering her grandmother at first by washing it with a sponge and replacing it in the dishwasher. The fact was, she did feel guilty about not calling Drew this morning. She'd seen the look of terror on Cole's face last night as she'd come into the room. Everyone had done their best to comfort the boy, but he wanted Drew, although he was being stubborn and refused to ask for his uncle.

"He's got enough on his plate today." Sam picked up the silverware basket and noticed there were bits and smears of food on those as well.

Nana sat at the table, placing her cup down and a second one on the placemat across the table. "Or maybe it's because you haven't realized that nobody ran that dishwasher yet."

Sam's back stiffened as she examined a piggy plate with a smear of bacon grease on it. The memory of her loading the dishwasher last night because she couldn't sleep came back to her, but she hadn't run it because it was noisy and she didn't want to keep Nana up. Her shoulders slumped in defeat.

"Fine." Sam stomped over to the table and sitting down roughly. "I'm a horrible person. I don't want to talk to Drew. There, I said it. Okay?"

Rose smiled as her granddaughter buried her head in her hands. "I'm not going to tell you what to do. I know men can be a handful. And I got a good look at how much of a handful Drew was the other night when I found you two in my guest room."

"Nana!" Sam's face started to burn as she lifted her head and stared at her grandmother in horror. "Please, that was embarrassing enough!"

Rose giggled as she sipped her coffee. "I'm sorry dear, but I just want to see you happy. And that's what I saw last night at the fair. You were happy. Not as happy as the night before, but still happy."

Sam picked up the coffee cup, more for something to hide her face behind. She gulped some to wash down the mortification she was feeling right about now.

"What happened," Rose asked, the playful teasing no longer in her voice. "Was it because he was nearly killed?"

Sam stared down at her cup, tracing the edge of it with her finger. The idea of losing Drew terrified her, but that's not the reason she wasn't talking to him.

"No, that's not why." Sam explained what Drew said last night after the intruder escaped. "Drew wants to leave Ember Falls and take his sister and Cole with him. I can't really blame him. His childhood in this town was a nightmare, and he came back because his sister was murdered, but I thought he and I might be starting something here, something that was worth fighting for. He'd leave that in an instant if he could just convince his sister and nephew to move with him."

Rose reached out across the table to take her granddaughter's hand. "I suppose that after last night, Ashley might consider it. Is that what has you worried?"

Sam sighed. "No. It's the fact Drew doesn't want to be here. He'll stay for his sister. He'll stay for his nephew, but he won't stay for me." She walked to the window, looked out at the yard, and watched a pair of birds pecking around on the grass. With blue feathers on their backs and wings, their bellies were white with a touch of bright orange. They both bounced around each other for a few moments, until the darker one flew off, leaving the other one behind.

"He and Ashley still fight all the time," Sam said. "You should have heard her last night when he walked in. She was so upset that whoever it was got away, she was blaming Drew, saying how he couldn't even get that right."

Rose leaned back in her chair. "She was upset. Before he came back, she was pacing back and forth, worried sick over Drew. I heard her say to Lily how she couldn't stand to lose Drew now that she finally got him back. Of course, she also threatened to kill Lily if she ever told Drew that."

Despite herself, Sam laughed a little. "Yeah, she's good at hiding how glad she is that Drew is back. So good, I'm afraid she's going to convince him to get out once we catch whoever killed his sister."

Rose made a shooing motion with one hand. "Nonsense. Drew isn't going to leave his sister and he's certainly not about to leave Cole. You saw them yesterday. He adores that child. His face lit up whenever Cole laughed."

Sam smiled at the memory of Drew watching Cole with the animals. It was the first time the boy really laughed and seemed like a kid his own age.

"I know," Sam said. "It just hurt to hear him say that last night. I just…" She shook her head and turned around again to face the window. "Am I being nuts? Am I making too much out of this?"

Sam felt her grandmother's arm slide around her waist. "As a matter of fact, yes."

Sam's eyes widened in shock, but she couldn't muster any anger at her grandmother's bluntness. Nana wasn't one to pull punches.

"Sweetie, Drew was terrified for his family. He's

probably doubting his ability to keep them safe. I don't blame him. As much as he loved his sisters when he was young, I think he loves that little boy even more. And he probably blames himself for Kelli's death."

Sam sighed, knowing it was true. "I wish he wouldn't."

"Yes well." Rose went to the table and picked up her coffee mug. "I wish you wouldn't feel so worried about me that you felt as if you were anchored here in Ember Falls." She carried it over to the sink.

"I'm a big girl." Rose retrieved her keys from the counter. "I can take care of myself. I don't want you to think that I don't love you living here with me. I do. Although there are times you do cramp my style, like the other night."

"Nana," Sam whined.

"Hush," Rose said with a pointed finger. "Maybe Drew just had a moment of panic. Maybe he really does want out of Ember Falls. Like you said, who could blame him? But have you ever thought that maybe if he decided to leave, he'd want to take you with him?"

As her grandmother started to head for the front door, Sam stood rooted to the same spot in the kitchen, blinking rapidly. When she heard the front door open, she ran to catch up with her grandmother before she left.

"What? Go *with* him? Leave Ember Falls? But, we've only known each other... I can't imagine... I couldn't leave you and—"

"Stop." Rose held up a hand like a crossing guard halting traffic and gave her that no nonsense look that had Sam stopping in her tracks and closing her mouth. "I hate to be the one to tell you, but you're in love with

Drew Duncan and he's in love with you. So go take a shower, get dressed and go to see him. Work it out. Find out where his head is at. He's what you want, so go fight for it. Or don't." Rose gave a casual shrug. "But don't use me as an excuse. Now, I've got to go meet some friends at the Adirondack Diner. I'll be back soon and I expect you to be gone. Help yourself to more condoms before you go."

Before Sam could think of anything to say, her grandmother was gone, leaving her alone with nobody to argue with but herself.

****

The police had spent three hours going through the house, finding nothing of use and making a mess in the process. It was nearly eleven by the time they left, and Lily, who seemed more upset over the mess than she was over the intruder, had gone to work cleaning.

She sent Drew and Ollie to work in Ashley's room, getting rid of the glass and shards of shattered mirror. As the pair worked, Cole stood by the doorway, wanting to be close to Drew, but remaining silent.

The same could not be said for Ashley, who continued to bitch at her brother, asking how he could have missed. Ollie pointed out that since Drew hadn't returned fire, he technically hadn't missed. That didn't seem to placate Ashley at all. It wasn't until Ollie handed her the ruined picture frame that she stopped taking swipes at her brother. The shard of glass had put a scratch down the center of the picture, right through the image of Kelli. She excused herself, wiping at her cheeks.

Lily insisted on doing the vacuuming herself, but had Ollie and Drew move the furniture so she could make sure she got each and every nook and cranny. They took Ashley's bed apart last, standing the mattress up. When they did, Ollie inhaled deeply through his nose.

"Are you sniffing Ashley's bed?" Drew said in a hushed voice.

Ollie shrugged. "It smells like her perfume. Cherry Blossoms."

Drew snickered and Ollie's face burned red.

By the time Lily was satisfied they had done enough for the night, it was nearly one in the morning. They put Cole to bed, but he was up fifteen minutes later, complaining his stomach was once again hurting. He stood on the landing to the stairs in his Spiderman pajamas, pressing a hand to his stomach for effect. Nobody believed him, but since nobody else felt like sleeping, they brought him downstairs.

Everyone spent the night in the living room. Cole ended up on the couch, his eyes glued on Drew and leaning on Ashley. He'd asked her to rub his belly like she had in the car while listening to Lily tell a story about his mother from when the two of them had first become friends. One by one, they'd all fallen asleep where they sat or lay. Drew was the only one who hadn't nodded off.

When Cole woke at six-fifteen, he had a panicked look in his eyes, feeling his aunt's arm on him, but he'd calmed down as he saw Drew was still awake. No words were spoken as he settled back down and fell back to sleep.

They were all up by eight, each with sore muscles and necks, but nobody complained. Lily enlisted Cole's help to make breakfast for everyone while the others began to make phone calls.

Ashley was on the phone with an alarm company, then with a local handyman they'd used before.

Ollie called his mother, then the station. He talked in hushed tones, looking toward Drew as he listened.

Drew called Sam, but got her voicemail. Leaving a message, he spoke with McAlister Security, making arrangements for security to come to Ember Falls. He'd spoken at length with the General, who promised he'd be on the plane with some men that afternoon. He thought about trying Sam again each time he was off the phone, but decided that was just a little too pathetic. Still, he needed to hear her voice.

Lily prepared French toast, with powdered sugar, plenty of coffee, bacon, eggs, and fruit.

Nobody ate much, except Ollie, who cleared his plate, took seconds and made sure to finish off the bacon, saying it was a sin not to.

Throughout breakfast while they watched Ollie eat, the phone kept ringing. The police called to speak to Lily as the homeowner. The moment she hung up, it rang again. They fielded calls from the insurance company, the bookstore, Ashley's boyfriends, a few friends of Lily's who heard what happened and called to offer their support, the police department again, and the handyman.

When the phone finally went quiet, the doorbell rang.

Cole hadn't realized he was holding his breath until Drew told him to relax. "If they come back, I doubt they'll ring the doorbell."

It was a pair of officers assigned to patrol the area. They stopped in to see how things were and both Ollie and Drew went to speak with them. As they spoke, the doorbell sounded again. This time it was the handyman. Ashley greeted him and called Lily over, but she was interrupted by the phone ringing again.

"Hello," she answered. "Oh, hi. Yes, thank you. I'm afraid you called at a bad time." She paused as Ashley yelled for her from upstairs. "What?" She said, clearly distracted. "Oh sure. He's right here, hold on."

She turned and held out the phone to Cole who blinked in surprise. "It's for you," Lily said. "It's someone from your old school, Mr. Mongello."

Cole accepted the phone. "He was the principal."

Lily ran upstairs as Ashley yelled for her again.

Taking the phone into the kitchen, Cole raised the phone to his ear. "Hello, Mr. Mongello. Thank you for the flowers you sent."

"Well hello, Cole," said a voice Cole recognized immediately. All the air was sucked out of the room as Cole started to shake and sweat. A warm wetness spread across his crotch area as he lost control of his bladder. "I heard about your mom. Such a pity."

Cole tried to move, tried to call out to his uncle, but it was as if he'd been pulled out of his world and into an alternate dimension. He could vaguely make out the voices of his uncle and Ollie talking to the two officers in the living room, but couldn't make out a single word they were saying. The handyman with his Aunt and Lily walked above him, but even though they were only one floor up, he might have been on the other side of the country. Urine dripped down his leg, but had no ability to stop it.

Memories of cheap whiskey and a basement kept extra chilly flooded Cole's mind. The beat of Cole's heart slammed in his chest, and his pulse pounded in his ear like their old water heater. He was back in that cold room with the man who still haunted his nightmares. Cole closed his eyes to memories of what he'd seen in that cellar.

"You still there Cole?" His stepfather said. "I'll assume you are. I can hear you whimper. Now I want you to listen up. You remember that deal we made? About how you'd keep your mouth shut? I know you do, and I know you remember what I promised you I'd do. Don't you?"

There was a pause as the memory of that promise came flooding back into Cole's head, the images he'd seen that night rose to the surface of his mind and Cole's breakfast nearly came up as well.

"Don't you!"

The shout had Cole moving, away from where anyone might see him. He found himself in the laundry room and collapsed to the floor, pulling his knees up to his chest, but kept the phone to his ear.

"I'll take your whimpering as a yes. Let me get to the point of my call. It occurred to me that you might think since some rank amateur slit your mother's throat that you might now believe the original deal is no longer in place. After all, I can't hurt *her* anymore. I'm sure I don't have to remind you what I would have done. You know full well, don't you?"

Cole didn't answer with more than a nod, something his stepfather couldn't see, but Cole was convinced Edward Hunter was right there, inches from his face.

"I'm sure you do," Edward said with a snicker. "My secret remains *my* secret. If I find out you talked to anyone, and I'll know because I *always* know, then I'll come to my old home town myself. You're living with your aunt now, aren't you? And that short little piece of ass, Lily. And then there's what I'll do to you. After I make you watch. Of course, maybe you'd liked that? You want me to come to town and give you a little reminder of what I can do?"

Cole shook his head, feeling as if he were chained up.

"How about this, Cole?" Edward said. "Why don't you go on with your cozy little life there in Ember Falls? You stick with your Aunt and her gal pal. I even heard your uncle is back. You stay with them and keep your mouth shut, and I'll leave you and your new little family alone. You talk?" There was silence for a moment, where Cole pictured Edward's sadistic smile. The silence was broken by a low, cruel laugh right before the line went dead.

With trembling hands, he shut the phone and tried to remember how to breathe. When the buzzer for the drier went off, he nearly screamed.

****

"So earlier when I was on the phone with my mom," Ollie looked around to make sure nobody was in earshot. "She told me McAlister Security is bringing equipment that will be able to tell if there are bodies underground. You really think they're going to find more bodies?"

Drew nodded. "Yeah, I do. I told you, there were those scratches on the wall. That old pack of cigarettes. You went and looked under those rocks and found a small box with plastic bags of keys, right?"

"Yeah, shush," Ollie said. "Only a few people

know about that right now. We're still trying to identify exactly what those keys go to. We're thinking padlocks, like the ones you'd use on a chain, but we're not sure yet. Old fashioned ones, maybe? And I know what you're thinking, but I think we would have noticed if other women had gone missing."

Drew remembered the scratches on the wall. None of them looked new to Drew. Would Kelli have been the start of a new block of five? "When you were there, did you sit on that rock? The one by the cigarettes?"

Ollie shook his head. "No, why would I?"

Drew kept an eye out for Cole, expecting him to pop out at any moment. The kid hadn't wanted to be left alone since last night. Maybe he was up with Ashley.

"I did." Drew recalled the memory. "It was the perfect spot to sit, have a smoke and just gaze out on that area of ground. Somebody kept going back. There's something there. It's a gut feeling."

Ollie didn't look convinced. "I just don't know if I'm buying that. Look, I believe in instinct, but if we're dealing with a serial killer, wouldn't we have noticed? People would have reported missing women."

Drew shook his head. "Not if the victims were people nobody ever misses, like prostitutes, homeless people, transients. Ember Falls isn't far from Albany or other places where people like that are more common."

Ollie considered it, frowning. "But Kelli doesn't fit that profile. It's a *small* town. People knew she was home. The fact she was your sister *made* people talk. And I happen to know she was asking people about your case. She even went to the hospital."

"Really?" Drew folded his arms and tried to picture

his timid sister asking questions. "I didn't know that."

Ollie nodded. "I think she thought if she could prove you were innocent, you'd be more likely to come back. She thought that was the only reason you stayed away." He held up his hand to halt Drew's protest. "Hey, I know you would have come back the moment she asked, but she didn't. Plus, I think she wanted to do that for you. Besides, if it was some psycho who likes killing women, why come here and not hurt anyone while he was alone with them? He could have taken them all out. I know you know that because it scares the hell out of you like it does me. So if it is a serial killer, how is the break-in connected?"

Drew shook his head and sat on the couch. "I don't know. That part doesn't make sense. We've been over the house and nothing was taken, at least as far as I could see. You know, if we'd found something in that box like hair or clothing or something, I'd think maybe the killer was breaking in to get his keepsake, and maybe blitz killing two women and a kid doesn't fit his ritual, but I doubt Kelli had any keys like the ones you're talking about. They were all the same?"

Ollie nodded. He held his fingers out about an inch apart. "Smaller than a door key, steel, not bronze, and with those little loops on the end. And the rod part was hollowed. They're strange little keys. Kind of like the ones you'd expect to see enchanted and flying around a room to protect a stone that helped you live forever, but without the wings."

Drew stared up at him, with a wide-eyed, open mouth which clearly said, "What the hell are you talking about?"

Ollie shrugged. "You know...the scene where

Harry had to get on a broom…yeah, I'm still a nerd."

Taking out his cell phone, Drew looked up pictures of old padlock keys, bringing up images of heavy-duty locks, with small keys that matched the description Ollie had given. They didn't have the teeth normal keys had, but a single tooth at the bottom. The end where you held the key was a circle. He held up the cell phone to Ollie. "Like this?"

Ollie scanned the picture, nodded. "Very close. You'll see it yourself, but that's close."

As Drew closed the image and put his cell back in his pocket, he heard banging from upstairs. Drew jumped up from the couch.

"Relax," Ollie said. "It's just the handyman."

"Sorry, I'm jumpy." Drew looked around, wondering if Cole had the same reaction. Where was the kid? Hadn't he last seen him go into the kitchen with the phone in his hand?

"Cole," Drew called. He waited a beat and called his name again. The only answer was more banging from upstairs. He turned to Ollie. "You see him come out of the kitchen?"

Ollie shook his head. "Maybe he went up the back stairs."

Drew walked to the kitchen, not finding Cole there, and went to the window and looked out to the back yard, although he doubted Cole would go outside after last night. In fact, Cole had barely left his sight since.

Drew walked back over to the stairs, opened his mouth to call up and was interrupted by more banging. When this round ended, he yelled up for his sister.

Ashley came running to the top of the stairs. "What? Did they catch the bastard?"

Drew shook his head. "Is Cole up there?"

Ashley frowned and called for their nephew. They both waited a moment, but there was still no answer. "Hold on."

His heart beat faster as he waited for Ashley to find him.

"I don't see him! Lily!"

Ashley thundered down the stairs, Lily on her tail. "He's not up there in the bedrooms or bathrooms."

Ollie came running up to her. "I checked downstairs in the cellar and the bathroom down here. Nothing."

"Oh God, where could he…"

"Ashley, get in here!" Drew called from somewhere in the kitchen.

Ashley pushed past Ollie and ran to find her brother. The kitchen was empty, but her brother was in the laundry room.

Drew knelt on one knee. He held the portable house phone in his hand. "This was on the floor."

"The principal from his old school called," Lily said. "It was just as the handyman arrived, so I handed Cole the phone."

Drew scowled and handed the phone to Ollie. "We need to know who called here. Look here." Drew pointed to the floor." There was a drip of a light, yellowish liquid. Drew touched his finger to it and sniffed. "Urine."

Ashley blinked in confusion. "I don't understand."

Drew spotted a basket of dirty clothes was on the floor. Normally, the baskets of laundry waiting for the wash were left on a nearby table. Drew reached over and grabbed the set of Spiderman pajamas that was on top. "Aren't these the ones Cole was wearing? Does he have more than one pair of these?"

Ashley shook her head. "No, just the one."

Drew felt the pajamas, felt the wetness, sniffed them. "They're soaked. I don't know who that was on the phone, but it wasn't his ex-principal and whoever it was, scared the piss out of him."

He pushed past Ashley who was shaking, tears rolling down her cheeks. "Trace that phone call," Drew said to Ollie as he raced upstairs. He skidded to a stop at the foot of Cole's bed and reached underneath.

Ashley was by his side within seconds. "What are you looking for?"

Drew looked under the bed to make sure he hadn't missed it, and then he looked up at his sister. "Cole's backpack. He kept one there, hidden with money in case he got so scared he needed to run."

Getting up, Drew pulled out his own cell phone and dialed Cole's phone. It went straight to a voicemail that wasn't set up. Drew ended the call and made another one, this one to McAlister Security.

"John, this in Drew Duncan. ID number seventeen-oh-one. You know that phone we got my nephew? Can you activate it if it's off?" Drew listened, his eyes locked on his sister. He shook his head. "Yeah, he's gone missing, but I think he took the phone. Get it locked in so if he turns it on we can get a location. Be ready to listen in, but don't signal him. Just let me know."

Ashley started to pace back and forth as Drew finished up on the phone. She jumped when the doorbell rang.

Chapter 20
The Wheels on the Bus

Cole had run out through the yard, through the broken fence in the back. Uncle Drew had placed it back up and in place, but hadn't secured it, allowing Cole to slip through easily. Within a few moments, he passed the large, empty house behind Lily's and down the block.

He looked over his shoulder every few seconds as he rushed, nearly tripping two or three times. Wearing a pair of jeans from the laundry, a t-shirt that had a small tomato sauce stain on it, and his backpack. He didn't slow down until he realized he had no idea where he was. A trail veered off into a wooded area, and Cole followed it.

Edward Hunter knew where he lived.

He'd never be safe and neither would anyone who lived there. They didn't know what kind of monster Edward was.

As the image of his former stepfather filtered into his mind, Cole's knees buckled. Tears streamed down his face as he sobbed. Hugging his knees to his chest, he started to rock back and forth in place.

Cole couldn't let anything happen to Aunt Ash, or Lily, or even his Uncle. Uncle Drew was tough. He'd been a Marine, fought in a war and faced bad guys with guns and everything.

But none of the people his uncle fought were like the monster he and his mother lived with. As much as his mom feared Edward, even she never understood.

Only Cole knew.

Something moved behind Cole, making him scream and crawl on his hands and knees several feet. Panting, he turned to look and fell over like a turtle on its back. He struggled to get up and managed to wrestle himself free of his backpack. As Cole tried to scramble to his feet so he could run away, something slowly came out of the bushes.

At first it was only small, brown eyes blinking at him from the shadows of the brush. Cautiously, a small baby deer crept out of the bushes. It was about a foot tall, with light brown fur on its legs and back, with a design of white dots that matched the fur on its belly, chest and just underneath it's tiny mouth. The fawn's black nose twitched as it ambled forward, letting out a soft bleat as it looked around, uninterested in Cole.

Cole sat transfixed at the tiny deer moving around on unsteady legs. It would let out a small cry every few moments and only glanced at Cole when he moved.

Cole struggled to his feet, careful not to move too quickly so as to not scare the baby deer. The first thing he did was check to make sure he hadn't wet his pants again. The fact he had done it once was humiliating and enough reason to never face his uncle again. Once satisfied his pants were dry, he turned his attention to the tiny fawn.

"Are you looking for your mommy?" Cole kept his voice gentle as he spoke. The fawn let out a small whine.

Cole crouched down and crept forward, trying not

to startle the baby deer. He held out his hand and continued to speak softly. The deer reacted by calling out again. To Cole, each squeak from the fawn sounded more and more as if was calling out, "Mom."

Flicking its tongue out to lick its own nose, the fawn sniffed at Cole tentatively. It bleated again, raising its chin up as it moved forward another inch.

Slowly, Cole stroked it between its eyes. "It's okay. I won't hurt you. You're going to be all right." Cole's hand moved to its neck as the fawn nuzzled into his touch.

"You miss your mom too, don't you?" Unaware he was crying, Cole sat down and gently pulled the fawn into his lap. He continued to pet the animal as he spoke to it. "Do you want to hear a secret? At night, when I can't sleep, I talk to her. I know I'm silly, right?" The fawn bleated again. "I miss her. And maybe... I don't know... Maybe I'm a little mad at her, and I feel bad about that. I wish she could tell me it was all right."

Cole leaned down to kiss the baby deer who licked at his face, making him giggle.

Something moved in the bushes. Cole held onto the fawn, unwilling to let any harm befall his new friend. He hushed the baby deer as it cried out, although it made no attempt to escape, even when an adult deer pushed through the bushes.

Cole gasped as he stopped shaking. "Is that your mommy? Did you just wander off?" The fawn continued to make the same noise as the adult deer approached.

Cole gently helped push the fawn to its feet. It stumbled forward and was greeted by the large deer. They touched noses and then the older animal looked up toward Cole. For a moment, he wondered if the deer might attack. Perhaps it didn't like a human boy touching its baby.

Instead, the adult deer trotted off. The baby deer glanced at Cole one last time before following.

Smiling, Cole imagined telling the story to Aunt Ash, Uncle Drew and Lily. He imagined the smile on the face of Sam and her Nana, and wondered what sort of silly joke Ollie would make.

Then he remembered he'd run away and most likely would never see them again. Pulling his knees to his chest, Cole wept.

****

Drew came down the stairs with his gun drawn. He glanced toward the kitchen where Ollie emerged in an identical stance. With one nod toward each other, they approached the door. Ashley followed her brother, ignoring his silent signals to go back up to one of the bedrooms. Both he and Ollie exchanged an eye roll as they reached the door.

Using nonverbal cues, Ollie and Drew worked as a unit, positioning themselves on either side of the door. With a nod from Drew, Ollie carefully reached forward, twisted open the lock, and opened the door.

It took a moment for Sam to register the fact both her partner and the man she'd taken to bed had a gun pointed at her. Instinct made her want to reach for her own sidearm, but before she could move, both Drew and Ollie lowered their weapons.

"Jesus," Sam said. "The bad guys don't ring the doorbell, guys."

Drew pulled her in. "Cole's missing."

Sam's eyes widened as her they went from one

face to the other. "What happened?"

As Drew explained what they knew, Ashley sobbed. She buried her head on Ollie's chest as he stroked her long hair and promised they'd find Cole and make sure he was safe.

"I have someone working on tracing the call," Ollie said. "They said it might take a little time to figure out where it came from, but it wasn't local. It was from a cell phone, they think from Cheyenne."

"What?" Ashley's head snapped up as she stepped back from Ollie. Her face flushed red as her back stiffened. "That's where Cole and Kelli lived with that bastard. Edward Hunter. There's no fucking way that's a coincidence."

"I know," Ollie said. "I'm trying to figure out if he had anything to do with Kelli's murder, but he certainly didn't do it. He was locked up for assault. From what I've been able to find out, he isn't exactly rolling in the dough. I can't see him being able to afford to hire a hit."

Drew let go of Sam's hand and paced. He scowled as he played things out in his head. "Cole wasn't taken from here. Nobody that grabbed a kid from his home is going to let him change his clothes and grab his bag. Cole ran."

"Why?" Ashley's face was white. "What did that bastard say to him?"

Drew shrugged. "We're not going to know until we find Cole and ask."

Ashley started to pace, kicking the ottoman and cursing. "First his mother was killed. Then some bastard broke in here last night. And then this son of a bitch called. Who can blame him for panicking?"

Lily lowered herself into a chair, her knees no longer able to support her weight. "Oh God, it's my fault. I never met his stepfather, never heard his voice. He sounded so nice and polite on the phone. He said his name was Mr. Mongello, Cole's old principal. Kelli mentioned his name, said he was nice." Lily sniffed as she looked up to Drew and Ashley. "He sounded kind. And the handyman was here and...I just handed the phone to Cole. If I'd waited, I'm sure I would have realized...seen Cole's reaction. I'm so sorry."

Drew knelt before her and took her hand. "Stop. You took Kelli and Cole in, and made them your own. There's a reason why my sister asked all of us to take care of Cole. You love him. He's yours as much as he's mine and Ash's."

Ashley didn't speak, but put her hand on Lily's shoulder.

Drew stood and called McAlister Security to see if they had any location on Cole. They promised the moment they did, they'd notify him.

"Record everything," Drew ordered. "I'm going to look for him. On foot."

"Wait for me," Sam said. "I'm coming with you. Two sets of eyes are better than one."

"I'm going to get some other units looking for him and then drive around," Ollie said.

"I can't just sit here and not do anything," Ashley said. "I want to go with you."

Drew didn't object. "Someone needs to stay here in case he comes back on his own."

"Are you all right on your own?" Ollie said to Lily

Lily picked her purse up and pulled out a small, silver Colt .380. "I had it locked up since Cole moved in with us, but I took it out last night. I'll be fine. I've been shooting guns longer than the two of you."

Drew nodded as he motioned for Sam to follow him. "Let's go find him."

****

Cole wasn't sure how long he sat crying like a little baby, but he knew he couldn't stay in the bushes forever. He still had no idea where he was going. If he were older, he'd go join the Marines like Uncle Drew. That would take him far away from Edward and keep his family safe.

He hiked up the trail, avoiding the main road, keeping himself hidden from the people and traffic, until he seemed to run out of trees and bushes. At the highway, cars flashed by in both directions. He stood by the corner and waited until the light changed before crossing the street.

As he did, a red Buick screeched to a halt just inches from slamming into him.

"Hey kid, get out of the road!"

Wide-eyed and shaking, Cole bolted across the intersection as fast as he could. Leaning on his horn, the driver continued to curse him out as Cole made it to the other side.

Cole rushed down the road, paying no attention to the street signs. He tried to ignore the weight of the backpack and the tightness in his chest from panic and exhaustion. Drained beyond belief, Cole stopped and hunched over, his hands on his knees as he panted and tried not to vomit all over the sidewalk.

As he slowly caught his breath, Cole glanced around, unsure of where he was. He'd only been in Ember Falls a little over a month and most of that time was spent at home. The street looked vaguely familiar, but Cole wasn't sure where he'd seen it before. More importantly, he still had no idea where to go from here.

The people passing by were varied. A mother out shopping with her daughter, a man in a suit walking with a briefcase in hand, and a few teens standing and laughing together, smoking cigarettes. A city bus approached from the distance. Cole rushed to the bus stop.

A woman with long, dark hair with strands of gray was also waiting for the bus. She wore unflattering jeans, a striped shirt and carried a large, white leather purse. She was aggressively chewing gum, which cracked and popped every few seconds.

Cole had only ridden on a public bus when he and his mother first came to Ember Falls. When they arrived, both Aunt Ashley and Lily seemed completely shocked to see them, but welcomed them into the house despite the late hour. They'd fussed over Cole, who hadn't known what to say, so he'd stayed quiet.

Cole shook off the memory as the woman reached into her purse and pulled out a small, plastic card. *Was that how you paid on a bus?*

The woman smiled again as she snapped her gum. "You okay, kid?"

Cole forced a nod. "Do you know how much the bus is?"

"Two dollars, sixty-five cents. You don't have money?"

"No, I do." Cole pulled out a few of the twenties from the wad of cash his uncle had given him.

The woman gasped. "You're kidding, right? You can't get on the bus and hand him a twenty. You need exact change if you don't have one of these." She held up her card. "And in actual change, not paper. Where are your parents?"

Cole started to panic. "They're divorced and I'm going to see my mom, but I left my card at home. I don't want to call them because they'll be mad. I keep forgetting it."

The woman frowned. "My name is Linda. What's yours?"

Cole hesitated a moment. "Andrew, but people call me Drew."

Linda nodded. "You're not running away from home, are you Drew?"

Cole shook his head. He made sure to sound and act polite because adults trusted kids more if they were nice. "No ma'am. My father's a cop and had to go to work today. So I'm going to go to my mom. I just don't want to get yelled at because if I call, one of them has to leave work early."

Linda crossed her arms and pursed her lips. "You got any quarters or dimes?"

As Cole's face burned red, he looked down in his bag, but knew he hadn't bothered to take any change and Uncle Drew hadn't given him any.

"Relax, kid." Linda cracked her gum. "I'll take care of it. Just put that money away where nobody can see it. You know there are dangerous people out there."

Cole nodded. "I hope I never meet any."

****

Drew and Sam cut through the yard like the night before, only this time their weapons remained holstered. The first thing Drew did upon reaching the back yard of the empty house was try the door. It was locked, completely empty and he was fairly sure Cole wasn't hiding inside. They went around to the front and he repeated the same process on the front door. It was also locked.

"He had to come out through the back," Drew said as Sam came up on the front porch with him. "Ollie and I were by the front door, talking with two cops. He didn't go by us and I would have seen him if he went out the back door and around to the front of the house."

Sam looked down the block both ways. "You're probably right. So which way did he go?"

As Drew tried to decide, he heard the yapping of a small dog. The lady they'd seen last night was passing by, walking her dog. She was dressed in a bright blue, velour sweat suit. Her dog was a black pug that kept pulling toward Drew and Sam. The woman picked the dog up and eyed both Drew and Sam with suspicion.

"Ain't nobody livin' there," she said.

Drew walked forward, keeping his hands by his sides and visible. "We know that. We're looking for my nephew. He's eight, almost nine. Light brown hair. Would have had a backpack with him. I don't suppose you saw him?"

The elderly lady scowled, looking him up and down. "People seem to disappear on you. First that pretty girl you took to the dance, now your nephew. What you gonna do with him?"

Drew face started to burn. "Keep him safe from the bastard who killed his mother. Now did you see him or not?"

The woman's cheeks turned pink. "I don't like language like that."

Drew started to open his mouth to use more

language she wouldn't like, but Sam stepped in. "Ma'am, please. I'm a police officer. Last night there was a break-in and the boy is scared. We're just trying to find him and bring him home."

As the woman considered, the black pug wiggled around, yapping loudly. "Calm down Greta, calm down. You're gonna fall."

The dog refused to stop moving and soon slipped from her grip. It landed on the dirt with a yelp that was more surprise than pain. It ran in a circle a few times and then lunged toward Drew.

Leaping up, its front paws landed on Drew's lower leg. It continued to bark as its entire butt wiggled, begging for Drew to pet it.

Impatient with the delay, Drew scooped the puppy up and handed it to the elderly lady amid a flurry of licks from its tiny tongue. "We've got to go."

Hazarding a guess, Drew started to head north. Sam fell in step beside him.

"You're going the wrong way," the lady called.

Both Drew and Sam stopped and spun around. "What?"

The old woman sighed and pointed south. "Kid went that way. Fast as a bullet. Kept tripping as he looked behind him. I guess if Greta likes you, maybe you're not out to hurt the kid, but I'll tell the cops if I hear…"

Drew cut her off by kissing her cheek and scratching the dog's neck. "Thank you."

Both he and Sam hurried in that direction as the woman placed her hand on her cheek where Drew kissed her. "He didn't stay on the road. He went down the trail into the trees."

Drew called out a second thank-you and led Sam off the road into the woods.

****

Linda used her card to pay the fare for both her and Cole, telling him once they sat at the back of the bus it was her good deed for the day. As they rode, Linda kept talking to him, pausing only to chew and snap her gum. She couldn't help but notice how Cole, who she referred to as Drew, kept very quiet, answering mostly in nods and shakes of the head.

If he spoke, he kept his response to as few words as possible. She told Cole about her job working the morning shift at a local motel and how she first learned how to take the bus when she was about his age. Mostly, she talked about the love of her life, her new grandson, who was only five weeks old and cute as a button. Even though he mostly looked out the window, Linda was sure little "Drew" was listening. He was very polite and thanked her sincerely for her assistance, but otherwise, just listened.

After about ten minutes, Linda worried if he wouldn't prefer her to be quiet and was just too shy and polite to say so. She stopped talking for a moment as she reached into her purse and pulled out another stick of gum. Unwrapping it, she tossed it in her mouth and chewed, the gum snapping as she did. She was about to toss the wrapper in her purse when she spotted Cole glancing her way. She held up the wrapper. "I'd offer to share, but this is nicotine gum. It's not healthy for kids. I'm trying to quit smoking and this is the only thing that makes it less than pure torture."

Cole leaned forward, curious. "Is it really hard to quit smoking?"

Linda nodded, chewed, and snapped. "You better believe it. I've tried before, could never make it past two weeks. Hated it when my son started, but it's hard to yell at him for doing something he's seen me do my entire life. But Mindy, that's my daughter-in-law, she hates cigarettes and made him quit before they got married. He was like me. He'd quit, go back, quit again, go back again. Took him over a year to get it to stick."

Linda paused for a moment as she peered out the window while the bus came to a halt. Satisfied this wasn't her stop, she snapped her gum and continued as if she'd never paused.

"Now, I thought Mindy was being a little hard on my boy, but I know she loved him and just wanted what's best. She told me, when we have kids, I don't want them to see their daddy puffing away. I used to say, 'Well, when you give me a grandchild, I'll give it a go.' And wouldn't you know it if she didn't remember my saying it when she gave me the great news. I don't blame her for not wanting it around the baby, but Lord is this the hardest thing ever. Still, I've managed to stay without 'em since he was born. Cut down a lot over the pregnancy, which was hard enough, but quitting is even worse." She shrugged. "So be smart and don't ever start. Once you do, it's crazy hard to stop."

"My Uncle Drew just quit. I'm allergic and it makes me sneeze."

If Linda was surprised by Cole's sudden talkative nature, she didn't let it show. "Good for him. I imagine he must be crabby as hell, but that'll pass. So be patient if he gets angry a little easier than normal. He using gum too? Or the patch? That's something like a Band-Aid they stick on your arm to help with the cravings like the gum."

Cole thought about it. "I don't think so. I did hear my Aunt talking about how he used something like a chilly chicken or something."

Linda's eyes widened in amusement as she snapped her gum again. "Did she maybe say, quit cold turkey?" Cole nodded, and she laughed. "Oh sweetie, that just means he just up and decided to stop. Bless his heart, I don't know how. I guess knowing you were allergic was enough. I guess he must really love you then. Least he could do since your mama named you after him."

Cole smiled as Linda snapped her gum again.

"You sure you didn't miss your stop?" Linda asked. "This line only has three more before it turns around. I've only got two more myself."

Cole made a show of looking out the window and pretended as if he knew where he was supposed to get off. "No, I'm good. This is my stop now. Thank you again. And good luck with the quitting."

Linda smiled as Cole went to the door. "You take care of yourself now, Drew."

Cole waved goodbye as he got off the bus. He could still hear the snapping of her gum as he heard a familiar voice from behind him.

"Cole? What are you doing here, young man?"

Chapter 21
A Code for Dummies

"You want to tell me what's going on, Cole?" Rose Henry said. She stood with her arms crossed and one eyebrow arched. With all the poor boy had been through, she knew she shouldn't be enjoying the look of wide-eyed, open-mouthed, caught-with-your-hand-in-the-cookie-jar look, but she just couldn't help herself.

They stood outside a strip mall that had a hardware store, pizza place, nail salon, and the Adirondack Diner.

She could practically see the steam coming out of Cole's ears as he tried to figure out how to explain away his presence so far from home. He kept mumbling things like, "Well um…" and "I uh…" If it weren't for the fact his family was probably worried sick, it might be adorable. Maybe someday, she'd be able to tell them all about this and see them laughing, but she had a feeling today wouldn't be the day.

Just as Cole opened his mouth to try again, Rose held up her hand. "Just save it. Do you have any idea how worried your aunt and uncle are? It's just lucky I was coming out of the restaurant and saw you." She reached into her purse and pulled out her cell phone. "Now, what's your home number?"

"Um…" Cole looked around as if the answer would be floating in the air. "I uh…I don't know."

Rose scowled. "Now listen here, kiddo, don't try

and pull that on me. I can call my granddaughter and she'll have your uncle's telephone number. But then when I tell your family what happened, I'll have to add the part in about how you pretended not to know. And don't"—she took a step closer—"even think about bolting. I may be old, but that don't mean I'm slow. Now spill or I call Samantha."

Cole's eyes were full of wide-eyed terror. He turned ghost white and trembled. For a moment, Rose was afraid she was really going to have to chase him and that wouldn't end well for either of them.

"Cole," Rose tried to soften her voice as his eyes filled with tears. "Come here." Gently, she pulled him to a nearby table in front of the pizza place. "Talk to me. What's the matter?"

"Excuse me." A man in a jacket and tie came over. Rose spotted his sidearm strapped to his belt under his gray jacket. "Cole Duncan?"

"How can I help you?" Rose asked.

The officer smiled. "I work with Officers Miller and Rossi. You're her grandmother, right? She's shown us pictures." He took another chair from a nearby table and sat down without invitation. "My name is Officer Miranda. I'm actually off duty, but Ollie called in a few favors because Cole here is missing."

Rose scrunched her face up as she tried to recall the name Miranda. She hadn't met many of the officers that worked with her granddaughter, but Sam did mention them, and she knew she'd heard the name Miranda before. "Did your wife just have a baby?"

The Officer smiled. "Yes ma'am. A little girl named Francesca. But we should get you and the boy to the station."

Rose frowned. "I can't just take Cole home? I've got my car just over there."

The officer rose. "Nobody's there right now. There's been some sort of break in the case. I was just told if we found the kid to take him right to his uncle at the police station. The whole family is there with the chief now."

Cole's eyes widened. "They know who hurt my mom? What happened?"

The officer held up his hands. "Whoa, I don't know the details, kid. I've been out looking for you. But I can take you to your aunt and uncle. They'll be happy to see you. C'mon."

Rose held Cole's hand. "I feel like I should stay with Cole."

He motioned toward the parking lot. "I promised I wouldn't let the boy out of my sight, but you're welcome to ride with us. I'll return you back for your car once the kid's back with his family."

Rose nodded. "All right."

****

Within a few moments, both Rose and Cole were tucked into the back seat of the officer's Buick, Cole's backpack on the seat between them as the officer climbed in the front. Pulling out of the parking lot, he turned off the main highway and onto a back road.

Cole glanced at the scenery through the window as the officer chatted with Rose about the baby, midnight feedings and sleepless nights. Cole wondered what the break in the case was. It had to be big if everyone was there and not looking for him. Uncle Drew told Cole, *"If you run, I'll find you, because you won't be running from me."*

So why wasn't his uncle looking for him?

A cold, sick feeling started to overcome Cole as he eyed the officer.

Cole grabbed his backpack and edged it closer. Reaching inside, he felt around for the cell phone. Just as he pulled it out, Miranda's eyes narrowed and found Cole's in the rear view mirror.

"Whatcha' doing there, kid?"

Without answering, Cole hit the power button.

"Oh," Rose said looking over. "Good, you're going to call your uncle. They'll be relieved to hear your…"

Miranda slammed on the brakes, causing Cole and Rose to crash forward into the front seats before bouncing back. Cole dropped the phone as the car swung sharply off the road behind an old, abandoned warehouse. Screeching to a stop, Miranda opened the door and came around to the side as Cole scrambled to find the phone. He had it in his hand as the door opened and the officer shoved a gun in his face.

"What are you doing?" Rose pulled Cole close to her.

Miranda pointed his weapon at her and gave her a warning glare. He grabbed the phone from Cole. "Did you send a text?"

Cole didn't answer, he just stared up defiantly.

Miranda put the gun to Cole's head. "Let me ask again. Did. You. Send. A text?"

Rose cried and begged Cole to answer.

Cole glared. "No."

Miranda glared back. "Now, why do I not believe you? What's the code to the phone?"

Cole jutted his chin out, but remained silent.

With a sigh, the gun was pointed at Rose instead.

"All right," Cole yelled. "I'll tell you, don't hurt her."

With a smug smile, the officer held the phone out and waited.

"It's one-two-three-four," Cole said.

With an eye roll, Miranda keyed the code into the phone. He scanned the screen, saw the app for texts and opened it up. There were no new messages. Hitting the power button to turn the phone off, Miranda glanced at Cole. "You've got a stupid password. One-two-three-four. What a joke." He shoved the phone into his jacket pocket.

Cole refused to make eye contact. "I'm only a kid."

****

Broken twigs, branches, and small footprints told Drew they were on the right trail. There was one footprint in front of him, clearly indicating Cole had gone to the right, toward the main road. That was good. He had a trail to follow, but looking at the size four imprints on the ground, Drew was reminded how small Cole was.

"Drew," Sam said. "I promise you, we'll find him. He'll be okay."

Drew stood up, but refused to face her. "If we don't, it's going to be my fault."

"No, it's not," Sam assured him, taking his hand and placing herself directly in his line of sight. "Drew, you've done everything you could for Cole. And you'll continue to once we find him."

He jerked away, wanting to find something to pound on. "I haven't figured out a way to get Cole to trust me. I haven't made him feel safe in his own home."

Drew started to move again, covering ground quickly. Eventually, they came out on Route 9. They stood on the corner looking around, but didn't see him. There was no sidewalk once you crossed going north and south, as they led to the intersections of the main highway. That left two other directions.

"He had to come out this way. Do you think he would have crossed the street?"

Sam looked at the busy highway. "I hope not. Let's start asking people if they saw him. Shoot me his picture."

They split up, one going west, the other east.

Most people only took a quick glance at the picture and shook their head, but a few took a moment and studied it, apologized and promised to keep a lookout for the boy. Nobody recognized Cole, but sometimes Drew recognized the moment his face clicked in their memory, usually followed by a hasty retreat. Drew didn't give a shit as long as they looked at the picture on his cell phone. He'd know if they'd seen Cole. He'd see it in their eyes.

And he did.

He was a tall black man who resembled a linebacker, with a shaved head and a neatly trimmed goatee. The man would make an intimidating figure if not for the fact that on his shoulders sat a little girl of five in a pink dress. Both father and daughter wore matching plastic tiaras as they had come out of Tea Room for Tots where they'd enjoyed some father-daughter time.

Careful to keep balance of his daughter, he studied the picture on the screen. The man narrowed his eyes, the glimmer of recognition flashing in them. "Yeah, I saw him. I was in there with Tamara," he said with a rumbling, baritone voice, turning slightly to the right toward the playhouse. "We were having our tea and doing nails."

Drew looked at the man's fingertips, which were covered in magenta nail polish sloppily applied.

"I heard cars screeching and horns blaring so I looked out," the man continued.

Drew's heart lodged in his throat.

"Relax," the man said. "He wasn't hit, but I got a look at his face when he turned cause the uh…" His eyes went up to his daughter for a moment. "When the A-S-S in the car that almost hit him began cursing him out."

"That spells ass," The little girl squealed, followed by a fit of laughter.

The man rolled his eyes. "Great. Anyway, the kid managed to get across the street. I went to check on him cause he didn't look good, like he was going to be sick, but by the time I got someone in there to watch Tamara and got out here, he was gone."

Drew nodded, wanted to curse himself but stayed mindful of the little girl within earshot. He quickly sent Sam a message that he found someone that saw Cole. "Do you have any idea which way he went?"

The big man sighed. "I can't be sure. I thought I caught a glimpse of him over there." With his huge chin he gestured across the bus stop.

"As soon as I saw him," the man continued, "The bus came and blocked my view. When the bus pulled away, he was gone. Now I can't swear on a stack of Bibles that it was the same kid I saw cross the road, but if it was, he got on the bus."

"Thank you so much," Drew said and texted Sam who came running. "And thanks for trying to help."

The man nodded. "Having a kid changes your world. I hope you find him. Can I ask what happened?"

Drew sighed. "His mom died recently, then our house was broken into and he got scared."

The man gave the little girl a ride as he shook his head. "People are assholes. Good luck finding him. I've got to get this little munchkin home."

The man walked away with the giggling little girl yelling out, "asshole," as they went.

Drew quickly filled Sam in on what he'd learned. Sam sent a quick text to Ollie before they navigated their way across the street to the bus stop.

As Drew tried to remember what might be along the bus route, a white SUV pulled up. Ollie was in the driver's seat, his tired eyes hidden behind sunglasses, and his normal, quirky smile noticeably absent from his face. Ashley occupied the passenger seat, her cheeks still glistening from freshly shed tears. Sam and Drew climbed into the back seat together. Drew gave them a detailed but succinct rundown.

Ollie put the car into park, hit the emergency lights and pulled his cell off the dash holder. "I'm going to call in and have someone find out who drove that bus, see if they can tell us where he got off."

"Good," Drew said as he leaned forward from the back. "I'm guessing he didn't know where he was going, so let's drive the route in the meanwhile. We can stop if we see anything that might have caught his eye. Or maybe he got out somewhere and is walking again."

As Ollie made his call to the EFPD, Drew turned to his sister. "We're going to find him. He got scared and ran, but we'll find him."

Ashley, normally the hothead, had no spirit left in her. At first she sat with a vacant expression on her face, listening to Ollie sounding assertive as he gave instructions. Just as Ollie finished, she turned to Drew and took her brother's hand. Her eyes were moist and her lip trembled. "What if we don't?"

Before Drew could answer, his cell rang. It was McAlister Security. He quickly hit the speaker phone. "Yes?"

"It's Ari." It was a name nobody except Drew knew, but everyone in the car was rapt with attention. "I have good news and bad news." He spoke with a crisp tone flavored with a Middle Eastern accent. His voice was calm and professional as he spoke.

Ashley tensed as Ollie pulled his shades off. Sam simply moved closer. Everyone seemed to hold their breath.

"Talk to me," Drew said.

"The phone turned on for about two to three minutes. We are working on a location."

Drew exhaled. "Good, that's real good. What's the bad news?"

Ari paused. "Whoever keyed in the code, used the one marked as a dummy code. Any chance he might forget the proper code? I've got it as 5-3-5-5-4."

Drew shook his head. "No, that spells Kelli, his mom's name. You said it was turned off?"

"Yes, but, that code lit up our monitoring division like a Christmas tree. The phone will look like it's off, but it really is not. As long as it has power, we should be able to track it to within five feet. We're working on getting a link to it. We can listen in and even talk to him. I should even be able to patch it through to you once I'm in the sit-room. I'm headed there now. Give me two minutes or so."

"Good," Drew said. "Link up using stealth mode."

"Very good," Ari said. There was noise in the background as if he'd just walked into a room buzzing with activity. "Let me contact you back in two minutes so I can link you into the system."

The called ended and Drew counted down the seconds.

"What's stealth mode?" Ollie said.

"When McAlister links up," Drew said. "They'll be able to hear what's happening around him, but Cole won't hear anything."

"Why not just talk to him," Ashley asked.

Sam leaned forward. "Maybe if Cole hears us, he'll throw the phone away so we can't track it."

True to his word, Ari called back at the two-minute mark. The background chatter sounded fast and agitated.

"I am here." Ari's voice held a note of weariness and grief. "Everyone is working hard to assist you in bringing Cole home. Does anyone there have a smart phone or Blackberry? I want to be able to link you in without losing the ability to talk to you. It will take me a few minutes, but I have Albert working on it himself."

Drew rattled off Sam's number. "What can you tell us, Ari?"

"We've been listening to the entire conversation from the moment that it came through," Ari said. "Your nephew is not alone. He is alive, but it would seem he is being held against his will."

Ashley let out a cry and everyone in the car tensed,

shifting in their seats.

"Is he all right?" Drew said. "What's happening? Who has him?"

"From what we have heard a man identifying himself as a Detective Miranda has them," Ari explained. "There is a woman with him who also appears to be held captive. They are in a vehicle of some kind, but we do not have an exact location yet. We should have GPS shortly."

"Oh God." Ashley started to rock back and forth. "Not again."

Drew told Ollie to drive as he tried to comfort his sister. Sitting directly behind the driver's seat, he took her hand and told her not to give up. "We've handled situations like this at McAlister Security before. You've got top of the line experts on our side."

"Drew," Ari said. "I've heard you had trouble there with the local law. Normally, we'd reach out to them, but if one of them has Cole…"

"Ari, this is Oliver Miller," Ollie said as he navigated his way back into traffic, which thankfully was light. "I'm a police officer here in Ember Falls. I know Officer Miranda. His wife just had a kid and they left on Friday to go visit his parents in Syracuse. I'm going to give you a number. It's for my mother who is the chief here in town. She's aware of the situation and will help in any way possible." Ollie waited a beat to give Ari a moment to prepare, then rattled off his mother's cell number.

Ari was quiet as he noted it. "Drew?" The implied question was clear.

"Do it," Drew answered. "Ollie is part of the family. I need a location."

"Hold on," Ari said. There were noises in the background. Ari gave orders while others replied. "We don't have an exact location as they are moving, but we know they're near a tower located on the corner of Lake Street and Excelsior Ave."

Ollie applied more gas and they surged ahead. They weren't far away and he'd get them closer so when they had an exact location, it wouldn't take them long. "That's the tower near the old sawmill. Not much out there. You have a trailer park, then a lot of farmland. Houses are pretty far apart."

Ollie took a right turn fast enough to make the tires squeal and skillfully blew a red light, slowing just enough to verify there was nobody coming on the quiet intersection.

"Drew," Ari's said. "We're almost ready to link up. We've also notified the General. He had their plane relocated to a small airport in town. He's bringing backup, but he's not there yet so you might be on your own. I've been listening to the feed. I think your nephew, what's his name again? Cole?"

"Yeah," Drew answered. "What about him?"

"Smart young man you've have there," Ari said. "He must know we are listening. He's feeding us details, but he continues to say things in a way that this Miranda, or whoever he is, doesn't get that he's giving us intel."

Drew couldn't help but grin with pride. "Like what?"

There was another squeal as they hit a left turn. This time fast enough so the right side of the car lifted a fraction of an inch off the ground.

"He keeps asking where they're going," Ari said.

"Of course this Miranda isn't telling them, but Cole just says, 'Are you taking us to that old red barn?' A minute ago, he asked 'If they were going to the rock place,' wherever that is."

Drew hit the back of Ashley's seat. "That's the rock quarry, up on Bellerose Way. There's a barn just down the road. Nobody's lived there for years."

Ollie increased speed, feeling more confident in where they were headed. He rocketed down Clinton Drive, adeptly weaving around any car in his path. He'd use his horn if needed when they got to an intersection, but only sparingly. It was important for them to hear what was being said on the phone, but even more important they get to Cole.

Ashley kept rocking back and forth, with her eyes closed and her arms folded. "That's my boy, that's my baby." As long as Cole could be heard, he was okay.

"Holy crap!" Ari said.

Drew was shocked at Ari's stunned tone. "What?" Drew yelled while Ashley's eyes snapped open. She was shaking her head, saying, "No, no, no," over and over again.

"Hold on a moment, Drew," Ari said.

It was like the air had been sucked out of the car. Everyone was silent as they listened and waited for the worst. The only sound was the roar of the engine.

On the phone, Ari yelled, his accent a little thicker as he barked out orders. "Repeat that and get the link going."

Drew held the phone up a little higher in the air, trying to pick up some clue to what was happening from the muffled voices coming from the connection. It was torture having to wait. Drew wanted to scream into the phone, but he trusted Ari. He needed to let him do his thing.

"I do not believe it," Ari finally said. His voice sounded excited and in awe, not distraught. "Cole started to mouth off. The woman tried to keep him quiet, but he kept going. Cole made it sound like he was just being condescending, but he managed to give a basic description of the kidnapper."

Ashley reached forward and grabbed the phone. "He's okay? Cole's still okay?"

There was a painful four-second pause. "Yes, we just heard Cole's voice again. I think Miranda stopped short, sent them flying forward as a way to make Cole stop talking, but your nephew gave us some good details. He said the kidnapper was too potbellied to be a real cop. Cole called him a bald walrus with glasses."

Drew squinted. *Bald walrus?* Weren't all walruses bald except for their whiskers? So was that Cole's way of saying whoever it was bald? Or balding?

Apparently, Sam was thinking along the same lines. "Vic Miranda has thick, black hair. He's too young to be going bald. And he doesn't have any facial hair."

"Son of a fucking bitch! Harrington! It's Harrington." Drew looked toward Ashley. "He was one of the detectives that tried to jam me up for Kelli's murder."

Ollie started to nod. "It fits, right down to the damn walrus description."

Drew glanced over at Sam, her lips pursed and brow furrowed. "You don't agree?"

Sam looked up, biting her lower lip. "I don't know. I've never liked Harrington or his partner, but I just don't think he's got the balls for it."

Drew scowled. "It's him. I'm telling you."

"We'll know when we get him." Ollie made a sharp right onto the Highway Route. It was a mostly empty stretch of road, with little activity on a Sunday. They were on the edge of Ember Falls.

"Drew," Ari said. "We are going to conference you and the General with us. He's still in the air, but should be landing soon. Your cell might sound as if the line is lost, but wait for the beeps. Hold on."

The background noise went silent. If he hadn't been warned, Drew would have sworn they'd lost the connection, instead they waited.

After about thirty seconds, Ashley started to worry. "Are we sure we didn't lose the…"

Drew's phone emitted a series of three quick beeps, followed by five seconds of silence and one long beep. "Are you reading me Drew? Who's in the car with you?" The General's commanding voice said.

"Here, sir." A sense of assurance washed through Drew at hearing the General's voice. "I've got Sam, Ashley and Ollie."

"Go to the main screen on your phone. Ari has the logistics app linked. It'll bring up a detailed map of the area." His tone was all business, as if they were about to deliver furniture.

Drew hit the home key and scanned the different app icons, locating the one that displayed a white box with the word "logistics" on it. He touched the screen, launching the app.

"It's opening now," Drew said.

The screen held an image of a local map with details of roads, streets, and business.

"Ari is working to get the app linked via satellite," the General said. "Once he does, you're going to see two dots. The green one will be you. The red one will be Cole. It'll take Ari a few moments to get the uplink working."

"Got it," Drew said.

"I've been briefed on the situation," the General continued. "I know this is different because it's Cole, but you've got this, Marine. Based on Cole's description, it sounds like he's been nabbed by one of the pricks who tried to pin this on you."

Drew nodded and looked to Sam. "That's what I thought. Sam seems to think he wouldn't have the courage to kill Kelli, though."

"I agree," the General said. "My take was he had the backbone of a jellyfish. His partner had the balls, even if he was a shit for brains. I'm thinking they might be in this together."

"I can see Wilson as the brawn." Ollie moved the vehicle down the road as fast as possible. "I've told my mom on more than one occasion he's a dirtbag, but that's not a good enough reason to get rid of him. I just don't know if I'm buying Harrington as the brains. He's an empty cheap suit. Any case they've closed is because of Wilson."

A small, high-pitched beep emanated from the cell. Drew looked down at a map, which now showed two moving dots. "We got a location on Cole. He's traveling northwest on Route 7. We're gaining on them." His eyes followed the small red dot. "They changed directions. They're on Euclid Road heading west. There's not much out there." Drew watched, waited.

Instinct told him Harrington was getting close to his destination. "He's off Euclid. The app didn't even show a street, but there must be some dirt road out there. He's going north. I think they're slowing...No...They stopped." Drew tapped the screen, making it larger. "About three miles off Euclid. What the hell is out there?"

"From what I'm seeing," Ari said, "it looks like just a few hunting cabins. It certainly seems like an isolated place."

"Oh, God," Ashley said. "That can't be good. I've seen movies. Isolated is bad, right?"

Drew reached out, took her hand. "Listen to me. They didn't kidnap Cole and bring him all the way out here just to kill him in private. They want him for another reason. And we're almost there."

Squeezing Drew's hand as if her life depended on it, she managed a small nod.

"Drew," Ari said. "Your second cell is about to ring. That will be the link to hear whatever we can pick up on Cole's cell. The audio only goes one way, so you do not have to worry about anyone hearing you; however, keep in mind it will not do any good to yell and curse the phone."

It was going to be torture to hear Cole's voice when he was scared and in danger and they still weren't with him. The fact was they were still at least twenty minutes away, even with Ollie breaking every speeding record. A lot could happen in that time. They could end up being too late. It was possible they could have to sit helplessly as they heard the child they all loved executed. If that happened, he was positive it would completely destroy Ashley.

Drew promised he would do the same to Harrington and anyone else responsible for this hell.

"Ari." Ollie leaning his head back toward the phone. "Do we have any idea who the other woman is? Is there a chance she's in on it?"

"No," Ari replied. "I do not believe this is true. She's mostly been quiet, but when she speaks, she is clearly frightened. The man, this Harrington you say? He keeps referring to her as "'old woman',", but nobody has said her name."

Sam quickly answered her cell when it rang. At first, there were only heavy footfalls, the creaking of floorboards and shuffling sounds.

"Ouch! That's too tight!" Cole cried.

Ashley's head snapped up, her eyes finding her brother's. Cole was alive.

There was a high-pitched smacking sound followed by a cry of pain. The bastard slapped Cole's face. He glanced down at the phone. They were close.

Five more minutes and you're gonna get yours, buddy.

"Leave him alone," said a woman's voice. Everyone's brow furrowed as they listened. The voice had a familiar sound to it. "He's just a boy."

There was another slap, and from the cry of pain, it was clear the kidnapper slapped the woman. Cole's voice was indignant with fury.

"You think you're tough," Cole yelled. "Just wait until my uncle gets here. He'll kick your ass."

Another slap. "Shut up, kid. Your uncle ain't coming."

There was a muffled sob and when he spoke next, it was clear from the shaking in his voice Cole was terrified. "Yeah he will. They all will. Uncle Drew, Aunt Ash, Ollie and Lily will come and get me. They will! Nana's granddaughter will come for her!"

"Shut up or I'll kill you now!"

Cole sobbed, but someone shushed him. "It's okay, Cole. I know Sam will come for me. I know she will."

Sam's face had gone white and she nearly dropped the phone. "Oh, God, he has Nana!"

Chapter 22
And How Does That Make You Feel?

Cole was scared.

The man with the gun used plastic ties to bind Cole's hands behind his back, smacked his face, and threatened to shoot him. At one point, the man pulled his gun out and pointed it right at both Cole and Nana, promising he'd blow a hole in their heads.

Cole had no idea where he was, no way of knowing if his uncle was really on the way to save him or what would happen when Uncle Drew got here. He knew he could die. So yeah, Cole was scared.

He'd been scared before, terrified beyond all reason, but this was different.

Whoever this man with the stupid mustache and stupid bald head was, he wasn't Cole's stepfather. If Edward Hunter was here, Cole would be petrified to where he might piss his pants again.

Whoever the man with the gun was, he was no Edward Hunter.

The man paced back and forth on the wooden floor of the small cabin. Nearly everything was the same color wood. There were two doors, one in the front and one in the back. The three windows had thick, red curtains on them that were full of dust.

"Where are we?" Cole said, his voice loud and clear.

"I told you to shut up," Harrington snapped.

Cole looked around. "I've got to pee. I don't even see a bathroom."

Harrington pulled a small flask from his pocket and started to unscrew it. "It's a Goddamn hunting cabin. There's no fucking bathroom, except the trees out there."

The man took a long drink and replaced the flask. He ran his hand through his hair and continued to pace.

"Do you pee on the trees by the back door, or the front?"

Harrington stopped pacing and looked at Cole, his mouth open. "What the hell does it matter? They're all trees."

Cole shrugged. "I'd use the trees in the back. There are no windows back there."

Harrington glanced toward the back door, which was between the small kitchenette and bed. "So?"

Cole shrugged. "I don't want you to watch while I pee."

Harrington shook his head, pulled out his flask and drank again. "Forget it kid, you can just pee your pants, I'm not taking you out."

Cole sighed. "Who are you waiting for?"

Harrington replaced the flask. "What makes you think I'm waiting for someone?"

Cole narrowed his eyes. "I'm not stupid. You're not doing anything."

Harrington moved closer. "You want me to do something, kid? Because I can, you know. Maybe you need to ask less questions and answer the ones I asked you earlier."

Rose looked over and shushed Cole. She was

worried about making the man with the gun angry, but the more he watched him, the more Cole realized the man wasn't going to shoot them.

The man pulled out the flask again and tipped it all the way back. When he pulled it back, he shook it. "Dammit."

He went to the kitchenette and started to pull open cabinets. They were mostly bare, but there were a few canned goods, spices, and a box of rice. The next set of cabinets held paper plates, old, ugly tin cups, and a few pots. Finally, in the third, he found three glasses and an old bottle of whiskey. Harrington didn't bother with a glass. He drank straight from the bottle.

After two deep swigs, he put the bottle down on the kitchen counter and pulled his cellphone out of his pocket. He flipped it open and stared at the screen. "Fuck. I should have known we'd get no reception out here, especially on this cheap piece of crap."

Cole started to panic. If the man's cell phone didn't work here, did that mean neither would his? Did that mean Uncle Drew wouldn't be able to find him?

He had to find out.

"How old is that thing?" Cole said. "I thought only old cells had the flip thing."

Harrington held up the phone and walked to the other end of the cabin, searching for a signal. "It's new, just cheap. Damn." He snapped it shut and put in his pocket.

"Mine is brand new," Cole said. "My uncle just got it for me."

Rose shushed him again, giving him a wide-eyed look of disbelief. "Cole, please. Don't upset him more."

Harrington smiled and pulled out Cole's phone.

Powering it on, Harrington studied the screen. After a few moments, he smirked. "You're right kid, mine is a piece of shit. I'll just borrow yours."

As he turned his back to dial, Cole allowed himself a moment to grin. Rose looked at him as if he'd lost his mind, so Cole forced the smile off his face.

"Yeah, it's me," Harrington said. "Where are you?" He listened a moment as he walked back to the counter and grabbed the bottle. "No, I asked him already. Kid had no idea what I was talking about."

Keeping the cell to his ear with one hand, he took another long swig with the other. "No fuckin' way. I'm not doing it. I don't care." He took another drink. "Well, fuck." He looked over at Cole and Rose. His cheeks getting a rosy tint to them. "Yeah, you can do that. I took them. You want to make sure, you do it yourself. I can't. What are you going to do anyway?"

He made a face of disgust. "Well, you can try. And if not, I'll walk away and Wilson can do whatever. I want no part of it."

After ending the call, he walked over to Cole with the bottle in his hand. "You're in for it now, kid. You think I'm bad? Just wait two more minutes."

Would his uncle get here before whoever else was coming? Who was he talking to? Cole tried to think of a way to get the man to keep talking, to give up more information, but his mind was blank.

Harrington wasted the next two minutes drinking the whiskey. The bottle was half empty by the time the back door opened.

Cole had never seen the man. He had a full head of blond hair, and stubble as if he hadn't shaved in a few days. He wore a black t-shirt and jeans. He was big and muscular, much like Uncle Drew.

Cole did recognize the woman.

"You! You pretended to be nice! You said you were sorry! You're a liar!"

Diana looked almost amused. Her eyebrows went up and she smiled. "Cole, sweetie, I was sorry for what happened to your mom." She managed to force her smile into a phony frown as she approached Cole. She knelt on one knee and tried to look sympathetic. "I hated it when your mom was killed, but she wouldn't listen to me. Really, it's not my fault what happened. It's hers. I tried to help her."

Cole lunged forward, but all he managed was to fall out of the chair. Rose tried to tell him to calm down, but he wouldn't listen.

"You're a liar!"

"I'm not lying," Diana insisted. "I tried to help her fix her pathetic life. I wanted to help her become strong. To not be scared to walk down the street. She thought Edward was going to come back here, but she was safe. As long as she stayed in town, Edward wouldn't come to Ember Falls. But she couldn't just deal with life. She wanted your uncle back in town. The moment she decided to start asking questions, she signed her own death warrant."

As Cole screamed at her to shut up, Diana rose and looked to the man who came in with her. "Wilson, get him up. Now."

Cole continued to struggle as Wilson reached down with one hand and lifted him. Too furious to be afraid, Cole kicked his leg.

"Ow!" Wilson smacked Cole's face hard, much harder than Harrington had. Then he put his huge hand on Cole's throat and started to slowly squeeze.

Cole's eyes bulged as Wilson slowly increased the pressure on his neck. Rose screamed for the man to leave him alone as Cole's air supply was cut off. His vision blurred and there were three of everything.

"Enough," Diana said.

Wilson sighed and let go.

Cole gasped for breath. His chest was on fire as he gulped down air. He looked into Wilson's eyes. This man was different from Harrington. The other man would hurt Cole if he had to. Wilson wanted to.

"I'm the one who slit your mom's throat." Wilson's tone so casual he might have been bragging about his golf swing. "Then I jabbed the knife into her chest. She knew she was dead. It was fun."

Harrington paced behind him, still chugging straight from the bottle. He was sweating and refusing to look.

He started for the door, but Diana stepped in front of him. "Where the hell do you think you're going?"

Harrington jutted his chin toward the door. "Right out back. You don't need me in here. You've got Wilson. Besides," He looked toward Cole. "I've got to pee."

He tried to go around her, but Diana put a hand on his chest. "You're not going anywhere. Put that bottle down and knock it off."

"I don't want to see this." Harrington tried to push by Diana.

"Too bad." She grabbed the bottle out of Harrington's hand and put it on a nearby table. "You knew what would happen when you grabbed him. It's not like we can let him go."

Harrington clenched his fists. "I'm not psycho boy there." He pointed toward Wilson. "Ever since he killed the kid's mother, he's been itching to do it again. He talked about doing them all the other night, how he could have taken his time and done it slow. You should have heard the perverted things he wanted to do."

Diana rolled her eyes. "Oh, please. You don't think he told me? Who do you think told him not to?" Her eyes slid toward Wilson. "And if the idiot hadn't left his damn cell in his car, I could have warned him to get out of the house, which is why we're here."

Wilson shrugged. "If you let me do things my way, I'd have taken care of that fuck Duncan myself."

Diana sighed before moving back toward Cole. She was pleased to see the fight in his eyes replaced with fear. Wilson had a way of doing that.

"Now, Cole," she said in a gentle voice. "I just need you to help me out. Your Mom was asking some questions and poking around. She told me she had something interesting and had it safe. Where is it?"

Cole shook his head. "I don't know what you're talking about."

Diana smiled. "I believe you honey, I do. But she had something. I want you to think. It could be a little thing, one of those tiny plastic things you stick in a computer. Or maybe a few pieces of papers. Anything. Did she give you something? A flash drive? A box or book?"

Cole kept saying no. He was crying again. They were going to kill him if Uncle Drew didn't get here soon.

Diana frowned. "Oh, sweetie, I wish I could just believe that, but it's too important. You've got to tell me, or something bad will happen."

Cole racked his brain, but there was nothing that he could remember. The fact was, his mom hadn't given him anything since they got home. She didn't even have a computer or a cellphone. She'd used Lily's to send Uncle Drew that e-mail.

"I don't know," he whined.

With a sigh of disappointment, Diana stood up straight. "Cole, I want to give you every chance to think about it. So while you do, Wilson's going to show you what he plans to do to you if you don't remember."

Wilson smiled and stepped forward. "'Bout time."

"But I really don't know," Cole cried.

Diana shrugged. "You may be right, but we have to be sure." She looked to Wilson. "Move him so he can see the woman. Then have your fun."

Grinning, Wilson reached into a leather sheath on his belt and pulled out a knife with a four-and-a-half-inch blade. He went behind Cole and shifted his chair so he was looking right at Rose, then leaned into Cole's ear. "Let's see how loud the old lady can scream, kid."

Rose's eyes widened in terror.

Diana's cell beeped.

"You can't get a signal in here with those cheap things," Harrington said.

"It's a text you idiot." Diana opened the flip case. "They take less bandwidth." She opened the text app and her eyes scanned the message. "Shit!"

Wilson put the hand with the knife on Cole's shoulder. "What's the matter?"

Diane shoved the phone in her back pocket and started for the door. "Someone's coming! Grab them! *Now!*"

Seizing Cole, he pulled him off the chair and threw him over his shoulders like a bag of potatoes, not bothering to be gentle. "Deal with the old hag," he told Harrington.

They both quickly followed. Wilson moving effortlessly with Cole and Harrington struggling with Rose. Within seconds they were outside and Wilson caught up with Diana. Both Wilson and Diana headed to a red Nissan parked close to the woods while Harrington pushed and shoved Rose toward his brown Buick.

Harrington stopped short at the sound of a car moving against the dirt road. Ollie's SUV skidded to a stop and the doors swung open.

Harrington looked over his shoulder and yelled out. "They're here!"

Chapter 23
Promises Kept

"Stay in the car, Ashley!" Drew barked out the order just as Ollie swung the car behind the small cabin. Drew had his Beretta ready. Harrington held onto a white-faced and shaking Rose. About twenty feet away, Wilson and the woman they'd heard on the link raced toward their car.

Nestled into a small nook of tall trees, there was only one path for a car to get to and from the rear of the small cabin. With a sharp turn of the wheel, Ollie blocked the only possible escape route for their two vehicles. It also exposed the side of the car both he and Drew were on to direct gunfire, but it protected Ashley and Sam.

"Sam, you and Ollie handle Harrington and Nana," Drew said as he opened his door. "I've got Cole."

Seatbelts were unbuckled and everyone quickly exited the car. "Get back in the car, Ash!" Drew ordered again, right before he banked left.

"Not gonna happen," Ashley replied under her breath. She dashed to the right, and followed her brother.

Sam and Ollie moved as a unit toward Nana and Harrington. Both hands steadily on her Glock, Sam stayed on Harrington's non-gun side. "Get your hands off my grandmother, Harrington!"

The detective tightened his grip, as if Rose were his lifeline. His face an ugly shade of purple, and sweat poured out of him.

"You and you're partner back away!" He turned toward Ollie, then Sam, and then back again. "You let me get into my car and leave. I'll let her go down the road."

Sam shook her head. "Not going to happen."

Harrington shoved the gun into the back of Rose's neck. Sam winced as Nana cried out in terror, but didn't falter. Her gun stayed aimed at Harrington's chest. She knew she couldn't let the detective leave with her grandmother.

"You've got no chance, Harrington," Sam said. Despite feeling shaken to the bone, Sam's voice was steady and sure. "It's over."

"Bullshit," Harrington yelled, spit flying from his mouth as he shouted. "I'm going to run and you'll never see me again."

Sam needed Harrington's focus on her, so she took a sharp step forward. "You're out of options. The moment you pull that trigger, you die. We've got backup on the way. Not cops. Men with semi-automatic weapons. They'll be here within minutes. They'll have snipers who can take you out at four hundred yards."

Sam really had no idea how many people the General was bringing, or when they'd get here, but she knew it sounded good. Harrington had known about Drew working for McAlister Security, so why not use it?

It was working. Harrington was totally focused on her. Tunnel vision had kicked in.

"Once they get here," Sam continued. "They'll take

you down if you give them a shot. All they need is a small opening and boom. You're a big fucking target hiding behind a little old lady. You won't even know you're dead. You're only chance of surviving this is to let Nana go and surrender."

"No! No! No!" Harrington shook his head, closing his eyes as he tried to deny the reality around him. "I ain't going to jail. They won't let me survive in there. I've got to get out of here."

He was losing it, so Sam kept pushing. "You may not even last that long. Look at you, you fat fuck. You're soaked with sweat. You're shaking. Your face looks like a plum. You're going to drop dead of a coronary any second now. Drop your weapon and let her go. Because I promise you, if you hurt her, I will shoot you in your fucking balls."

"No!" Harrington's eyes snapped open. He raised his gun toward Sam and fired.

The moment the barrel of Harrington's weapon wasn't pointed at Rose, Ollie came in from the other side, grabbing Sam's grandmother and pulling her to the side. Ollie quickly shielded Rose with his body.

Sam stepped to the side as soon as the gun moved toward her. Harrington's shot went wild, hitting the rear view mirror on the driver's side of Ollie's car. Before the detective could take aim again, Sam opened fire, putting a solid four rounds in his chest.

Harrington stumbled back several feet, the gun slipping out of his hand. His mouth opened and closed like a fish out of water as his eyes darted back and forth, searching for an answer as to what happened to him.

His knees buckled and he went down. With one

final death heave, William Harrington went still forever.

Sam kicked his gun away and checked for a pulse. There was none.

Satisfied he was no longer a threat, Sam raced over to her grandmother. She wept in Ollie's arms and trembled when Sam took her. "It's over. It's okay, you're safe now, Nana." Sam looked around. "Where's Drew?"

****

Drew couldn't shoot without the risk of hitting Cole, who was twisting and turning, trying to get away, calling out for help whenever he could catch his breath. His little hands were still bound together, but Cole was determined not to make it easy for Wilson, hitting his kidnapper with his fists whenever he could.

Diana and Wilson darted into the woods.

Cole was slowing them down, but Wilson wouldn't just drop him. He knew the boy was his trump card, but Drew was slowly eroding the considerable lead Wilson started with.

Each time Drew heard Cole yell, it tore a hole in his heart. He wanted to call out to him, but he didn't want to clue Wilson in on how close he was. He needed a few more feet. *Just get a little bit closer.*

"He—help!"

Cole tried to pick his head up. He knew Uncle Drew was coming. That's why they were running. He balled his hands into fists and slammed them down on the small of Wilson's back. The man was solid and it hurt Cole's hands, but he did it again, and again.

"Knock it off you little shit!" Wilson lost his balance for just a moment, but quickly recovered. "I swear I'm going rip your head off when…"

Cole hit him one last time, hard enough to cause Wilson to lose his footing for a moment, slowing for only a few seconds.

It was all the time Drew needed.

Leaping through the air, Drew slammed into Wilson's legs, taking both him and Cole down. All three of them rolled down the hill until they came to a stop.

Both men started to smash their fists into each other, struggling for their weapons. Wilson pulled his gun out, but Drew kicked it away.

Immediately, they both started to struggle for Drew's Beretta. It went off, the bullet hitting a nearby tree. Legs, arms, and even heads struck out in powerful blows.

Cole scrambled away, screaming when someone grabbed him by his hair. Diana pulled him to his feet. "You stupid, little…"

"Get away from him, bitch!"

Ashley's fist slammed full force into her face. Diana stumbled backwards, falling to the ground. Ashley grabbed Cole, pulling him away.

Wilson and Drew crashed into each other. Somehow, Drew's gun was gone, but Wilson managed to pull out his knife.

"Hey, kid," Wilson called. "Want to see what I did to your mom?" With a bloody smile, he surged forward.

With Cole's scream ringing in his ears, Drew moved with lightning speed. Each blow was like a sledgehammer. Bones cracked and blood poured.

Wilson was like an animal, injured and desperate to kill. *"I'm going to gut you and your family!"* Wilson rushed forward, aiming for Drew's heart.

In one liquid motion, Drew grabbed the hand that held the knife used to kill his sister, twisted around, and brought it sharply up.

Wilson's mouth filled with blood as the blade, still in his own hands, ripped into his heart. He gazed down at his chest and laughed at the sight of it.

Giving the blade one brutal twist, Drew let Wilson fall to the blood-stained grass and went to his nephew.

Cole pulled away from Ashley and crashed into Drew's chest. "You came for me! You came for me! You promised you'd come and you came!"

Drew dropped to his knees in front of Cole and pulled him into an embrace. "I'll always keep my promises to you."

****

Sam rushed into the woods, gun drawn, searching for the others. Ollie and the General were by her side, flanked by members of Ember Falls PD and McAlister Security, dressed in black and carrying semi-automatic weapons.

Sam's heart had gone to her throat when she'd heard the gunshot. Who had taken that bullet? Was she about to find poor Cole dead? Or Drew?

She knew they couldn't have gotten far. It all happened so fast. Harrington's body was still warm on the ground when backup arrived and the shot rang out.

With her heart pounding, Sam realized how completely terrified she was that something might have happened to Drew. How the hell had she managed to fall in love with him so quickly?

"There!" Ollie pointed ahead, through a small bank of trees. Three people were huddled together under a tree.

Drew and Ashley were side by side, comforting Cole as Drew used a knife to free the boy's hands. If it was strange to see Ashley in tears and being tender to the brother she was normally snarling at. It was even stranger to see Cole clinging to each of them. The boy was clearly shaken, and who could blame him? But he was safe.

Sam started to smile, but in her heart she ached. She could only imagine that now Ashley herself would want to leave Ember Falls. From her violent childhood, to her sister's murder to today, this town held one cruel memory after another.

Could Sam leave her own grandmother to go with them, even if Drew asked? God, she'd want to, but how could she leave her grandmother alone after today? It was too much. She didn't want to lose *either* of them.

Somehow, she'd have to find a way to have them all. It was as simple as that.

Sam spotted Wilson. His ripped shirt was completely covered in dark red stains and there was a very long blade protruding from his chest. They'd have to check him for signs of life, but there was no chance he'd survive that sort of injury.

Drew was covered with blood. His lip was spit and there was a small trickle of blood from his temple, but Drew was concentrating completely on Cole, patient and gentle, reassuring the boy everything was okay.

Diana was bloodied, her normally beautiful face snarling as she glared toward the Duncan's. She reached down to the grass, picked up a gun lost in the struggle with Wilson, and started forward.

"Gun!" Sam yelled as she and everyone else

surged forward.

Drew's eyes snapped up, understanding the tone in Sam's warning. He followed her line of sight. With Diana advancing on them, he pushed Cole and Ashley behind him, shielding them with his body.

"Drop it," Ollie ordered. He and three officers from EFPD fanned out to the right, as Sam moved to the left, flanked by three McAlister Security men and the General. Within seconds, they had Diana covered from multiple angles without having to worry about catching the Duncan's, or each other, in a crossfire. "Drop it now or die."

With a curse, she dropped her weapon and raised her hands. The men in black ops gear kept their weapons trained on her as the officers moved, searched her and placed her in cuffs. She listened with disdain as Ollie read her rights aloud, then with one last scornful glance toward Cole, she said, "Lawyer."

Chapter 24
Looking to the Future, and Digging up the Past

Pulling into the driveway, Sam walked to the back of the house and started up the stairs on the side of the garage that led to the apartment where Drew had been staying. Just as she reached the top of the stairs, the door opened.

Drew was dressed in a casual black suit and tie. The top buttons of the white shirt had been undone and the knot of his tie loosened considerably. Sam was hit with the urge to push him inside, rip his tie and shirt off the rest of the way, and then keep going, but she decided against it. At least until they talked.

Drew didn't make things easy as the first thing he did was pull her into a long, deep kiss.

"Oh no, I'm leaving," a little voice said.

Sam pushed Drew away and looked over his should to see Cole sitting on the couch. Her face burned as Cole slid off the couch and moved to the door. Sam winced when she saw the bruises still visible on his neck, but she was pleased to see him here with his uncle. "I'm going inside to do homework. I don't need to see you guys try and fit in each other's pants."

"Huh?" Sam said as Cole pushed past them. "Where did he learn that from?"

Drew held up his hands. "Don't blame me. That's his aunt. How's your Nana?"

Sam smiled. "She's rarin' to go. I just got back from taking her to the doctor, who gave her a clean bill of health and a prescription to go out and dance her fanny off in two days at her weekly Friday Hoedown." Sam didn't mention the fact her Nana had humiliated her by requesting the doctor write a prescription for her granddaughter to liberally dip into her condom stash. The suggestion had both Sam and poor Doctor Langdon turning deep shades of red.

Drew laughed as he invited her into the garage apartment. Sam stepped inside, her chest tightening as she noticed Drew's suitcase open on the table. She'd realized he'd never unpacked, and it was clear he was still living out of it. As she took a closer look, Drew shrugged out of his jacket and pulled off the tie.

"You um…" Sam swallowed and then started again. "You're not moving into the house full time?"

Drew tossed the tie on the small table in the middle of the room. "Nope, and thank God. That couch is killing my back. I stayed there a couple nights, but Cole seems all right. Besides, Lily installed a security system. McAlister did it yesterday."

Sam nodded, looked around. With the exception of the punching bag, Drew hadn't done much by way of settling in. It shouldn't surprise her. The apartment was small and cramped. There was no stove or oven. She'd been in the bathroom and it was tiny. She'd go nuts here. "You could move into the room Kelli was using."

Drew shrugged as his cell rang. He looked at it, scowled and hit ignore. "I could, but…It feels weird, sleeping in the room where my sister did right before she was murdered." Drew shook his head. "Besides, Ash and I butt heads too much. We're getting along better, but she doesn't want me living with her. She yells every time I take a beer."

Sam forced a smile. "She just likes giving you a hard time."

"No kidding," Drew said. "It's her favorite pastime. And I love her and all, but there are times I need a break. By the way, have you heard anything about Diana? Has she spoken to the DA?"

Sam shook her head as she continued to examine the space Drew had been living in. The punching bag he installed could easily be taken down, and the few weights taken with him when he decided to leave. "No, she's keeping mum. She's going before the judge on Monday, so we'll see. I'm sure she'll try and get some deal to roll on whoever else was working with her."

Drew nodded as he changed out of his dress shirt.

Sam eyed his suitcase again. "So, you're moving?"

Drew's cell rang again. This time, he didn't even bother looking at it. He just shut it off and put it in his pocket. "Soon, I hope. Come on."

He grabbed her hand and pulled her toward the door.

"Wait," Sam said. "I think we need to talk."

Drew yanked her close and crushed his mouth on hers. Her body heated up as she melted into his arms.

"So do I." Drew grinned. "But not here. Just c'mon."

Still protesting, Sam let Drew pull her down the stairs and into the back yard. "Drew, stop. Where are you taking me?"

"Right here." Drew brought her to the back of the yard, grabbed the part of the fence in the back he'd broken recently, moved it to the side, and pulled Sam through the gap. "Or rather, here."

Sam looked around, feeling more confused by the moment. "What are we doing here?"

Drew gestured toward the empty house in front of them. "Guess what I bought today?"

Sam started to blink rapidly as she stared at the house, then at Drew, then back at the house again. "You bought that?"

Drew nodded. "A buddy of mine from McAlister knows a lot about houses. He and I did a walk through yesterday. I got the owner on the phone. He's been trying to unload it for a while. We're still working on the details, but I went to the local bank to work out being able to qualify for a loan."

Sam's hands covered her mouth. "Drew, that's so great. You're really going to buy this house to be near Cole."

Putting his arm around Sam's waist, he climbed the steps to the back porch. There was a big window, so Sam was able to peek inside. The kitchen was huge. It was old and badly needed to be modernized, but it could be amazing. She could make out a nice sized great room, and what looked like a formal dining room. It was all empty, out of date, and just bursting with potential.

"I imagine Cole must be thrilled." Sam continued to look inside, imagined different things that could be done, and wondered how much of her input Drew would welcome.

"Yeah, he was. He and I did a walk through together. He already picked out his room." Drew shook his head and laughed. "Little brat thought he could lay claim to the master bedroom. But we worked that out. I figured this way he can live here, and with Ash and Lily. We'll knock the back fence down so he can come and go between us easily enough. And this way, Lily doesn't get stuck with the kid when Ash and I kill each other from living together."

Sam finally looked up. "Wow. It's a big step. So when do you make an offer?"

Drew grinned. "Well, that depends on a few factors. I'll pass credit because I still officially work for McAlister, but I know I'm going to need to have another job. After the bank, I dropped Cole off and went to see Chief Miller. She wants me to come to work as a detective in the EFPD. Isn't that a kick? She may have to get clearance, but she thinks it'll be a good fit."

"Wow." Sam's eyes went wide. "That's a big bombshell to drop. When did that come up?"

Drew shrugged sheepishly. "She called late last night, wanted to talk to me. Now that I've been cleared in the death of Wilson, she wants to pursue this. She needs to fill the shoes of both Harrington and Wilson. Bad news is you might lose a partner. I heard Ollie was interested."

Sam nodded. "He's mentioned that. I like working with him, but he'll make a great detective."

"Then there are the inspections." Drew continued. "I've got to have it tested for mold, structure, termites, electrical, roof. Something called a radon test, whatever the hell that is." He slipped his hand into his pocket. "And the most important inspection there is."

"Oh?" Sam thought as she continued to look inside, wondering what the bathrooms looked like. "What's that?"

Drew took her hand and pulled her away from the window. "Yours. You don't think I'd be stupid enough to put money down on a house for us without you loving it."

"Drew, it's your... Wait, did you say a house for us?" Sam suddenly became very aware of her own heartbeat. She gazed at the house for a moment before turning back to Drew.

"Yes, I did." Drew held out a small, black velvet box. He popped it open and inside was a gold ring with a pear-shaped diamond. "I know we haven't known each other long, but I know what I want and I've learned you have to make the life you want. I want *you*. I want to build a life with you. To have a family with you. To help raise Cole with you. I want this to be our home."

The entire world seemed to stop as Drew dropped to one knee. "What do you say?"

"Oh." Sam's heart raced. "Yes. Yes. I want that life."

Drew slipped the ring on her finger, rose and kissed her. It was a perfect moment, ruined by an annoying sibling.

"Drew." Ashley was standing at the foot of the porch, with her cell phone in her hand.

Drew sighed as he turned toward his sister. "You've got lousy timing, you know that, Ash?"

Ashley just rolled her eyes. "Yeah, yeah. You two can play hide the salami later. Ollie is on my phone looking for you. He said he tried your cell twice."

"I know," Drew said. "I ignored him. We're not partners yet."

"Whatever." Ashley tossed him the cell. "He says

it's important."

Drew sneered as he put the phone to his ear. "Yes, Ollie. What's going on?"

In a moment, any trace of joy drained from Drew's face. He listened intently, stepping away from Sam. "How many?" He shook his head. "Jesus Christ, but that means…" He stopped to listen, scowling. "Are you sure?"

As Drew continued, Sam and Ashley exchanged bewildered looks. Neither of them had any idea what was happening, but they were pretty sure it wasn't good.

With narrowed eyes, Drew continued to listen. "When will they know for sure?" He gripped the banister of the porch. "Fine. I'll be down soon." He ended the call. For a moment, it looked like he was going to throw Ashley's cell, but he handed it back to her instead.

"What is it?" Sam said. "What's wrong?"

Drew blew out a breath. "You know that area where they found Kelli?"

Both Sam and Ashley nodded.

"Well, they just found something else there. McAlister Security brought in equipment to search the area on Monday. I've been kept out of the loop. So has Ollie since you two have been on administrative leave. He's back as of today."

Sam nodded. "I would have been too, but I took Nana to her doctor. What did they find?"

Drew glanced, not toward his new fiancée, but to his sister. "Bodies. Six of them. They've been there for some time, they think. They're still working on unearthing them all but they got one up that's been buried for years. About seven years and three months."

Sam blinked. "They can't have that kind of time estimate that fast, I don't care what equipment they brought in."

"It's not the equipment that's telling them that," Drew answered. "They're pretty sure the first body they uncovered was Molly Winters."

Epilogue
You Didn't Think This Was Over, Did You?

When Chief Ann Miller finally stepped in front of the cell, it was difficult for her to keep on her 'cop' face when the sight of Diana filled Ann with contempt and disgust. Kelli Duncan had been her patient, yet she took part in a plot to kill her.

What's more, the fact that she'd nearly killed a child made Ann want nothing more than to lock her away in a dark room for the rest of her miserable life, but she'd listened to the recording from Cole Duncan's phone. It was clear that whatever was going on was bigger than two dead detectives and a therapist who betrayed her duty to help and not hurt.

She stayed silent, deciding instead to wait for Diana to speak first. She didn't have to wait long.

"What are you doing here?" Diana sneered. "I don't have my attorney."

Ann crossed her arms and scowled. "You don't *have* an attorney. You fired both of them. Do you have a personal attorney that you would like to contact? Or do you need a recommendation?"

Diana scoffed at the thought. "Take an attorney based on the recommendation of the chief of Ember Falls PD? Not on my life, which is what it would amount to."

Ann stepped closer to the cell. "You're going to

need someone to enter the plea for you. And you should know that the DA plans to ask for no bail." She paused for a moment. "And when you are remanded into custody, you'll await trial in the state penitentiary. No protective custody."

Diana's eyes widened as she took a sudden step forward. "If you do that, you're signing my death warrant."

Ann arched an eyebrow. "Am I?" She shrugged. "I suppose that's possible. It certainly seems to me like there was someone else pulling the strings. I suppose they may want to shut you up. Too bad they don't know you're too stupid to talk to the only person who can keep you alive." Ann turned to start walking away. "Have a good weekend. It's likely to be your last."

Ann counted the seconds before Diana's panicked voice rang out. *"Wait!"*

Ann stopped, taking her time before she turned around and walked the four feet back to the cell. This time, Diana stood by the door to the cell, her hands gripping the bars as if they were the only things keeping her from being swept away.

"You have something to tell me?" Ann glanced at her watch, as if she had an appointment to get to.

Diana folded her arms over her chest. "To you? No. I'm not trusting anyone in an Ember Fall's uniform. But if you get me a deal, I'll spill my guts. I know where all the bodies are buried."

Ann tried to look bored. "So do we. Right where Kelli Duncan was left. We found them."

Diana grinned. "No, you don't. You think it ended with them? That was just the beginning."

The implications of her words slowly sank in.

"What are you trying to say?"

Diana jutted her chin out, feeling more confident that she finally had a hand to play. "That's all you're getting until I know you can keep me alive. You prove to me you can, I'll give you something that goes way beyond Ember Falls."

Coming soon from Vincent Morrone:
Part 2 of the Torn Saga:
Torn in Two

A word about the author...

Born and raised in Brooklyn NY, Vincent Morrone now resides in Upstate NY with his wife (although he can still speak fluent Brooklynese). His twin daughters remain not only his biggest fans, but usually are the first to read all of his work. Their home is run and operated for the comfort and convenience of their dogs.

Vincent has been writing fiction, poetry, and song lyrics for as long as he can remember, most of which involve magical misfits, paranormal prodigies, and even on occasion superheroes and their sidekicks.

As they say in Brooklyn: Yo, you got something to say? Vincent would love to hear from you at Vincent@vincentmorrone.com

http://vincentmorrone.com/
https://twitter.com/Vince524
https://www.facebook.com/Morrrone

www.ingramcontent.com/pod-product-compliance
Lightning Source LLC
Chambersburg PA
CBHW050026030726
47506CB00001B/144